This was a Meredith that Shane had never seen before…

A bell jangled as she opened the store's glass door, waltzing toward him like sunshine on the darkest of days. As her shoes tapped on the damp boardwalk, he launched off the seat and with a bow, held out his hand.

Meredith lifted a slender eyebrow, perhaps sensing his sarcasm. He could not stop the rolling crest of emotion threatening to take him over. The snow did not touch him, the wind did not chill him as she laid the palm of her hand softly against his. Time stopped, Shane's soul stilled and her gaze found his.

Wide-eyed and as startled as a doe by a hunter, she did not move. Nor did he. A second stretched into a moment without heartbeat or breath, and he felt as if eternity touched him…

New York Times Bestselling Author
Jillian Hart

Patchwork Bride
&
Calico Bride

H HARLEQUIN® LOVE INSPIRED® CLASSICS

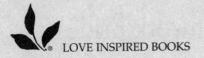

LOVE INSPIRED BOOKS

ISBN-13: 978-1-335-45459-1

Patchwork Bride & Calico Bride

Copyright © 2019 by Harlequin Books S.A.

The publisher acknowledges the copyright holder of the individual works as follows:

Patchwork Bride
Copyright © 2010 by Jill Strickler

Calico Bride
Copyright © 2011 by Jill Strickler

www.Harlequin.com

Printed in U.S.A.

CONTENTS

New York Times bestselling author **Jillian Hart** grew up on her family's homestead, where she helped raise cattle, rode horses and scribbled stories in her spare time. After earning her English degree from Whitman College, she worked in travel and advertising before selling her first novel. When Jillian isn't working on her next story, she can be found puttering in her rose garden, curled up with a good book or spending quiet evenings at home with her family.

Books by Jillian Hart

Love Inspired

The McKaslin Clan series

Visit the Author Profile page at Harlequin.com for more titles.

PATCHWORK BRIDE

A man's heart deviseth his way:
but the Lord directeth his steps.
—*Proverbs* 16:9

Chapter One

Angel Falls, Montana Territory, April 1884

Lord, what have I gotten myself into?

With the crisp April wind in her hair, Meredith Worthington braced her hands on her hips and glared at the mud-caked fender of their ladies' driving buggy. The vehicle was currently mired in the deep mud in the country road. Totally and impossibly stuck and she didn't know what to do. How would they get home from school?

This had never happened when she was at her finishing school back east. Then again, she never would have been allowed to drive a horse and buggy along the busy city streets. A lady was expected to be driven, not to do anything as garish as handle the reins herself.

"This is a fine mess I've gotten us into," she muttered, sloshing through the mud in her new shoes. "Me and my bright ideas."

"You wanted to drive." Her littlest sister rolled her eyes. "In fact, you insisted on it."

"Don't remind me." Not a request she'd regretted because she'd been wanting permission to drive for a long while, but why did this happen on her first day? She stared at the axle nearly buried in mud. Who knew the mud puddle would be that deep?

"I bet you miss Boston now." Wilhelmina, Minnie for short, hopped in the shallow mud at the shoulder of the road, making little splashes with her good shoes.

"Miss that place? Hardly. Finishing school was like a very comfortable, very pleasant prison." Meredith puffed at a hunk of hair that had fallen down from her perfect chignon, but the stubborn curl tumbled right back into her eyes. Much better to be home in Montana, even if she had to figure a way out of the very mud her mother had warned her against.

She winced, already hearing the arguments. Her independent ways were not popular with her family. If she didn't get the buggy home and soon, she feared she would not be allowed to drive ever again. And if she couldn't drive, how would she secure employment and get herself to work every day? Her dreams may be as trapped as her buggy.

"A prison? I'm telling Mama you said that."

"You will do no such thing," she informed her sister, who squished around in the ankle-deep mud quite as if she liked it. "If you don't stop playing and help me, we will be stuck here forever."

"Or until it starts to rain." Minnie looked up from making shoe prints in the soupy earth. "It looks like a storm is coming. With enough rain, the mud will thin down and we can get the wheels out."

"Yes, that's exactly what I want to do. Stand here in the mud and rain for hours." She tugged affectionately on Minnie's sunbonnet brim. "Any excuse to stay out of doors, I suppose."

"What? I *like* outside. I don't know how I shall ever survive when Mama sends me away to school." The girl wrinkled her freckled nose at the thought of the expensive and well-respected finishing school where two of their other sisters were currently attending. "Was it really like a prison? Is that why you don't want to go back?"

"No, I just didn't like feeling as if I were a prized filly being prepared for a contest. Everyone was set on getting married, as if that is all a girl can do." Her parents said that an appropriate match was the most important thing a girl could accomplish, and sadly, her mother was bent on finding her a suitable husband.

Forget suitable and appropriate. She wanted true love in her life, the kind that surpassed reason, a riot in the heart and soul, an eternal flame of regard and feeling that out-shone all else. *That* would not be easy to find.

The cool wind gusted, reminding her she was about as far away from her dream as a girl could get. She swiped the curl out of her eyes again. Those rain clouds definitely appeared foreboding. She may as well concentrate on the goals she could attain.

She braced her hands on the buggy's muddy wheel well, ignored the muck that squished between her fingers and called out for Sweetie to get up.

"We are never going to budge it. Our horse isn't strong enough. We ought to unhitch Sweetie and ride her home. We can get Papa and Eli, and they can come pull out the buggy." Minnie grinned, proud of herself for solving their problem.

"Do you want to give Mama heart failure?" The girl, she feared, was a lost cause. "Our mother would never recover if her very proper daughters rode the countryside perched on the back of a horse for all to see."

The old gray mare gave another valiant try. The wheels rocked just enough to give a girl hope, but they could not escape the bonds of mud. Exasperated, she blew the lock of hair out of her eyes again. "Minnie! Why aren't you helping? Do you want to stand here all afternoon?"

"Look, I made a smiling face." The girl grinned ear to ear, pleased with the imprint of eyes, nose and a curving mouth her shoes had made. "I don't recognize those horses. Do you reckon that's the new deputy? He looks in charge."

"What are you talking about?"

"The two horse and riders." Minnie pointed down the road.

Riders? Meredith peered over her shoulder, squinting through the weak shafts of disappearing sunlight. Sure enough, two riders ambled close on horseback, but her gaze found and stayed on only one of them. He wore a black Stetson, a black coat, denims and boots. Dark hair tumbled over his high forehead to frame blue eyes. Awareness crashed through her hard enough to wobble her knees. It was like she knew the man, as if she had known him somewhere before.

"Good afternoon, ladies." He tipped his hat, amusement curling up the corners of his mouth. "Looks like you have a problem."

A problem. Meredith opened her mouth, but nothing happened. No words, not a sound, not even air. Her entire head had gone blank, as if she had forgotten every word in the entire English language. She straightened, the mud sucking at her shoes and clinging to her skirts, and swiped at that curl with one hand.

"Yeah, we're stuck!" Minnie spoke up.

"So I see," he drawled, just short of mocking, as he dismounted, his boots landing with a splatter in the shallow end of the mud hole. "April is going out like a lion. We've been battling hard rains all over the territory."

"Where you are from?" They weren't locals. Angel Falls was a small enough town that she would have seen him before. His was a face she would never forget. Was he passing through or had he come to work on the new railroad grade up north?

"I'm from Virginia." Blue eyes twinkled handsomely as he plunged closer, disregarding the mud sticking to his boots. He gestured to the much older man still mounted behind him. "Braden is from Texas."

"You're both far from home." A strange skitter of sensation traveled down her nape. One of warning, or of something else? It didn't feel comfortable and she took a step back. Something felt out of place. Should she refuse his help?

He stalked closer, impressively strong. Even wearing a coat, he gave an impression of power and confidence. There was no mistaking he was a man who worked hard for his living. He had edge to him. It was in the day's growth shadowing his granite jaw and the sense of worldliness he carried easily on his wide shoulders.

"I'm Shane Connelly." He tipped his black hat, revealing more of his face. What struck her most was the chiseled high cheekbones that gave him character. With his dark blue eyes, straight no-nonsense nose and hard slash of a mouth, he could have been a dime-book hero come to life. A down-on-his-luck man of principle who was capable of defeating any bad guy.

There she went, being far too fanciful again. The trouble was that she read too much. Was it her fault that men were better in books than in real life? He was obviously trouble on two feet, and she could well imagine what Mama would say if she were to learn she was accepting such a man's help.

"I'm Minnie." Her little sister spoke up, clearly interested by this turn of events. "Can you get our buggy out?"

"I plan to try." He swaggered over to inspect the front

wheels and as he bent, his coat shifted, revealing an inlaid silver belt buckle and a gun.

She gulped. He was armed, a rarity for those riding these peaceful country roads. Proof the man was not as civilized as seemed.

"You managed to get the wheels wedged in good." He straightened, shooting her a breezy grin bracketed by dimples. "It might take some muscle to get this out. Good thing for you Braden and I came along."

"I suppose so." She took a step back, her pulse thudding in her ears as he approached. My, he was certainly tall and imposing. She bumped into the buggy's fender. She wasn't entirely sure she should let them stay. "Thank you for going to the trouble."

"Oh, we don't mind." He went toward her like a predator scenting prey, his Stetson slanted at a jaunty angle, his chiseled jaw rock-solid. He didn't blink. It didn't seem as if he breathed.

"But I do." If she was going to be a woman of independence, then she ought to solve the problem herself. After all, she intended to be driving her own buggy working for the Upriver School District this summer, God willing. She could not depend on a rider happening along to help her then, could she? No. Besides, she didn't like the look of these two strangers. With their trail dust and unshaven jaws, they could be anyone—drifters, thieves, escaped convicts from the territorial prison.

Fine, they did not look *that* disreputable, but there was something amiss about Shane Connelly. "I'm not used to being beholden to strangers."

"Then you might want to keep the buggy wheels up on the grass and out of the mud hole next time."

"And risk turning over in the ditch?" As if she hadn't thought of that for herself. She didn't remember asking for his advice or for the way he bent to inspect the rigging. "I know how to drive."

"I see that." A friendly smile flirted along with his dimples. A hint of kindness, not meant to make her feel chastised or defensive.

She wanted to be defensive for some peculiar reason. "For your information, my cousin was blinded and her parents killed when their buggy overturned. I was trying to be prudent."

"Then the mud was the right decision." Good humor beamed across his granite face, softening the lean planes and hard angles and turning his eyes an arresting midnight blue.

"You have a smear on your face."

"I do?" She gulped, watching as the distance between them began to vanish. He stopped a hand's breadth from her. My, but he was close. As he unfolded a clean handkerchief from his pocket, time screeched to a halt. Something deep within her shouted to turn and flee while she could, but she did not move as the piece of muslin brushed against her cheek.

Should it surprise her that his touch was gentle? She'd never been this close to a man her parents did not know. Her cheek tingled from the dab and scrape of the cloth. He folded his crisp white handkerchief and rubbed again at her cheekbone, close enough that she could smell the rain on his coat. Near enough that she could see the individual stubbles of his unshaven jaw and the threads of gold in his breath-stealing blue eyes.

Should she be noticing such things? Aloof, he tucked the handkerchief into his pocket and took several steps back. Now that he was not so near, the breathless feeling should go away, shouldn't it? Oughtn't her pulse rate return to normal?

"I had best see to your buggy, miss. You need me to carry you over to the grass?" His baritone held a smiling quality as he took another step back, his gaze never leaving her face.

An odd feeling, being peered at like that, as if she were something worthy to be looked at. Vaguely she remembered the buggy and her little sister somewhere nearby watching, cleared her throat and tried to do the same with her cluttered mind. "No, I'm not afraid of a little mud."

"A little? You look like you were in a rolling contest with a pig and won. No offense, miss."

"None taken." Why was she laughing? She looked down helplessly at the drying mud on her light yellow silk overskirt. Mama would definitely get the vapors when she saw this. "I feel as if I should lend a hand. At this point, I cannot get any muddier."

"Don't be too sure." He knuckled back his hat, revealing dark brown hair that was thick, untamed and a little too long for decent fashion. "I was wrong about you. At first look I mistook you for a vain, helpless miss, but you are clearly a country girl."

"Surely I am at heart." There was no way he could know how wrong he was. She worried that no matter how hard she tried to be otherwise, she would always be Robert and Henrietta Worthington's daughter, expected one day to be the perfect wife living an impeccable life of giving parties, raising well-mannered children and upholding the family's fine reputation. She feared her dreams of teaching children would never be realized.

"It'll only take a moment to hitch up." He whistled to his horse.

The wind gusted, batting the troubling lock of hair back into her eyes. She swiped at it, wondering how she must look standing in the mud with her hair a tumble and her skirts spattered enough to hide the intricate shirring and stitching and expensive satin hem. Easy to see how he could mistake her for a country girl, which she truly longed to be. Her friends, Fiona, Earlee and Kate, were country girls and some of the best friends a girl could have. She wanted nothing more than to be like them.

The spotted bay gelding trotted obediently forward, nose outstretched, nickering low in his throat in answer to his master. Shane took a moment to stroke his horse's nose, and Meredith remembered his gentle touch. Another shiver slid down her spine imagining being taken up in his arms. If a girl were to lay her cheek against his broad chest, she might feel safe and sheltered. Maybe even treasured.

There she went, spinning daydreams again.

"Are you coming, Braden?" Shane knelt to squint at the buggy's rigging, his horse nibbling at his hat brim.

The other man didn't answer, only nudged his big black horse forward. This one appeared much older, his face weathered and not a hint of softness on his features. When he rode by Meredith, it was like an arctic wind blowing by, cold and impersonal. Definitely not a friendly man.

The first drops of rain pelted from the sky. They struck the ground like wet bullets, tapped on her bonnet and *plinked* in the enormous puddle at her feet. The prairie stretched around them to the horizon without more than a single barn in sight, one big curtain of rain. With no one else on the road, she suddenly felt vulnerable. A small hand crept into hers—Minnie's.

"Do you reckon they are outlaws?" Her littlest sister's whisper was incredulous, and her big blue eyes widened with excitement.

It was hard to tell the manner of man Shane Connelly was, and even harder to guess at the older man who was hitching the two horses alongside their gray mare. But

Shane must have heard Minnie's whisper, for he glanced over the wheel well and let his eyes twinkle at her. Humor danced in those dark blue depths and told her all she needed to know about the man.

"No, I reckon he's a never-do-well with an appalling reputation," Meredith answered wryly.

"True." Shane's gravelly tone deepened as he chuckled. "I am one sorry renegade."

"Are you like Robin Hood?" Minnie boldly asked. "Do you help those down on their luck?"

"I have been known to aid a lovely country miss or two, if the peril is great." When Shane rubbed a hand over his gelding's muzzle, a softness came over him.

A kind man, then. Hard not to like that.

"You've got a pretty horse," Minnie spoke up. "What's his name?"

"This is Hobo. He's an—"

"Appaloosa." The single word tumbled across Meredith's tongue. "He's beautiful."

"You know of the breed?"

"My father has a fondness for Western lore," she answered, her face heating. Was she really blushing? "Perhaps I do, too."

"Perhaps?" He questioned, his dimples deepening.

"Fine. I love everything Western, but it's not ladylike to admit it and my mother would have an apoplexy if she heard me say it."

"Then it's best not to tell her." He winked, and opened his mouth about to say something else when the other man hollered out to him.

"That's enough, Romeo. I've got the horses hitched. Time to push."

"Gotta go." Shane waded to the buggy box and positioned his hands on one side of the soiled fender. "You two ladies might want to hop onto the grass."

"I told you. I intend to help." She mimicked his stance on the other side of the buggy by bracing her feet and placing her hands. "If this happens again, I want to know what to do."

"I really don't think—" His argument was cut off as a "Git up!" from Braden rang from the front of the buggy.

Horse hooves clamored on sodden, wet earth. The vehicle rocked forward and then back. Another "Git up!" and the buggy rolled forward again. The mud gripped the wheels, refusing to let go.

A little help please, Lord. She prayed and pushed with all her might, fearing there was no way the vehicle would move. She fought visions of their little driving buggy stuck here in the middle of the main road to town for the rest of the rainy season. Folks would have to somehow maneuver around it, muttering about that Worthington girl who had the poor sense to have dropped out of finishing school.

"Harder!" Braden shouted as he tromped through the mud and grabbed the bumper nearest to her. Even Minnie took a position and pushed. The buggy rocked again, almost out, before it sloshed back into the muck.

She hardly noticed because what was she watching? Shane. Out of the corner of her eye, his grimace fascinated her. All her friends, except for Fiona who was engaged, agreed no man ever had been as handsome as Lorenzo, the most gorgeous boy in their class at school. But now she begged to differ. Shane Connelly was stunning, but something beyond his physical good looks made him captivating—some strength of spirit, she suspected, and a steadfast character, she hoped.

The buggy lunged forward, suddenly rolling up out of the muck. Mud flew off the fast-turning wheels and sprayed like slop across her face, cold and wet. Too late, she realized she was the only one standing directly behind one of the wheel wells. Ooze clung to her eyelids and dripped like thick cream frosting down her face. The earthy taste seeped between her lips. The cold weight pressed on her, penetrating her bodice and weighing down her skirt.

"Oh, Meredith," Minnie soothed, shocked. "Your dress is ruined."

Humiliation seeped into her, as cold as the mud. She swiped the yuck from her eyes with her sleeve and only managed to smear it.

"Whoa!" Shane and Braden shouted together from a fair distance away, stopping the horses on the uphill slope of the road. When young Mr. Connelly turned around and spotted her, a wide grin stretched his mouth and he shook his head slowly from side to side. "Something tells me you are a whole peck of trouble, Miss Meredith."

"She is," Minnie spoke up, sounding pleased as punch. "It's her first time driving the buggy alone."

"Minnie, don't tell him that." Really, she looked bad enough without adding "idiotic, inexperienced driver" to the list. That was what she felt like. Out of her element, when she wanted to fit in so badly. Too badly—maybe that was what the Lord was trying to tell her.

"You are a right mess." Shane pulled out the handkerchief again and wiped the white surface across her eyes. This close, she could see there were green threads, too, in his deep blue irises, to match the gold ones, and something noble within.

There she went, being fanciful again.

"The good news is that your horse and buggy are fine, aside from the mud." He folded the cloth to scrub at her nose and cheeks. His nearness was a funnel cloud, pulling her helplessly toward him. "You, miss, I'm not so sure about. Maybe Braden and I had best see you home."

"No!" That came out a mite defensive, but she could imagine Mama's reaction. "Please, if our mother knew there was a mishap, she wouldn't let me drive again. It's imperative for me to become a better driver."

"You don't sound like a country miss to me." His gaze narrowed, his presence and his sculpted features steeled. "Who are you?"

"Just Meredith." That was who she wanted to be. She needed to be herself, not her father's daughter, not her mother's achievement, but someone real. This man, who rode where he wanted and who did as he liked, would never understand.

"All right, then, Just Meredith." His grin returned, crooked and dimpled. "Let's get you in the buggy and on your way home."

Chapter Two

Just Meredith was beautiful, no doubt about it. Shane glanced over his shoulder to make sure the gray mare pulling the buggy was managing all right. The spring storms had turned the roads to every kind of muck, although judging by the downpour it was hard to call this brand of cold spring.

"Stopping to help those girls made us late for our next job," Braden commented drily as he tucked the much-folded telegram for the riding directions back into his slicker's pocket.

"Helping them was the right thing to do." It wasn't something they hadn't done before in their travels. "We couldn't leave them there."

"I'm not arguin' that. Truth is, this new stint has me worried. Heard the wife is a whole peck of trouble."

"Wife? I thought that we were working for a mister, not a missus."

"Shows what you know about marriage." Braden cracked a rare smile. "I say we give it a trial before we commit. I don't want to get knee-deep into a job, figure out it's more trouble than it's worth and then tear myself up trying to figure if I should run for my sanity or stay and finish the job the right way."

"I see your point." Shane was new at this. Not green, but not experienced either. He'd only had a year of apprenticeship under his belt since he'd hooked up with the best horseman this side of the Mississippi. He'd left everything behind in Virginia—family, reputation, duty—to learn horsemanship the real way. It had been the roughest year of his life and the best one. Finishing his apprenticeship was all that mattered. So why was he thinking about the woman and not the upcoming job?

Another glance over his shoulder told him why. There was something special about her, something extra—like a dash of both sweetness and spirit not often seen. "Just Meredith," she'd called herself in a dulcet voice that made him think of Sunday-school hymns and Christmas carols. And pretty? She put the word to shame with those blond ringlets tumbling down from beneath her plain brown hood and eyes the color of the sea in the rain. She was a rare beauty with creamy skin, delicately cut features and a mouth made for smiling.

He liked country girls the best, he'd learned long ago, not missing the perfectly mannered and prepared debutantes who were part of his world back home. It heartened him to see honesty and goodness in a female. It was far preferable in his opinion to the veils of pretense that filled his growing-up years.

Out west, things were more likely to be what they seemed and the people, too. He liked the image of Just Meredith in her simple but elegant brown coat, pretty yellow dress and sincerity. She made quite a picture holding the reins as the chilly weather battered and blew. With the smears of green in the nearby fields and the world of colors blurred and muted by the rain, she could have been the focus of an impressionist watercolor. A prized painting meant to be cherished.

"You're watching me," she called out above the twists and gusts of the wind. "You think I'm a bad driver and I'm going to get stuck in the mud again."

"No, but I *am* keeping track of the mud holes. I don't see a thing you can get mired down in, at least not yet." He let Hobo fall back alongside the buggy. "You're doing pretty good for it being your first day driving."

"You may be fibbing." The look she threw him from beneath her brown hood was a challenge.

He laughed. He liked the dazzle in those interesting gray-blue eyes. "I'm trying to be encouraging. Keep to the positive. Avoid the fact we nearly had to go in search of a pair of oxen to free your buggy."

"Thanks for not mentioning it." When she grinned, she was like a sunbeam on this dismal day.

"You still don't figure on letting your mama know about this?" He couldn't resist asking, not that it was his business.

"What she doesn't ask about, I won't have to tell her."

"And what if she notices the mud?"

"That's the flaw in my plan. I'm hoping Mama doesn't notice. She could be busy and not even hear us driving up."

"She will be watching, Meredith." The little girl wrinkled her nose. "Nothing gets past Mama. You ought to know that by now."

"That won't stop me from trying." She laughed. At heart she was not a deceitful daughter but one apparently amused by her mother. "If Mama revokes my driving privileges, then I won't learn enough about driving to make it on my own come June."

"Why June?" Call him curious. He couldn't help it. Something tickled in his chest like a cough, but maybe it was interest.

"That's when the summer school term begins." A ringlet bounced down from beneath her hood to spring against her cheek. "I'm studying for the teachers' exams. If I pass, I hope to get one of the smaller county schools just north of here."

"A schoolteacher." A fine ambition. He couldn't say why that pleased him either. He wasn't looking to settle down, not with his long apprenticeship hardly more than half over.

"But Mama doesn't know," the little girl added impishly. She was a bit of trouble, that one. "And no, Meredith, I won't tell on you, but it's likely to kill me."

"I wish you had never overheard me talking with my friends. You can't keep a secret to save your life." Meredith wrapped an arm around her sister's neck and hugged her close, an affectionate gesture. "I'll never forgive you if you blurt it out and ruin my plans."

"It won't be easy." The girl rolled her eyes and huffed out a sigh, as if her life were truly trying indeed.

"It seems you keep a lot of secrets. The mud incident, the teacher's exams." He swiped rain from his eyes. "It won't be as easy to hide an entire job when summer comes."

"Oh, I know. I don't want to deceive Mama. That's not what I mean to do. I want my own life is all."

"I've known that feeling."

"How can you? You're a *man*."

"True enough, but why do you say it like that? Like being a man is a bad thing."

"Not bad, exactly. I'm just exasperated." She blew the curl out of her face, but it just sprang back. Did she dare take both hands off the reins? No. Sweetie was as gentle as a horse could be, but doom had a tendency to follow her around. She had no intention of letting anything else go wrong.

"Meredith often gets exasperated," Minnie explained with a little girl's seriousness. "Mama says it's because nothing is quite to Meredith's liking."

"That's not true," she hotly denied, as she always did. "Okay, so maybe it's true sometimes. It's just that boys have it easier. They can do what they want."

"That depends." Shane's voice dipped low, butter-smooth and warm with amusement. "My mother thought I should join my father in business and one day follow in his footsteps. Carry on the family legacy."

"Drifting from town to town?" The quip escaped before she could stop it. What was wrong with her?

"I wasn't always a saddle tramp." Those crinkles around his eyes deepened, drew her closer and made her want to know more.

She shouldn't be curious, not one bit, not one iota. The dashing, mysterious, slightly dangerous young man was not her concern. Although it was easy to imagine him lassoing wild horses, fighting to defend the innocent or performing some noble act. Beneath the stubbled jaw and traveling coat, he might be full of honor, a real-life hero with the rain washing away the mud on his boots.

She tried to imagine what her best friends would say. Earlee, the most imaginative of the group, would pen him as an intriguing hero of a fantastic tale. Lila, ever the romantic, would compare him to the most handsome boy in their high-school class, Lorenzo. Kate and Scarlet would heartily agree and start dropping hints about the status of their hope chests, the reason they met every Saturday afternoon to sew for a few hours. A sewing circle of friendship and of hope, they tatted doilies, embroidered pillowslips and pieced patchwork blocks for the marriages they would all have one day.

Yes, this chance meeting was going to be a huge topic of conversation come Saturday.

The rain turned colder, falling like ice, striking the great expanse of prairie with strange musical notes. Beauty surrounded her, but she could not take her eyes from the handsome wanderer.

"What did you do in your former life?" Was that really her voice, all breathless and rushed sounding? Her face felt hot. Was she blushing? Would he notice?

"Back home, my father and grandfather are lawyers, although now they have many partners to manage the firm." He let his horse fall back, to keep pace beside her. "As the oldest son, I am a great disappointment traveling around on the back of a horse."

"I think it takes courage to follow your own path." Courage was what she was trying to find for herself.

"Could be courage. My father called it stupidity. My mother said it was stubbornness. She was none too happy with me when I left, since she was in the middle of planning my wedding to a young lady of their choosing."

"You ran out on a wedding?"

"I never proposed, so I didn't see as I had an obligation to stay for the ceremony." Dimples belied the layer of sorrow darkening his voice.

"Your parents had your whole life mapped out for you?"

"Mapped out, stamped and all but signed and sealed." Understanding layered the blues in his eyes and softened the rugged, wild look of him. "Something tells me your parents adore you. They want the best for you, and that's not a bad thing, as long as it's what you want, too."

"Tell that to Mama."

"Sounds like our mothers are cut from the same cloth."

The howl of wind silenced and the veil of rain seemed to vanish as he leaned over in his saddle, close and closer still. The sense of peril returned, fluttering in her stomach, galloping in her veins and did she turn away?

Not a chance.

"No one I know has a mother like mine." Strange they would have this similarity between them. "Is yours overbearing, impossible, full of dire warnings and yet she'd throw herself in front of a train to save you?" she asked.

"Yep."

"Does she drive you beyond all patience with her meddling and fussing and trying to do everything so your life is easier?"

"That would be an affirmative."

"And you love her so much you can't bear to say no and disappoint her?"

"In the end, I did say no and it broke her heart." No way to miss the regret. It moved through him, deep like a river, reflecting on his face, changing the air around them. "It was hard for her to let go, but I wouldn't be the man I wanted to be unless I made my own life. She'll come to see that in the end."

"So she hasn't forgiven you?"

"Nope. Not yet. But I'm confident she will come to see I was right."

"That wasn't the answer I was hoping for." If only following her own path would not potentially cost her her mother. "I'm praying my experience will be different from yours."

"Your mother doesn't want you to be a teacher?"

"She doesn't want her daughters to work." She hadn't corrected his misimpression of her as a simple country girl, so how did she explain her mama's view of society and a woman's role in it? "My only hope is that Papa will understand."

"Then I'll pray for that, too." Serious, his words, and so intimate that it was as if they were the only two people on the entire expanse of the plains. Completely odd, as she'd never felt this way with anyone before. It was as if he'd reached out and taken her hand, although they did not touch. A tug of warmth curled through her, which was sweet like melting taffy and enduring in the way of a good friendship.

"Meredith!" She felt a tug on her sleeve. "Don't forget to turn."

She blinked, the feeling disappeared and the world surrounding her returned. Wet droplets tapped her face, the jingle of the harness and the splash of the horse's hooves reminded her that Minnie was at her side, home was within reach and the time to say goodbye to this man had come.

"Is this your driveway?" Shane broke the silence between them, one brow arched with his question.

Did he feel this way, too? As if he did not want the moment to end?

"Yes." The word rasped past the regret building within her. She drew Sweetie to a stop, knowing he would go his way, she would go hers and she would never see him again. Her spirit ached at the thought. "Where are you headed?"

"To a ranch somewhere in these parts." He knocked off the rainwater gathering on the brim of his hat. "Since we're running late, we might as well see you to your door. Braden, is that okay with you?"

"Goin' this way anyway," came the answer as the older, gruff man pulled his mount to the roadside and consulted the telegram in his pocket.

"Guess that means we don't have far to go." He shivered when the wind lifted, knifing through his wool coat.

Nearly wet to the bone, he ought to be eager to get into dry clothes and thaw out in front of a fire. Gazing down at Just Meredith, he wasn't in much of a hurry. "You ladies must be freezing. The temperature is falling. I could dig a blanket out of my saddle roll. Might keep you warmer."

"That's very gentlemanly of you, but we'll be fine."

"Meredith!" Minnie protested. "I'm cold. Look. It's starting to *snow*."

"No wonder I'm half an icicle." Nothing like a joke to warm a fellow. He twisted in his saddle to tug on the ties and pulled a folded length of red wool from beneath the oiled tarp protecting his things. "This ought to keep you two ladies a little more comfortable."

"Thank you, Shane."

He liked the way she said his name with a touch of warmth—unless he was imagining that—and a bit of respect, which he didn't mind at all. He gave the blanket a snap, settled it over the ladies' skirts, nearly falling out of his saddle to hand over the edge to Meredith so she could tuck it around her and Minnie. Leaning close, an odd sense of warm curled around his ribs, something tender and fine like first light on a spring morning.

Once she had the blanket settled, she gathered the reins in her slender, smooth hands. In retrospect, maybe he would have thought about that more and realized it was a sign. That a country girl's hands wouldn't look soft and pampered instead of callused and rough from work. But the bit of warm felt cozy in his chest, a nice and wholesome thing, so he didn't think too much as he followed the buggy off the main road and down a narrower drive curving between a copse and tall fencing.

Braden signaled him. "I don't want you gettin' too friendly with any of the neighbors."

"Are you tellin' me you want me to be rude?" He angled

his brim against the driving snow tapping against his hat and stinging like icy needles on his jaw.

"Not rude, no. But I want your mind on horse business."

"It will be." The chance to keep learning at Braden's heels was all he wanted. So why did his gaze stray to the buggy? Although he couldn't see Meredith from this angle, he wanted to, as surely as he sat in the saddle. That could *not* be a good thing.

"I know how it is. It's only natural to take interest in a pretty gal. But remember, we move on. Our commission here is only two months at the most."

"I know that." He knew what was important and why he was here. He had learned a lot, and on this assignment he would have more responsibility and a real opportunity to use what he had been taught. "I know what you're asking, Braden, and you can count on me. I'm not going to leave you with all the work while I chase after a pretty calico. I'm not that kind of man."

"I'm still waiting to see the brand of man you are." Braden, tough for his years, iron-strong and jaded, had a look that could pare like the sharpest blade. "You have potential, Shane, but you're a blue blood. I'm waiting to see which wins out."

"I'm not playing at this. I'm here to work." He still had a point to prove. Right now his work was the only importance in his life. He squared his shoulders and did not flinch when arctic blew in on the wind. The curtain of snow thickened, obscuring Meredith's driving buggy and the rest of the world from sight.

Home was nothing more than a hint of a roofline and a glint of windows through the whiteout. The weather could often be a surprise in Montana Territory and she liked that about this part of the country. Here, you could build a fence, but you couldn't fence in the prairie. The adventurous part of her, the one Mama did her best to lecture right out of her, thrilled in the feel of the icy wind and violent snow.

"Uh-oh." Minnie stood up, gripping the dashboard, to squint in the direction of the front porch. "That's Mama. Do you think she will notice the mud?"

"How could she not?" Meredith drew poor snow-covered Sweetie to a stop and set the brake. Beneath the blanket, the mud thick on her coat and skirt had frozen, crackling as she moved. The good news was that snow had iced over it, so it was almost impossible to see the dried brown beneath.

Please, Lord, let Mama be understanding. She laid the reins over the snowy dash and squinted into the white haze. She saw nothing but shadows and no sign of handsome Mr. Connelly.

"Allow me." His voice rolled through the storm. A gloved hand caught hers, and in the thick of the storm she could make out the cut of his wide shoulders and the hint of his square jaw.

When her hand settled against his broad palm and she felt the power there, awe thrilled her. He was a perilous man because he made her feel both safe and in jeopardy in the same breath. Simply allowing him to help her from the buggy was like taking a grand adventure. For a moment she floated, caught in midair as if defying gravity before she flew downward and her shoes touched solid ground. The veil of snow had thickened, obscuring him completely, and when his hand released hers she felt alone.

"Girls!" Mama's shrill voice dwarfed the howling late-spring storm. She barreled into sight, well-wrapped against the cold, marching down the walkway like a general at battle. "I have been worried sick! Where have you been? And who are these *people?*"

Although it was hard to tell in the snowfall, Meredith could well imagine Mama's curled lip. Mama did not approve of strangers, particularly strange men who were not in the same social class. Meredith winced, picking her way through the ice toward the lee of the house, where the snowfall thinned.

"We wanted to make sure your daughters arrived home safely." Shane Connelly appeared, dappled with snow, safely seeing Minnie onto the pathway. He faced Henrietta Worthington as if he were not intimidated by four-star generals. "The storm has turned treacherous."

"Indeed!" Mama disregarded him with a turn of her shoulder and hugged Minnie against her. "I have been half ill with worry. Where have you been?"

And today had started out so well, she thought. "We had a bit of trouble with the mud."

"Did I not warn you? Don't think I didn't notice the mud caked all the way up to the dash, young lady. I knew it was a mistake to let you drive." Mama grabbed Minnie protectively and pointed her toward the steps and the front door with a motherly push. "I suppose I owe these people some sort of thanks for seeing you home."

How embarrassing. Meredith's face burned. It was not respectful to correct her mother, but the argument sat on her tongue. A muscle ticked in Shane's jaw, and she felt his muscles bunch in his arm. Tension. Maybe a sign of hurt.

"I'm sorry," she said quietly but he seemed so far away. Maybe it was the snow's veil putting distance between them, but probably not. Mama's opinion of him had altered everything. The closeness and the taffy-sweetness within her had died. Was there any way to repair it? "I am grateful for your assistance, Mr. Connelly."

"It was nothing."

"It was gallant. And muddy."

"In truth, I did not mind the mud." Any hint of a smile was gone. His striking blue eyes had shielded, his handsome face as set as stone.

Of course he would be unhappy with the way Mama treated him. Who wouldn't be? Anyone would be offended. Meredith ached to set things right, but how could she? She would have to speak to her mother later for all the good it would do, and that wouldn't mend things at this moment. She longed to say something to Shane, but he stepped quickly, deliberately away. His unflinching gaze hardened.

This was why she wanted to be her own woman and not her mother's daughter. She wanted to stand tall for what she believed in without apology. She loved her family, but she was embarrassed by them, too.

"I can have Cook reheat some stew," Mama announced in her superior way, thinking she had been so kind to the rough-looking men. "You may circle around to the back door. Take off your wraps and boots first. Be mindful of your manners. I'll expect you to keep your hands to yourself, no pilfering the silver, and you must leave as soon as you are finished eating."

Meredith watched another muscle jump along Shane's clenched jaw. If only she could melt into the snow and disappear. She couldn't believe Mama had said such a thing. Whether these men were down on their luck or simply passing through, they did not deserve to be spoken down to. "Mama, you must mean to say how happy you are that these fine men offered to help Minnie and me. It probably inconvenienced them and since it's nearly dark, perhaps they would like to join us for dinner—"

"That is not what I meant!" Mama gripped her shoulder and firmly guided her up the steps. "What has come over you, Meredith? In the house, now, and start your home-work. I'll deal with you later."

"But, Mama—"

"And change that dress. I want this understood. You will never ask to drive that buggy again." Her mother drew her-self up full height, not in an understanding mood. "Now, inside before you catch your death of cold. I must have a few words with these people."

"I'm sorry." It was all Meredith could offer Shane. She watched a hint of understanding soften his iron gaze be-fore she stumbled over the threshold and into the warmth of the house. The door slammed shut behind her and she felt Minnie's hand curl into hers.

"It's too bad we'll never see them again." She sighed. "But wasn't it something to see his Appaloosa?"

Chapter Three

Shane swiped snow from his face, ignoring the icy pin-pricks against his skin and the letdown within. He might have known. Just Meredith, as she'd claimed, was a far sight more. This was the Worthington estate and although he couldn't see more than a hint of a roofline, the long stretch of lamplight windows gleaming through the storm suggested not a simple house but a dignified manor. Meredith was no country miss.

"I'm Mr. Shaw," Braden attempted to explain to the dismissive Mrs. Worthington. "I'm the horse trainer."

"The man my husband hired?" The woman drew her chin up and looked down her nose at the rough and ready pair. "And the one who gave my daughter special attention? Is that your assistant?"

If looks could maim, he would be in need of a pair of crutches. Shane stepped forward. He was no longer Aaron Connelly's grandson, not in these parts. He was a horseman and proud of it. "Yes, ma'am. I'm Shane Connelly."

"You were being awfully forward with my daughter." Mrs. Worthington barreled fearlessly farther into the snowfall to meet him, her apple-cheeks pinched severely and her gaze hard with accusation. "Tell me I am wrong."

"I was helping her out of the buggy and through the storm. That was all."

"And that's the way it will stay if you wish to work here. Do we have an understanding?"

He held his ground, fighting down the urge to argue and correct her misimpression. He may have been enjoying the pretty miss's company, but that was all. If he felt anything more, then he refused to admit it. It stung to be reprimanded when he'd done nothing wrong, and he couldn't explain the tightness within his chest. Nor could he remember being offended by a woman so quickly. He wanted the job here and he did not wish to disrespect a lady. He was not raised that way, so he did not argue with her. "Yes, ma'am."

"Fine. Mr. Shaw? If you two will take the mare and buggy to the stables, you'll find Eli waiting. He'll show you around, get you acquainted with our expectations before he leaves us for good at the end of the day. I'll tell Cook to keep the stew warm for when you're ready. Use the back door only."

"Yes, ma'am."

Although Shane couldn't see Braden's expression, he could sense a wariness. The hardest part of their job wasn't the horses but the people who owned them. He swiped snow from the old mare's forelock, taking care to keep the cold wet from falling into her eyes. She was a sweet thing, watching him patiently with a liquid brown gaze and a quiet plea.

"You did a fine job today," he assured her as he took hold of her bridle. It was the mare that had fooled him into believing Meredith's pretense. This was no fine pedigreed animal, but an elderly mare with a slightly swayed back. Strange that she was the driving horse of choice for the Worthington girls and not some fancy pony.

His nape prickled as if Meredith Worthington was watching him from one of those dozen windows. He studied what he could of each glowing pane but caught no sight of blond curls or her big gray-blue eyes. Probably just his imagination or the wish that people—especially women—could be what they seemed at first sight. That was why he wanted to spend his life training horses. A horse didn't put on airs, put you down or figure they were better than you because of the quality of their possessions.

"I plan to tell Worthington I want a trial period." Braden fell alongside, leading both horses by the reins. "I'm not sure about that woman."

"She was protecting her daughters." Akin to the way a mother bear defended her cubs.

"Sure." Braden nodded, his jaw tense. "But one thing needs to be made clear to Robert Worthington. I came to work with the animals, not to be nitpicked to death by a lady who has nothing better to do with her time."

"You're still ticked from our last job."

"True enough. After those difficult people, we deserve an easier assignment." Braden shook his head and rolled his eyes. "Not sure if we're going to get it this time."

"No, I don't think we are."

Lord, please let this work out.

The first outbuilding they came to was a well-built barn with a wide breezeway marching between big box stalls. Several horses poked their noses out into the aisle to nicker a welcome to an old friend and to greet new ones. Hobo sidestepped, head up, cautious as he looked around.

"Whoa there, buddy." He left the old mare standing to lay a hand of comfort on his boy's neck. Snow tumbled from his black mane.

Best to get these horses rubbed down, dry and stabled and no sense in hurrying. His stomach might be rumbling, but he wasn't looking forward to heading up to the main house to eat. Meredith would be there. That made his gut clench tighter.

Maybe it would be best to avoid her, he decided, if that could be possible as long as he had a job here. That young woman had as good as lied to him. He'd had enough people in his life being less than honest, and he wasn't looking for more of the same.

"Ho there." A man about his same age with a friendly grin and a trustworthy look hiked down the main aisle. "I'm Eli Sims. You must be the new trainers. Good to meet you. Let me lend a hand with your horses."

Braden stepped forward to ask a few details about Mr. Worthington, as Shane knelt to uncinch saddles and unhook harnessing. He kept half an ear to their conversation but couldn't seem to concentrate. At least he hadn't been fooled by her for long. Not that the not-so-country girl was on his mind. He was doing his best to purge every thought and image of her from his brain.

Whether or not he was successful was another question entirely.

Meredith couldn't forget the look on Shane's face when Mama had spoken down to him, which was by her guess the exact moment he realized she was not the country miss he'd assumed her to be.

Did he hate her? Was he the kind of man who would understand? She hadn't meant to mislead him. Was her parentage her fault? Hardly. They lived in the country, so she technically was a country girl. It wasn't a lie she had let him believe, but she hadn't corrected him.

She regretted that now. She stared out her bedroom window instead of at the history book open on the desk. She could not concentrate and let her gaze wander over the roll of high prairie and the rugged Rocky Mountains hugging the horizon. Sunset dusted the snowcapped, craggy peaks with dabs of mauve and streaks of purple.

"Meredith." Matilda, her older sister, poked her head around the door frame. "Mama wanted me to come fetch you. Dinner is about to be served."

"Dinner." She was not in the mood. "I don't suppose I can have a tray sent up here?"

"Mama is mad enough as it is. I wouldn't ask if I were you." Sympathy softened Tilly's features, making her almost pretty in the lamplight.

If only a fine beau could see Matilda as her sisters did, with a beauty of spirit, a sweetness of temperament and a generous soul that made her the finest catch in all of Angel County. Men were notoriously shallow, as Meredith had decided, and so dear Tilly was still unmarried and, worse, unbeaued at the age of twenty. Not a single man had come courting, when marriage and a family were all that her sister desired.

"Then I suppose I'll survive dinner." With a wink, Meredith closed her textbook, pushed back her chair and climbed to her feet. The sun was going down on the day and on her hopes. Her one chance to prove herself as a sensible driver to her parents was over. "Do you think it will be the topic of conversation? My big failure as a driver."

"You may have to endure a few comments from Mama, but Papa believes a woman should know how to drive," Tilly encouraged. "Remember how he bought Sweetie for me, so I could be more independent? And that means—"

"You can drive me," Meredith finished, reaching out to squeeze her sister's hand. "The certification exam is coming up. Will you find a way to help me take it?"

"I'll drive you there and back myself, even if I have to defy both our parents to do it." Voices at a whisper, they meandered down the long stretch of hallway. "There is always the hope that the new horseman will be as helpful as Eli has been."

Eli was a gem and while it was a boon to him that he was joining his brother's teaming business, she seriously doubted that Shane Connelly was going to go out of his way to help her. The disbelief on his face flashed back to her as they'd stood in the falling snow. Would he understand, especially after the way Mama had treated him?

She hoped so. There had been a spark of something between them on the ride home. She shivered remembering the warm taffy sensation his nearness had brought her. She was still dazzled by his dimpled smile, the snapping connection when their gazes met and the tender touch of the rough and rugged man.

"I hadn't realized Papa hired two horse trainers." Matilda's comment echoed in the stairway as they descended to the main floor. "Minnie says the older one is a little scary."

"Not scary exactly, just distant and in charge." In truth she hardly had an impression of the older horseman. Shane had so dominated her senses at the time that no one else could matter. She could not tear his image from her thoughts, and her gaze shot to the windows hoping to catch a single sighting of him.

"Girls, there you are." Mama bustled toward them, skirts swishing, floorboards shaking, cups rattling in their saucers on the dining-room table. "Hurry. We are waiting the meal on you."

"Sorry. I was lost in my studying." And wondering about the new horse trainer, but she kept that to herself. She felt Tilly's hand on hers give an encouraging squeeze. Glad she wasn't alone, she headed toward her chair. Papa and Minnie were already seated. Meredith cast an apologetic look at her father, who looked stern as she slipped into her chair next to Minnie. Definitely not the best of signs.

"I heard you had some trouble today, young lady." His deep voice seemed to fill the room, although he spoke softly. Papa had a presence, too, a formidable one when he wanted it. "Something about nearly ruining the buggy and being covered with mud."

"We came back in one piece." The last thing she wanted to do was to disappoint her father. She set her chin, determined to accept with grace the loss of her driving privilege, which was sure to be coming. She tried to be upbeat. "All's well that ends well."

"It certainly was not." Mama's chair scraped as she settled up to the table. "Anything could have happened to you. You could have been killed or maimed."

"I was careful. We are fine." Humiliation rolled through her. She was a sensible girl who got good grades. She needed practice driving, that was all. She swallowed hard against the rising sense of failure that seemed to fill her to the chin.

"Not fine enough," her mother argued. "Your dress was near to ruined, Meredith."

"I know." Mortified, she folded her hands, preparing for grace. She felt bad enough, seeing herself from Shane Connelly's point of view. She could have had "loser" painted on her back in scarlet letters. Not merely a loser, but a failure and a disappointment. Papa appeared so grave and Mama furious.

"I'm sorry." The apology wasn't easy. "You are right. A more experienced driver would not have gotten stuck."

"It was all the mud's fault." Minnie spoke up. "Meredith isn't to blame. It could have happened to anybody."

"Not anybody." Was that a hint of amusement in Papa's

voice? "For instance, I drove that stretch of road home and I had no problem avoiding the mud holes."

Doom. Meredith hung her head, knowing the official pronouncement was imminent. She would be banned from the family's horse and buggy forever.

"Dear Father," he began to pray instead using his most serious voice. The room fell silent except for the creak of the back door opening, muffled by the closed kitchen door.

Was it Shane coming in for his dinner? Were those his boots thudding with authority against the floorboards in the other room?

"Please bless this food we are about to partake and know that we are grateful for Thy bounty." Papa's brow furrowed in concentration, his face set with sincerity.

I should be paying attention. She did her best to rope in her thoughts, but her disobedient ears continued to strain for the texture of that low, deep voice talking with Cook. It had to be Shane's because her soul knew it, the rise and fall and rumble.

Please help him to forgive me, Father, she asked silently.

"Although we are far from perfect," Papa continued, "You forgive us and continue to bless us with Your loving kindness."

Was it her imagination or did Papa wink at her? It was hard to tell because he was so very somber as he finished his prayer.

"Guide us to Your will, Lord, and Your eternal light. Amen."

"Amens" rang around the table, but the faint low rumble of Shane's chuckle was the only sound she heard. It rolled through her like a spring breeze, welcome and refreshing. Why did he affect her so?

"Meredith!" Minnie nudged her with an elbow. "Pass the gravy."

"Right." She shook her head, trying to scatter her thoughts, but Shane remained front and center, the tap of his boots against the floor, the deep note of his "thank you," and the final squeak of the closing door more drawing than the delicious scents steaming up from the serving platters and her family's conversation.

"I know how you feel, Henrietta," Papa said to Mama as he plopped a spoonful of mashed potatoes onto his plate. "But this is the best horseman around. Even our dear Thad recommended him. Braden Shaw and his apprentice are genuine wranglers. They've broken and trained horses from Texas all the way to Canada. They've been all over the West. Can you imagine? Just like in my favorite novels."

"Novels are made-up fiction," Mama pointed out as she always did from her end of the long table. "Just you mind that. Real horses kick and bite and run away with their drivers. Remember what happened to you? You were nearly killed handling an unbroken horse. I hardly think we need animals like that in our stables."

"That's why we have a horse trainer, my dear. Besides, I'm fit as a fiddle and fully healed. As Meredith says, all's well that ends well."

"All ends well only with eternal vigilance, heaven's guidance and common sense." If a corner of Mama's mouth upturned as if battling good humor, it had to be Meredith's imagination. "I know where this is going, Robert, and no, I refuse to reconsider. Meredith will not be driving that buggy again anytime soon."

Meredith was certain Papa winked at her as he handed Minnie the bowl of mashed potatoes.

"I would like to learn to drive." Minnie dug into the

potatoes with unladylike zeal. "Do you think Shane could teach me?"

"Wilhelmina!" Mama's fork and knife tapped against the rim of her dinner plate. "Such talk! You are far too young, and no, I know what is coming next. You may not learn to ride horses either. A Worthington lady does not resort to such behavior."

"But, Mama, I don't want to be a lady."

The back of her neck tingled, as if someone were watching her. Shane? His path from the kitchen door to the bunkhouse would take him through the garden and right past the dining-room windows. Sadie, their maid, would have given them their meals in a basket. Hired men were not allowed to eat in the house. Was he standing outside looking in, and what was he thinking of her?

She craved the opportunity to talk with him. She glanced over her shoulder, searching through the glass for the sight of his black Stetson and his striking face. But all she saw was the turn of his back and the impressive line of his shoulder as he strode away.

He had understood about her mother when they had spoken before. Surely he would do so again. And if she ought to be wondering why his opinion of her mattered, she didn't want to analyze it and took the potato bowl from Minnie instead.

"Why don't you tell us all what Lydia's letter said," Papa began as he cut into a slice of roast beef. "I brought home the mail today and there was an envelope from our girls."

"And another letter from the school's headmaster." Mama's mouth pursed as she held out her hand, waiting for the potatoes. "Angelina is on warning. She was caught smoking behind the outhouse again. Another stunt and she will be permanently suspended."

"Did you truly think finishing school would change

her?" Tilly said in her gentle way. "She doesn't want to be there, Mama."

"I know how that feels." Meredith handed over the bowl and accepted the beef platter from Minnie. She forked a slice of meat onto her plate, remembering how restricted she had felt, how smothered. "Sometimes a girl just has to be who she is, or she feels as if her heart will die."

"Nonsense." Mama dished up with a clink of the spoon against her china plate. "We have a family obligation and standards to uphold. We may have moved out West for practical purposes, we are still considered a part of good society. We must not allow our conduct to slide."

Mama cared far too much what certain people thought about her. Life in St. Louis had been much different, and her mother had been happier with her numerous clubs and charities there. They had moved to take care of cousin Noelle when she had been blinded in a buggy accident, and her parents—Mama's brother—killed. But what the Worthington girls had seen as an adventure, Mama had viewed as a necessary duty, a hardship she struggled to rise above.

"I hope you do not rue the day you dropped out of that fine school." Mama's pronouncement was punctuated by another dollop of mashed potato hitting her plate. "Now, back to Lydia's letter. Your dear sweet sister writes that she loves her teachers and her coursework this year is most enjoyable."

Meredith glanced over her shoulder again. The pathway was empty and all sight of Shane gone. She felt as if something important, something she couldn't describe, had slipped away.

The bunkhouse smelled like fresh lumber, coal smoke and boiling coffee. Shane pushed back his now-empty dinner plate on the plank table and took in his new home. Much better than their last place with separate rooms for sleeping and living, comfortable chairs near the generous windows and a woodstove. Cozy enough to spend a comfortable evening reading and plenty of room for at least a half-dozen hired men. The place echoed around them.

"Looks like Worthington is hoping to be a major operation one day, judging by the size of this place." Braden ambled over with the coffeepot and filled both ironware cups. "Good for him. I had a chance to ride around the spread. He's got some prime land for raising horses."

"And plenty of it." That took money, and judging by the looks of things, the Worthingtons were rolling in it. Memories of the life back home, the one he'd been dying to get away from, hit him like a slap to the face.

"Tomorrow we look over the horses we've come to train." Braden set the coffeepot on the stove with a *clunk*. "Caught sight of the two-year-olds in the paddock. Fine-looking bunch. Robert Worthington has a good eye. Shouldn't be too hard of a job, if we can answer to Worthington only. That wife of his…" Braden didn't finish the sentence, shaking his head.

Shane didn't need to be a mind reader to know what his boss was thinking. Braden had issues with women, especially the domineering type. Thinking of his own mother, who managed her family and alienated his father with her overbearing determination to have everything her way, Shane couldn't blame him. It was the reason he'd chosen his own path in life. He pushed out of his chair and opened the door a crack. With the fire going full bore, the well-built house was sweltering. "At least we can leave when our work is done, and sooner if you decide to."

"There's nothing better than freedom," Braden agreed, swinging into his chair. He dug into the sugar bowl and stirred a couple teaspoonfuls into his coffee. "It's why I'll always be a bachelor."

"Always? That's a mighty long time."

"And well worth it. I can come and go as I please, do what I want without being henpecked to death by a woman." He slurped the steaming coffee, a man content with his life.

"Or lied to." Hard not to talk about what had been on his mind all afternoon, since they'd come upon the young ladies in the road. Just Meredith, she'd been then, pretty as a picture in her pretty yellow dress and gold locks tumbling down from her hood, flyaway curls that framed her beautiful heart-shaped face like a dream. She looked sweet with that swipe of mud on her peaches-and-cream cheek and wholesome, so determined she was to help free the buggy.

Captivated, that was a word he might have used to describe her effect on him. That was before she'd gone from Just Meredith to a Worthington daughter, one of the richest families in the county and, according to Braden's research, the territory. The way she'd tricked him taunted him now, reminding him of how easy it was to get the wrong impression about someone. He tugged the sugar bowl closer to his cup and stirred in a heaping spoonful. Coffee steamed and the strong rich brew tickled his nose.

"You aren't thinking about the Worthington girl, are you?" Braden stared at him over the rim. The rising steam gave his piercing look a menacing quality.

"Don't worry about it." He had been, so he couldn't lie. "It's nothing."

"Make sure it is. This is the first time I've seen you show interest in a calico since I've known you." Braden took another slurping sip. "I feel beholden to warn you to stay away from her. She's the boss man's daughter. That's a brand of trouble you don't want to get tangled up in."

"Not intending to." The hot coffee scorched his tongue and seared his throat and shook him out of his reverie. He was here to work and to learn. Braden was one of the best trainers in the country and he wasn't going to mess up this chance to work with him. "I suppose Meredith Worthington is eye-catching enough, but I've seen who she really is. Nothing she can do from this point on can make me see her differently. She's not pretty enough to distract me from my work."

"Good to know." Braden nodded once, turning the conversation to tomorrow's workday, which was scheduled to start well before dawn.

Shane didn't hear the muffled gasp on the front step or the faint rustle of a petticoat. The gentle tap of the falling snow outside and the roar of the fire in the stove drowned out the quiet footsteps hurrying away through the storm.

Chapter Four

Meredith shook the snow from her cloak at the back door in the shelter of the lean-to before turning the handle. Clutching the covered plate, she eased into the busy kitchen, where Cook scrubbed pots at the steaming soapy basin and barked orders to their housemaid, Sadie, who scurried to comply.

Sadie never missed anything and glanced at the full plate Meredith slid onto the edge of the worktable. "They don't like cookies?" she asked.

"Something like that." Still smarting from the conversation she'd overheard, she numbly shrugged out of her wraps and hung them by the stove to dry. Shane's words rang in her head, unstoppable. He wasn't going to understand. He didn't want to be friends. He didn't think she was pretty.

She squeezed her eyes shut, facing the wall, glad that her back was to the other people in the room so no one could see the pain traveling through her. It hurt to know what he thought of her.

"Meredith?" The inner door swung open, shoes beat a cheerful rhythm on the hardwood and Minnie burst into sight, cheeks pink, fine shocks of dark hair escaping from her twin braids. "There you are! You are supposed to help me with my spelling. Mama said so."

"I'll be right up." Her voice sounded strained as she arranged the hem of her cloak. She could not fully face her sister. Pressure built behind her ribs like a terrible storm brewing. Shane's tone—one of disdain and dismissal—was something she could not forget. He'd said terrible things about her. So, why did pieces of their afternoon together linger? The way he'd swiped mud from her cheek, leaned close to tuck his blanket around her and the steadying strength of his hand when he'd helped her from the buggy hurt doubly now. Why it tormented her was a mystery. She didn't know why she cared. She no longer wanted to care. A man who would say that about her was off her friend list.

"Meredith?" Minnie asked. "Are you all right?"

"Couldn't be better." Fine, so it wasn't the truth, but it would be. She was an independent type of girl, she didn't go around moaning the loss of some boy's opinion. She was strong, self-reliant and sure of her plans in life, and those plans had nothing to do with some horseman who was too quick to judge. He undoubtedly had a whole list of flaws and personality defects.

"Good, because you looked really unhappy." Minnie crept close and took her hand, her fingers small and timid. "Are you terribly upset at losing your driving privileges?"

"A little." A lot, but she would deal with that when the morning came, when she had to be driven to town like a child. With Eli gone, Shane would be the logical person to take his place.

Oh, no. No, no, no. Her pulse stalled, her knees buckled, and she grabbed the wall with her free hand for support. However could she endure being close to him and, remembering what he'd said about her, pretending not to? Sitting there next to Minnie on the backseat through the silence of the drive to the schoolhouse staring at the back of his head?

"I think Papa understands." Minnie's grip tightened, the melody of her voice ringing with loving sympathy. "Maybe he will let you drive again after the roads firm up. The mud won't last forever."

"Yes, sure." She squeezed her sister's hand, so little and trusting within hers. She loved her sisters; she was so blessed to have each and every one of them. "Now, let's get you upstairs and we will see how well you know your spelling lesson."

"I studied and everything." Minnie wiggled her hand free and skipped ahead, rattling the china in the hutch.

"Minnie!" Mama admonished as the kitchen door swung open. "No running in the house. How many times must I tell you?"

"I forget." Minnie meekly skidded to a stop in the dining room, although her fast walk held quite a bit of a skip as she headed toward the staircase.

"Walk like a lady!" Mama peered around the edge of the sofa in the parlor, her sewing on her lap. "Do not forget you are a Worthington. We glide, we don't gallop like barnyard animals."

"Yes, Mama." Minnie grabbed the banister and pounded up the steps, perhaps unaware how her footsteps thundered through the house.

"Quietly!" Mama's demand followed them up to the second story, where Minnie popped into the first doorway on the right and jumped onto the foot of her bed. The ropes groaned in protest.

Did Minnie's window have to have a perfect view of the new bunkhouse? Meredith stopped at the small desk, pushed up to the sill and stared beyond the greening leaves of the orchard to the glowing squares of lamplight. Behind those muslin curtains was the man who'd maligned her, who'd judged her and whose words she could not get out of her mind.

I've seen who she really is, he'd said. She wrapped her fingers around the back rung of the chair until her fingers turned white. The pain returned, digging as if with talons around the edges of her heart. How could he judge her like that without giving her the chance to explain?

"Meredith? The list." Minnie bounced impatiently on the feather mattress.

The list? She shook her head, an attempt to scatter her thoughts, but they remained like hot, red, angry coals glowing in her skull. She glanced at the book lying open on the desk before her and concentrated on the words printed there, forcing all thoughts of Shane Connelly from her mind.

She chose a word randomly from Minnie's spelling assignment. "Insularity."

"Insularity," Minnie repeated, taking a deep breath, pausing as she wrestled with the word. *"I—n—s—"*

It wasn't fair. He wasn't fair. Her gaze strayed to the windows of the bunkhouse, where the bracing scent of fresh coffee had filled the rooms and carried out the cracked open door.

"—i—t—y," Minnie finished. "Insularity. It means to be narrow-or small-minded."

Not that a certain horseman came to mind. She cleared her throat, grateful when no emotion sounded in her voice. She chose another word from the list. "Supposition."

"S—u—p—" Minnie's dear button face furrowed in concentration.

Meredith did her best to stare at the word on the page, checking carefully to make sure her baby sister got the spelling right. Was it her fault her eyes kept drifting upward? It was as if there was something wrong with them, as if Shane Connelly held some sort of power over her ocular muscles tugging them in his direction.

"—*n*." Minnie sounded proud of herself. "It means to draw a conclusion or an assumption."

That was exactly what had happened today. Shane had met her mother, seen the family's rather extravagant house and assumed she was the same, a pampered young lady of privilege who was not good enough for an honest man like him. The talons of pain clutched tighter, as if wringing blood. She didn't want to think why this mattered so much.

"Prejudice," she squeaked out of a too-tight throat. She felt as if she did not have enough air to speak with. As if all the surprise and shock of what she'd overheard had drained away, leaving no buffer. She had not leaped to conclusions about him, although she was happy to do so now.

"*P—r—*" Minnie paused, scrunching up her face as she tried to visualize the spelling. "*—e—j—*"

What was she doing, fretting about a saddle tramp? She didn't care what he thought of her. He was clearly not the type of person she wanted to befriend, and if a tiny voice deep within argued, then she chose to ignore it. He'd insulted her, hurt her feelings and now her dignity. Well, she was hurting, and she had better things to dwell on than a man like that.

"*—i—c—e*." Minnie finished with a rush. "Whew. I almost always get that one wrong."

"It's tricky," Meredith agreed, gathering the book with both hands and turning her back to the window. Forget Shane Connelly. That was certainly what she intended to do from this moment on.

A knock rapped against the open door. Her oldest sister hesitated in the threshold. "Hey, are you busy?"

"I've spelled three words in a row correctly!" Minnie gave a hop, beaming with pride.

"That's what happens when you study first," Tilly teased in her gentle way, love obvious on her oval face. Her brown curls bounced as she bounded forward with a sweep of her skirts and plopped on the free corner of Minnie's bed. "I overheard Papa and Mama talking. I have a suspicion Papa will be able to make things right."

"In time for school in the morning?" Meredith asked.

"Probably not that soon."

Of course not. However soon her father talked her mother into changing her mind, it could not come fast enough. First thing tomorrow she would have to face Shane. Dread filled her. The thought of him waiting for her alongside the buggy, reaching out his hand to help her up, being able to listen in on her conversations with Minnie from the front seat, filled her with a burning mix of confusion, hurt and rage.

Well, she didn't care about his hurtful words. Her pride was wounded, that was all. So what if he didn't like her? Why would she want him to? She simply didn't have to like him. She pulled out the chair and sat down, her spine straight, her back to the window. What she needed to do was to banish all thoughts of the man from her head.

Pleased with her plan, she could focus on her sisters' conversation.

"No, Minnie, I can't drive you tomorrow." Tilly smoothed a wrinkle in her skirt. "I wish I could, but I promised Mama I would help her finish your new dress. You are growing like a weed, little sister."

"I am." Pleased, Minnie grinned, showing off her adorable dimples. "Pretty soon I ought to be tall enough to ride a wild mustang. Then I could help break next year's new horses and Papa wouldn't have to hire anyone to do it."

"I don't think that's likely to happen, not if Mama has anything to say about it." Worrying the discussion would turn to the hired men, Meredith changed the subject. "What about the day after tomorrow? Can you drive me then, Tilly?"

"I have a meeting at the church that afternoon, but I think we can work it out. Unless Mama has objections about the road conditions. After all, you can't miss going to your weekly sewing circle." Her older sister stared at her intently, as if trying to see at something beneath the surface, something Meredith did not want anyone to know. Tilly shook her head, as if she could not figure it out. "I understand not wanting one of the new hired men to drive you. I'm shy around strangers, too."

Shy? That was hardly the problem. She thought of how she'd bantered with Shane, how he'd made her blush and laugh and quip. She feared her face was heating and her emotions would show and her sisters would guess at the truth.

You don't like him, Meredith, she reminded herself. *It's impossible.* He's *impossible.*

"Oh, Meredith wasn't one bit shy when they met up with us on the road," Minnie burst out. "She and Shane talked practically the whole way home."

"Is this true?" Tilly studied her again, her curiosity greater and her scrutiny more intent.

Heat burned her cheeks. She could feel her skin across her face tighten. Surely she was blushing. A dead giveaway. "I was polite to him, nothing more. I assure you of that."

"But you're blushing."

"Because I feel uncomfortable." That was true. Uncomfortable with the way Shane made her feel, with her hurt dignity and with this discussion. "You know I have plans that have nothing to do with finding a man to marry me right out of school. What would I want with an iterant horseman who is here for two months at the most and then he'll leave, never to be seen again?"

"I wasn't thinking of that." Tilly shrugged, her slender shoulders sagging a notch. The hint of sadness that overcame her was heart-wrenching. "I was wistful, that is all, hoping that true love would come your way, since it is sure not to be coming to mine."

"Don't say that." Meredith slipped onto her knees before her sister, gathering her slim hands in hers. "There is always hope for true love. Emmett is simply busy with his business."

"Oh, he was never truly interested in me. I was the one. It was all me. I mistook his politeness for more, that's all." Although her chin came up and she pasted on a smile, there was no disguising the hint of heartbreak on Matilda's dear face, a sorrow she kept hidden. "A girl has to have wishes, or what else does she have?"

"God. Family. Principles." Mama thundered into the room. They had all been so engrossed they hadn't heard her until she towered over them, glowering. "Some men are more appropriate to love than others, my girls. Now, why aren't you studying? And, Matilda, shouldn't you be downstairs sewing?"

"Yes, Mama," they muttered in unison, Meredith leaping to her feet, Tilly pushing off the bed and Minnie bouncing once before hopping two-footed to the floor.

Meredith glanced over her shoulder, drawn by the lit windows gleaming in the dark evening, unable to stop a deep pinch of regret and, to be honest, a wish that Shane had not been Papa's hired man. That they had parted ways at the driveway and he had kept riding so she would have been left with the romantic tale of their brief meeting, a moment in time when she could have forever believed in the man and his dimples, his good humor and character. She could have lived the rest of her days with the legend of their meeting and what she had believed him to be.

Now that she knew the truth, there was no legend, no sweetness, no tale of romance. Just the broken pieces of what had never been.

In the long gray shadows of dawn, Shane dragged on his boots by the back door, head pounding and eyes scratchy from what fell far short of a restful night's sleep. He'd been fitful, unable to drift off on the top bunk of what was a comfortable feather tick, in clean muslin sheets and plenty of blankets. After a hard day's ride he should have slept hard enough that only Braden's rough shaking by the arm could have woken him.

"Quit dragging your feet and let's get the morning started." Braden growled as he jammed one arm and then the other into his riding jacket. "We've got work to do."

Not that he minded work. No, he thrived on it. He loved every aspect of horse care from the shoveling to the riding. But this morning a dull ache stabbed his temples as he finished tying his boots, winced when the wind caught the door and smacked it against the wall. He grabbed his coat.

Dawn hadn't yet softened the night's shadows, but already the horses were stirring, some more enthusiastic than others, nickering for attention and feed. Braden led the first animal out of her stall—a demure white mare—and cross-tied her in the breezeway.

"Get to work." Braden handed him a pitchfork and left him to take care of business.

A lot must have been on his mind last night because it tried to surface as he worked. He dug the tines into the soiled straw and hiked it into a pile. He worked with quick, even strokes, lifting and turning the fork, making fast work of the roomy stall before moving onto the next. Was Meredith far from him mind?

Not a chance.

Worse than that, he couldn't stop thinking of home. As merry golden light fell through the cracks in the walls and the double doors open on either end of the barn, he lost his battle to keep sad things buried. Maybe it was this place, he conceded, with its impressive stone-and-wood manor house. The no-expenses-spared stables and fine pedigreed horses reminded him of his family's stable back home. Not that Father was a horseman by any means, but he took pride in owning the best driving horses in White Water County. Appearances were everything in his family.

His guts still twisted up remembering the pressure he'd felt as the firstborn. The love he'd tried so hard to earn most of his childhood until he finally figured out that if you had to earn it, then it wasn't love. Not the real thing, anyway.

Although he'd been gone a while, he missed his family. Just because he couldn't get along with them didn't mean a lack of love. He thought of Grandmama and her kitchen full of delicious smells and her plain house full of blooming flowers. Mother with her narrow view of the world and her belief that she ought to control what she could of it. His younger brother who was always in and out of one scrape or another. Hard to imagine him buckling down to work in Father's and Grandfather's firm and being groomed for politics. He missed the boy's constant ribbing and antics.

Homesickness tugged at him. There were good things he missed—wrestling with his brother, riding with his dad, his mother's cookies and his grandmother's understanding. Sure, he missed home, although he did not want to be there.

"Time to harness up the gray mare for the schoolgirls."

Braden's announcement rang through the barn like a death knell.

Shane grimaced. In truth, he'd been hoping to put that task off as long as possible. Nothing to be done about it but put aside his pitchfork, leave the rest to Braden and go in search of the old, placid mare.

Sweetie greeted him with hopefulness. Recognizing the gleam in those big brown eyes, he searched his pockets for a sugar cube. She took it daintily from his palm, a polite girl. Hard not to like her. Her beauty wasn't in long, perfect lines or the quality of her breeding, but in something far more important. He led her gently through the barn to the buggy he'd washed while his hands froze in yesterday's last bit of daylight and slipped a collar over her neck.

"Whatever happens—" a voice broke the silence behind him "—don't let Meredith talk you into driving."

"Yes, Mr. Worthington." He'd met the patriarch of the family late last night after all the barn work was done. He didn't have an opinion of the man one way or the other. Worthington hadn't been as off-putting as his wife and was far friendlier. Shane gave the mare a pat. "I expect the roads to be tough going, so I'd like to get an early start."

"Wise. I'll inform the girls." Robert hesitated like a man with something on his mind.

Here it comes, Shane predicted. He buckled the gray mare into the traces, bracing himself for whatever warning or judgment the wealthy man was about to make. Most likely a threatening warning to stay away from the Worthington daughters.

"It was hard to let Eli go. He had been a fine employee. Always took care of my horses and my girls. I never gave either of them a moment's worry when they were in his care." Robert cracked a smile, a masculine hint of Meredith's, and he had the same stormy blue eyes.

This job meant a lot to him so he would take the warning on the chin. Not let insult to injury show.

"I can read between the lines," Worthington went on. "The mud on the girls. Mud on the buggy. And poor Sweetie was barrel high. I noticed you cleaned the buggy, boots and tack without saying a word. You helped the girls when they needed it, and I'm much obliged. I can rest easier knowing they are in safe hands with you at the reins."

Sometimes folks surprised you, Shane thought as he gave the last buckle a tug. Maybe this would be a better assignment than he'd figured, not that he was looking forward to driving Miss Meredith Worthington around town. But this was what Worthington wanted, so he would do it to the best of his ability. "I won't disappoint you, sir."

"You say that like a man who has no clue what he's in for." Worthington shook his head, retracing his steps. "Meredith is not happy about this. Consider it a word of warning."

Meredith. As if his thoughts had summoned her, she bustled into the barn, dusted with snowfall and clutching a big stack of schoolbooks in the crook of her arm. If the scowl on her beautiful face was any indication, she was about as thrilled with the situation as he was.

Chapter Five

Her plan to banish Shane Connelly from her thoughts backfired like a Winchester with a jammed cartridge. Meredith swiped snow from her face as she took smaller and smaller steps toward the waiting buggy. He was there, as remote as stone, as unmoving as marble. He did not even seem to be breathing.

Perhaps it was especially difficult for him to be anywhere in proximity to her. She pushed Minnie ahead of her, gently nudging her along so she would reach the buggy first. She'd worried over this moment all night long, whenever dreams would pull her from her sleep, taunting dreams of Shane's smile, his dimples, the snap of aliveness she'd felt in his presence. Regret had chased her all night long, keeping her sleep fitful and dawn a welcome release. She'd risen out of bed, dreading each step she took, each word to her sisters, every bite at the breakfast table because it led her all inexorably here to this unstoppable moment as he helped Minnie into the buggy's backseat and then held out his gloved hand.

Memories of that hand in hers mocked her. Worse, he gazed past her, as if she didn't exist to him. Much worse than she'd anticipated. She didn't have to worry about meeting his gaze and being reminded of his words last night. She ignored his hand and clamored into the buggy of her own accord, settling her skirts and reaching for the lap robe before he could help.

You can be tougher than this, Meredith. She set her chin, focused her gaze forward, aware of his hesitation, so near to her she could hear him breathe. His gaze scorched her, raking the side of her face like a touch. If she turned and dared to face him, would she see regret softening the rugged angles of his handsome face? Or would she see his disdain?

His opinion of you doesn't matter, she told herself, curling her fingers tightly around the hem of the robe. She was independent. She should not need any man's regard, and it irked her beyond all reason that his opinion did matter. Somehow the air turned colder, the morning less bright as he took a silent step away and settled with a creak of leather onto the front.

"What about the roads?" Minnie scooted forward and laid her arms against the back of his seat. "Are we going to get stuck again?"

"We'll have to wait and see," came Shane's reply, warm and friendly as he gathered Sweetie's reins. "The snow is too wet for the sleigh and the road is too soft for the wheels. It ought to be interesting."

"I trust you." Minnie grinned at him, flashing her adorable dimples. "I know you're a really good driver. I can tell because Papa hired you."

"Then I'll try not to let you or your papa down." Shane released the brake and gave the thick leather straps a careful slap. The old gray mare stepped out into the yard, eager to lift her nose to the flyaway snowflakes tumbling from the sky. An arctic wind fluttered her mane and ruffled the edges of the lap robe, letting in a cold blast of air.

"That's good, because I don't want to be late. I have a spelling test this morning and I can't miss it," Minnie chattered on. "I really worked hard and I know every word perfectly."

"You do?" Shane seemed interested in a kindly, brotherly way.

If Meredith didn't have her heart set against him, then she would have liked how he treated her little sister.

"It's the very first time I have studied so hard." Minnie swiped snow from her eyes. "I always pretend to study, but Mama keeps getting really mad at my grades. I have to go to finishing school in two years, and my marks are abysmal. That's what Mama says. I don't think they are all that bad. I would rather be riding horses than sitting in school."

"That's the way I felt, too, shortcakes. I finished school first, and *then* I started working with horses." He turned his attention to the road ahead of them, the half-frozen mud clutching the buggy wheels like glue. The old mare struggled, lowering her head to dig in with all her might.

"You called me shortcakes." Minnie's grin stretched from ear to ear. She knocked the snow accumulating on her pink cap. "How come?"

"'Cuz you're cute and you're sweet."

"I am?" Pleased, her grin went dazzling. No doubt about it, in a few years she would be breaking more than a few young men's hearts.

"I would appreciate it if you were not so familiar with my sister." That cool voice could only belong to Meredith. How he could ever have mistaken her for a sweet country miss was beyond him. He didn't have to look over his shoulder to know she had her chin up and a regal look on her beautiful face.

"The apple didn't fall too far from the tree?" he asked. With a gasp, she fell silent. He gave thanks for the whipping wind and thick snow sailing into the buggy. He had his opinion on many things, such as a fancy summer buggy being used for winter driving, but he kept his tongue. He tried to convince himself it didn't hurt that she obviously didn't like him. As he guided the mare down the snowy landscape, doing his best to guess where the higher ground beneath the snow might be, he felt her disregard like the beat of the wind.

Admit it. You don't like disliking her. He'd been captivated by the country beauty in the road yesterday, but what he'd told Braden was also true. These days he was a working man, not his father's son, and pretty debutantes like Miss Meredith Worthington had to stay out of his reach. He'd learned his lesson about debutantes the hard way. His brief fiancée, Patricia, had only cared about having material things and more of them than her friends, and he did not want to go down that path again. Regardless of how beautiful Meredith was or how fascinating, she was not the kind of woman who could capture his heart.

Not that he was looking for one.

The mare heaved, struggling with the weight she pulled. The ground was not fully frozen, and mud sucked at the wheels, making the going rough. Without a word of reassurance for the fine Worthington girls in the backseat, he hopped out of the buggy to lighten the load and gripped the icy trace. He walked beside Sweetie the rest of the way to town, glad to be battling snow and the road instead of thoughts of Miss Meredith and her cool disdain.

The school's bell tower could be seen from the town of Angel Falls's main street, rising like a ghost above the two-story buildings and playing peekaboo through the veils of snowfall. Meredith thought of her friends and wondered if they would already be gathered in the schoolhouse, or would Providence be with her and she would arrive first so that no one would be able to notice the new driver. Watching the stiff line of his back and the way he purposefully ignored her had not put her in a pleasant mood. She wondered if she should ask him if she could help, too, but could not summon up the will to speak to him. If only she was as tough as she wished to be.

They turned the corner and the schoolyard came into view. Well-bundled students marched along the streets. Horses and vehicles clogged the roadway as parents dropped off their children for the day. Screams and shouts rose like shrill music as snowball fights dominated the well-covered lawn, gangs of girls clustered together to laugh and share news, and the first series of bells tolled from the tower.

"Shane is a really good driver." Minnie clutched the lap robe and shivered in the cold. "We didn't get stuck once and we got here really fast. Ooh, look, there's Maisie." She leaned over the side to wave at her friend.

Not only was he a good driver, but he was kind to their dear mare. His soothing tone, his care when she struggled, the way he laid a hand on her neck when a snowball from the schoolyard flew into her path all spoke well of him. She'd paid attention to the way he'd handled the horse all the way to town, realizing that as a driver he had done so much more than hold the reins and tug on them now and then. It bothered her greatly that she could learn much from him, the one man she did not ever want to talk to.

Sweetie stopped in front of the school. Finally. Meredith hopped down, not bothering to wait for the new driver's assistance, and slung her book bag over her shoulder. She did not require his assistance. Her dignity may still be smarting, but he did not seem the least bit affected. He stepped away from her and gave Minnie his attention.

"Meredith!" Fiona waved, trudging through the snow, her lunch pail swinging from one red-mittened hand, her book bag from the other. "I just finished blanketing Flannigan. Could you believe all the vehicles stuck on the road? I didn't think you would make it."

"We have a new driver who is surprisingly competent." Surely Shane could hear her. He was merely feet behind her, helping Minnie from the buggy, so close the hair on the back of her neck tingled.

"So I see." Fiona, happily engaged, glanced curiously at the hooded figure who was mantled with snow. "Oh, he's good-looking."

"Is he? I thought so when I first met him, but then I changed my mind." He was beyond what a sane woman would call handsome; he was magnificent. The steady strength, the quick world-changing grin added to his gentle manner would make the toughest female look twice. But she could not bear to let him think she thought him so fine.

"Isn't he your type?" Fiona asked. "Handsome, rugged, very manly?"

"My type?" *Please, don't let him have heard that, Lord.* She glanced over her shoulder to see Shane handing Minnie her lunch pail with a big brother's kindness. A smirk tugged at the corner of his mouth.

He *had* heard her.

"Oh, he's all right," she said, letting her voice lift on the wind, knowing full well Shane could hear her. "But he's not fine enough to interest me."

"Meredith! What a thing to say, and I think he heard you." Dear gentle Fiona was shocked. She skidded to a halt, jaw dropped, eyes wide with a sad censure. "I've never known you to be mean before."

"I—" The excuses died on her lips. Cold quivered through her, burrowing deep into her bone marrow and further, as if into her soul. She'd only meant him to know that she hadn't been thinking about romance, that she hadn't been hoping he was interested in her. She wanted him to know that he'd hurt her, but the words had come out wrong, and now she'd made matters worse.

The man drove her crazy.

Shane's gaze fastened on hers, holding her prisoner as time stilled. Snowflakes tangled in her lashes, but she could not break away from the compelling mix of hurt and sadness darkening the wondrous blue of his eyes. She could feel his emotions as clearly as her own. It was the oddest sensation. The connection they'd forged upon first sight remained, but it was wounded, no longer light and full of laughter but of something grave.

I'm sorry, she wanted to say, but before she could, he broke away. The wind gusted and the snow fell harder as if even God were ashamed and trying to steal him from her sight.

"Fiona! Meredith!" Scarlet Fisher emerged from the storm, her bag swinging from her shoulder, her beautiful red hair dusted with snow from her walk through town. "Who was that?"

"Nobody." The word was out before she could stop it. Meredith drew her scarf over her face. She could hide her humiliation from her friends, but not from herself. How could she have done such a thing?

"He's almost as handsome as Lorenzo." Scarlet shook the snow from her knit cap and fell into stride alongside them. Snowballs flew over their heads and little kids darted into their path as they waded through the yard toward the schoolhouse's front steps. "Is he Eli's replacement?"

"He must be," Fiona replied, "although Meredith doesn't seem to like him."

"What's not to like?" Scarlet asked. "Did you see his shoulders? He looks like a hero out of a novel."

"You always say that." Fiona rolled her eyes, although she was smiling. Ever since she had become engaged at Christmastime, she had been a lot happier. It was good to see. "Sometimes men like that are even real."

What they needed was to change the subject, Meredith decided and took charge of the situation. "Did either of you figure out the last math problem in our homework assignment?"

"Who cares about our homework?" Scarlet grabbed Meredith's hand, staring in the direction of the school steps. "Lorenzo."

Sure enough, Lorenzo Davis stood off to the side, chatting with a few of his close friends. Their nemesis, Narcissa Bell, was easy to spot as she laid a possessive hand on Lorenzo's arm, as if staking claim.

Fiona said something, words lost in the wind and snow and the fuzz in Meredith's brain. Of all the sounds in the school yard, it was a single note of baritone, low and gentle, that rumbled to her ears. It was Shane speaking to the old mare, encouraging her through the combination of deep mud and spots of ice the busy road had turned to.

The snowfall hid him, but she could picture him perfectly, his straight impressive posture, powerful and so caring as he walked alongside the mare. Other horses neighed in frustration, other drivers shouted in exasperation, and even a whip crack or two snapped out. But Shane's comforting voice did not show impatience or frustration or cruelty.

You do not like him, Meredith. She stared at the ground where the snow grabbed at her shoes and her ruffled hem, sick with regret. She'd never been so disappointed in herself. Had he taken her words to heart, the way she had his?

Or was he tougher, able to disregard the hurtful comments from a girl he'd found less than worthy?

From a girl who had just sounded extraordinarily like her mother. The realization punched through her like a physical blow. Her knees weakened, shock rolled through her and she'd never felt so bad. One thing was for certain: Shane Connelly brought out the worst in her.

Perhaps it was her duty to bring out the best.

"Meredith." A sneering voice broke into her thoughts, a familiar and unfriendly voice. Narcissa Bell gave her perfect blond ringlets a toss. "I heard your father hired a new horse trainer. When my father was looking for a new trainer, he had considered the same man but found someone much better. Too bad your papa couldn't afford to do the same."

"Leave her alone." Scarlet, fearless as always, shouldered up to Narcissa hard enough to knock her back a step. "You ought to be more careful. Your jealousy is showing."

"As if I could be jealous of her." Narcissa dropped her tone, so it wouldn't carry to the crowd she had been with. "Lorenzo is as good as my beau. I don't see him hanging around with your circle. Meredith isn't so much."

"If you can't say anything nice, then maybe you shouldn't say anything at all." Fiona led the way up the stairs. "C'mon, Meredith."

"Poor Lorenzo." Meredith followed her friends, her shoes slipping on the icy step. She was aware of Narcissa's glare, the quick glance up and then down at her new hat, her elegant traveling coat and the new dress Mama had finished the other day with the ruffled and embellished hem finer than even Narcissa's.

She had learned a lot of lessons living in this small town, ones she had never learned at finishing school where Mama had wanted her to turn out so fine. Clothes did not make the person, material possessions did not matter, certainly not in the way that God cared about. As she shrugged out of her wraps in the crowded vestibule, she was aware of each rustle of the green velveteen gown, every ivory button, every inch of imported French lace.

"This time she's probably telling the truth," Scarlet said as she hung up her practical brown coat. "You know, one of these days, she's going to snare him."

"Poor Lorenzo," Fiona agreed, hanging up her old dove-gray coat with care. She smoothed the wrinkles from her plain gingham dress. "It's important to be with someone kind you can trust to be good to you."

"You would know all about that," Scarlet answered, gathering up her book bag, adorable in her blue flannel plaid dress, trimmed with wooden buttons and matching ribbon. "Your wedding is three weeks away. Are you getting excited?"

"Nervous. Marriage is a big change. But I'm excited, too." Fiona reached out, taking Meredith's hand. "You are off in a daze again. Are you still worried about your homework?"

"I'm always worried about my schoolwork." At least that was true, and a good way to avoid admitting her most cherished goal had not been on the forefront of her mind. Shane had.

Right now he was battling the road and weather conditions right along with Sweetie, his shoulders as unbowed as his spirit as he guided her on the long trip home. His work was harder because Papa would not let his girls be seen in the serviceable but plain sled with the right runners for this weather, a vehicle made for hauling hay to the animals.

I wish I were a simple country girl, she thought, because then Shane would still like her and she would not feel as if she stuck out here, among her friends and the place she loved.

"Meredith." Lila, keeping her voice low, opened her bag and pulled out a comb. She began to fluff at her sleek cinnamon-brown hair. "Love your dress. Is that the one your mother just finished?"

"No one can embroider like Mama." She felt self-conscious of the fluffs and the flourishes and the rose embroidery in matching silk thread that adorned the bottom tier of the skirt. It was lovely, but it didn't fit the image of the one-room schoolteacher she wished to be—the woman she wanted to be. She set her book bag on the desk, which she shared with Scarlet, and gestured toward the empty seat where the rest of their friends should be. "I guess both Kate and Earlee are having trouble making it."

"Kate has a long way to travel on worse roads," Scarlet agreed. "I notice none of Earlee's sisters and brothers are here. They have to walk all the way in."

"I wonder how Earlee is?" Lila asked, leaving unsaid what they were all thinking. Her lot in life was the hardest among them. If she was on the road right now attempting to reach town, then perhaps she would be meeting Shane on the way.

Shane. Even the thought of him weighed on her. *It doesn't matter what he thinks of you,* she told herself, but she knew that it was a lie.

It mattered, and much more than she could explain.

Meredith Worthington was a piece of work. Shane blinked hard against the snowflakes diving at his face and eyes, swiped them away with the cuff of his coat sleeve and tightened his trip on the trace. Not even the weather of the morning's hardship could drive her from his mind.

The morning's traffic to town had broken the crusted ice and churned up doughy mud that grabbed hold of his boots with every step. A mean wind sliced through his layered garments, cutting clean through to his bone marrow. A sky cold as steel and as light as snow made the world one ball of white, except for the mud tracking ahead of them.

Sweetie nickered and stopped in her traces, her harness jingling. The mare shook her head, snow flying off her mane, as she surveyed the road ahead. She remembered the exact spot and direction she had become stuck the day before. Nervous, she didn't want to take another step forward. He patted her neck, hoping to give her comfort.

"You're scared of that happening again, but I'm with you this time." He kept confidence in his voice so the mare would hear it. "Trust me, girl."

The mare nickered, leaning into his touch. Her brown eyes and curled lashes searched his, tentative and worried. She must have been frightened, held captive by the buggy she could not budge. She was trying to let him know it.

"We'll keep to high ground as best we can," he promised, putting all his understanding in his voice and gentle pressure on the bridle, waiting until she was ready before he whistled and led her through the muck. Snow crunched beneath one boot as he took to the shoulder, eyed a deep ditch, and felt thick mud ooze beneath his tread. Sweetie quivered with nerves as she picked up her pace, half in a panic as she clamored and slipped in the icy and slick mixture.

"That's a good girl," he praised, stepping fast to keep up with her. Something grabbed hold of his toe and with a sucking sound, his boot slipped right off. His stockinged foot squished in the freezing muck.

"Whoa," he called out, holding on, ignoring the stunning cold of his exposed toes as each step he took made his sock wetter and icier.

Great. Just what he needed. Once he had the mare safe on firmer ground, he set the buggy's brake and splashed back to tug his boot free. Bending over, vulnerable in the road, awareness snaked down the back of his neck. Unarmed and defenseless, he whirled in the road, sensing he was no longer alone.

Chapter Six

❧

"That almost happened to me!" A little boy who couldn't be more than six or seven broke through the veil of white. A knit blue cap crowned his head and matching mittens covered his hands, where he held on to a small bundle wrapped against the weather—schoolbooks, Shane guessed. The family was on their way to school. The boy skidded to a stop in the mud. "What are you gonna do about your sock, mister?"

"Probably take it off before I put my foot in my boot." He liked kids, and this one with a single tooth missing and a dimple in his chin looked as likable as can be. "You're mighty late for school."

"We all are."

We? Shane glanced as far as the snowfall would allow. Sweetie nickered, sensing what he could not see. A few seconds later shadows began to appear in the whiteness. A row of children stair-stepped year by year, a family of nine brothers and sisters, mostly sisters.

"Well, gotta go." The boy grinned up at him, wiggled a tooth with his tongue that was getting loose and plunged ahead into the mud, choosing the deepest puddle to wade through with more splashes than a rampaging buffalo could make.

"Edward! How many times do I have to tell you?" A slightly amused voice rose above the whispering wind and tapping snowflakes. "Stay out of the mud."

"But I couldn't help it, Earlee!" The little guy called over his shoulder as he splashed along, not repentant in the least. The storm closed around him until he was a shadow and then nothing at all.

"Pardon us, please," a young lady, tall and willowy, halted next to him. Other children said a simple country howdy as they passed. The oldest one of the bunch squinted at him carefully. Blond curls peeked out from beneath her knit cap. "That's Meredith's family's horse and buggy. You must be Eli's replacement."

"Lucky me." He didn't believe in luck, he believed in the Lord, but it was the only comeback he could think of. Eli was the fortunate one, blessed enough to be well away from Meredith Worthington.

"I'm Earlee Mills, one of Meredith's friends. You aren't from around here, are you?" She knocked a thick pile of snow off her hat and curly bangs, studying him with clear gray eyes.

"Nope." He took a step back, boot in hand, sizing up this friend of Meredith.

She was obviously no debutante, he decided, noticing the old wool coat fraying at the hem and the simple calico dress, unadorned by any lace or ribbon beneath the coat's snowy hem. Although mud obscured most of her shoes, what he could see of them looked worn and aged, as if those shoes had been handed down more than once, as did the cap and mittens she wore, the red yarn fading in places.

"I don't suppose it's a good sign that you have Sweetie. Meredith's first day of driving must not have turned out too well." The other children had disappeared, but this young lady lingered, concern wreathing her oval face. "Oh, dear. Poor Meredith. Driving meant so much to her."

"So I've heard." This was Meredith's friend? Something didn't add up. Wouldn't Miss Hoity-Toity want a more socially prominent friend? "You must live just up the road?"

"Quite a ways. Our farm is almost a mile beyond Meredith's."

"That's quite a way." A farm? No doubt about it, this was a country girl, unlike Meredith of the sad eyes and sharp retorts. "But you are friends?"

"Of course." She took a step away from him. "Why wouldn't we be?"

"No reason. Just fact-gathering." He looked down at the muddy boot he held. "Meredith is an interesting character, isn't she?"

"Interesting? She's fantastic." She glanced over her shoulder. Her brothers and sisters were out of sight, but she felt the pull of responsibility. She didn't have time to figure out this stranger. "I didn't catch your name."

"Connelly. But I doubt Miss Meredith will use my Christian name if she talks about me."

"Why not?"

"She's a tad angry with me, although I don't know why," he confessed.

Was that a twinkle in those dazzling blue eyes? Something glinted deep in the iris, beyond flesh and all the way to the spirit. He was a charmer, and if she wasn't mistaken, he held a spark for Meredith.

There I go, weaving stories again. She took a step backward, slogging through the sludge. She was given to tales of romance and fancy. Her mind had always been prone to it. But she had not imagined the hint of warmth when this Connelly character had spoken her friend's name. A warmth and a reserve, a strange combination. She would have to get the full tale from Meredith at a later time.

"I'm late, so I had better go. It was nice meeting you, Mr. Connelly." She lifted a hand in farewell, the snow already closing around her. Aside from the echoing pattering footsteps of her siblings on the road ahead, she could have been alone as she walked on, cocooned by the storm. Perhaps that was why her thoughts turned to the letter in her pocket, the one she hoped to post after school. Although it was only two pages of parchment, it weighed down her pocket and the corners of her heart as if it were two hundred.

This was the consequence of harboring a secret crush. No one, not even her circle of best friends, knew she had started corresponding with a man. Last February a letter had come to her family addressed to her cousin, who was no longer living with them. Since she did not know where Euen had moved on to, she returned the letter with a note of her own to the sender, Finn McKaslin.

Even thinking his name sent little tingles of life through her soul. He was twenty-one to her eighteen, and she well remembered him from the days when he'd attended Angel Falls's public school and all the times she spotted him around town. Folks called him trouble and he was surely that, but she could see the pain in him, the heart and the tenderness. He was capable of so much, and she believed a great goodness lived inside the man. In spite of his mistakes, she cared.

While Finn had met a sad end, he had once been funny and full of life. Handsome didn't begin to describe him. With his midnight-blue eyes, thick dark brown hair and his strong frame, *magnificent* would be a more fitting word to describe him. *Superb* would do nicely, too. Even *extraordinary*.

The letter in her pocket felt heavier, and Earlee supposed she could not hide the truth from herself. *And certainly not from You, Lord.* She was ignoring one teeny-eensy fact. Finn was currently incarcerated in the territorial jail over in Deer Lodge. He had responded to her letter, he'd written her in return, asking for news of the town. She had written to him with friendliness only, but she couldn't deny that in her soul, in places she did not dare look, were buried tiny seeds of hope for more.

"Earlee!" Her sister Beatrice called, her annoyance echoing through the storm. "Hurry up! We're late enough. Don't make it worse."

"Coming." She strode out, walking faster, forcing her thoughts to the school day ahead and the arithmetic lesson she was likely missing. Her friends would already be warm and tucked into their seats at school. Her steps lightened simply thinking of them.

If only she could get him out of her mind, then she could do a better job at her schoolwork. Frustrated, Meredith blew a curl out of her eyes and stared at her slate, wishing she could make sense of the scribbles of the vocabulary words she was supposed to be learning. Too bad the letters were incomprehensible squiggles and lines her brain did not want to decipher. And why?

Because Shane Connelly would not vacate her brain.

I could never like a man like him, she told herself. Why couldn't she feel this way toward Lorenzo Davis? It would give Mama fits of bliss. She peered through her lashes across the desk, past Scarlet bent over her vocabulary list to the handsome young man who her mother had deemed the most acceptable boy in town. The Davis family had come from Connecticut and a respectable banking fortune, and since Papa owned the bank in Angel Falls, Mama had blessed the match.

The only problem was, Lorenzo, as cute as he was, had never turned her head, not seriously, and she had never done the same for him. No, if he had eyes for anyone, it was Fiona, but as she was marrying someone else, he was likely to be single for a long while.

Someone bumped her elbow, startling her out of her reverie. Had she been staring at Lorenzo? She hadn't meant to. She noticed Scarlet inching her slate closer on their shared desk. A note was written there.

Lorenzo? Scarlet winked, and the sparkle in her eyes put a nuance to the word.

No, Meredith wrote on her slate. She was not sweet on the poor guy.

The horse driver guy? Scarlet scribbled.

"Class, your attention please." Miss Lambert stood to ring her handbell. "It is three-thirty. You are dismissed for the day."

Shoes thundered against the floorboards as several dozen students flew out of their desks, talking all at once. Meredith grabbed her book bag and shoved her slate into it. She moved fast, but she already knew it would be nearly impossible to evade Scarlet's curiosity. Or Earlee, who had mentioned meeting Shane on the road this morning when they had been eating lunch.

Just because she had managed to change the subject at the time did not mean she was free from questions about the man. As much as she loved her dear friends, they had one-track minds when it came to boys. How long she could delay having to mention anything more about the horse driver guy was anyone's guess. She grabbed her last book and launched out of the desk.

"Minnie!" She spotted her sister in the crowded vestibule where the girl was chattering away with her friend Maisie. "I've got to run up to Lawson's. Tell Connelly to come fetch me there."

"Why don't you do it yourself?" Minnie tugged on her mittens. She beamed adoration for the horseman. "He's so nice. I'm sure he will. He's right outside waiting for us."

"You have him take Maisie home first." That ought to keep him busy for a while and delay having to face him. "Then you can swing by the mercantile."

"I'm surprised you aren't rushing out to meet the guy. Talk about handsome. Wow." Earlee sidled up to her, coats in hand. "Here, I fetched yours, too."

"Thanks, Earlee." Resigned, she accepted the garment and slipped into it, making her way toward the door. A glance over her shoulder told her that the rest of the gang wasn't far behind. "I'm going to pick out more material for my quilt. I've changed my mind about the border fabric."

"Hey, I can come with you. I've got an errand at the post office." When Earlee smiled, the whole world shone. "Besides, I have to come lend a hand. You know how I love looking at all the fabric."

"You and me both." Snow pelted her face as she tugged up her hood. The steps were slick beneath her shoes as she trudged down to the yard along with a long line of students. Kids ran off screaming and laughing, snowballs filled the air and a long parade of horses, vehicles and waiting parents lined the road. Judging by the tap-tapping of her pulse, Shane Connelly had to be close.

Best just to keep walking and not look to the left or right. Straight ahead, that way she could ignore him. She didn't have to remember how she'd acted this morning as long as she didn't have to see his face.

"The horse driver guy is amazingly gorgeous," Scarlet said. "He's waving at you, Meredith."

"So? It's my plan to ignore him." Forever, if she could get away with it.

"Why?" Lila fell in stride beside her. "He looks nice. Not as handsome as Lorenzo, but who is?"

"I suppose that's in the eye of the beholder." Fiona joined the group, pulling on her mittens as she waded through the snow. "I happen to think my Ian is the most handsome of all."

"True love will do that to a girl," Earlee commented with a dramatic sigh.

"Do what? Make her blind?" The words were out before Meredith could stop them, sarcastic and cynical even for her. What was the matter with her today?

There was only one answer. Shane Connelly. He was what had happened to her, stirring her up, twisting her inside out, making her sound like her mother. She could feel his pull like gravity tugging against her, and she set her chin, refusing to look at him. Did it stop her from wondering about him?

No. What was he thinking as she marched past? Was he glad she kept going?

"Meredith." Lila laughed. "What has happened to you? You've gotten cynical."

"Unrequited love can do that to a girl," Scarlet answered before Meredith could.

"It's not unrequited love." Honestly. Where had Scarlet gotten such an idea? "For your information, Shane Connelly isn't the slightest bit interested in me."

"He sure has eyes for no one else," Earlee commented with a sigh. "Look at the way he watches you. I could pen a story about this, with love triumphant and a happy ending."

"Love triumphant?" Her shoe slipped in the snow, sending her off balance. She caught herself and remained upright, although she felt as if she were falling as she turned to catch a glimpse of the man.

Across the expanse of snow and distance, she spotted him standing tall and regal, the wind tousling his dark locks and whipping the hem of his coat. His gaze hooked hers, shrinking the distance, silencing the noise, arrowing straight to her soul. She felt touched, impossible from such a great distance, but she could not halt the sensation. She felt exposed in places she never knew existed within her, the corners of her heart, the rooms of her soul.

"I think we have another romance on our hands," Lila announced, hands clasped with glee.

"And another wedding to sew for," Fiona added with a happy lilt, as if she were smiling all the way to her soul. "Who would have thought Meredith would be the next of us to marry?"

"I'm not marrying anyone." Really. She was a practical woman these days and she would prove it, if only she could pull away from Shane's gaze, from the sight of him offering his hand to her little sister and helping her onto the backseat. Minnie chatted with him a moment, and try as she might she could not rip her attention away. Through the tumbling flakes and the span of the road, she felt close to him and the sight of his smile traveled through her like music and hope.

But hope for what? She believed in true love, but knew how rare it was. A chance for such a blessing came perhaps once into a person's lifetime. She did not begin to think for one minute that Shane was that chance.

"But you want to marry someday, right?" Lila asked.

"Sure, when the time is right. In the meanwhile, I have plans. You all know that. I've been studying for the teachers' exam for months."

"Which you will pass easily." Earlee, ever sweet and

supportive, took her arm and gave her a squeeze. "You will make a great teacher, Meredith."

"That's the plan." She focused her attention on the intersection ahead, but her senses were still off-kilter and she could feel Shane's presence like a physical tie stretching between them. Was he watching her? The back of her neck prickled and would not stop.

"Just because you have planned one future, it doesn't mean something better can't happen." Fiona's tone held a smiling quality, and it reminded Meredith that once she'd said the same thing to Fiona. "God might have other plans for you. Better ones. That is exactly what happened to me."

"Shane Connelly is not my future. You all know we have something better to talk about. Fiona's impending wedding." Meredith rolled her eyes, hoping that would effectively divert her friends' attention and her own thoughts from the handsome horseman.

The conversation changed tracks as they walked together, laughing and chatting down the town streets, but her thoughts and her sense of Shane did not.

He could see her through the mercantile's front window at the fabric counter, chatting with one of her friends from school, the one with brown hair. The others must have gone on their separate ways while he'd been delivering Minnie's best friend home. Because the girl lived a few blocks behind the town's dress shop, he figured the purpose of such an errand was so the little girls could chat and giggle together a bit longer before being parted for the day. Even now, Minnie was in the backseat scribbling a note to the friend they'd just dropped off.

Females. He shook his head, deciding they were an enigmatic bunch. He pulled his watch from his shirt pocket and frowned. Braden had expected him back by now. They had been evaluating the yearlings, two-year-olds and the new horses Worthington had purchased earlier in the year. Work was waiting and Miss Meredith did not seem to care, concerned as she was with fabric. She did look a fine sight at the counter in her beautiful dress and soft bouncing curls trailing down her back.

You are not going to let her distract you from your work, Shane. He'd made that promise to Braden and to himself. But she could tempt the sun from the sky with her loveliness. Her words this morning had hurt him, but they had shown him something, too.

"Does she always take this long?" he asked, glancing at his watch again.

"Yes." Minnie rolled her eyes. "Sometimes she takes longer. She's taking her time on purpose, you know. She's mad at you because you're driving instead of her."

"I don't think that's why she's mad at me." He shivered as the wind gusted, and he felt the cold driving through his layers of wool and flannel, more than he usually did. He'd spent the morning feeling her contempt with every step, every block and, finally, every mile between them.

"Trust me," Minnie confided. "She's real upset about the driving thing."

"Yep, I noticed that."

"Except she's not very good at it." Minnie put down her pencil, glad to have someone to share her secrets with. "Yesterday after school, she had to have one of the boys at school help her rehitch Sweetie to the buggy and then she backed into the hitching post in town. That was before she got stuck in the mud."

"That's one tough day." Why couldn't he look away? It was as if every molecule he owned longed for the sight of Meredith. She was pure as spun sugar with her pretty face bright in laughter. Unaware he was watching her, she accepted a wrapped bundle from her friend behind the counter and lifted a long slender hand in goodbye.

She has captured me, he thought, as surely as if she'd hobbled him like a horse at the ankles. He watched, enchanted as she whirled toward the front of the store, giving him a perfect view of her flawless face, the breadth of her smile, the shimmering brightness of her merriment. Her long skirts swirled and swished as she paced closer to the door. She shined as if she brought the lamplight with her.

This was a Meredith he'd never seen before, another side of the puzzle that was the woman. A bell jangled as she opened the store's glass door, waltzing toward him like sunshine on the darkest of days. As her shoes tapped on the damp boardwalk, he launched off the seat and, with a bow, held out his hand.

She lifted a slender eyebrow, perhaps sensing his sarcasm. He could not stop the rolling crest of emotion threatening to take him over. The snow did not touch him, the wind did not chill him as she laid the palm of her hand softly against his. Time stopped, his soul stilled and her gaze found his.

Wide-eyed and startled, she did not move. Nor did he. A second stretched into a moment without heartbeat or breath, and he felt as if eternity touched him. It was only her stepping up into the buggy. She looked away, her hand slipped from his and it was as if the contact had never been. They were once again separate. She, with her chin in the air and he, standing below her on the boardwalk with weak knees.

"Shane?" Minnie gripped the back of the front seat bouncing in place as he took his place at the reins. "Can we swing by Maisie's house again? Please, please, please? I've got to give her this."

"A note? But you just saw her." He released the brake,

trying to pretend he was not shaken, but his voice came out thick and raw.

"But it's important," Minnie pleaded. "Please?"

"You were in school all day with her." He gave the reins a snap, checking over his shoulder for traffic as the mare moved out, pulling them along behind her. "Can't it wait until tomorrow?"

"No, or I wouldn't have asked you."

What he would give to be as thick-skinned as Braden. Then it would be easy to disappoint the pixie with the fairy-tale freckles and eyes just like Meredith's.

If he turned his head, he could barely see Meredith out of the corner of his eye sitting as regal as a princess clutching the wrapped bundle on her lap.

"Fine," he said to the little girl. "But I'm going to need something in return."

"Whatever can I do for you, Mr. Connelly?" Minnie asked primly, bouncing on the seat.

"I'm partial to molasses cookies. Put in a good word with Cook for me, would you?" While Minnie laughed in agreement, he noticed the hook in the corners of Meredith's rosebud mouth. She fought a smile she could not fully suppress, and to him it was as if spring had returned.

Chapter Seven

The shady outline of the house appeared in the twilit snowfall, telling her they were home. She gathered her things the moment the buggy stopped rolling and hopped down before Shane could reach her. He looked busy enough tending to Sweetie; perhaps she had a rock in her shoe with the way he knelt, the mare's hoof resting on his knee.

Ignoring the temptation to gaze upon him a few moments more, she offered Minnie a hand. She had to make sure the girl did not slip as she landed with a two-footed thud. The flakes were larger and wetter, hitting like little slaps against her hood and her face, smacking in imprecise rhythms against her coat and the ground. Warming, the snow had grown slick and dangerous.

"Sorry I couldn't help you," Shane shot over his shoulder, apologetic and sincere. A furrow dug into his forehead. Worry for the horse?

"Is Sweetie all right?" she asked, concerned. She adored their little mare.

"Just a little heat is all, I think." The concern returned to narrow the hard ridges of his face and made more prominent the high cheekbones and the straight blade of his nose. "Tomorrow you fine ladies will not be riding in that buggy."

"You mean we have to use the barn sled?" Minnie skipped over to the kneeling man and rubbed her hand across Sweetie's flank. "The one used for hauling hay?"

"Depends on what the weather brings." Shane gently returned the mare's hoof to the ground, rubbing her comfortingly. "If there's more snow, then yes. If the weather warms, it will be on horseback."

"That would be great. Wouldn't it, Meredith?" Minnie's dimples flashed.

"Either choice would give Mama the vapors." She should be turning on her heels and putting as much distance possible between her and Shane. So why were her feet carrying her toward him?

Dumb decision, she told herself. The man was nothing but trouble. The kind of trouble she knew best to avoid. "Papa won't allow it."

"The mare is fine today, but drive her tomorrow in worse conditions and she could founder." The disdain evaporated, replaced by a grim set of his expressive mouth, and she realized his feelings were over the horse's welfare and not because she was anywhere near him.

A tiny fission of relief rippled through her, like the wind through the snow. Odd, the effect this man had on her.

"What's founder?" Minnie asked. "It sounds bad."

"It means to go lame." He rose to his full six feet. "Don't worry, I'll take good care of her. She needs a bit of rest and some pampering. She's an old mare and we don't want to ask too much of her. Unless you don't care what happens to her."

"Of course we do." She stroked her fingertips along Sweetie's neck, smiling when the animal leaned into her touch with a nicker. Such a sweet girl, really. "We want the best for our Sweetie."

"Don't let anything happen to her, Mr. Connelly." Minnie wrapped her arms around the mare's front leg, holding on tight. The horse lipped the brim of her cap with affection.

"I won't, shortcakes. And you might as well call me by my given name." He gave her braid a tug. "Don't forget your promise to me, now."

"Not on my life." Minnie flushed, gazing up at him between her long curling lashes. She released the horse and took off, book bag bouncing on her shoulder. "I'll go talk to Cook right now!"

Fine, so he was kind to Minnie. He was probably the kind of man who was great with children. She could admit that he wasn't *all* bad. The deep fading notes of Shane's chuckle rumbled through her, scattering her senses, drawing her to him like the snow to the earth. Vaguely, she heard Minnie shut the front door with a thud and she realized they were alone. With the curtains of white cocooning them from sight of the house, they could very well be the only two people on the high Montana prairie.

"Thank you for being so nice to my sister."

"No need for thanks. She's a good kid, and I'm not as bad as you think." Dimples hinted, bracketing his mouth with the promise of more. "I don't know how, but you heard what I said about you last night. Isn't that right?"

It was hard to read the tone of his voice, for it was dangerously light and bordering on amusement, but the set of his features and the lines of his face remained like stone.

"The bunkhouse door was open," she confessed. "The cookies were still in the oven when Sadie bundled up your meals. She wanted you to have dessert, but she was busy helping Cook with the dishes, so—"

"You volunteered." He finished her sentence, nodding slightly. He laid a hand on Sweetie's withers, a touch to let the mare know he hadn't forgotten she was standing hot and lathered in the icy winds. His attention did not flicker, his gaze latched on to Meredith's in understanding. "You came to serve us dessert? You? Did your mother know?"

"Don't act so surprised. I wanted to ease Sadie's workload a bit, that was all." Snow flocked her curls, enveloping her with purity and drawing the feelings he had refused to acknowledge a little closer to the surface. She flushed, as if embarrassed. "I wanted to apologize for how Mama treated you. That's why I volunteered. I felt so bad about what she said to you, and the way she said it. But things didn't work out according to plan."

"That's fairly obvious since I never did get any of the cookies."

"I'll make sure you get double dessert with your supper tonight." She cast her gaze downward at her shoes, where she toed the snow. Her hair fell around her, soft bouncy curls around the most beautiful face he had ever seen. She appeared troubled, and vulnerable.

"Braden was concerned you would distract me from my work. That's what you overheard. Do you want to apologize for what you said about me in the school yard?" He had to ask. He had to know if she forgave him.

Her toe stilled. She pulled herself up like a ballerina, elegance and grace, and her blue eyes began to sparkle like an ocean storm. The corners of her mouth tipped into a full-fledged grin, dazzling in its honesty. Trouble glittered there along with a measure of amusement.

"*That* I am not sorry for," she trilled, spinning in the snow to waltz away from him. "Now we're even."

"Even?" The way a woman's mind worked puzzled him greatly.

"We've both agreed we are not interested in the other whatsoever, so now we may as well call a truce."

"A truce?" He knew from the sound of her gait that she was on the steps.

"As long as it's not terribly disagreeable to you." She disappeared into the storm, lost to his sight, her voice as buoyant and as warm as a May breeze.

"Not too terribly disagreeable," he admitted. "Marginally bearable."

"Good. Then we're in perfect agreement."

He searched for the hint of her shadow, the movement of her skirts. The lamplight at the window glinted off a golden curl, the only sign of her in the storm. He did not know why she drew him. But if the grin on his face and in his soul were any indication, he was in trouble. Big trouble.

"Have a good afternoon, Just Meredith."

The door swung open and heavy footsteps tapped onto the porch. "What is going on out here?" Mrs. Worthington demanded. "Meredith, why are you speaking with this person? You could catch your death standing in the cold. Get inside before you freeze clean through."

"Yes, Mama." There wasn't a contrite note to her words as they died on the wind. The door creaked shut, and she was gone. The brightness within him, the one she had put there, remained.

"C'mon, Sweetie." He knelt to unbuckle the traces. "Let's get you washed, rubbed dry and tucked in your warm stall. What do you say?"

The mare nickered in agreement, and they headed off together, side by side as the snow warmed, and crystal drops of ice rained down on them.

"It's lovely fabric, Meredith." Tilly's gentle alto chased away the icy remains of Mama's mood. Their mother had long since retreated from the parlor although her reprimand had not.

"Meredith, it would please me if you did not talk with the hired men." She could still hear the authority and ring of Mama's footsteps as she'd crossed the wooden floor of the parlor. "I'm in the middle of tea. Now I do not wish to be disturbed again."

She had disappeared down the hall to the solarium in the north wing. Now and then women's voices merry with conversation drifted down the long hall that separated the wings of the house. Mama was hosting another gathering of her friends, all the finest wives of the wealthiest families in Angel County. She knew her mother meant well, but how on earth was she going to avoid speaking with Shane? Especially now that her pride was no longer hurting?

"I liked it better than the silk Mama insisted on." Meredith turned her thoughts back to the fabric she was showing her sister. She thumbed the purple cotton fabric with the tiny sprigged rosebuds. "Lila pieced a patchwork quilt years ago done in calico fabrics and I've always admired it."

"Calico quilts can make a room feel cozy and snug." Tilly's understanding was worth more than all the money in the world. "It will make a nice addition to your hope chest."

"My far-in-the-distant-future-perhaps chest," she corrected, lifting the folded fabric and giving it a shake. The plentiful yards tumbled over the sofa in a cascade of ivory cotton and miniature green leaves. "Maybe it will be for my first place when I'm on my own as a teacher."

"Your plans may change." Tilly took an end, holding it out. "The right man may come along and save you from my fate."

"You are not a spinster yet, Matilda." She ached for her poor sister, whose beauty ran deep, but it was a sad state of the world that many men did not measure a woman for her internal beauty. The one slight interest Matilda had from Emmett Sims, a local teamster, had faded away. While she had never expressed her disappointment, Meredith knew it was there, a secret sadness her older sister did her best to hide. She did not know how to comfort her and sighed. "And even if we both grow old without husbands, there are much worse fates."

"True. There is pestilence and plagues." Tilly gathered up the material in her arms, drawing yard after yard into a messy bundle. "Or we could take up smoking."

Thinking of their rebellious younger sister, they burst into laughter. Their peals echoed against the coved ceiling.

"Can you imagine?" She helped Tilly with the last bit of fabric. "Mama would burst."

"If we did that, we would have to take up horseback riding, too."

"Maybe chewing tobacco."

"We could learn to spit."

"So much for the family's reputation."

"From couth to uncouth in sixty seconds." Tilly gasped, sputtering. "It would be a total waste of our finishing school."

"True." She led the way through the dining room, the last vestiges of laughter fading. "Have you ever thought how different our lives would be if we weren't Worthingtons?"

"Now and then." Tilly's smile remained, but it had turned sad. "Emmett and I—"

She didn't finish. She didn't have to. Events might have turned out differently for Tilly. He was a teamster, a common occupation about which Mama had made her opinion very clear. Meredith couldn't help her suspicions. "Do you think our mother said something to discourage him? The way she's treated Shane makes me wonder. Do you think she did the same with the Sims brothers?"

"Who knows?" Tilly shouldered open the kitchen door. "If Emmett didn't care enough about me to stand up to Mama, then…" She said no more, turning away, disappearing into the kitchen.

Meredith caught the door. She didn't know what to say to ease her sister's devastation. She wished there was a way to piece those broken dreams back together for her.

"I'll be happy to get this washed up for you, Meredith." Sadie's voice rose above the clatter Cook was making at the stove. The scent of baking pork roast filled the air. "This is lovely fabric. It will be a perfect match with those blocks you are piecing."

"Thanks. I think so, too. Would you like the scraps when I'm done?"

"Oh, I would love them. Thank you." Sadie curtseyed, her accent sweet as the delight on her face. Soft auburn curls tumbled down beneath her ruffled cap. "It will go well with the scrap quilt I'm making."

"You've started a quilt?" Sadie was another sad story. The girl was the same age as Meredith and her friends, but she was an indentured servant, working off the cost of her steamer and train fare from Ireland. She was poor without family to help her and without the chance for an education. The difference in their lives, although they were a month apart in age, reminded Meredith how fortunate she was. Why the Lord had blessed her well and not Sadie, she did not understand. "I would love to see it."

"Truly? I can show you on Sunday." Her only day off. "I've just started piecing my first blocks."

"The beginning is always so exciting."

"Yes, and—"

"Sadie!" Cook bellowed. "I'll not have you wasting time like a lazy lout. Get over here and scrub these pots."

"Yes." Sadie bobbed her head in acquiescence, shot Meredith an apologetic shrug and gathered the big ball of fabric into her arms. She disappeared into the lean-to where the washtubs were kept.

"Out!" Cook commanded with a straight-armed point. "I have work to do."

"Sorry." Tilly and Meredith together backed out of the kitchen. Pots clanged and banged, the sound chasing them through the dining room.

Against her will, her shoes skidded to a stop at the wide windows. She could not say why as she looked over the garden and glimpsed at the barns. Ice clung to everything, sheeting the glass panes, dripping from exposed tree branches and varnishing the great expanse of snowy ground. Shane was out there, lost to her sight. She didn't know why her thoughts returned to him now, but thinking of him made quiet joy whisper through her. She was Just Meredith to him again.

He caught glimpses of her through the rest of the afternoon. When he hauled buckets of water from the pump behind the main barn, the windows of the house glowed golden through the gray, catching his attention, a haven of light and shelter in the freezing storm. Ice beat against his face as he caught sight of her sewing industriously while Minnie paraded around the parlor with her slate in hand, perhaps practicing her spelling homework.

Later, after nightfall and several trips with the wheelbarrow to clean the stalls, he saw Meredith at the dining-room table, bent over her schoolbooks. The ice-glazed glass made the scene ethereal, as if out of a dream. The way she sat, spine straight, arms folded primly on the table before her, made her endearing, an image he carried with him back into the horse stables when he took up his pitchfork.

"Tomorrow we start working with the yearlings in the morning. The two-year-olds in the afternoon." Braden sauntered up to fling forkfuls of clean straw into the newly mucked-out stall. "We'll be up and at work by five to get a full twelve-hour day in. I want to get our work done as fast as we can. The missus paid a visit to me today, and I'm already eager to be outta here."

"Can't blame you there." He could well imagine what the woman had told a rough-and-ready like Braden. All he had to do was to imagine what his own mother would have said. She looked down on anyone who performed manual labor. According to her last letter twelve months ago, she looked down on him, too. "Some folks put a lot of importance on the wrong things."

"That's why I work with horses." Braden shook the last of the straw free from the tines and backed down the breezeway. "Horses make sense to me. People don't."

"Some people," he agreed. He forked soiled bedding from the adjacent stall into the wheelbarrow, and the yearling filly he'd tied in the aisle watched him curiously as he worked.

"I'll have this done in a jiffy, girl." He kept his voice low and friendly. Tonight she was interested in him, someone fairly new. The sweet little thing had been well-treated. She didn't shy when he'd approached and she showed no fear now of the pitchfork or his swift movements as he tossed the last of the bedding into the barrow. "Are you going to let me teach you all about a bridle tomorrow, pretty filly?"

Her brown eyes sparkled, liking the sound of his voice. He leaned the pitchfork safely against the wall out of her reach and curled his hands around the worn wooden handle of the wheelbarrow.

"At least you've been well-treated here," he told her as he puffed on by. A full load of dirty straw was a heavy one. "I have a feeling that's the only reason Braden and I are staying."

The filly nickered once as she reached out with her nose to try to grab the hat off his head. Her whiskery lips clamped on his brim, but he was quicker, dodging her just enough that his Stetson escaped any teeth prints.

"That's the truth," Braden called out, his boots pounding closer, and fresh straw landed with a rustling whoosh in the filly's stall. "Any serious trouble from that woman and we're gone. So don't get too attached to this place. Or, more importantly, to anyone here."

"What makes you say that?" Shane set down his load to heave the end door open.

"I got eyes." The force of Braden's frown could be felt all the way down the aisle.

"I'm not attached. I'm not going to get attached."

"See that you don't. Final warning."

"Don't need for a warning." Shane gripped the handles and put his back into setting the wheelbarrow in motion. The front wheel squeaked across the threshold. Stinging pellets of ice slapped across his nose and cheeks and bulleted against his coat.

The instant he was free of the door, where did his gaze inexorably go? To the big window where Meredith now stood beside the dining-room table, gathering up her books and slate, chatting away with her older sister, laughing and full of life.

His chest hitched. Surprised, he shook his head, forced his attention away from her and swiped ice off his brim. Braden didn't know what he was talking about. He and

Meredith were worlds apart. More than social status divided them.

He manhandled the wheelbarrow across the crackling ice, his boots sliding out beneath him as he went. Perilous going. Keeping himself upright and in control of the wheelbarrow ought to be enough to keep his mind off the girl but it wasn't. Ice skidded down the back of his neck, needled through the layers of his clothes and numbed the tips of his fingers while he worked, emptying the contents of the wheelbarrow into the manure pile, one forkful at a time.

His teeth were chattering when he finished. Only a single lantern burned in the end aisle of the stable. Braden had gone through and carefully put out all the others, making the horses safe for the night. Shane stowed the fork and the wheelbarrow in the stable, and after waiting for Braden to lock up, led the way back to their quarters. The ice was softening, the downfall changing to freezing rain rather than ice, making the going so treacherous they skated the last ten yards to their front door.

"I'd best go fetch our meal." He didn't want Sadie coming out from the main house and risking a fall on his account.

"I was young once, too." Braden almost cracked a smile before he turned stoically into the bunkhouse and kicked his boots against the door frame to beat off chunks of ice.

It was worth the inclement weather and the near fall into a berry bush for the chance to see Meredith's smile one more time. He didn't figure she would be in the kitchen—she wasn't. But she was nearby. He could hear the low alto of her voice through the kitchen door. That was enough.

He took time checking through the heavy basket to make sure nothing was missing. He made sure there were two servings of pork roast, mashed potatoes and dinner rolls and went in search of the dessert. Molasses cookies, just as he'd asked for. Two dozen of them, just as Meredith had promised.

Happiness he didn't understand accompanied him through the storm. Rain tapped off his hat as he reached the bunkhouse door. He spotted her in the dining-room window, ready to draw the curtains. He couldn't be sure but he thought he saw her smile. A truce, she'd said.

That sounded mighty fine to him. He was looking forward to it. He stomped the ice off his boots, stumbled through the front door and into the bunkhouse.

Chapter Eight

"**I'**m sorry," was all that Tilly had said the moment they'd spotted Shane seated on the high front seat of the buggy, driving two of the draft horses kept for farm work up to the house. "I know I promised to drive, but with the roads in a worse condition than ever, I just don't feel up to it."

"It's all right. I have set my mind to endure the man." Meredith had closed the front door behind them, seized her sewing basket and clomped down the steps into the cold rain. Framed by a silent, steel-gray sky, he'd tipped his hat at her as solemn as a judge except for the mischief sparkling in his eyes of midnight blue.

Mama had waved them off with dire warnings about the road conditions. The moment Shane extended his hand to her to help her onto the seat beside him, summer washed over her. She settled her skirts, taking care to smooth the blue flannel fabric so it wouldn't wrinkle. When Shane leaned close to tuck a warm blanket over her, she took the length of wool from him and tucked it in herself. Just because she'd declared a truce did not mean she wanted him any closer than he had to be.

The ride had been a bumpy and a muddy one, and with Shane sharing the seat with them, she and Tilly didn't take time to chat. Fiona's little rental house came into sight and the usual excitement trilled through her. She couldn't wait for the wagon wheels to stop turning and had the blanket off her before Shane could lend her his hand. As his strong fingers wrapped around hers, the sense of summer returned.

Surely, a flitting sense of whimsy, that was all. Nothing to worry about.

"Have a good time, Miss Meredith." His dimples ought to be against territorial law for the effect they had on a girl.

"I intend to, Mr. Connelly." She shivered in the wind, waiting for him to hand down the food hamper and her sewing basket. She hardly had time to think of him again because the front door flew open and Fiona rushed out to meet her.

"Meredith! We were beginning to worry." She wrapped a shawl around her shoulders, hurrying through the mash of melting snow, ice and thawing ground. "But you're here safe and sound after all. Thanks to your very capable driver."

"He's just doing his job." Honestly, she had to set her friends straight about the man before they started planning her and Shane's life together. She waved to her sister, let Fiona wrestle the food hamper away from her and they tripped up the steps together. "Don't get any ideas. Shane is here only for a few months. Maybe less if their work is done sooner."

"He's gallant." Fiona tumbled through the doorway into the cozy front room. "Did you all notice Meredith's new driver? He's escorting her around again today. On a Saturday."

Before she could get a word of explanation in, Scarlet called out from one of the chairs set in a circle around the tiny sitting area. "Fortunate for you, Meredith. I wouldn't mind a handsome driver of my own."

"Wouldn't we all?" Kate glanced up from her embroidery work. "I love my dad, he's such a dear to drive me all the way to town and back, but I wouldn't mind my own driver. Let's say he could be a tall handsome stranger with dark eyes and a mysterious past."

"Oh, I could write a story about that." Earlee squinted as she threaded a needle.

"That's the only way I'm going to have a happy ending considering the boys at school. We don't have much to pick from," Kate quipped. "Aside from Lorenzo, who else would you marry?"

"Luken Pawel," Lila answered immediately, setting down the calico dress she was basting. "What? You all don't need to look so shocked."

"You're always going on about how Lorenzo is utterly too-too." Meredith shrugged out of her coat and sat in the chair by the door to unbutton her muddy shoes. "I thought you only had eyes for him."

"*Aside* from Lorenzo, she said," Lila clarified, eyes twinkling. "If he and his family moved back east, I would have to set my sights lower, to be sure. It would take me a while to get over the heartbreak, but I would eventually move on. There are other handsome men in town."

"Not *that* handsome." Kate giggled as she pulled a long strand of green embroidery thread through her hoop, fussing with it so it would lie just right. "Face it, the pickings are slim."

"That's because we've known everyone forever," Earlee added. She tied a slipknot at the end of her needle and thread. "This is a small town, and we've grown up with the same guys. It's hard to foster any romantic feelings over the boy who spilled ink on your favorite dress, or put a salamander in your lunch pail."

"James Biddle did that." Scarlet set down her crochet hook. "I was seven and I may have forgiven him a long time ago, but forgetting is another thing. If Lorenzo moved away, then I would simply pine for him and grow old as a spinster. We may as well face it, girls. There is a shortage of decent, solid bachelors in this town. If you're picky about looks, then it's even slimmer pickings."

Meredith took a moment to gaze at the circle of best friends. Five of them had been together since their first day of Sunday school when they were just little girls. When her family moved to town over five years ago, she had been welcomed into their midst with loving arms. She felt as if she had always been a part of their friendship, the kind of bond that would always endure. As she slipped into the last available place beside Earlee on the horsehair sofa, overwhelming gratitude breezed through her.

God had been looking out for her the day He led her to their circle, and she felt His presence greatest when they were assembled together.

"We all can't have handsome strangers ride into our lives the way Fiona and Meredith have." Kate debated the placement of her needle before pulling it through her hoop.

"Whoa there." Meredith pulled out her latest patchwork square and her threaded needle. "Don't put me in the same category as Fiona. There's a big difference. She's about to be married. I am trying to make peace with a man my father hired. There's a big difference between the two."

"Make peace?" Fiona returned from the kitchen with two cups of steaming honeyed tea. "Are you two getting along now?"

"I'm trying, but he's an impossible man," she quipped. She smoothed her sewing on her knee and studied it as if it held all the importance and Shane Connelly none. *Here it comes,* she thought, *the place where her friends begin imagining what isn't there.*

"That's what I thought, too, when I was getting to know Ian." Fiona set one of the cups on a nearby foot-stool that served as their coffee table. "He was impossible and maddening and wonderful. And that part of things hasn't changed."

"But your feelings toward him did," Lila pointed out, returning to one of the long skirt seams of her new dress. "The same thing could happen with Meredith."

"I wouldn't hold my breath if I were you." Meredith pawed through her basket for a stack of small fabric squares she had cut out over several sewing circles past. She considered the different colors of calico and chose a blue piece to add to her square. "He isn't at all interested, just like I'm not interested in him. He's said so."

"Not interested in you?" Fiona straightened, taking care not to spill the cup she held. "I don't believe that for a second."

"Believe it. He said he can't be distracted from his work."

"Oh, Meredith. I'm sorry." Fiona's dear face wreathed with concern. Her sympathy was mirrored on the rest of her friends' faces. Needles stilled. Sewing projects were set aside.

"So that explains what you said about him." Fiona nodded, as if it were all making sense to her. "Well, he doesn't sound like the nicest man."

"Yes, that's what I thought, too. But I think he really is all right. We've called a ceasefire of sorts." Meredith blushed, feeling too many curious and caring gazes on her. She carefully pinned her piece into the block, eyeing the quarter-inch seam allowance. "Like I said, he'll be gone soon, and that's enough about me. Fiona's wedding is coming up. Are you starting to get nervous?"

"Not one bit. I've never been more sure of anything in my life." Her beloved friend wasn't fooled, judging by the way the sympathy on her face changed to understanding. "A few more weeks, we'll all be graduated, I'll be married and then Ian will be able to move in here as my husband. Let me take this tea in to Nana and I'll be right back."

Fiona swept from the room to open one of the doors that opened from the sitting area. Meredith caught a glimpse of a well-appointed bedroom. Ian had moved his grandmother out to live with them, and Fiona cared for the elderly woman who was in fragile health. Never had her friend looked so happy. Becoming engaged was a definite improvement to Fiona's life and Meredith knew the marriage would be a great blessing for her.

"The right man will come along one day for each of us. I have to believe that." Earlee's head was bowed over her work as she stitched a simple princess collar to the child's dress—she worked on her family's sewing as often as she worked on projects for her hope chest.

"Amen." Scarlet double crocheted, the lacy doily taking shape as she turned it, double crocheting again. "Isn't that why we're all sewing? We have hope."

"Hope." Meredith repeated the word as she took up her needle. Words from Scripture came to mind. *Now faith is the substance of things hoped for, the evidence of things not seen.* She had wishes for a happy future. Maybe one day a handsome, good man who would ride into her life at just the right moment with midnight-blue eyes and a dashing grin, the man who would capture all of her heart.

Why was she picturing Shane? She should not be remembering the scent of hay on his coat and sweet mystery she felt whenever their hands touched. He was still a stranger, a saddle tramp—he'd admitted that himself—someone simply passing through.

She wanted so much more in a man, in a husband, than that. Fiona took her place at the circle and the conversation turned to the wedding plans. While they sewed and talked, rain drummed on the roof and tapped at the windows, making their ring of friendship cozier.

He could see her through the small front window of the shanty, golden hair burnished by the lamplight, transformed by happiness. She might look like a country miss with her simple braid trailing down her back sitting in a typical country home with her sewing on her lap, but when Meredith relaxed and in laughter let her true beauty show, she was extraordinary. She shone like a single star in a sky without light, her luminous goodness a guide for a man alone in the dark.

He waited in the rain until the gathering was over. As the front door opened and the young ladies tumbled out into the cold, gray world, they brought their laughter and life with them. Bonnets and skirts swirling beneath their coats brought color to the dismal afternoon, and their merry farewells and promises to keep for Sunday school tomorrow rang like music. A pair of oxen and a wagon pulled up, loaded with fence posts from the lumber yard. A fatherly man tipped his hat in greeting before extending a hand to one of the girls and driving off with her. She kneeled on the wagon seat, facing backward, waving goodbye to her friends.

A pair of Meredith's friends disappeared around the corner to the stable. A buggy waited in the shelter, perhaps the vehicle they had driven from town. Meredith waved gaily to them before grasping the last girl by the arm and pulling her to the wagon.

"We're giving Earlee a ride," she explained as she handed up the hamper and basket.

"Fine by me." He nodded at the familiar blonde. "We met in the road the other day."

"We did. Thank you for letting me come along this afternoon. It will save me a good mile of walking." She climbed onto the seat beside Meredith, casting her a secret glance. Females were such a mystery to him, he didn't even try to guess what either of them were thinking. Braden was right. Horses were better. You knew where you stood with horses.

He gathered the reins, directing the matched bay Clydesdales around in a circle and back toward home. As he listened to the girls talk about someone named Fiona and a sweet grandmother, he kept his eyes on the road. He ought to be wondering about how Braden was fairing. They were not making the desired progress without the two of them working side by side. Worthington had him driving his daughters all over the county, or at least it seemed that way. When Meredith's laugh trilled, warming the air, a piece of loveliness he enjoyed listening to, he had to admit he didn't mind. But it was a distraction from his work.

She was a distraction, her voice stealing his focus and forcing him to listen to her. Maybe it wasn't the girl that lassoed his attention, but what was missing in his life. He had been lonely this past few year, leaving all his family behind and some friends who hadn't understood his decision. Moving place to place every few months didn't make it easy to establish new friendships.

Maybe loneliness was the reason he felt drawn to her. Maybe it was as simple as that.

"This is where Earlee gets off." Meredith turned to him, her shoulder brushing his arm, the brief contact sweet and comfortable as homecoming.

"Whoa." He drew back, slowing the big animals, who pranced in place and huffed great clouds of breath in the cold. The girls exchanged goodbyes while he gave Earlee his hand. Shyly she avoided his gaze, thanked him and splashed to the ground. She waved, hurrying down an intersecting road, a small figure on the roll and dip of the vast high plains, leaving him and Meredith alone. As he picked up the reins and guided the horses on, he was acutely aware of the rustle of her skirts as she resettled them, the small sigh as she swiped rain off her nose, the faint scent of rosewater.

He should not be noticing such things.

"Do you want to take the reins?" He handed them out to her, when he should have stayed silent. But the hope splashing across her dear face told him he'd done the right thing.

"Do you mean it? You would let me drive?" Her gloved hands were already reaching out, eager for the lines. "I might have to alter my opinion of you."

"No need to go to such extremes."

"I wasn't intending a radical change. Just a tiny step up in my tolerance of Shane Connelly." She bit her bottom lip, as if doing her level best not to break into laughter.

"Tolerance?" He could joke, too. He laid the thick leather straps across her palm. "I thought we agreed to be friends."

"I don't remembering using that word, and I certainly didn't mean we should become kindred souls." Mischief teased the corners of her mouth as she leaned forward to take the reins. Her slender fingers took hold just behind his, and for a moment—one brief span of time—it was as if they were connected by more than the leather straps. "I knew a man like you has his uses."

She was baiting him on purpose. She could not disguise

the merriment dancing in her gorgeous blue eyes or the curve of her mouth that she could not hold straight.

"Is that a hint of regard I hear in your voice?" He shook his head, scattering rain off his hat brim.

"No, perhaps the wind is distorting my words."

"It is not distorting my eyesight." He released the lines, leaving them in her dainty hands, hands that he suddenly wanted to cradle within his own. A crazy wish. "You have to know the impact you have on a man."

"Me? What impact could I have?"

"The sight of you can distract a blind man from a mile away." He moved his hands over hers, to adjust the tension of her grip, ignoring the wish taking form and life. "Women with your beauty put us men at a disadvantage. You have been so angry with me, and it wasn't fair. You were the one who caused it. You're pretty enough to befuddle the most stoic of men."

"You think I'm pretty?" Astonishment rounded the soft contours of her mouth. Didn't she know what she was? As beautiful as a princess in a storybook.

"No." He said the word with much emphasis, doing his best to hide the feelings he could not possibly have. "*Pretty* isn't a word I would use to describe you. *Stunning* and *amazing,* maybe. But no, not *pretty.* Remember that the next time you come upon a poor man trying to hold on to his senses."

"Is that what you're doing now? Holding on to your senses?"

"No, because we have a truce."

"Can I ask you something, Shane?"

"Sure." He'd bared enough of his soul. A little more wouldn't hurt.

"Are you in need of glasses?"

"Not to my knowledge."

"A doctor's examination?"

"Nope, I'm fit as a fiddle and my mind is, too." He reached over to draw on the left rein. "Perhaps it's my good taste that is questionable."

"There's no accounting for taste?"

"Yes." The smile blooming through him was like nothing he'd known before. Being with her was like Sunday morning and Christmas Eve all rolled up into one. He leaned to tug on the right rein, guiding the horses. "Best to keep the wagon out of the mud this time."

"It's worse today with the thaw." Up ahead was the mud hole that had claimed her buggy. The entire way was soupy and sloppy from the fence pole marching down the field on one side all the way to the section posts on the other. "There is no way to see the worst of it. It's danger lurking in the depths. That's what I discovered the last time I drove."

"You want to keep to higher ground." He leaned closer yet and the brush of his arm to hers became a steely pressure that scattered her wits. His breath fanned the loose tendrils from her braid. He tugged on both reins, taking charge of the horses. "You see the wagon tracks on the other side of the bog? Keep your eye on them."

"I'd rather keep my attention on the mud." It felt as if no space separated them, as if he were pressed up against her from the powerful length of his thigh to the forceful curve of his shoulder. Her wits were definitely gone right along with every lick of sense.

"Look beyond the problem, Meredith." He guided the horses to the left, toward what she was sure was danger. "Try to get the wheels out of the ruts. Line them up and give the horses more speed."

"Speed? I would rather go slower when the wagon mires down and tips and we go flying out of the seat and onto the ground." Had she really said that? She heard shades of Mama. "It's true. When a girl grows up she turns into her mother. It's happening already."

"Then you had better start listening to me."

"I don't think that's a good idea either." The quip died on her tongue as his hands closed over hers, bands of warm strength that felt intimate in spite of his gloves and her mittens. It was as if they touched skin to skin.

When he gave the reins a smart snap, the movement traveled up the lines through the bones of her fingers, along her arms and inexplicably working its way into her heart.

"We're going to turn over." She felt dizzy and off balance. Was it the wagon? Or her senses?

"We're going to be fine. Trust me."

Trust him? The notion sent her into a panic. The wagon bounced, the wheels splashed and mud flecked up from the horses' hooves. The horses charged forth, trudging through the mud hole with grim determination. One wheel rose up on the high side of the shoulder, tilting the vehicle to the side. She definitely felt as if she were falling, but then the wagon settled with a thud, level and safe. They were on the other side of the mud hole. The horses plodded forward, and Shane released her hands.

"You did it, Meredith. Good job." He didn't move away.

This close, she could make out the gold and green flecks in his stunning blue irises and see the faint hints of a day's growth beginning along his rock-solid jaw. If she looked hard enough, she could see deeper into him. There was a sadness like shadows in his eyes and a hint of lonesomeness she did not understand. Why could she sense these things about him, things she did not want to know?

"Would you come with me to Sunday school tomorrow?" She blurted out the question, surprised by her boldness. Heat stained her face, so she turned her attention to the road ahead and the horses ambling along, the reins heavy in her hands. She felt the tactile brush of his gaze on her face, his curiosity and something deeper she didn't understand.

"Why are you asking me?" He sounded as surprised as she was.

"I know what it's like to move to a new place and to feel as if you are on the outside looking in." She liked to think that was really the reason why she had asked him. "Everyone knows one another and have friends, but not you. So I thought you might like to come along. As a friend and not as my family's hired man."

"I would like that very much." Buttery warm, that baritone, ringing so low she could hardly hear it.

"I only ask because you've been so nice to me," she told him, hearing the defensiveness in her words, feeling it creep through her. It had to be the truth. It wasn't as if she was sweet on the man. He had been kind to let her drive. She needed the practice and she appreciated his help.

"Sure, I understand that." He didn't sound troubled by it. "I have need of a friend, Meredith. I'm starting to like you."

"You're not too bad, yourself." They shared a smile as the house came into sight, their ride together at an end.

Chapter Nine

There was something sacred about the light on a Sunday morning, something special that no other day in the week had. Glad to soak in the peace, Shane guided the Worthington family surrey down the muddy town street. The shops were dark and the boardwalks empty. Only those headed to church followed the road through town to the white steepled church on Third Street where families flocked toward the front steps and children raced around in their Sunday finest on the sodden lawn. He drew the vehicle to a stop near the front stone walkway and hopped into the road with a splash.

"Hurry, young man." Henrietta Worthington held out her gloved hand. "I will not be late for my ladies gathering."

"Sorry, ma'am." He ignored the censure in her voice. She had been the one running late, forcing the horses to wait and criticizing his driving all the way to town. On top of that, the roads had slowed them. The church bells pealed, tolling the hour, as he aided the woman over to the grass, leaving her to help down the oldest daughter, Tilly, who thanked him primly, and Meredith, who did not thank

"Howdy," he called out and tipped his hat. The horses jerked the surrey forward, and in the crowd of so many people it was Meredith his gaze arrowed to. Meredith his pulse slowed for. She was with her friends now, chatting excitedly with them. The swish of her bright pink skirt, the lark song of her laughter, her wholesome joy stood out to him like color in a world of gray. He eased the horses to a stop alongside the road in full view of the woman.

Even when he turned his back to her to climb down and tie the team, his ears searched the winds for the melody of her voice and the music of her laughter. He glanced over the backs of the horses as he blanketed them, captivated by her straight, willowy posture, the tumble of her gold hair and the graceful way she moved with her friends toward a door at the side of the church. He stopped breathing when she disappeared from his sight. He stood aching for her like nightfall missing the sun.

It's not as if I'm sweet on the girl, he told himself as he crossed the road. He could always hope the tangle of emotions locked away in his chest had more to do with his lonesomeness than true interest. And if a tiny voice at the back of his mind wanted to argue, then he simply did not have to listen.

"I saw you at the school yard the other day." A female voice cut through his thoughts.

He blinked, turned on his heel, not knowing exactly where he was. He'd been so wrapped up in his thoughts that he hadn't realized he was standing on the church lawn. The grass squished and squeaked beneath his boots. Someone—one of Meredith's friends?—was hurrying toward him. She had dark hair and finely tailored clothing. Pearls gleamed at her throat. Gold glowed from the rings on her hands and from the expensive brooch pinned to her cloak. With her carefully coiffed appearance and a

Godey's Lady's Book look, she was the kind of girl his mother would rave over.

Not one of Meredith's friends, if he remembered right.

"Aren't you the Worthingtons' new driver?" She flashed him a coquettish smile and tilted her head to one side, as if doing her very best to appear charming. "I'm Narcissa Bell. I know your name is Shane Connelly because I overheard Meredith say so."

Narcissa Bell. That name sounded familiar. It could have been mentioned in one of the conversations he'd tried not to listen to while conveying the girls around. He scanned the churchyard, looking for help. Of the people streaming past either toward the church's front steps or the basement, not one of them looked his way. Looked as if he was on his own with this problem.

"I couldn't help noticing how you handle horses." Her compliment was a purr.

Great. He knew exactly what she was up to. Not that a girl of society would be interested in a working man, so there had to be some other motive.

"You have a strong way with them and a gentle touch. I admire that so much." She batted her long dark lashes, gazing up at him sweetly.

"Gotta go." Escape was his only response. He hoofed it away as fast as he could. He didn't want to look back, but he was fairly sure the girl followed him.

"Shane! There you are." Meredith marched through a small crowd of schoolboys, scattering them as she advanced like Sherman on Atlanta. Fire blazed in her eyes and her dresses snapped with the fury of her pace. "What are you doing? I have been waiting to introduce you and here you are making cozy with Narcissa."

"Shane and I were having the most wonderful conversation." Narcissa caught up to him and grasped his arm, holding on with a surprising amount of strength for such a fragile thing. "I'm so sorry he forgot all about you, Meredith, but as you can see—"

"Excuse me, miss." Heat burned across his face as he twisted away from the girl's iron clutches. Never had he been more uncomfortable in his life. One girl using her wiles on him, the other enraged and passersby were starting to notice.

"I'll be happy to walk in with you." Narcissa tripped after him and he moved his arm before she could latch on to it again.

"Go ahead. I don't care." Meredith turned on her heel, her face red, her lovely hands fisted. She stormed away, back stiff, shoulders bunched, her skirts rustling furiously.

"Excuse me." With a curt nod, he broke away from the manipulative debutante. He had to run. Meredith might be willowy and petite, but she was a powerful force. He caught up to her at the open door.

"It wasn't my fault," he quickly explained.

"When it comes to *boys,* it never is." She emphasized the word with a hint of distaste, as if to make clear he'd gone down a step in her estimation.

"I'm no boy." He settled his hand on her shoulder, knowing she would turn toward him, knowing there were more emotions buried beneath her anger. He wanted her to understand. "I see what that girl is trying to do to you. I'm not interested in her."

"This is not about interest." Pride. Meredith's chin went up and she spun way in a swirl of golden curls and pink satin. "I only wanted to warn you, but I can see you've made up your own mind about Narcissa Bell."

"She approached me. I'm perfectly innocent."

"If you want to resume your acquaintance with her, you might want to sit well away from me," Meredith tossed airily over her shoulder as she led the way down the narrow stairs. "Narcissa and I have never gotten along since she insulted my sisters and spread horrible rumors about me when I was new to school, but if you want to befriend her, be my guest. That's your choice. Maybe you were made for each other."

"I didn't mean to betray our friendship." He gentled his voice. He'd forgotten how childhood rivalries could be, how cruelties could build upon cruelties. He'd felt the sting of those once as a boy. He hadn't forgotten. He hated that Meredith was so upset. Surely she wasn't jealous. He puzzled on that as he held up his hands. "We're in a church. Surely you can forgive me?"

"Only because it is my faith."

Was that a hint of humor warming the chill from her voice? She'd relaxed a little, he realized, as she trailed a hand down the banister and hopped off the last stair. They had entered a great room divided by several different sets of clustered chairs. In the far corner young children gathered around a kindly but harried-looking woman who must have been in charge of the little ones. In the center of the room milled the middle-grade children. The final group in their teens looked up to study the stranger in their midst. He recognized many faces from the school yard and noted a few men who looked to be close to his age, about twenty.

"This is Fiona's fiancé, Ian McPherson." Meredith gestured toward a tall, quiet-looking man with a friendly manner. "He's fairly new to our group."

"Good to meet you, Ian." He held out his hand.

"Good to meet you. We're a small group here, but a friendly one." Ian's grip was firm and there was something about him Shane immediately liked. The two of them might have been friends, if time in this town wasn't so limited. "I hear you have taken over Eli's old job."

"What do you do?"

"I work north of town at the lumber mill." Ian drew a dark-haired young woman dressed in gingham to his side. The couple radiated happiness. An engagement ring glittered on her left hand.

A middle-aged woman clapped her hands. "School is about to start. Come and take your places."

Where had Meredith gone?

"Hi, Shane." Narcissa Bell again sauntered by and batted her lashes.

He could feel Meredith's glare of daggers from six chairs away. Poor Meredith was not having a good day. He stepped around Narcissa, hoping to sit with his chosen girl, but her friends surrounded her, taking all the nearby chairs. He noticed the class was segregated by gender— girls on one side, boys on the other, so he joined Ian and Eli Sims. He settled in, greeting Eli, but his attention remained on Meredith.

She didn't look happy with him. Was she truly worried about that Narcissa girl? Didn't she know that her honest, wholesome beauty was far superior? A strange ache settled deep in his chest, one of admiration and respect, he insisted stubbornly, because it could not be anything else. He could not allow it to be.

As the Sunday-school teacher opened her Bible, all he could focus on was the way Meredith sat straight and proper, her attention devout on the open volume she held on her lap. Was it his fault he noticed the vulnerable curve of her nape, the lovely line of her slender shoulder and the soft angle her arm made as she bent over her Bible?

Lord, what are You trying to tell me? He pondered that question, fighting gentler emotion he did not dare acknowledge.

"'Strength and honor are her clothing,'" the teacher

read from Proverbs, *"'and she shall rejoice in time to come. She openeth her mouth with wisdom; and in her tongue is the law of kindness. Favor is deceitful and beauty is vain, but a woman that feareth the Lord, she shall be praised.'"*

Meredith remained in his sight and in his thoughts all morning long, as did his gentle feelings for her.

The image of seeing Narcissa hanging from Shane's arm burned like a coal-hot brand. It stung all the way to her soul. The scorching did not abate through the lesson or Sunday service. Meredith fidgeted on the hard pew, frustrated. She didn't know what strange emotion was troubling her, but it burrowed into her and would not let go. It was an unwelcome agony and she did not like it.

This *is what came from dealing with men,* she decided. It was a good thing she had set her sights on teaching instead of settling for the first guy who would propose to her. If she got this agitated over a man she hardly liked, think of what it would be like when she did like one?

She was starting to rethink her views on romance. Maybe being a spinster wasn't such a bad idea.

"Meredith! What's wrong with you?" Mama hissed. "Stand up."

Right. The final prayer. She bobbed out of the pew, the last to stand. But were her thoughts contemplative on this morning of worship?

Not a chance. She wished her gaze would not slip from the reverend at the pulpit, across the rows to where Shane sat. He certainly looked fine in a black muslin shirt and matching trousers. She rarely saw him without his hat, and the thick tumble of his dark hair became fascinating and so did the cowlick at the back of his head.

Stop looking at him, she told herself. If she kept gaping at him, then people would mistakenly start to think that she liked him. She clasped her hands and bowed her head, determined to let only holy thoughts into her brain.

"Let us pray," Reverend Hadly began. "Heavenly Father, we ask for Your loving guidance. As we go through our busy and demanding week, please help us to remember to put on a mantle of kindness."

Only holy thoughts, she reminded herself. But one broke through, and it wasn't faith-centered. Shane drew nearer. She sensed him like the ripple of a breeze from the windows. Her eyes opened; she could not stop them. He padded soundlessly down the aisle, his wool coat clutched in hand and his Bible tucked into one of the pockets. He honestly was the most dashing man in the church, perhaps in the entire town. Maybe it was his classic good looks and his high cheekbones that made him irresistible. She rather thought it was his square jaw hinting at his good character that made it impossible to look away.

This was not fair. Caring about him was not her fault. She was helpless to stop it. A girl did not have a chance around him. She had tried her best to dislike him and if she could not do it, then no one could.

"Meredith!" Mama hissed again, nudging her arm.

She snapped her eyes shut, but did the awareness of him end?

Not a chance. She felt the touch of his gaze against her cheek as he came closer. His shoes whispered on the floorboards and the air around her shivered from his movements.

Just ignore him, she told herself. Could she help it if the hair on her arms prickled as he passed? Perhaps it was a gust of wind blowing through the church and no possible reaction to him.

Mama's elbow bumped her sternly, more serious this

time. Clearly her mother did not understand the consequences of being around a man like Shane. She sighed,
forced her attention to the front and gave thanks that Shane
was safely out of the church. She knew because her mind
could focus on the last of the prayer.

"As You have drawn us with loving kindness, help us
to remember to see You in all we meet," Reverend Hadly
implored. "Amen."

A chorus of "Amens" rang out. The service was almost at an end.

This was like torture. Meredith opened her eyes, feeling a little light-headed from her ordeal. Rustles echoed
through the sanctuary as heads were raised, hands reached
for hymnals and Mrs. Tilney at the organ began the first
strains of "Amazing Grace." Voices lifted with the melody, but all Meredith could think about was Shane out in
the rain.

"Meredith, I've decided to get a new beau." Narcissa
leaned across the aisle, not even bothering to sing. "Shane
is so handsome. You can have Lorenzo if you want."

"I don't want either of them." It felt as if she were telling a lie, and she wasn't. She didn't want a beau. She certainly did not want Shane. She wanted to be an independent
woman in complete control of her heart and her life. "Go
ahead and set your cap for him. I don't care."

"I'll have him wrapped around my little finger in no
time. Just you wait and see." Narcissa's nose went up in
the air. Her face crinkled unpleasantly as she gave a dis-
paraging grimace. "There's a reason some girls can't catch
themselves a beau."

What she needed at this exact moment was the perfect
comeback. Just this one time to really put Narcissa in her
place. But could she think of a single word?

No. Meredith bit her bottom lip. Her feelings simmered

and yet her mind was as blank as a clean slate. Completely frustrating. Especially because she'd had no trouble doing the same to Shane the other day.

"Meredith!" Mama nudged her with her elbow, leveled her with a warning look and returned to singing the final chorus with great zest.

"...was blind," Meredith joined in, but she couldn't properly concentrate on the song. Narcissa's smugness kept floating across the aisle to her like a foul odor. Finally, the hymn was done and the service ended.

"I don't know what's come over you, young lady," Mama huffed, shaking her head severely. "You are in church."

"Yes, I realize that." She doubted her mother would ever understand. She felt miserable, and not because Narcissa had declared her intentions for Shane—surely that could *not* be it.

A hand settled on her shoulder, and there was no need for words. Meredith turned around and smiled at Lila, who was with her family.

"Are you all right?" Lila whispered.

A single nod was all she dared, with Mama listening in. Lila's face wreathed with empathy. No doubt she had overheard Narcissa's whispers across the aisle and was offering unspoken comfort. There was nothing like best friends. Lila's kindness and solidarity was the perfect antidote to Narcissa's declaration.

Rustles and voices filled the sanctuary. Worshippers began filing into the aisle, ready to head home. Meredith gathered her Bible and her wraps. She waited until Mama was occupied with Minnie and slipped into the aisle.

"Some people have all the nerve." Fiona fell in beside her. "I heard what she said. Do you really think she's going after Shane?"

"It doesn't matter to me." There was that feeling again, that she was telling a fib. It was the truth—Shane's love life was none of her business. She didn't want him. Correction. She didn't *want* to want him.

"You would think Narcissa would be happy trying to torture us all with how close she is to Lorenzo." Lila slipped into stride with them. "Lorenzo has never beaued her anywhere. Not even to church."

"*You* would notice," Kate added, peeling away from her family to join them. "How long have you had a crush on Lorenzo?"

"Since I was seven. It's a romance that is never meant to be." Lila shrugged.

"Meredith," Scarlet stepped in to say, "you know Narcissa's interested in your driver guy only because she thinks you are."

"Then maybe I should pretend to like Luken so she would throw herself at him and leave poor Shane alone." An extreme plan at the very least, but it sounded very tempting.

"If I were writing the story," Earlee began as she squeezed into line with them, "Narcissa would be the villain who would try to steal the hero away from the heroine, but she would get her just reward in the end."

"What reward?" Scarlet wanted to know.

"Well, that's the fun about being a writer." When Earlee smiled, the whole world brightened. "She could trip, roll down a muddy hillside and land in very thorny brambles. But I would hate to do physical harm."

"It's not terribly Christian," Kate admitted, gesturing around at the stained-glass windows and the crucifix on the wall.

"No physical pain, then." Lila paused, considering.

"Maybe the hero could see her for what she truly was, turn his back to her and marry the heroine."

"You aren't saying I'm the heroine, right?" Meredith interjected.

"It's a story," Earlee assured her.

"Based on actual events," Lila went on to say. "I think you should have the mean things she does come back around to her."

"Great idea." Earlee nodded. "And the hero and heroine live happily ever after."

"I don't believe in fairy tales." Meredith broke through the doorway and lifted her face to the sky. A fine gray mist drizzled from leaden clouds, but May's touch was in the greening trees, the spears of daffodils poking up in the border beds and the robins taking flight from the lawn.

The promise of summer was everywhere. And Shane was waiting for her, watching for her, and lifted his hand. Too bad he looked exactly like her idea of a perfect hero. They were a fairy tale that could never be.

Chapter Ten

Shane closed the gelding's stall gate, taking time to double-check the latch. The big Arabian nickered, poking his nose over the half door to make sure there was no grain to be found in Shane's hand.

"Sorry, buddy. You already had your share." He rubbed the animal's nose, laughing as the velvet lips nibbled at his gloves, which very well might have smelled of grain. "I'll be back with your supper later, big guy."

The gelding shook his head, as if he understood perfectly, and nickered to his next-door neighbor, as if to start a horsey discussion. Shane grabbed the empty bucket and damp towels, the curry comb and the hoof pick and headed down the aisle.

"Shane?" Her voice welcomed him, as refreshing as first dawn's touch on a waiting world. She'd changed out of her Sunday best into a simple cotton dress, adorned with dainty touches of lace and silk. She carried a small basket in hand. "I know you are supposed to fend for yourself on Sundays, but since you drove us to church because Papa was busy, we ought to at least provide you with lunch."

"I can't argue with that." His stomach rumbled in agreement as he shouldered open the tack-room door to lay down his load. "That fried chicken smells mighty tasty."

"I made it myself, because Cook has the day off."

"You cook?" He poked his head around the door.

"Don't look so surprised." Her laughter rang like the sweetest music. "Cook taught Tilly and me. Things are different in Montana Territory than St. Louis."

"That's where you're from?"

"Yes. Both Matilda and I are not looking for the socially advantageous marriage our parents think we should have." She untied her hood and shoved it out of the way, revealing her rosy cheeks and sparkling spirit. "Mama is stubbornly holding on to hope, but society seems less important here. Maybe because there are so few families who are rich."

"Is that why you have the friends you do?" He thought he already knew the answer, but he wanted to hear it from her lips, to *see* the measure of her not just to know it.

"You mean because I had no other choice, so I settled for whoever I could find in this small town?" She looked at him as if he were an idiot. "Really. That's what you think of me?"

"I've sat in the front seat of the buggy driving you around. I think I have a notion of who you are." He was close enough to brush one of the many stray curls out of her eyes, of her endless blue eyes a man could fall right into and become lost forever.

"Then you know I love my friends as if they were my own family." She held out the basket to him, blindly, as her gaze was held by his and she was helpless to look away. Maybe she did not want to. "When I moved to this town, my circle of friends welcomed me without question. I remember standing in the basement of the church, feeling unsure and surrounded by strangers. Mrs. Hadly had split up my sisters by age group, and this girl with red hair patted the empty seat beside her and smiled at me. After class Scarlet introduced me to the rest of the gang and when I started school the next day, they greeted me like old friends."

"They welcomed you without question." He tucked the basket in one arm, riveted by her, unblinking. The way his gaze remained locked on hers felt as if a deeper bond, a greater connection was forged. "I've known that feeling before."

"Then you understand."

"Unconditional acceptance and love. The best kind of friendship there is." His stomach rumbled again, breaking the moment. He looked away, as if a hint embarrassed. "I'm obviously starving. Would you want to stay with me while I eat? I'd offer to share, but I'm sure you already ate your dinner. We could keep talking."

"I would like that." She glanced around and spied the ladder ascending to the loft. "How about the haymow?"

"My favorite place."

"Mine, too." Rain tapped lightly on the roof, serenading her as she seized both sides of the ladder and hiked her foot onto the bottom rung. "That's another blessing living in Montana. There are so many opportunities to do different things. Back in the city, we had a small stable for our carriage horses, but that was all. Here we have barns and horses and land to roam."

"And your mother allows this?"

"There are so many of us, Mama can't keep us all in check at the same time." She hoisted herself up to the next rung, carefully moving her hands one at a time. "You'll see when my other sisters come home from boarding school. It's a madhouse when we're all together."

"If I'm still here, that is." He waited patiently on the ground below, with his back turned to her. He seemed smaller from so high up, but not diminished. "Braden says we're making fast progress with the horses' training."

"Yes, I suppose you always have to keep on eye on your next job." Sadness hitched in her throat. Odd, because of course she knew he wouldn't be staying in Angel Falls. She raised her foot onto the next narrow rung and pulled her weight over the lip of the loft and onto the hay-strewn boards. "I'm up. You can look now. Next time I'll borrow a pair of trousers."

"I can't imagine what your mother would think of that."

"She would have an apoplexy for sure. Although Kate wears her brother's trousers when she rides her horse, and Earlee does the same when she helps with the barn work." My, but he could climb quickly. She backed up as he hopped onto the mow, basket and all. She wandered around, looking for the best place to sit. "Now it's your turn."

"Mine?" His forehead furrowed as he carried the basket, hay crackling beneath his boots.

"Your turn to talk." There was already a horse blanket spread on the hay. She watched as he set the basket down on a corner of it.

Light spilled through the cracks in the wall boards and the spaces between the walls and the eaves. This close to the roof, the rain whispered and sluiced with the cadence of a sonnet, rising and falling in the most pleasant way. She spied a small writing desk on the corner of the blanket. *This must be Shane's own hideaway place, where he spends his spare time. Curious.*

"I'm not sure I have anything interesting to say." He unlatched the wide door and drew it open. He didn't seem to realize how fascinating he was. "I'm not a terribly interesting man."

"Interesting is in the eye of the beholder." She knelt and

settled her skirts, aware of how impressive Shane looked staring out at the gray-and-green world. His hands were planted on his hips, which showed off his amazing shoulders and the strength in his arms. His feet were braced apart, emphasizing his height and power.

Meredith, you are staring at him again. She blushed, thankful he had his back to her and didn't know. She cleared her throat, hoping she sounded perfectly normal because she certainly didn't feel that way. "What about your friends?"

"Right." He pushed away from the open door, outlined by the falling rain as he paced toward her. "It's a long story. Are you sure you want to hear it?"

"Positive."

"I might bore you." He folded his long legs, swept off his hat and reached for the basket.

"If you do, I'll stop you." As if this man could possibly bore her. He had set her world upside down the moment he'd ridden into it.

"Don't say I didn't warn you." He winked, his manner light, but there was something deeper, something private that remained just out of sight. He lifted the basket's lid. "Just before my twelfth birthday, many of my father's investments went bad and we fell on hard times."

"I'm sorry. That happens to a lot of people."

"And we were no exception." His voice stayed steady, betraying no emotion. "We had to rent out our house in order to keep it, so we moved in with my grandmother."

"And you left your friends behind?" she guessed.

"Worse. I had no friends to leave behind." He kept his face down as he pushed aside the cloth keeping the food warm, speaking casually, perhaps thinking she could not hear the shades of strain hidden behind his words of the lingering hurt he must be trying to hide. He pulled a plate from the basket. "When our financial situation changed, the friends I had grown up with turned their backs on me."

"How awful. You had to be crushed."

"Something like that." He unwrapped the plate of fried chicken. "I can still remember standing in the front yard waiting for Ted and Zachary to come home from school, the school I'd been forced to quit because we could not pay the tuition. It was raining just like it is today, a fine drizzle that wet your face and misted the world. It was cold and turning colder, but I refused to go inside because my mother was upset packing up our house and because I was lonely staying home from school. I wouldn't wait to see my two best friends."

"But your family losing money changed things with them?"

"Yes. When they came down the road driven in their family carriage that day, their driver didn't stop. They didn't lean out the window and wave, shout some remark or even throw a spit wad. You know how little boys are. Ted saw me and turned away, as if he were ashamed of me. Zachary sneered as he rolled past, and called out something unkind. He made it clear I was no longer their friend."

"That had to devastate you."

"I never forgot it." He withdrew a second plate from the basket, hardly paying attention as he set it on the blanket. The memories had changed him, drawing layers of emotion and sadness she'd never seen before. "Two weeks later we moved into my grandmother's house. I was feeling as lonely as a boy could be. Two kids from across the street came over to see what was going on. When they saw I was their age, they invited me to come play tag with them. Neither of them cared about my family's name or what my grandfather did for a living. We're friends to this day."

"Is that what the writing desk is for? So you can keep in touch?"

"Yes. Eventually my family's finances improved, and we moved back into our house a few years later. Warren, William and I have been corresponding ever since. Some friendships are able to survive time, life's events and even great distances."

"Yes, and whenever you're together again it is as if no time has passed and nothing has changed." She leaned forward to help him by lifting the cloth from the plate. "Such is the nature of real friendship."

"I can't argue that."

"You know what this tells me about you?"

"I'm afraid to guess." His dimples returned, edging out the sadness of his story and leaving the hope.

"That you have more character than I gave you credit for."

"Did you just pay me a compliment? Or did my ears deceive me?"

"I'm as astonished as you are."

They laughed together. She couldn't hold back her admiration or the strange power he seemed to have over her affections. Like a rope binding her heart to his, when he felt, so did she. His gladness rolled through her and they smiled together as if in synchrony, as if friends for real.

"And I have even more news," she confessed. "I officially have no reasons left not to like you."

The sunlight broke through the doors, spilling across them like a sign from above. They laughed together, their chuckles echoing in the peaked roof of the loft and drowning out the rise of birdsong from the green fields.

Hitching up Sweetie had not been nearly as difficult as she feared, not with Shane teaching her. She pulled the last strap through the buckle, securing the buggy's traces to the mare's thick leather collar.

"Did I do it right?" she asked.

"Perfect," Shane praised from the other side of the horse. "How does it feel to have hitched up your first buggy?"

"Liberating." The floor bit into her knee, so she stood and dusted off her skirt. Bits of dirt and scraps of hay tumbled off the cotton, swirling like dust motes in the sunshine. "Thanks to you, all the lines and buckles and pieces are no longer completely mystifying. Now I can hitch up any horse, no problem."

"You're one step closer to your plans." Over the top of Sweetie's broad back, he tipped his hat to her. "Well done. Soon you will be driving your own buggy across the plains."

"I wish. I still have examinations to pass, and they are usually very hard." The mare nickered as if wondering why she was standing still if she was hitched to go somewhere, and Meredith rubbed her shoulder comfortingly. "It's getting closer, and I'm getting more nervous. What if I don't pass? I'm starting to see doom. All the ways things can go wrong."

"Don't worry. You will do fine, the same way you do everything."

"You're just saying that. You don't know me that well."

"I know you're smart and hardworking." He laid his arms across the horse's back and leaned close, resting his chin on his hands. "I know you enough to guess you are at the top of your class."

"Earlee always gets the top grades, but I come close." Just thinking about it made nerves settle into her stomach, hopping around like trapped grasshoppers. "I've been wanting this for so long and suddenly it's almost here. If

I pass the exam, I can have my own little schoolroom this summer."

"Summer? Doesn't school usually start in the fall?"

"Yes, but some areas can't afford to pay a teacher or there are too few students for a district. Summer school helps to bring education to the rural areas. It's a great place for a beginning teacher."

"You light up when you talk about it. Why do you want to be a teacher?"

"Because education can better a child's life. I believe everyone should have the chance to learn." A curl tumbled into her eyes, as one always did, and she brushed it away, totally unconscious of the adorable gesture. She tucked the lock behind her ear. "I took my schooling for granted until I moved here and saw life from a different perspective."

"My move to Charleston to live with Grandmother did the same thing for me." His throat closed, full of so many things he couldn't admit or felt too bashful to say. It was fine to have material things, but a man could not build his character accepting inherited money that he had not earned. That was another reason he had walked away from his family. He supposed Meredith felt the same, and he admired her for seeing the work she could do in the world instead of closing her eyes to the need.

The door at the other end of the barn opened with a wrench of wood and a drum of boots. Didn't sound like Braden back early from town. That meant the intruder could only be Robert Worthington.

"Meredith!" Harsh tones reverberated the length of the structure. "Are you out here?"

"Uh-oh." Across Sweetie's withers, Meredith stepped back, panic pinching her lovely features, animating her in the most darling of ways. "I'm not supposed to be here, but mostly I'm not supposed to touch the horse or buggy."

"I'll take care of her," he whispered back. "Go on. Talk to your father."

"Thank you." Her sincerity washed over him as surely as the spring breeze at his back, and he felt her gratitude in his inner-most heart. She seemed to take the light with her as she scurried away on pretty kid slippers, leaving him as if in winter's gloom.

The mare curved her neck to toss him a questioning look, as if to say, "What's going on? Aren't we going some-where?" He reached to unfasten the buckles holding the collar to the buggy traces, working fast. Those striking boot steps had stopped midway through the barn, danger-ously close. Not that he intended to deceive Worthington if he should question him, but if the horse was unhitched in time and back in her stall, the man might not think to ask a question he would not have to answer.

"But, Papa!" Meredith's protest rang in the breezeway.

She was probably being sent back to the house. Shane lifted the collar from Sweetie's neck and hung it on the nearby hook. Lighter steps tapped away, her gait dimin-ishing with distance. She must be gone. The barn door squeaked closed and he led Sweetie back to her stall.

"Connelly." Robert Worthington's voice boomed in the stillness, chasing a sparrow from a perch on the grain barrel. Horses stirred in their stalls and many poked their noses over the bars of their gates, nickering and whinny-ing at the disturbance. A sign of anger in the man's voice.

Even Sweetie skidded sideways, suddenly nervous. Shane laid a hand on her neck, murmuring low to her.

"I'm in here, sir." He opened the gate and Sweetie hur-ried into her stall.

"I need a word with you." Worthington pounded closer, his boot steps preceding him. He came into sight still in his Sunday's finest—a waist coat, pleated trousers and shin-

ing boots. He was no longer the doting, easygoing patriarch, not with anger tight on his face.

"What do you need, sir?" Shane checked Sweetie's latch
and pushed away from the stall.

"A moment of your time." Robert glowered. "I don't
know how to say this."

"Clearly something is wrong. Let me guess. You were
concerned about your daughter being alone in the barn
with me without a chaperone. Is that right?"

"That's it." Robert pounded closer, closing the gap between them. With every step he took, the disapproval lining the man's face became deeper and more apparent.
"Meredith is a good girl, but she is headstrong and naive."

"I would never do anything to insult or harm her or
any of your daughters." He had done nothing wrong, so it
was easy to meet the man eye to eye and ignore the tension thick in the air.

"I believe that." Robert came to a stop outside the stall,
his tone dark. "Which is why you will understand. I have
to insist that you limit your interaction with my daughter
to strictly the business I've hired you for."

"You hired me to train your horses."

"No, I hired Braden for that. You, as his assistant, will
do the various menial tasks around this place. If you cannot, I will hire someone who can." Shoulders back, chin
up, unflinching, Robert looked like a man who meant what
he said. "Is that clear?"

"Of course. I don't want to lose this job for Braden." He
thought of Meredith in the house. He didn't want her punished for spending time with him. They had been talking,
nothing more. Surely no one could believe differently. "I
meant no disrespect to you or to Meredith."

"See that it stays that way." Worthington jammed his
fists into his pocket, his gaze narrowing as he looked

Shane up and down. "Don't take this the wrong way, son, but you're young and you have little to show for yourself. You're learning a trade. For that I commend you, but do not misunderstand my daughter's propensity for befriending those less fortunate than herself."

"Less fortunate?" He blinked, a little puzzled because he had thought the father was concerned they had been alone together and for his daughter's reputation. Apparently the greater issue was their budding friendship. "I don't understand, sir."

"The man who wins my Meredith's hand will not be an itinerant saddle tramp working a few months out of the year, living hand to mouth, with nothing to offer. Now do you understand?"

Now it made sense.

"You are as clear as a bell, sir." Anger built like a fire behind his sternum, but he tamped it down. He should have been prepared for this. He should have seen it coming. He couldn't say it didn't hurt.

"It's nothing personal, son." Robert wasn't a cruel man, and his tone softened a notch. "Things might be different if you had the right family connections and a fine spread of land to call your own."

"I can't say that I do, sir." Not anymore. He had given up that life. He was no longer that man. He was twenty years old. Worthington wasn't exactly wrong. He'd built up a savings, but he had no plans to settle down. He *was* sweet on Meredith. He felt closer to her than he should.

"Otherwise, you have done a fine job for us. I hope there are no hard feelings." Robert dipped his chin in a formal nod before pivoting on his heel.

Hard feelings? Shane blew out a breath, determined to hold on to his dignity. Best to let the man's words roll off him instead of take them to heart. He couldn't say that if he was in Robert's shoes he would have done anything different. Meredith was amazing, worth protecting, worth the sting he felt on his pride.

He was a wanderer, that was part of his job. He was itinerant, he had no home and every material possession he owned could be tied to the back of his saddle. It shouldn't matter that he'd been told not to be friends with Meredith. The weeks would soon be ticking by until it was time to leave. There was no future for them anyway, and he didn't want one. He wasn't looking for anything serious. Not now. Not at this place in his life.

The sting remained like a welt, tender and inflamed, as he headed out into the yard. Leaves rustled overhead and the breeze sang through the blades of grass at his feet as he made his way to the bunkhouse. The sunshine winked on the windows of the house, drawing his attention, forcing him to glance at the big window where Meredith could be seen sitting at the dining-room table, laying out a piece of material. Her oldest sister stood nearby. The two young women commented, studied, furrowed their brows and Meredith moved around a few pieces of fabric. The sisters smiled, as if pleased.

Shane twisted away, realizing he was staring. The woman had more power over him than he'd realized. He forced his feet forward where the bunkhouse and a good book awaited him.

Chapter Eleven

"Girls!" Mama's call rang through the morning stillness. China cups rattled in their saucers as she barreled into the dining room. "Hurry and get ready or you'll be late for school."

"I wouldn't mind being late." Minnie dropped her fork on her plate with a *clink*. "I have a quiz today."

"And let me guess. You didn't study?" Meredith took one last sip of apple cider before pushing away from the table. "I would have helped you."

"But I didn't want to do it." Minnie flashed her dimples and bobbed out of her chair. "What I want is for summer weather to come, so I can play in my tree house."

"That is hardly ladylike." Mama drew herself up, shook her head with disapproval and gave Minnie a loving nudge. "Off with you, now. Gather your books and put on your wraps. Sadie! Where are the girls' lunches?"

The kitchen door swished open and the maid, hair curling from the kitchen's heat and looking frazzled, scurried into sight, carrying two small pails. "Here you are, ma'am. Is there anything else you'll be needin'?"

"No, go back to your work, Sadie." Mama took possession of the tins. "Meredith, why are you daydreaming again? Stop staring at the window and get ready to go."

Had she been staring? She hadn't noticed. Meredith blinked, realizing she was indeed facing the window, and launched out of her chair. A strange flickering feeling traveled through her as she followed her mother through the parlor. It wasn't a bad feeling, just a novel one that was as pure as the morning's gentleness and as uplifting as the budding lilacs waving their tiny perfect flowers in the breeze.

Shane. She could see him through the parlor window driving the buggy to the front door. He perched on the edge of the seat and the wind tousled the ends of his dark hair. The new day's light bronzed him as if he'd come straight out of a painting.

"Did you not hear me, child? Goodness, you are preoccupied today."

"Sorry, Mama." She took the coat her mother thrust at her and jabbed her arms into it. Something was definitely wrong because it was the strangest phenomenon that the closer Shane came to her, the more she was aware of him. The tug he held on her heart increased. Her thoughts centered on him. Her senses filled until he was all she could see—not the door opening, not Minnie jumping down the steps and skipping along the walk, not Mama kissing her cheek and wishing her a good day—just him.

Only him.

It was as if something had gone wrong with her entire brain and she was helpless to stop it. She hardly felt the bricks at her feet or the change in the wind that May day brought. The air evaporated from her lungs, leaving her breathless as her hand settled into his. His fingers closed around hers, and the connection between them became more powerful, as it did every time they touched. She did not recall climbing into the buggy or settling on the cushioned seat, only that his hand released hers, he moved away and she felt the purest of lights the heavens had to offer.

It wasn't until she was halfway to town that she realized Shane hadn't bid her good morning or greeted her with a smile. He hadn't turned around once in the seat in front of her. His attention remained focused on the roads. Mud still splashed beneath the wheels, but the sun was out and drying the land. Everywhere mist rose in great cloudy ribbons from earth to sky, and beside her, Minnie scribbled a note to her best friend, preoccupied with the secrets little girls shared.

Town came into sight with children straggling toward the school. The bell was ringing by the time Shane pulled to a stop behind a long line of buggies. Horses stomped impatiently, parents called out goodbye and students scurried toward the front steps as the last toll of the bell clanged.

"We're gonna be tardy, Shane!" Minnie folded her note into her pocket and held out her arms.

"Sorry about that." In his big-brother way, the man swooped Minnie safely from the seat to the soggy grass and gave the ribboned end of one braid a tug. "Do good today, shortcakes."

"I will!" Minnie beamed up at him as if he'd been personally responsible for hanging the sun. She spun away and sprinted across the lawn. "Maisie! Wait for me!"

Chuckling, Shane turned back to the buggy, back to her, the essence of him so attractive and powerful it was nearly too much to bear. She felt ensnared by invisible bonds she could not describe or understand, and she wanted nothing more than to capture the closeness they had shared yesterday in the barn. To reestablish their fun banter and trade a laugh or two.

The trouble was, he did not seem to feel the same. He did not meet her gaze. His smile faded as he held out his hand dutifully, as silent as stone.

"I hope you have an enjoyable day with the horses." She floated instead of stepped from the buggy. When her shoes touched the ground, it came as a surprise. Being near him scrambled her senses, there was no denying it, even if he did not feel the same. She could no longer deny she liked him very much.

"I hope your day is enjoyable as well." Oddly formal, he didn't look at her as he spoke. He turned away and climbed into the front seat, intent on straightening the reins, which were straight and orderly to begin with. What was going on?

The male brain made no sense at all to her. He was simply going to drive off as if they were complete strangers, and after the time together they had shared? Fine, let him. A smart girl wouldn't give the guy another thought. A sensible girl would march to the schoolhouse, where class was about to start any minute.

Because her shoes were not taking her in the direction of the front steps, she was obviously neither smart nor sensible. Her feet took her right back to the buggy and Shane. He looked up from releasing the brake, startled to see her standing there when he'd thought she had gone. His arresting blue eyes could stop the sun from rising, which was probably why she was standing in front of him and not acting like herself at all.

"Is this because I said I liked you?" she blurted out, wishing for the first time she had paid attention to her roommate Elizabeth Barker back at finishing school who had much experience and endless advice on dealing with the male gender. Shane paled, so perhaps she had been a bit overly bold. Did that make her fall silent?

Not a chance.

"You hardly so much as glanced at me this morning." She gripped the side of the buggy and met his startled gaze. "You were talkative with Minnie and friendly with her. Then in nearly the same breath you became with me as formal as a judge."

"I'm doing a job, Meredith. That's all." Strain bracketed his mouth, a poor imitation of the dimples that she liked so well. Apology shone in the depths of his irises and in his heart, which she could feel.

"I don't understand. Of course you're doing a job. Why else would you be driving us around?" If hurt lodged like a stone behind her rib cage, she did her best to ignore it. "You're one of those fly-by-night men, aren't you?"

"Fly-by-night?" A corner of his mouth quirked upward.

"You think a female is getting too close and you race off like a mustang being chased by a mountain lion."

"And why would I do this?" The other corner of his mouth twitched, as if he were fighting amusement and, judging by the set of his eyes, sorrow.

"Because I said I liked you yesterday. Remember?" She couldn't believe it. She smacked the flat of her hand against the side of the buggy, mad at herself. "I was talking about friendship. That was all. Surely you know that."

"I do." He swallowed hard, a man wrestling with something important. "I'm not sure friendship between us is a good idea."

"Why not? You don't like me?"

"Not like you?" He took in the endearing look of her, the vulnerability revealed in her question and in the wobble of her lush bottom lip. "Impossible. Life is better around you, Meredith. But as your father reminded me, I am here to do a job, not to make friends."

"My father? Papa talked to you?" She looked angry. "I made him promise not to."

"He was only looking out for his daughter." The wind tousled a row of bouncy corkscrew curls into her eyes and before she could brush them away, he reached to do it. His fingertips grazed the petal-soft curve of her cheek, the shell of her ear and felt the impact of her sweetness. Tenderness, unbidden and new, rose up in him like a hymn too beautiful to quiet, too reverent to stop.

"What did Papa say?" Worry crinkled her forehead in the most darling way. "He insulted you, didn't he?"

"He said nothing that wasn't true. You have plenty of friends." The words tore at him, but he managed to say them with a shrug. He was a man unaffected. "You don't need me."

"I do."

"No, you don't." He hated doing it because he didn't want to hurt her, but he raised the reins and shielded his heart. "In a couple weeks, you will be teaching school somewhere far out on that prairie, and Braden and I will be working in Butte. There's no sense in getting attached."

"But, Shane, I don't see why—"

"Have a good day, Miss Meredith." He slapped the reins. Sweetie stepped forward with a slow plod. The buggy rolled a few yards away from her, shielding him from her sight.

All she could see was the black back of the vehicle slowly maneuvering away from the crush on the road—and away from her. Just like that, he'd driven away. Cast aside their friendship because her father had spoken to him.

Not exactly a man capable of great friendship.

"Hey, handsome!" A superior-sounding, very familiar voice lifted above the noise of the street and the shouts of kids scrambling toward the schoolhouse. Narcissa Bell stepped onto the side of the road and waved boldly. "What's your hurry? I'll see you later!"

Had Shane waved back? Had he acknowledged her in some way? Meredith worried, seeing red as Narcissa smiled. A satisfied look passed across her smug face.

"Shane is utterly the cutest." Narcissa's chin went up

in the air, her narrow smile triumphant as if she knew exactly how deep the barb went.

Anger roared through her, but she held it in and kept the lash of the anger inside her, silent and hidden. The last thing she wanted was for her archenemy to know how much it hurt. How could Shane end their friendship, and go looking for another? And with Narcissa of all people.

No, he wouldn't, she decided, remembering the strength of character she'd witnessed in him. Narcissa was simply going after what she wanted. No need to be upset over her. It was enough to watch the buggy rolling farther away down the street, hesitate at the corner and then turn out of sight. Why did it feel as if her very essence longed after him? As if her spirit wished for the company of his?

They weren't even friends anymore. She brushed at the curls that had fallen in her face again, remembering the blissful kindness of his touch.

"Meredith? Are you all right?"

She felt a tug on her sleeve. Kate stood beside her with concern on her face and a question in her eyes. Was she really standing here pining after a man for all to see? The sun was in her eyes, causing them to tear a little, and she blinked hard, turning on her heels, lifting her chin, shoring up her dignity. "I'm all right. Just lost in thought."

"You're going to be late. We'd better go in."

"What? Oh, right."

The school bell had long silenced. Narcissa was the only other student in sight scurrying up the front steps. Miss Lambert held the door open, gesturing impatiently. "Hurry, girls! You don't want to be marked tardy."

Meredith felt Kate pulling her along. She was aware her feet were moving. The schoolhouse loomed up ahead and so did the disapproving countenance of their teacher.

"Guess what?" Kate whispered as they rushed up the

stairs. "There's a new girl in school today. She's got the desk behind Earlee and me. She looks nice."

"Great." It was as if Kate's words had no meaning, for nothing seemed to be able to penetrate her Shane-centered thoughts. She darted past the teacher, shucked off her coat and hurried to her seat.

He couldn't get Meredith out of his mind. Hours had passed since he'd driven away from her, and still her image of vulnerability and hurt stuck with him. He tipped his hat lower to shade his face against the cresting sun and checked the tension of the longe line. The black filly walked in a large circle, ears up, head up and her gait as smooth as silk.

If only he could enjoy the moment with the horse, the sense of accomplishment he got from seeing an animal progress and the shared camaraderie. He ought to be at peace, happily at his work. But he felt twisted up inside. Losing Meredith's friendship tore him apart. He'd only been doing them both a favor. Mr. Worthington was right. It wasn't practical to form attachments when both he and Meredith had plans to move on.

This wasn't about friendship, he admitted to himself, but something more. That was why he'd agreed with Robert Worthington. The father had recognized what the daughter had not. Shane had never been in love, but he suspected he had taken the first stumbling steps on that path.

"Pretty day, isn't it?" Braden sauntered over from the barn and leaned on the corral rails, eyes on the horse. "I didn't think warm weather would ever come."

"I was beginning to think the same." Shane glanced around. It was hard to believe that snow had blanketed the ground days before. The grass sprang beneath his boots as he turned in place, handling the longe line, keeping the filly at a disciplined walk.

Around him the landscape was stunning, some of the most beautiful he'd seen of all his travels. The roll and draw of the prairie and hills were pleasing, the depth of green in the fields unparalleled, the perfect blue of the cloudless Montana sky breath-stealing.

He could get used to it here. Birds chorused as they perched on the branches of the trees in the orchard. In the next paddock over, the spring's crop of foals stretched their long legs in bright green grass and budding buttercups. Even the wind felt warm as he shucked off his coat and kept the line he held taut. The filly had come a long way, stepping up to a trot when he commanded it.

"Good girl," he praised. "That's it, nice and easy."

"You've done a good job with her, Shane." Braden ducked between the fence boards and into the corral, a coiled lasso in hand. "She's come along very well, but you would do better if you kept your mind on your work."

Guilty. Shane winced, because he couldn't deny it. "I know. If I'm distracted, the horse will be, too."

"Right. When you're done here, come help me saddle up the white gelding. You're doing good work, Shane. I'm handing over half the two-year-olds to you. We'll see what you can do on your own." With a wink, Braden strode away, his compliment a strange contrast to the frustration and sense of loss Shane had been wrestling with.

Keep your mind on your work and not on the woman, Connelly. He whistled to the filly, watching her gait change as she slipped into a graceful canter. As much as he loved his work, he could not get lost in it. Meredith remained as if she were a part of him.

Concentrating on her schoolwork proved haphazard at best. Meredith rubbed at the dull ache in her forehead, turned the page of her spelling book and stared at the word on the top of the page.

"Time for lunch." The teacher's handbell jingled merrily, and all around her students burst out of their desks, conversation erupted and footsteps pounded down the aisle to the front door, where warm sunshine beckoned.

Finally. She closed her book, blinked to refocus her eyes and gave thanks that she had an hour to rest her weary brain. It took an astonishing amount of energy to keep her mind on the day's tasks.

"At least we don't have school tomorrow." Scarlet stacked her books on her side of the desk. "A day off."

"For you, not for me." She hopped to her feet, glad to leave her work behind, and grabbed her book bag from beneath her seat. "This time tomorrow, I'll be halfway through my teachers' examinations."

"Me, too." Earlee hooked her bag over her shoulder. "While you all are playing, Meredith and I will be finding out if we have what it takes to be teachers."

"As if the answer isn't already perfectly clear." Fiona smiled sweetly.

"Yeah, you two are the smartest in our class. You will do fine." Lila rolled her eyes. "The rest of us will be the losers because you both will leave us behind to get your own little schools. You will have your own careers."

"You make it sound so romantic." Kate sighed as she fished her book bag out from under her desk. "I have no idea what I'm going to do after we graduate."

They hadn't taken a step down the aisle before they heard a familiar, sharp-toned voice.

"Don't even look at me." Narcissa's words were pitched to rise above all the other sounds in the emptying schoolhouse. "Does it look as if I want to be friends with you? What is your name?"

"R-Ruby." It was the new girl, seated in the last desk of the row, looking miserable with her head bowed. Meredith had been so involved with her worries and her work that she had forgotten about the morning's addition to their school.

"I'm going to call you Rags. Look at that dress." Narcissa sneered, pleased with herself as she turned up her nose. "C'mon, girls. Let's go."

A few giggles and twitters filled the air as Narcissa and her group of friends clomped down the other aisle, leaving behind the lone girl with her head still down. A blush stained her fair face as she closed her tattered spelling book, clearly a volume handed down many times. She wore a faded red calico dress, which did not look as if it had been made for her because the fabric was bright red where the seams had been let out. The cuffs of her sleeves did not reach her wrists. The several patches on her skirt were made from a different fabric and were impossible not to notice.

Meredith stopped in mid-aisle. Kate lifted one eyebrow in silent question. Lila gave a little nod. Earlee and Fiona smiled. Scarlet, ever bold, turned on her heels and marched back to the new girl's desk, shoes striking like a hammer in the otherwise empty classroom. "Ruby?"

"Y-yes?" The girl didn't look up at them. Her face was still red as she kept her hands busy with a battered bag she had in her lap.

"Would you like to sit with us at lunch?"

Meredith saw the surprise and then gladness on the new girl's face. Ruby was really very lovely with porcelain features and wide, unguarded eyes.

"Oh, yes. I would like that very much." She swept into the aisle with her bag in hand. She had the friendliest smile. The dress she wore didn't fit much better when standing. The tops of her patched shoes were visible, as were her white stockings. "I'm afraid I've never been to a place like this before, so I don't know what to do with myself."

"You've never been to school?" Meredith had to ask, curious.

"No, I learned at home. My family used to live up near the Canadian border. There was no school nearby." Ruby blushed again. "I resolved not to make a fool of myself, but I think I just did it again, didn't I?"

"Not at all," Meredith assured her.

"Not a bit," Earlee seconded.

"Not even a little," Lila chimed in.

"Come on. We always eat lunch in the shade of the maple trees," Kate explained.

"And when we're done eating, we work on our sewing projects," Fiona continued.

"And talk," Scarlet finished, leading the way down the aisle.

"You all sew?" Ruby's face lit up as she followed them. "I'm not very good. What are you all making?"

"A quilt." Meredith plucked her lunch pail from the shelf above the hanging coats. "What's your current project?"

"Me? I'm afraid I don't have one right now." Ruby blushed again, perhaps embarrassed, hiding her face as she chose a battered tin pail from the shelf. "I did it again. I can't believe I said that. I'm just really nervous."

"It's okay." Earlee gestured at her own dress as they all trooped down the front steps and into the sunshine. "I get nervous like that, too. I'm letting out a dress for one of my younger sisters."

"Do you live in town?" Scarlet wanted to know.

"No. My pa took up a claim on a farm." Ruby shrugged shyly. "This is such a big town. I've never been around so many people."

A big town? Meredith bit her bottom lip to keep from

pointing out that Angel Falls, while a nice place to live, was a small settlement and their school humble enough to house all classes in one room.

"You must have lived in a very small town," Meredith said as they settled on one of the benches beneath the circle of maples. The younger children were cross-legged on the grass, pails scattered about, nearly done with their lunches. Some of the boys were already playing kickball.

"There was only a mail stop and a general store," Ruby explained as she took a spot on the bench next to Earlee. "It was a day's drive from the ranch Pa worked on, so we didn't go there very often."

"This must be a big change for you here." Lila empathized.

Meredith took the last space on the edge of the bench and tugged the lid off her tin while Ruby answered.

"Have you told your mother about the test tomorrow?" Scarlet leaned close to whisper.

"No. I've been dreading it, so I put it off." As if she didn't have enough eating her up inside with Shane on her mind. "It appears as if I'm out of time. I have to tell her before I leave to take the test in the morning."

"What if she forbids you to go?"

"I don't know." Meredith looked unhappily down at the meal Cook had prepared and Sadie had packed. Delicious aromas lifted from the cloth-wrapped food, but she wasn't hungry. Her stomach was tied up in far too many knots.

"You will think of something," Scarlet encouraged.

"I had better." Her plans for her entire future were at stake. Good thing Shane had taught her how to hitch up the buggy. If worse came to worst, she could drive Sweetie to town on her own.

Bless him for that. She plucked a leg of fried chicken out of the pail and did her best to join in with her friends' conversation.

Chapter Twelve

Not being pals with Meredith was like slow agonizing torture. The instant he'd spotted her tripping down the steps, her school day done, he read her unhappiness. Her head was down, her walk sedate. He hated seeing her like that. When she waved goodbye to her friends as they all parted ways, they promised to send prayers her way. Battered with regret, he hopped from the seat, boots striking the sun-kissed grass, seeing the crinkle of tension at the bridge of her nose and bracketing her rosebud mouth.

"Hi! Can we take Maisie home today, too?" Minnie reached him first, hand-in-hand with her best friend. The little girls giggled, twin braids bobbing,

"Sure thing, shortcakes." With an eye on Meredith, he helped the little girls into the backseat.

"Thanks ever so much." Minnie beamed at him, as cute as a button.

"You are ever so welcome." He winked to make her beam brighter. Hard not to grow fond of the kid. He would miss Minnie when he had to move on. He never had a young sister, but he reckoned it would have felt something like this.

He felt Meredith's approach. Every step she took closer

seemed to move through him like meter through a poem, the rise and fall of the cadence like that of his heart.

Don't let her know you are broken up, too. He tucked his feelings down deep and drew himself up to his full height. He was a disciplined man, but his resolve wavered as she glided to a stop before him. She did not hold out her hand, and he did not reach for her.

She pushed past him, gripped the side of the buggy and handily hoisted herself up, skirts swinging, lunch tin clanging, school bag dangling. Her silence said everything. She didn't need him, didn't want him. He couldn't say it didn't hurt. She smiled warmly at the little girls on the seat next to her, laughing at something Maisie had drawn on her slate.

Hardening his heart, he took his seat and the reins and sent Sweetie into the street. He was the driver, nothing more. That was what he had told her he wanted. If he felt the sting of her gaze on his back, he did his best to ignore it. If she was unusually quiet, he told himself it was not the sound of her voice he missed.

The streets were busy now that the warm weather had decided to stay. He had to wait at the intersection, enduring Meredith's glares and her silence. It felt as if ten years had gone by before the long queue of horses, wagons and buggies ahead of him dwindled, and he could finally turn onto the main street.

In front of Maisie's house, the little girls said goodbye. Meredith didn't so much as glance at him. He knew because he kept her in the corner of his eye.

There was no doubt she was mad at him. But that was not the reason she worried her bottom lip. Maybe she was anxious about her examination tomorrow. She had so much on her shoulders. A friend could help her by listening, maybe getting her to grin. He was not a friend, so he could not. He hated that no smile touched her rosebud-shaped mouth.

That he should even notice her mouth. It gave the sweetest smiles on earth and, he reckoned, perhaps the sweetest kisses.

Definitely don't think about kissing her, Connelly. If being friends was banned, then kissing would be absolutely prohibited. But as Minnie waved, hanging out the window, and he nosed the mare down the street, he could think of nothing else. Meredith's kiss would be soft as sun-warmed silk, as sacred as the most cherished of hymns. If he were allotted only one kiss in his entire lifetime, then hers would be the one he would choose.

He took the back roads to the church, where the oldest Worthington daughter was waiting on the top step. Tilly gathered her things and offered him a cordial smile that did not touch her eyes. She hopped in beside Minnie, hardly taking his hand. She didn't look any happier than Meredith did. But he was the driver and nothing more, so he gathered the reins and guided Sweetie toward home.

"How did the Ladies Aid meeting go?" Meredith's words penetrated his senses. Of all the noises in town and on the street, he could not shut out the sound of her voice.

"It was okay," Tilly said in the way women did when things weren't all right.

"What happened?" Meredith's question held tender sympathy, and that was what he liked about her the most. That she held a beautiful capacity to care.

He halted Sweetie at the end of the street, checked to see the way was clear and chirruped to her. The wind gusted through full leaves of the trees lining the road, and the music of children's laughter blotted out the older Worthington sister's answer. His every sense strained to hear Meredith's response, but the outside world seemed to work against him. A shout rang out from the main street, and several horses began to bay angrily. A woman came out her front door three houses up and began shouting for her children, her angry calls completely drowning Meredith's side of the conversation. Disappointment twisted through him, leaving him more frustrated than he'd started out.

Maybe he shouldn't be listening in. He knuckled back his hat brim, let the breeze fan his face and gazed up at what he could see of the blue sky beyond the buggy's fringed top.

Father, I'm feeling a tad lost. Please guide me. Even the smallest sign will do. No answer came on the summer-like air scented with green growing grass. They'd left the town behind them, where fields grew green and lush and the river roared on one side. Meredith was talking about an unnamed teamster Tilly was sweet on. The rushing roar of the upcoming falls drowned out the girls' conversation again.

Maybe that was sign enough. He didn't want to admit it, but perhaps he ought to work harder to close off his feelings and keep his desire to right what was wrong for her under control.

"What are you going to tell Mama?" Minnie asked, her words audible as soon as they'd left the falls behind them.

"I don't know," Meredith said, her lovely alto made him come to attention, spine straight, shoulders set. Maybe this was none of his business and he oughtn't be eavesdropping, but did that stop him?

Not a chance.

"I'm going to take the exam, whatever she says."

Yep, he wanted to help her. He wanted to be more than a friend to her. He wanted to be the man she turned to. But it wasn't meant to be. Just the driver, he gripped the reins more tightly and kept his attention on the road. Only on the road. Now and then an occasional note of her voice rose up to him like a little piece of music.

He'd never been so glad to see any building as he was the sight of the Worthington estate. Relief rolled through him. He pulled the mare to a stop. Tilly was out of the buggy before the wheels stopped turning. Minnie leaped out on her own, hollering a thanks to him. Only Meredith moved slowly, reluctant to face her mother, he reckoned, and not to prolong the presence of his company.

He could have wished her good luck, assured her he would say a prayer for her. He could simply reach out to squeeze her hand.

He did not. He sat straight as a fence post on the seat listening to her go. It was the little things that got to him now—the rustle of her skirts, the tiny intake of her breath that was nearly a sigh and the tempo of her gait on the walkway as she left him behind.

"Get a move on," Braden drawled, peeking around the garden gate. "We get the two-year-olds saddle broke, and I'm thinking it's time to reevaluate. Maybe make the decision to move on."

"Because of Mrs. Worthington?" He kept his voice quiet so it wouldn't carry to the house as he drove Sweetie toward the barn.

"That woman sat down with me today and gave me a lecture." He shook his head, looking as if he'd had enough. "I won't be impolite to a woman, but I was sorely tempted. She decided to have a say in how the horses are being trained."

"Does Mr. Worthington know about his wife's involvement?"

"He's about to." Braden, voice pitched low, pushed away from the gate. "I'll be waiting in the small corral."

"I'll be there."

He drove Sweetie into the shade of the barn. Looked as if he didn't need to worry about being here for much longer. He swung down and freed the reins through the loops on the dash. The wind gusted, carrying the faint murmur of women's voices from the house. Meredith's.

"Mama, no. Please. I have to do this." The gentlest plea he'd ever heard sailed over, wrapping its way around him. Heaven knew how anyone could say no to her.

"A Worthington daughter does not work." The mother's pronouncement rang with unyielding certainty and loud enough to clearly carry all the way from the parlor, across the flower garden and to the barn. "I expect you to deport yourself in a way that's appropriate to this family. A common schoolteacher, Meredith. Really. Where do you get your ideas, my precious girl?"

Whatever the woman's flaws, there was love there, too. He could not fault the mother for that.

Work was waiting, so he led the horse into the barn by the bridle bits. His sympathy for Meredith remained throughout the afternoon and long into the night, keeping him from a sound sleep.

The last thing she wanted to do was to disappoint her parents. Meredith set her morning cup of tea onto its saucer with a clink and tried to will the fog from her brain. After an upsetting evening with her parents, she'd tossed and turned most of the night and had awakened tired and groggy. Not the way she wanted to start this day, of all days. She listened to the mantel clock ticking off the minutes, knowing every moment that passed brought her closer to acting on her decision. Mama was so not going to like it.

"Meredith, why aren't you eating?" Her mother's tone jarred her out of her thoughts. "You haven't touched your breakfast."

"Sorry." She gathered knife and fork and stared at her plate. The food was delicious. Her stomach growled. She couldn't very well take her test without breakfast, so she cut into the stack of pancakes and took a bite.

"That's better." Mama approved with a nod. "A good girl doesn't mope if she doesn't get her own way."

"Although you've been known to, my dear," Papa quipped lovingly from the head of the table.

"I certainly have never moped, Robert." A tiny hint of amusement snapped between them. "I've been disappointed, perhaps, but a Worthington does not sulk."

Papa's chuckle was his answer as he turned back to his morning paper.

If it was only her mother who was against her becoming a teacher, then she knew she could have taken her pleas to her father. Papa had a hard time denying his daughters anything. But he'd sided with Mama on the subject, saying no girl of his would work. If she defied them, what would happen? She loved her parents. She didn't want to risk losing their regard. But neither could she let this opportunity pass her by.

I really hate being eighteen, she thought. Too young to be on her own, too old to let her parents decide the course of her life. She forked another bite of pancake into her mouth. The good food turned to sand on her tongue, nearly impossible to swallow. The clock had progressed another five minutes. If she wanted to get to the schoolhouse in plenty of time, she had to leave soon. Her palms went damp at the thought.

"You keep looking at the clock, Meredith." Mama and her eagle eye. She didn't miss much. "Do you have someplace to be? You know there isn't school this morning."

"I want to take the exam. You know this, Mama."

"And you know I forbid it. Don't think your father will

take you to town with him on his way to work. He and I have already discussed that. Matilda will be staying home with me this morning to finish reading for our book club. And since you are not allowed to drive, I'm sorry to say you have no choice but to spend your morning helping Sadie in the vegetable garden."

Was there any way to make her mother actually listen? Why was Mama's way always the right one, regardless of the consequences? "Times are changing. A lot of women are working. Earlee wants to be a teacher, too. Lila works in her parents' store."

"If your friends jumped off a cliff, would you jump, too?" Mama demanded. "I think not. Don't compare yourself to those girls, Meredith."

"Why not? They are my friends."

"They are not like our family. They don't have our responsibilities—"

"That is *such* an old-fashioned way to think." She pushed away from the table, torn apart by her wish to do as her parents wanted and by her own conscience. China rattled with the force of her feet hitting the floor. She drew herself up tall, hands clenched, pulse pounding. She felt as if she were tearing apart from the inside out. Why couldn't they understand? She wished more than anything that they would take a moment to see her—just Meredith—and not the daughter they intended to mold her into.

"Where are you going, young lady?" Mama's chair scraped. She was on her feet, her face blushing with anger. "You come right back here and finish your meal."

Her feet seemed to be moving of their own accord, taking her to the front door where she'd left her book bag packed last night. Ready to go, she unhooked her coat from the tree. She glanced over her shoulder across the long stretch of the parlor, and into the dining room where her family watched her, shock frozen on their faces.

She had never denied them before. Papa's newspaper had sagged to the table. The disapproval in harsh lines on his face hurt more than any punishment could. Tilly's fork had stopped midair and her sympathetic look was what gave Meredith the courage to slip one arm into her coat. Tilly understood. Minnie was the first to move, bowing her head to drag a strip of bacon through the syrup puddle on her plate, her shoulders slumped, upset by the discord in their home.

I'm upset, too. Meredith jabbed her other arm into the sleeve and quickly buttoned her coat. At least she would be able to hitch up Sweetie. That was the only saving grace. She had prayed with all her might last night and still the dream remained in her heart. God had not taken it from her. She grasped the bag's straps, twisted the handle and opened the door. *Please, give me strength now, Father.*

Mama's footsteps shot like bullets on the hardwood floor. As Meredith seized the doorknob, she glanced over to see her mother throw up the dining-room window.

"You, there! Young man," Mama called across the yard. "You are not to hitch up any horse and buggy for my Meredith this morning. Do you understand? She is forbidden to drive to town."

Oh, Mama. Did she have to think of everything? Frustrated and hurting, she gritted her teeth, squished all the rising pain down where she couldn't feel it and stormed through the door. The steps pounded beneath her soles as she tumbled out into the yard. For such a stormy day on the inside, it was gorgeous outside. The sunlight washed the fresh green world with a gentle warmth. Birdsong rose from the fields and trees, and lilacs nodded pleasantly in the wind.

Forbidden to drive. Mama's commandment matched the angry beat of her shoes as she stomped down the walkway. Now what did she do? Did she defy her mother in this, too? Or was that the reason she heard the back door open with a squeak? Had Papa come out to ensure she could not disobey and use one of the family horses?

Well, no one had forbidden her to walk. She stared at the road ahead, her shoes crunching on gravel as she stepped into the light. Mama's orders to come back shattered the morning's stillness, but she did not turn around. Anger burned at the backs of her eyes and her throat. Soon all she could hear was her labored breathing and her shoes against the hard-packed earth. Birds fluttered from fence post to field and horses grazing in the pasture looking up curiously as she passed. She felt so bad over how things had gone back home; it diminished the beauty of the morning and the hope for her day.

How was she going to do well on her examination now? All the studying she'd done through the last month of evenings had flown right out of her head. She couldn't remember a single fact of the Revolutionary War to save her life. There was only an empty space in her brain where the information should be. She was more upset over disobeying her parents than she'd realized. She had not wanted to dishonor them, but in the end she could not dishonor herself.

Horse hooves clinking against the road were faint at first and then grew into a steady ringing *clip-clop.* A vehicle's wheels creaked and rolled on the rutted road behind her. Was it Papa coming to stop her? The last of her hopes plummeted to the ground.

Sure enough, she recognized the matched bay Clydesdales drawing alongside her. Papa. Her dreams melted away. She felt wrenched apart, bereft as the wagon rolled to a stop beside her. It was not wrong, this future she longed for. But it was her own. She did not want to lose it.

"You might as well climb up, Just Meredith. I don't want you to be late." A wonderfully warm, familiar, deeply welcome voice spoke into her despair. A hand shot out, waiting for hers. The sunshine, low in the sky, threw blinding rays across him, cloaking his identity, but he was no secret to her.

Shane. Hope and joy leaped through her, lifting her spirit as she laid her palm to his. Once again Shane Connelly helped her into the wagon, the last man she would have expected to come to her aid.

"I can't believe you're here." She settled on the seat, adjusting her skirts, more breathless now because she was at his side. "Mama forbade you to drive me to town."

"But not to fetch the day's order of grain from the feed store." With a casual flick of the reins, he sent the horses moving forward again. "And had the order not been waiting, I would have helped you anyway."

"Why? You will probably lose your job."

"True. I know what it feels like to have to make a tough decision. It's not easy to do what you know is right and leave your family behind." The sun threw playful shafts around him, hiding him from her sight, but she could read his voice, sensing the layers of regret, of sadness, of resolve.

"It was hard for you to leave them, wasn't it?"

"The hardest thing I've ever done." His confession ached with emotion and made him larger than life, larger than any one man could be.

"I may have left them behind, but I didn't stop loving them." He shrugged, as if he'd been torn apart, too. "I wish my parents could have helped me find a middle ground. It wasn't as if I was running around behind their backs causing trouble. I simply wanted to learn to train horses."

"And I to teach." They were so alike. Amazing that he had come into her life when she'd most needed someone to truly understand. She wondered about God's hand in this and dared to say the words troubling her most. "I don't want this to cost me my family, the way following your heart has cost you yours."

"I don't want that for you either." He stared at the road ahead, but he was honest and he did not offer her false comfort. "Your family has one thing mine never had. Love. Your folks aren't going to be happy with you. They may never understand, but I'm sure they will always love you."

"Thanks, Shane."

He turned away and said nothing more. A terrible stinging plagued her eyes, and she blinked hard to keep back the tears. It occurred to her how sad it truly was that she had found her soul mate, the one man she'd always hoped she would find, and she could not count him as a friend.

Chapter Thirteen

"How did you think you did?" Earlee asked as they walked down the street toward Main, leaving the schoolhouse behind them. "The exam was hard. My brain hurts from thinking so much."

"Mine, too." Meredith rubbed her forehead, wishing she could soothe away her other troubles as easily. The sun was past its zenith, the afternoon was halfway gone and she dreaded what lay ahead. Even thinking of going home made her stomach tangle up in impossibly hard knots. "There were several questions I completely missed. I just know it."

"Me, too." Earlee lifted her face to the sun and let the wind breeze over her, tangling her pure golden locks. "I'm hoping what I got wrong isn't nearly as much as what I got right."

"We'll find out in two more hours." She was aquiver at the thought. Pass or fail, she still had to face her mother. The sunlight seemed to drain a few notches in intensity as she fell silent, watching the grass blades shiver in the breeze ahead of her feet.

"Can I ask you something?" Earlee broke the silence as they crossed the vacant lot at the end of the block. "I don't want to pry or anything, but I noticed something serious between you and your driver guy."

"Shane? There's nothing between us." This she knew for sure. She didn't even have to deny it. He'd made it perfectly clear—twice now. "He was helping me out this morning, that's all."

"But you like him. *Really* like him."

"I do not." There came the denial rushing like the updraft of a giant tornado. Heat blushed across her face like a sunburn. "Maybe that's a sign I do."

"I think so!" Earlee's good humor was a gentle one, laced with understanding. "Are you finding that it's complicated if you like someone? And that it's confusing?"

"I want to deny that, but I don't dare. I'm going to be honest with myself." She took a deep breath, hitched the strap of her book bag higher on her shoulder and stopped at the corner to check for traffic. "I like Shane in a way I've never liked anyone before and yes, it's confusing and complicated and horribly painful. I don't care for it."

"Me, neither." Earlee clapped her hand over her mouth, as if surprised she had revealed so much. "Oops. I was going to make this be a hypothetical discussion, but I let the cat out of the bag."

"I'll say." After a donkey and cart ambled by, she stepped into the road. "Who are you sweet on? I haven't noticed you talking with any boy at school."

"Oh. He's not in our school." Earlee blushed harder.

That explained it. Meredith searched through her mind, thinking of suitably aged bachelors in town. "Let's see. There's Austin Hadly, the minister's son."

"No. He's cute, but not the one. Not that he has ever noticed me." Earlee had turned bright red, clearly uncomfortable. "And if you try guessing, it will take you an eternity. He no longer lives in town."

"But he used to?"

"Yes."

They'd reached the other side of the street where the boardwalk led them past the milliner's shop and the post office.

"I need to check for our mail." Earlee hesitated, gesturing toward the small shop bearing the United States flag.

"You are trying to get out of answering the question." Meredith wasn't fooled, but she thankfully didn't probe. "I know how it feels. I'm not ready to talk about what I feel for Shane, not even with my best friends."

"Thanks for understanding. Some things feel that if you talk about them out loud, then they will somehow vanish or change on you." She knew her face was still red because she could see the tip of her nose. Strawberry red. Completely embarrassing and far too telling. "Shane likes you. You know that, right?"

"What? Shane? No." She shook her head hard enough for curls to tumble down from beneath her bonnet. The silk ribbons of her hat bobbled and swayed. She blushed furiously. That was telling, too. "He doesn't. He's told me so."

"Then either he isn't being honest with you or he isn't being honest with himself." She took a step toward the post office, knowing how it felt to wonder if a guy liked you and fearing that he didn't. "You should see the look on Shane's face when he thinks no one is watching."

"What do you mean?"

"He gazes upon you as if you are his dream come true. As if you are his princess at the end of a fairy tale. Don't shake your head like that. I've seen him."

"You, my dear Earlee, have a romantic streak a mile wide." Meredith looked wistful for one brief moment before shaking her head, as if discounting her wish, and wrapped her arms around her middle. "This isn't a dime novel or one of the lovely stories you pen. There is going to be no happy ending for Shane and me."

"I've seen the way you look at him, too." It was simply the truth. "A change comes over you. You look softer and somehow more like yourself. I've never seen you so beautiful, Meredith."

"Now I'm really blushing. You and your imagination, Earlee." She swept at the curls always falling into her eyes, and it would have been simple as pie to put words to page and describe the love brightening the blue of her eyes and denial negating it. "Oh, I guess my ride home is here after all."

"She says, and *then* she turns around to see the handsome man in the fine buggy pull to a stop behind her." Earlee lowered her voice, buoyant with happiness for her friend. In her stories, love always found its match and that love was always true. Every now and then it was affirming to see the seeds of it in real life, the proof that true love could exist and even prosper. "Your Shane is here."

"Shh!" She blushed again. "He might hear you."

"I guess I'll head home on my own." She didn't bother to disguise her gladness. "Have a very nice drive."

"Sure, considering the roads are much better these days. Just a little soupy in places." Meredith adjusted her bonnet bow beneath her chin. "And don't say it. I know what you're thinking. I can see it written all over your face."

"I wasn't talking about the roads."

"You couldn't be more wrong." She rolled her eyes, full of denial, turning just enough to spot Shane at the edge of her peripheral vision.

"The moment he is near, your spirit turns to him like he is the sun and you are the earth. Definitely like every romance I've ever read. Be honest with yourself. You're in love with him."

"I have to go." Love? That was a very powerful word and it hardly applied. It was ridiculous, that was what it was, but that was Earlee finding the beauty in anything—even if it didn't exist. She loved her friend, but she was sorry to say Earlee was exceptionally wrong in this instance. Somehow she scooted her feet forward toward the buggy where Shane waited, his face shaded by his Stetson and his unseen gaze a touch to her cheek, her mouth, her lips.

Now I'm *being fanciful,* she thought, waving goodbye to Earlee, who glowed happily, apparently sure she had things all figured out, before spinning around and hurrying down the street to the post office.

"How did it go?" Shane hopped down, not in the placid, doing-my-job way Eli Sims, her former driver, had done, but with a deliberate gentlemanliness that felt suspiciously like a courting man—although it could not be.

Whatever romantic fanciful tendencies Earlee had, perhaps they were as contagious as diphtheria. Meredith shook her head, hoping to scatter those thoughts right out of her mind, squared her shoulders and stepped into the buggy's shadow where Shane stood waiting for her.

"I have no idea if I passed or failed." She was talking about the test, but as he helped her into the buggy, dizziness swept over her, scrambling her senses.

"I'm sure you did very well." His words came as if from a great distance as the cushioned seat bounced slightly when he eased down beside her.

She gulped, surprised at the slight brush of his elbow against her sleeve as he took up the reins.

"There's no sense of you sitting in the back all by yourself and me being up here by my lonesome self." His baritone held a note she hadn't heard in it for a long time. Not since the first day they met. His combination of amusement and warmth and manliness could lull her into believing that Earlee was right. That he was attracted to her. Her heart fluttered, as if with wings.

"What are you going to do when you pass?"

"I suppose I will find that out in a little while. The superintendent said he will have the exams graded by three o'clock."

"We don't have to head straight back to the house." He knuckled back his hat like a Western hero. "We can wait her in town, if you like."

"Sure, but you are here to do a job, not to be friends." She longed for him to argue the point. "Waiting with me certainly is not part of your job description."

"I figured I'm fired anyway, so why not?" There was a deeper nuance to his words, a layer of affection that he could not hide.

If only she did not feel it, she thought. It was hard not to care for him in return. Shane snapped Sweetie's reins and led them rambling down the road through town.

Earlee nearly died when she saw the letter in the small bundle the postmaster handed across the counter. Finn McKaslin, Deer Lodge Territorial Prison, was written in a clear script in the upper left-hand corner. She couldn't believe it. He'd actually written back. She ran her fingertips over the letters of his name, atremble with too many emotions to describe easily. She knew good and well what her parents would say if they knew she was corresponding with a man in prison, but hadn't Reverend Hadly preached on Sunday to see God's goodness in all those we met, and to wear a mantle of kindness?

That is not *the reason you're glad Finn to wrote you, Earlee Elizabeth Mills.* She pushed through the door, held it for elderly Mrs. Finch and headed straight for the bench situated next door in front of the bakery. Ignoring the hustle and bustle of the horse-and-buggy traffic, the rattling commotion of teamsters hauling their loads down the street and the clip-clip of shoes on the boardwalk behind her, she carefully tore open the envelope. The parchment crackled like dried leaves she shook so hard.

The same clear intelligent handwriting covered the page. She leaned over the words, to shield it from passersby, and began to read.

Dear Earlee,
   I can't believe you actually wrote to me. I don't have a whole lot of spare time, being as this is a hard labor prison, but even here Sunday is a day of rest. I spent my free mornings in service and the afternoons writing to family and friends. Honestly, it's family. It doesn't matter how many letters I send out to friends, not a single one comes back. Not that I blame them. I messed my life up good, but I've never understood the meaning of friendship before or wished for it so much.

Poor Finn. Sympathy filled her. She glanced up from the letter, trying to imagine his life. Hard labor sounded awful, and so did his loneliness. She didn't know what she would do if something caused her to be parted from her friends. She felt so sorry for him, the young man she remembered as tall and broad-shouldered, muscled but not brawny. Before his trouble with the law, she'd had a crush on him with his bright blue eyes and dark fall of hair a little too long for fashion. The rumble of his deep voice could make a girl dream.

Now all his prospects in life and his chances were gone. It was good he saw the error of his ways and she felt the remorse in his words. She glanced across the street where sunlight reflected in the windows of the land office. Her throat ached from the lump of emotion settling there. She firmly believed there was good in everyone, and that everyone was worth a second chance. Maybe it was the dreamer in her or the writer wanting to pen a happier ending for him. She bowed her head and went back to reading.

Although your note was short, I was much obliged to hear about how you're doing and the town's news. Your letter was entertaining, I found myself smiling, and I thank you for that. I can't tell you what your gift of kindness means to me. How did the hunt for the calf turn out? Did you finish the dress for you sister in time for the Sunday service? I understand if you feel uncomfortable and decide not to write me, but I hope you do.

Hoping to be your pen friend,

Finn

She stared at his name, the confident swish of the letters and his vulnerable request on the page. He wanted to be pen pals. She thought of his friends who'd forsaken him and she pulled out a sheet of parchment, a bottle of ink and her pen. After loading the tip, she used the back of her slate for a lap desk and began to write.

Finn,

Yes, the calf story ended well. I didn't see the capture firsthand, but I heard about it from Scarlet Fisher, who lives next door to the Hoffsteaders. Late at night a clatter in the alley woke the Hoffsteaders from a sound sleep. The intruder in their backyard was threatened with a mop, since the family rifle was at the gunsmith's for repair, and the sheriff called. When the law arrived and one of the deputies lit a lamp, instead of the thief Mr. Hoffsteader had cornered on the porch, they found the runaway calf lounging on the swing. Mrs. Hoffsteader was beside herself because of the hoof prints in her flowerbeds and on the swing's cushion.

She lifted her pen from the paper, considering what to say next. She hoped Finn would smile at the tale, because it sounded as if he had little in his life that would make him do so. That was what she wanted to give him—a smile and a moment to forget his hardships. She bit her lip, gazed out at the street, watched an ox tied to a nearby hitching post attempt to eat a flower off a lady's hat, and let her pen guide the way.

I finished my sister's dress in time for Sunday school. That will teach her to daydream while she's ironing. I had to learn the hard way, too. I ruined two perfectly good dresses until I learned to keep my mind on the iron. The newest battle in my household is over who will do the barnyard chores. We have the cutest little batch of piglets born this spring, four dozen fluffy yellow chicks and twin calves that are too adorable for words. Add that to the new litter of kittens in the barn, and every morning the nine of us are squabbling over who gets to take care of what.

I won this morning and had the sweet privilege of feeding the calves. They have finally learned to drink from a bucket. Every time they spot a pail, their adorable brown heads rise up, their chocolate eyes glitter and they bawl in excitement. They run over on their spindly legs with knobby knees.

him until there was only her beauty and color and life. Just Meredith and his love dawning.

"I don't want to be friends with you." His confession was whispered, so no one but she could hear. "Do you suppose the soon-to-be schoolteacher would let a simple horseman come beauing?"

"You will have to ask her and see." Her answer twinkled in her eyes as blue as his future, and they smiled together. He dared to reach across the small table and cradle the side of her cheek in his hand. Never had he felt anything softer, never had he touched anyone so dear to him.

"Shall we go back to the schoolhouse and see just how well you did on your test?" he asked, knowing full well he was ten times a fool.

When she nodded, gently leaning into his touch, he lost control of his feelings completely. There was no way to hold back the depth and strength of his love for her. It rose up of its own power and accord, against his better judgment and a list of reasons he shouldn't get involved.

When he pushed his chair away from the table, he felt like a new man.

Chapter Fourteen

Banished to her room, Meredith plumped the pillow at her back, leaned against the window seat cushion and held her sewing hoop up to the lamplight. Tiny perfect stitches marched along the seam she'd finished sewing, bringing two more squares of her patchwork block together. Deciding the stitching was uniform and tiny enough, she smoothed the seam flat with her thumb and flipped the half-finished block over. The pretty cotton fabrics made her smile.

Fiona had talked her into buying the cheerful yellow sprigged, saying it was the perfect color to build a quilt around. She recalled how Lila had spotted the beautiful robin's-egg blue calico in a new shipment of fabrics in her parents' store and set it aside for her. Soft lovely emotions of friendship filled her whenever she gazed upon the pieces. Scarlet had helped her pick out the rose-pink calico and Kate, at one of their sewing circle gatherings, had pointed out she needed more contrast. So her father had driven them all to Lawson's mercantile after school one rainy day in February where she'd added the ivory, green and lavender calicos to the mix. Earlee wasn't satisfied until she dug out a bold purple sprigged lost in the bolts of cotton. The laughter and happiness of that afternoon shopping trip rang through her, a dear memory she wanted to hold close forever.

She chose a purple cut square from her fabric pile, judging it against the other colors of the block. The merry brightness brought out the flowery yellow and the leaf green of the adjacent pieces. She carefully pinned it into place, eyeing the seam allowance. The end of the school year was almost upon them, and she would no longer see her best friends every day. School would end, they would graduate and all go their separate ways.

As she had tried to explain to Mama hours ago, that was a good thing. They were growing up and into the lives they had been dreaming of. But with the gain came losses. Sadness chased away the memories as she knotted her thread and stitched the raw edges of the fabric. Her thimble clicked as she worked, loud in the silent room.

A rap against the window cannoned like a bullet from a gun. The needle flew out of her grasp, she jumped in place and her pulse took off like a runaway freight train. She drew back the curtain. A face reflected in at her through the shadowed glass.

Shane. Night was falling, cloaking him in shades of darkness. He'd never been more handsome to her as she unlatched the window and opened it with care. The wood frame did not groan, the hinge did not squeak and a pleasant wind blew in the scent of lilacs. The maple's leaves shivered as Shane leaned closer to the sill.

"How's the new schoolteacher?" He presented her a bouquet of fragrant flowers, the dainty little blooms the exact purple of the piece she'd been sewing.

"Fine enough." She accepted the blossoms and lifted them to her nose. The luxurious perfume filled her as if with hope. "It's the first big step on the road to my goals.

I wish it felt more like an achievement instead of a source of unhappiness for my parents."

"They want what they think is best for you." He brushed the sensitive curve of her chin with his knuckle. "They will come to accept this."

"I hope so. And if not—" Because that thought made her sad, she cast it aside, focusing on the man before her. How rugged he looked with his hat slanted at a rakish angle and a day's growth rough on his jaw. Lamplight flicked in the wind, lashing at the slash of his high cheekbones and revealing the steady glow of affection in his eyes. Affection for her right there, revealed for her to see, tenderness that stretched without words from his soul to hers.

A like regard budded within her, as pure as the blossoms she held and as fragile. Caring deepened, and she could not stop it. The backs of her eyes stung and she carefully laid the handful of flowers on the edge of her nearby night table, leaning away from the window and away from him. But the distance between them made no difference. Somehow everything had changed.

"I have money set aside to buy land of my own when the time is right." Manly, quiet strength radiated from him like light from a flame. Unaware of his own brightness, he humbly shrugged one shoulder, his gaze intensifying, his seriousness arresting. "There's a meeting between Braden and your father tomorrow. If all does not go well, we will be leaving. Braden intends to head south to start our next job early."

"So soon." She expected it, but it hurt just the same. Everything within her stilled. The wind whipped her hair into her eyes again, and she moved to brush those curls aside, but it was his hand grazing her cheek, his fingertips caressing a sugar-sweet path from her forehead to her temple.

"Beauing a woman is much harder to do from a great

distance." His words rumbled through her, layered with meaning and an affection he must have thought hidden in the dark.

"But I will not be staying either." Her fingers curled around his steely wrist, wishing she could hold him captive. "I have already inquired to several schools for the summer, and then I will be moving on to another permanent school in the fall."

"I could follow you." How certain he sounded, as if dreams were so easily set aside.

"But what about your apprenticeship?"

"I hate to end it, but I could." He winced, as if he were torn. "I've learned nearly all I have signed on to do."

"Then I think you should finish." She leaned into his touch. The wind stirred her golden locks against his knuckles. She unwound his fingers from her hair and cradled his hand in both of hers. "I am a very good letter writer."

"I'm sure you are." He stared at her smaller, paler hands clasped around his sun-browned, callused one, thinking how different they were and how like. Love enfolded his heart the same way her hands wrapped around his. "You would write to me?"

"I suppose I could be persuaded every once in a while to pen a note for you," she quipped, but she meant something more. He knew because he felt the same way.

"I'm glad to hear it." He lifted his hand, bringing her knuckles to his lips. "My understanding with Braden is done at the end of this year, and my traveling will come to an end."

"You want to train horses of your own?"

"I want to farm." He brushed a kiss to her fingertips, one by one. The tenderness taking over him was the sweetest thing he'd ever known.

Lord, she is the future I want. The prayer rose up with

all the might in his soul. *Thank You for leading me to Meredith*. He was about to start the best adventure of his life.

"Farm?" Her forehead furrowed. "You mean to raise horses?"

"No, to rescue them." His kisses stopped, but he kept their hands linked. "I always meant to have my own stables, but then I've seen a lot of sad things in my travels. Hobo is a horse I rescued last year from a man beating him in the middle of the road."

"What? Why would anyone do such a thing?"

"I don't understand it. I don't know." Sorrow etched into the counters of his mouth. "The poor animal was covered in saddle sores, half-starved, and had collapsed on a lonely stretch of the Wyoming plains. His owner had taken a whip to him while he lay helpless in the January snow. Braden and I came upon them and I offered the man the contents of my billfold. He took the two hundred dollars. I got the better deal."

"You saved Hobo's life."

"He saved mine. Because of him, I knew what I wanted to do. Find a nice spread to buy, raise crops and give horses a second chance. Everyone deserves a safe place to prosper." Never had the man been bigger in her estimation. He towered before her, framed by the window, dominating her senses. He was all she could see, all she ever wanted to see.

"Are you surprised?" he asked.

"No. I approve." She squeezed her fingers entwined with his. As she let go of his hand, the bond between them remained as enduring as tempered steel, proof enough that she was right. They were kindred spirits. Souls so alike they felt as one.

Footsteps echoed in the hallway. A floorboard squeaked. Panic lurched through her, but the gait was not Mama's.

"I'd best go." He pushed away from the sill. The leaves rustled, and a branch groaned as he shifted his weight. "Tomorrow."

"Tomorrow." She reaffirmed his unspoken promise with a single nod. Something tore apart within her as they parted. She closed the window and he disappeared from her sight.

A tap rapped on her door. "Meredith?"

"Tilly." She jumped to her feet and her sewing tumbled from her lap. She caught the fabric by an edge. "Come in."

"I thought you might like some company." Tilly slipped into the room with her embroidery hoop in hand. "It gets lonely being sent to your room for the evening."

"Yes, it does. I'm glad you came. I was working on my quilt." She held up her partially finished block, doing her best to take her mind off Shane and enjoy this time with her sister. There would not be many evenings left to spend talking and sewing together.

"It's cheerful. I love the purple." Tilly inspected the squares. "It's a happy coincidence it matches the flowers Shane brought you."

"How did you know?"

"They weren't there when I brought up your supper tray." Tilly settled back on the window seat. "How did he get them to you?"

"He climbed the maple." Her fingers tingled from his gallant, sweet kisses.

"Wow, he must have really wanted to see you." Tilly stared hard at her hoop, where a pair of love birds were taking shape out of carefully stitched colors of floss. "I thought you didn't like Shane."

"Once I acted out of hurt feelings, but I was wrong." It was her turn to blush, her cheeks turning a furious red. Every time they were together, she found more to admire and more reason to care for him. But she didn't know how to admit it, so she fell to silence and straightened out the tangle her thread had become.

She was thankful for Tilly, who didn't say another word as she bent her head to her needlework, saying in understanding silence what could never be said with words. They stitched the evening away in sisterly solidarity. Every fiber of her being yearned for morning when she could look upon Shane again.

"Good girl." Shane praised from the back of the black filly, patting her neck. The morning sun was burning off the dew and mist from the pond, and larks sang gloriously celebrating the new day. Robins hopped through grasses searching for breakfast and a jackrabbit hid in the bushes near the fresh young sprouts in the garden.

The filly shook her head, jingling her bridle bits, as if proud of herself, too. The wind stirred her mane and brought the scent of lilacs and voices from the house. Braden's deeper voice mingled with the conversation. When Shane looked up, he spotted Mrs. Worthington at the end of the walkway looking like a general at war, directing her youngest daughter into the waiting buggy. Minnie skipped along ignoring her mother's request to walk like a lady.

He smiled. He was fond of the littlest sister. He would miss her. The oldest Worthington girl walked into sight and took the front seat. She would be driving to town this morning, which was fine by him. He had a lot of work to finish up. The filly sidestepped, as if anxious to go.

"Whoa there." He increased pressure on the reins until she stilled and made her wait. Her ears pricked, and she stood at attention waiting for the signal to go. He gave it before she could move again, touching his heels to her sides and lifting in the saddle. Her trot was disciplined as she circled the corral. Posting in the saddle, he felt something in the air change and in his soul.

Meredith. The morning brightened as she swept down the front steps. Guarded by lilacs and accompanied by nodding daffodils, she was poetry in motion with her green bonnet ribbons trailing in the wind and her matching dress swishing at her ankles. He felt entranced, unable to look anywhere else.

"Meredith, you are to come straight home from school." Mrs. Worthington's command rose above the drum of the horse's hooves and scattered birds from the orchard trees. The jackrabbit ducked for cover. "Matilda will come fetch you. With our book club meeting this morning, that makes an unseemly amount of trips to town."

"We can always miss the meeting," Tilly answered from the buggy's front seat.

"That would be even worse. How else will I be able to keep up with the news in town?" A faint note of humor rang in the older woman's words, a hint she was not as hard as she seemed.

Still, Meredith dominated his vision. As if she felt his presence, she glanced directly across the driveway to where he stood in the middle of the corral. Time stopped. The world kept spinning, life kept moving forward but they—he and Meredith—did not. The distance of garden and yard and paddock between them vanished and it felt as it had when he'd kissed her every fingertip. She had agreed to wait for him. She had approved of his plans for his future; she knew he wanted to be a farmer. The smile that touched her lips let him know that her regard for him had not changed.

"Hurry up, Meredith!" Minnie hung out of the backseat, clinging to the frame. "We're gonna be tardy. I don't want to have to write lines."

"I'm coming." She tore her attention from him, and it ripped like a physical wound.

You are in so much trouble, Connelly. You are more in love with the girl than you think. The filly reached the end of the corral and he turned her smoothly, glancing over his shoulder to keep Meredith in sight. She clutched the side of the buggy and hopped up, settling her bag and her lunch pail, wholesome and golden in the pretty May morning. He could not gaze upon her enough.

Soon he would be leaving and all he would have were memories of her. His throat ached, growing tight beneath his Adam's apple. There would be letters and the hope of seeing her again, but the separation to come would not be easy.

"Connelly." Braden strolled into sight. "You've made fine progress with the filly."

"She's a great horse. It was a pleasure to work with her." The buggy rolled down the driveway, with Meredith hidden from his view. Minnie hung out the window, spotted him and waved her arms as if she were trying to scare cattle.

"Howdy, Shane!" she shouted.

"Think she's got a crush on you." Braden chuckled as he leaned his forearms on the top board of the fence.

"She's a good kid." He waved back, earning Minnie's wide grin. She disappeared inside the buggy as it bounced on the rutted roads and turned the corner. Trees hid the horse and vehicle, taking his heart with it.

"Minnie is not our problem."

"Don't even say it." Shane slowed the filly to a walk. "You were right. I shouldn't have gotten involved."

"I know you couldn't help yourself." Braden, tough as nails, was not a man to succumb to the charms of any woman, but neither was he unfeeling. "You gave your best attempt not to fall for her."

"It wasn't enough." He reined the filly to a stop. He couldn't help feeling he had made a mess of things, but on the other hand Meredith had been worth it. "Affection snuck up on me."

"That's how it happens. But I have to give you credit. It didn't affect your work. That's all I care about." Braden climbed between the boards and held out his hand to the filly. "You are a fine horseman, Connelly."

"Don't you mean I will make one someday?" He dismounted, his boots hitting the earth.

"Nope. I mean you are one." Braden smiled, a rare thing, and took the mare by the bits. "I'll take her in. I've got a little time before I meet with Robert."

"Do you think there's any chance we could stay on?" The road was empty, all sign of Meredith was gone, but he felt her like a sonnet in his heart, like a hymn in his soul. "There is still work to do here."

"We are at a good stopping place. The two-year-olds are saddle broke, the yearlings have most of the basics. We haven't finished what we've agreed to do, but I'm not sure I can take any more drama." Braden grinned over his shoulder. "The missus takes more work than the horses. We leave, and I won't have to worry about the smell of horse manure bothering her when she's gardening and the wind shifts."

"Or the sound of horse hooves interrupting her reading. You want to move on, regardless of what Robert says."

"That's an affirmative."

Shane knew it was coming, but the final answer hit like a blow. The idea of leaving Meredith behind was one thing, but the reality of it was another. The sun lost its warmth, the world its beauty and he felt alone in a way he'd never been before.

* * *

Meredith shifted in her seat, cradled her forehead in her hands and willed her mind on the open history book before her. But the facts of George Washington's presidency kept evaporating like smoke and refused to stick in her brain. What did occupy her mind? Shane astride the black horse, his face shaded by his Stetson, his wide shoulders straight and strong, her very own beau. She'd picked up a lilac blossom she'd pressed in her book and twirled it. The scent from the tiny petals launched her back in time. Instead of her history book, it was last night's history she reviewed—his story of Hobo, his dreams to farm and a sanctuary for abused horses.

Falling in love was not in her immediate plans, but she could no more stop her affections than keep time from ticking forward. She remembered the verse from Proverbs. *There are many plans in a man's heart, nevertheless the Lord's counsel—that will stand.* So much for her careful plans. She was not, in the end, in charge of them.

Something bumped her elbow. Scarlet nudged her slate across the desktop with a one-word message scribbled in the corner. *Shane?*

Meredith nodded, ready to scribble back an answer, but Miss Lambert peered their way. Oops. She returned her eyes to her textbook as Scarlet hastily erased the message with her slate rag. The wall clock counted down the minutes until lunch break. Restless, Meredith leaned forward to glance past Scarlet across the aisle to Fiona and Lila, who shared a seat. They were bent in study, Fiona's curly black locks hiding her face, and Lila absently winding a stray tendril around one finger as she read.

Two rows over, Lorenzo Davis was staring openly at Fiona, lost in the look of her, affection poignant in his gaze. Poor Lorenzo. He had always carried a secret love for Fiona, who never had been interested in him. Proof enough that plans did not often work out because God was guiding them all. Perhaps there would be someone for Lorenzo when he was ready. She knew the rest of their circle would be thrilled to be beaued by the handsome man.

Miss Lambert's handbell chimed above the sound of pages being turned and the industrious scratch of pencils on slates. Lunchtime. Movement erupted as students slammed books, launched out of their seats and conversations boomed. Meredith carefully set the tiny purple blossom on her page and closed the book.

"I'm starving." Scarlet shot into the aisle. "I have a treat. I brought everyone cookies—"

"*Excuse* me." Narcissa Bell pushed her way by, nose in the air.

"Honestly. What an attitude." Lila rolled her eyes in response. "That girl bothers me."

"Aren't we suppose to find the good in everyone we meet?" Earlee said sweetly, book bag in hand.

"Yeah," Kate agreed. "I'm sure there's a speck there somewhere, but we might need a magnifying glass to see it."

"A really big one," Ruby agreed as she joined them in the aisle. "Has she always been like that?"

Narcissa was already out of sight, having pushed her way through the tussle of the crowd. Meredith followed Fiona's gingham skirt between the desks toward the door. Sunlight glinted on the windows as they approached. "Is it me, or is Narcissa worse than normal?"

"Worse," Lila agreed.

"Worse," Scarlet seconded.

"Much worse," Kate chimed in.

"Makes me miss her usual disposition. Almost." Earlee smiled her contagious smile, making them all do the same. "I wonder what bee has gotten under her bonnet?"

"Good question." Meredith took her lunch pail off the coat room's shelf. "Maybe she's jealous she's not the first of our grade to get married like Fee is."

"Oh, I don't think she's jealous of me." Fiona, the dear that she was, grabbed her battered lunch tin and waltzed through the sun-washed door. "Although I did manage to find the best man in the county."

"Probably the entire territory," Kate agreed as they tromped down the stairs.

"Your Ian is to die for," Scarlet added.

Her friends' voices faded, coming as if from far away. The moment her shoe landed on the top step, she knew why. She felt his presence like grace to her soul.

Shane. He sat stride his Appaloosa at the edge of the road, mighty and forthright, everything a man ought to be. He tipped his hat to her, and the surprise and thrill of seeing him lifted her feet from the ground. She might very well have floated down the steps, for the lightness of her being, for the greatness of her love.

"Girls, it looks like Meredith has a beau." Lila could not mask the delight in her words.

"A beau?" Kate sounded confused. "I thought she didn't like him."

"Shh," Earlee whispered. "That's the way love works sometimes."

"Love?" Fiona sounded stunned. "Really? Our Meredith is in love, too?"

"What about her plans to teach?" Scarlet wanted to know.

Meredith hardly noticed her friends had stayed back, to let her go ahead. She was being pulled to Shane with a force that was beyond her will. He dismounted like a man who had been brought up on horses, striding across the grass toward her with easy, confident strides that made every other man in existence pale by comparison.

"Hello, beautiful." He gathered her hands in his, gazing as if he could never get enough of her. "Hope you don't mind I stopped by. I was in town on errands."

"I'm so glad you're here. Come join us."

"Your friends won't mind?"

She glanced around, but her friends—her dear friends—were nowhere in sight. This time alone with Shane was a gift, because she knew without asking this was their last day together. Sadness lay behind his smile and in his manner as his fingers twined tight to hers.

She led him to the steps, where they could sit and talk like any young courting couple. For fifty wonderful minutes, they were.

Chapter Fifteen

The first peal of the school bell came far too soon. Shane climbed reluctantly to his feet, hating that their time together was done. He held out his hand, assisting Meredith from the step. Children streamed around them into the schoolhouse, but he had eyes for only her.

"Braden and I have a lot to finish up before we leave." His throat felt full and his chest tight. The weight of what he wanted to say was lodged in his throat. "I'll be busy, but somehow I'll figure out a way to see you."

"I'm sure you will." She nodded, scattering her golden mass of curls that bounced and sprang when she moved.

"There's always the maple tree as a last resort," he quipped, fighting to keep things light. He did not want to waste the moments they had left with inevitable sorrows.

Something touched his elbow—not something, someone. The haughty girl, the one Meredith didn't like, settled her hand on his arm, an unwelcome touch.

"Hi there, Shane." She preened up at him, eyelashes batting. "Have you heard from your mother lately?"

"What?" He pulled away, shocked by her forwardness. "Excuse me, but Meredith and I—"

"I hope she isn't getting too attached to you." Narcissa,

honey sweetness and spite, turned to Meredith next. "My mother is friends with the Kellans."

"So what?" Meredith ignored her, turning away. The stream of kids broke around them, barreling up the steps, barring his way to her.

"For your information, the Kellans are close friends with the Connellys of Virginia." Narcissa smirked. "Don't you know your senators? We learned them last November. Senator Stuart Connelly?"

"My father." He broke through the trail of students to get to his beloved. He didn't know what the rude girl was up to, but he didn't like it. "I'm sorry, Meredith. I should have told you before this."

"I don't understand." Confusion hazed her clear eyes.

"Some say he'll go back home in time, after he's done having fun and sowing his wild oats. He's being groomed to take his father's seat when he retires. You know what that means. He will need a proper lady at his side, not a teacher." Narcissa, pleased to be the bearer of such news, smiled broadly as she tripped up the rest of the stairs. "I hope you didn't think his act was sincere."

"Act?" Meredith gripped the railing until her knuckles went white. "I don't understand."

"Don't believe her." Shane was at her side. The final clang of the bell resounded overhead. The sky remained as blue, the sun as cheerful, but everything had changed.

"She knew who you were all along." That explained a lot. Narcissa's attempts to get his attention and to get close to him. It all made sense now. Her anger when those efforts hadn't worked. And now the whole truth lay before her. His was no ordinary family. He was not the humble horseman he professed to be.

"There is no act, Meredith." The words rang with sincerity and might, a voice of an honest man. He squared his shoulders, back straight, iron jaw set. The only softness that remained was the plea in his loving eyes. "My intentions toward you are honorable. You know that."

"I apparently don't know anything about you."

"You know what matters. You know me." He laid a hand to his chest, as if to bare his soul. "I meant to tell you about my family, but—"

A handbell chimed furiously. The teacher glared at them. "Time to come in, Meredith. Girls."

Only then did she realize that her friends had held back, huddled together in the spill of sunshine, waiting and not wanting to interrupt. Their silent comfort and sympathy was a crutch she needed to lean on. She drew herself up, gathered her courage and faced the man who was full of apologies, almost as many of them as his unspoken truths.

"Let's go in," she told her friends. Turning away from Shane was like turning away from herself. Taking the first step toward the doorway was like ripping off a part of her soul. She left the real Shane Connelly behind as Miss Lambert shut the schoolhouse door.

"Maybe it isn't as bad as it sounds," Earlee soothed gently, rubbing Meredith's shoulder. "Maybe there's a good explanation."

"For betrayal?" She'd believed in him. She'd thought they were kindred spirits, two halves of the same soul. But he was exactly everything she didn't want—someone with prominence, power and more money than compassion. She wanted an honest man, but the man she'd fallen in love with did not exist.

It was all a lie, and she was the fool. She followed Earlee through the schoolroom, aware of Narcissa in the back row laughing.

He hated having to ride away. Every step Hobo took on the road to the Worthingtons' ranch, the image of Meredith walking straight-backed, slow and shaken, tormented him. That wasn't the way he'd wanted her to learn about his family. He tugged his hat brim lower against the change in the sun as his horse rounded the corner and the manor house came into sight. If only Narcissa had spoken earlier, he would have had a chance to explain. Surely Meredith did not believe he had ever been anything less than one-hundred-percent sincere.

"There you are." Braden emerged from the barn's breezeway, his jaw set, a harness flung over his shoulder. "I just put up the missus's horse and vehicle."

"Sorry to leave you on barn duty."

"It was never your job to begin with. I told Robert and the missus that they had better find someone quick. After today, neither of us will be here to play barn boy." Braden shook his head as he hung the freshly cleaned harness on its proper wall hook. "There's more trouble afoot. The missus came home in a very happy mood. She asked about you twice."

"You're right. That does not sound good." Either she had figured out he was courting her daughter or—

"Mr. Connelly?" The auburn-haired housemaid cleared her throat, framed by the wide barn door, her simple calico skirts rustling as she waltzed closer. "Mrs. Worthington is waiting for you up at the main house. If you would be so good as to come along with me?"

"Up to the house?" That was surely the last thing he wanted to do. A bad feeling gripped his stomach and clenched tight.

"What did I tell you?" Braden called after him. "Trouble."

That was an understatement. Henrietta Worthington waited for him on the porch in what looked like her Sunday best. He might not know much about ladies gowns, but there was no missing the elaborate silks and adornments out of place in this country setting.

"Mr. Connelly, do come in." With great courtesy, she gestured toward the open front door as if she were greeting nobility.

She knows, too. Reluctantly, he took the stairs. "Good afternoon, ma'am. What can I do for you?"

"Oh, no, that is entirely wrong. It's what *I* can do for you." She waited until he was through the threshold before following him in, completely ignoring the maid who trailed them. "Please sit down, make yourself comfortable. I have to say I'm most embarrassed that I didn't recognize you first off."

"Why would you?" He swept off his hat while he glanced around the well-appointed parlor full of fine furniture and expensive knickknacks that looked exactly like the ones his mother collected. "My father is notable. I am not."

"You are too modest, sir." She gestured toward the sofa. "Your grandfather was senator before him and best friends with a former president of the United States."

"The rumors of me following my father into politics are not true." Might as well stop that notion in its tracks. He considered the comfortable-looking sofa the woman kept nodding him toward, but decided to stay standing. With hat in hand, he watched dismayed as she began pouring tea. Tension banded his chest, making it hard to breathe. "Not to be rude, ma'am, but I have work waiting."

"Nonsense. A man like you doesn't stoop to manual labor." She plunked a steaming cup of tea confidently on the polished coffee table. "That Braden person can put up the horses. I'm sure you are used to a few finer comforts. I've instructed the maid to make up a room in the north wing—"

"Mrs. Worthington, no." He had no time for this kind of nonsense and had long ago lost the stomach for it. "Thank you for your consideration, but I am the same person I was when I came here. Don't put your maid to the trouble. I'll stay the last night in the bunkhouse."

"Nonsense. I've completely changed my mind about you leaving."

And about seeing her daughter, he guessed. He plopped his hat on his head, his boots striking the floor as he re-traced his steps. "My leaving is Braden's decision. I'm his apprentice. If I want to keep my job, I'd best get back to the corral."

"But—"

He seized the doorknob, yanked open the door and gave thanks for the blast of summery air. He breathed in the freedom of it and the tension released. Memories of growing up in a parlor full of rules and restrictions, his mother's endless list of criticism, his father's cool disdain and expectations, blew away like the dandelion fluff on the fragrant breeze. He followed the lilacs down the path, thinking of Meredith. Had she made the same assumptions her mother had? When she looked upon him next, would she see his father's son or the man he was striving to be?

Afraid he already knew the answer, he tucked his fears deep and took off for the stables where his work and his boss were waiting.

Late-afternoon sunlight slanted through the trees as the buggy jolted along the rutted driveway. Meredith rubbed at the pain behind her right temple, but the ache persisted right along with the one in her heart.

"Mrs. Bell was quite pleased to show up Mama at the book club meeting." Tilly reined Sweetie around the bend in the road and the stables and house came into sight.

"After all, Narcissa recognized Shane when we did not. Apparently she had seen a picture of him when she'd visited relatives back east last summer. A friend of a friend sort of a thing. That's why she recognized him and knew his name."

"Everyone knows?"

"You know how rumors spread."

"Mama knows." That was the part she was dreading most.

"She's ready to burst with excitement. One of the Virginia Connellys right here on our land." Tilly didn't look happy either. "She's already planning the wedding."

"Then she may as well plan for disappointment." Meredith dreaded every step Sweetie took toward the stately looking home flanked by trees and surrounded by flowers. She wished she could slow time and prolong the inevitable from happening. She'd been broken apart enough today. Mama stepping in to take control would be akin to rubbing salt in a fatal wound.

"You must really be mad at him. I thought he might have told you but sworn you to secrecy."

"No. I wasn't important enough to him for the truth." There had been plenty of opportunity, like last night when he'd brought her the lilacs. He'd told her a sad story about his heroism and a fine tale about his supposed dreams, but as sincere as he'd seemed at the time she knew him now to be false. He'd told her his family had fallen upon hard times, but that could not be true. Not if he were both a senator's son and a senator's grandson.

"I'm so sorry, Meredith." Tilly hugged her tight. "Maybe you can work things out?"

"What is there to work out?" She set her chin with all the determination she could muster. "He's a liar."

"*I* still like him." Minnie in the backseat leaned forward to poke her head in between them. "And you're wrong.

Shane wouldn't lie. Maybe it just seems that way. The truth can sometimes look bad because it's, well, it's the truth. A lie can look good every time."

"She has a point," Tilly agreed, but there was little hope in her tone.

Meredith didn't want hope, she wanted the hurt to stop. Everyone was quick to defend Shane, because he was from an impressive and influential family. But that man was a stranger to her. The buggy slowed as the driveway circled up to the house and Sweetie obediently stopped. They were home, but it was the last place she wanted to be. She lingered on the seat, unable to move. Minnie hopped to the ground and pounded up the walkway, her empty lunch pail jingling.

She couldn't delay the inevitable forever. Resolved, she curled one hand around the buggy's frame, lifted her skirt hem with the other, and scooted to the end of the seat. Shane was around here somewhere, so she was bound to run into him soon. Completely dreading that, she slid off the seat. She misjudged the distance to the ground and she hit it too hard. Her book bag slipped off her shoulder and crashed on the walkway. Her lunch tin rolled to a stop near the flowerbed.

"Here, let me," a deep baritone vibrated, a familiar voice, one she had once been so eager to hear. Shane knelt to retrieve her bag and scooped her pail by the metal handle. He strolled toward her looking like any horseman did, with a faint layer of dust on his muslin shirt and denims, his Stetson shading his face, a hint of stubble on his jaw.

It was a lie. She'd believed in him like a story in a book, something that was not real. She stared at his outstretched hands holding her things and remembered every time they had touched. He had made her believe.

Why did she still want the lie to be true? She could

not stop wanting to see the goodness in the man when it was the lies that mattered more. She took a step back, her throat closing tight. She had fought all afternoon not to let Narcissa's words bother her, but they rang through her mind with the force of a rushing river dammed for too long. *He's having fun and sowing his wild oats. I hope you didn't think his act of love was sincere.*

"Meredith, don't look at me like that. Please." The quiet plea rang like a prayer, an honest request from his soul. He moved closer, bringing with him only pain. "Let me explain."

"Maybe I don't want to." Her hands fisted. She straightened her spine and stood her ground. If she gave in one inch, then the pain within her would crumble. The lunch hour they'd shared talking of little things, horses and her sewing and bits of stories about her friends seemed a lifetime ago, last night at her window two lifetimes.

"What does that mean?" His forehead furrowed. Agony touched his voice. "You don't believe what that girl said, do you? There's no going back for me. I don't want that world. I have you now—"

"You do not have me." She lifted her chin, defiance in her glare but it was not strong enough to hide the pain.

"Meredith, my family is far away across the country and that's where they will stay. I should have told you about them. I know that. I don't deny it. But they are not real to my life. I told you I've walked away. I'm disinherited. I am making my own way." All he saw was her hurt, and he wished he understood why. "As for what that girl said, you know my life here has not been about having fun. Your mother has seen to that."

"Don't try to lighten the discussion." She took a step back, holding herself tense and rigid, as if her self-control was all she had. The perfect May day surrounded her with colors and life, flowers nodding, the breeze whispering, birdsong serenading, and yet she looked as if there was no beauty left to her in the world. "I'm sure you are very sorry, but you lied to me."

"How? I showed you who I am." He wanted to smooth the crinkle of agony out of her forehead and to kiss away the sorrow on her rosebud lips. Turmoil roared through him, bringing with it the knowledge he was about to lose her. She, who mattered most to him, and he didn't understand the reason. "Why is this hurting you? What have I done?"

"You were so harsh with me when you discovered I was not the country girl you mistook me to be, when I did not lie to you. I was simply being myself. You have behaved so much worse." She wrapped her arms around her middle, so alone and vulnerable, with her broken affection in pieces at her feet. "How can I ever trust you again?"

"That's easy. You can always trust me—"

"No," she interrupted, her world already shattered, her unrealized dreams of him already crushed. "You have been pretending all along. You told me story after story to make me fall in love with you—"

"You're in love with me?"

"Not anymore. That's destroyed, too."

She broke away, hearing the shards of those stories in her mind, defining tales of his character that she had trusted. Tall tales now of being rejected by his wealthy friends, of humbly living with his grandmother, of longlasting friendships and making a life for himself on his own. These were the keys that had opened her up, captured her affections and made her think they were soul mates, that only he could truly understand and love her.

She had been misled, and so much of it had been her own doing. Agony hammered through her as she tore up the steps, heaved open the front door. His remorse didn't stop her. She kept going, putting distance between them.

"Meredith! Why, you look positively wind-blown. Let's take a comb to your hair." Mama barreled over with the determination of a navy admiral, skirt snapping, the china figurines on the what-not shelves trembling. "It's nearly tea time and I thought this afternoon we would have a formal tea. I commissioned Cook to prepare a few refined desserts for the occasion."

"I'm not hungry." She had endured one battle. She did not have the energy for a second. "I'm going to my room."

"But I've invited a very special guest." Mama was delirious with happiness as she clasped her hands together, a woman who mistakenly thought an impossible prayer had been answered. "Someone I think you will be very happy to entertain."

"I am not going to marry Shane Connelly, so no matchmaking. Please." She circled around the couch to avoid her mother, and hurried straight to the banister.

"Meredith Henrietta Worthington! You come back here this instant." Mama's command echoed through the parlor and bounced against the walls of the stairwell, but Meredith kept going. Her eyes burned, her throat tightened and with every step she took up the stairs and down the hallway she left a piece of herself behind.

At least her room was private. She sank onto the edge of her bed, so hurt the tears would not come, the sobs would not escape. It was silly to hurt so much over a man. She was too independent for that, but she hurt all the same. She was not in control of her heart, not at all.

A light knock rapped at her door. Tilly slipped inside and held up her forgotten book bag. "You left this behind."

"Thanks." The word croaked out, heavy with pain. Surely Tilly had noticed.

Pity pinched her sister's face. Pity. Meredith bowed her face into her hands. Footsteps padded closer, the edge of the bed sank and Tilly's arm went around her shoulder.

"I know how it feels," Tilly confessed. "To fall so far in love, it's like you've both lost and found yourself at the same time. And then to discover you mean so little to him that he doesn't even look your way when he drives by on the street."

"You've been feeling like this all along?" Meredith choked out.

"Yes. Over Emmett Sims. For almost a year now."

"I'm so sorry, Tilly." No one deserved the sharp edges of a shattered love, edges that cut over and over again. "Does it ever end?"

"I don't know. I'll let you know if it does."

"That's what I'm afraid of." The injury reached into the deepest parts of her, places she didn't even know she had. Proof of how deep her love for Shane had gone, so quietly and lovely she hadn't even thought not to let him in. "I've changed my mind about love. It's bad. One should avoid it at all costs."

"If only we had known that from the start," Tilly agreed.

It was too late. Meredith took a steadying breath, wondering if Shane was devastated, too, or if he'd been able to go on with his work, his heart and his soul intact. She did not see the man with his head down, looking as if broken, standing at the end of the walkway where she'd left him, alone.

Chapter Sixteen

You have behaved so much worse. Meredith's accusations troubled him with every breath he took and every minute that ticked by through the worst afternoon of his life. While he'd been saddling one of the two-year-olds, her question filled his head. *How can I ever trust you again?*

He had his answer. She could not see beyond his family name to the man he was. He took a shallow breath, ignoring the squeeze of discomfort that had settled behind his sternum. The pain had made him numb, and perhaps he would stay that way. He had work to finish, which would give him time to figure out how to make this right. He had to get her to listen.

"Blow out your breath, Apollo." He gripped the cinch and splayed his hand on the gelding's ribs. "I know you don't like it, but we've got to get this nice and tight."

The big Arabian stomped one hoof and sidestepped, as if he didn't like the notion. Too bad he and Braden were leaving tomorrow. Not only did the horse need more training, but he was a kick to work with. Shane yanked a little harder on the cinch. "C'mon, big guy, let it out."

Footsteps tapped into his awareness, faintly echoing in

the empty stalls. Shane knew who it was without turning around. He'd been expecting a visit from Meredith's father.

"Connelly." Robert's tone had changed, and he was home from work early. Still in his suit and tie, the consummate bank owner tipping his hat to an equal—and not to the horse trainer's apprentice. A barn swallow flew in through one of the stalls, wheeled around and flapped back out again. Robert cleared his throat. "I'm looking for Braden. My horse and surrey are waiting."

"Did you find someone to take over the barn work?" Shane buckled the cinch, checked the strap, unhooked the stirrup from the saddle horn.

"One of my teller's neighbors has a son looking for work. He's to start in the morning."

"Good." He didn't have to turn around to read the discomfort, perhaps embarrassment, in the father's voice. He patted Apollo's flank and walked him a few paces. "I'll take the kid through the morning routine here. Make sure he knows how things run before we leave."

"I appreciate it." Robert fell silent, but he clearly had more to say.

Shane stopped the gelding and checked the cinch. Still nice and tight, so he patted the horse's shoulder. "Good boy, buddy. That was a good job."

Apollo preened, pleased with the compliment.

"Connelly." Robert blew out a sigh, as if he finally had figured out how to say what was on his mind. "About the way I treated you, told you to stay away from my daughter…"

"Said I wasn't good enough for her?" he finished helpfully, looping the ends of the reins through an iron ring in the wall. Leaving the horse secure, he turned his back. "I remember that talk very well."

"And I'm ashamed of it." Robert passed his hand over

his face. "I probably looked like a fool, saying those things to you. You clearly are a better man than me."

"Sir, I've been the same man all along. I haven't changed." He headed down the aisle, where Robert had left his horse and vehicle standing in the hot sun without care. "I'm still the horseman's apprentice."

"Not *just* a horseman's apprentice." Robert relaxed now that his apology was past. He followed behind, his manner friendly. "You're Stuart Connelly's son, Aaron Connelly's grandson. I read a newspaper article about you long ago. Something about charity work."

"Today I'm the one taking care of your horse." He held out his hand to let the stately gelding scent him. "That's all I am."

"I hope now that this misunderstanding has been cleared up that you will stay on." Robert seized the bridle. "Of course, you won't be expected to shovel horse manure and unhitch the family horses."

"As I understand it, we're leaving tomorrow." Shane frowned. Robert had the horse by the bits. Annoyed, he patted the Arabian's neck and clicked his tongue. The powerful horse turned toward him, breaking Robert's grip. Shane led the horse deeper into the barn.

"Is there anything I can do to change your mind?" Robert sounded sincere. He wasn't a bad guy, not at all. "I want to make things right between us if I can."

"Believe me, I would like to stay. This is a pretty piece of Montana you live in. I can't say it doesn't make a man feel right at home." He unbuckled the traces one by one and led the horse out from between the bars. "It's Braden's decision, and he's had enough. He's moving on, and I go with him."

"I envy you, young man. Long ago was the day I had the longing to do something different than work in my father's bank. I loved horses and dreamed of my own stables one day with the most beautiful Arabians grazing in my fields. I was forty years old before I brought the first broodmare to these pastures, and the most I can do is watch from the sidelines." Robert shrugged, looking wistful. "Maybe you can stay in Montana?"

"No. Our next job is in Butte, then we move on to Boise." He unbuckled the cheek strap and removed the gelding's bridle. "Not sure where to after that, but I think it's Salt Lake City."

"What about Meredith?"

Meredith. He squeezed his eyes shut to hide the crash of emotion. He felt sucker punched, but he didn't want that to show either. His voice sounded strained, and he hoped it could be attributed to the act of lifting the heavy horse collar off the Arabian's neck. "I suppose Meredith will be teaching school over the summer like she plans to."

"I thought the two of you were close." Not a father's ambition that spoke, but a father's love.

"I thought so, too," he said, keeping his back to the man while he slid the halter over the horse's nose and behind his ears. The coarse fetlock tickled the backs of his hands as he worked and the thought of Meredith angry and hurt destroyed him. He'd rather die than harm her, but that hadn't stopped it from happening.

"Perhaps I could talk to her," Robert suggested. "Maybe Braden could see reason to stay if more money was involved. If you would like to court my daughter, I would heartily give my permission—"

"Papa!" Meredith's dismay startled the horse and him. "I can't believe what I just heard."

The black's head came up and the powerful animal began to sidestep, nervously, about to bolt. Shane calmed him with a low murmur and a firm grip on his halter, drinking in the sight of his beloved. Like May itself, she swirled into the barn with a snap of her petunia pink dress and a sewing hoop clutching in one hand. Her hair a tumble, her bottom lip quivering with emotion.

"Meredith." A change came over Robert and his manner softened. The father's adoration of his daughter was unmistakable. "You surely have heard the good news. Your mother stopped by the bank on her way home from her meeting to let me know we have a very important person in our employ. I—"

"Papa, don't you dare try to distract me. You were trying to match me up with him." She held herself rigid, gesturing in his general direction as if she couldn't stand so much as to look at him.

Shane hung his head and led the horse away. The black went willingly and he left the father and daughter behind, their voices murmuring in the long stretch of the breezeway and bouncing off the empty walls of the stalls. Outside, horses grazed in summery fields and Braden's low mumble to one of the two-year-olds he was riding reminded him of what was at stake, more than his future and more than his heart.

He unhooked the stall gate, letting in the horse. Eyeing the paddock beyond and then his empty feed trough, the Arabian waited, giving Shane a look that clearly said, "I'm waiting."

"All right, buddy." He grabbed the grain bucket and upended it, the sound of cascading corn and oats drowning all sound of Meredith's voice.

I cannot lose her. He lowered the bucket to the ground. He would not admit defeat yet, not when there was still a chance. Latching the stall gate, he turned on his heel, determined to talk to her and explain, but she blocked his path.

"I'm sorry about my father." She faced him, jaw set

and braced as if it took all her strength to meet him. "Papa should not have been saying those things to you."

"About encouraging a match between us?"

"Yes." A muscle ticked along her porcelain jaw, a sign of how hard it was for her to be with him. She stood stone-still. A slight breeze played with the lace edge of her hemline and teased the flyaway tendrils from her single braid.

"I know he was not speaking for you, Meredith." He wanted to make her smile. "You are far too independent for that."

"At least you know that much about me." No smile, no softness, no hint that she intended to change her mind about him, or that she wanted to.

Please make her want to change her mind, he prayed. *Please, Lord, don't let me lose her.* He risked a step closer, the knell of his boots like a cannon strike in the tense silence between them. "I know a great deal about you."

"Is that so? Then you ought to know I am not going to believe your stories now."

"Stories. Fine, I'll admit it. I told you some stories." He fisted his hands, determined to take responsibility for his mistakes. He could be strong, too. "I wish now I had told you not parts but the whole of those stories. I'm sorry for that."

"All I wanted was the truth." Her blue-gray eyes shadowed and she spun away. "I can see that is not going to happen."

"Is that why you came?"

"No. I saw Papa arrive home and I knew what he was going to do the instant he went into the barn." She stared at the hoop she held, a colorful block of patchwork, and shook her head. She had obviously been in the parlor sewing. "You two didn't come to some kind of agreement, did you?"

"A betrothal agreement? No." He saw relief slumping her shoulders and the tension slipping from her jaw. He hurt to see how much she dreaded such an arrangement. She did not want him.

"Good. I caught him in time." She twisted away, her head down, an invisible barrier between them. Never had she been so distant. "My parents approve of you now."

"The only approval mattering to me is yours." There had to be a way to heal this breach between them. "I told you the truth and now I want to tell you the whole of it. The years we lived with my grandmother were the happiest of my childhood."

"I don't want to hear about them." She whirled at him, backing away. "I've had enough. There is no purpose in mending what is broken."

"I didn't mean to destroy your trust. My parents are not a part of my life, not anymore." He tugged off his hat, vulnerable, a man with nothing to hide. "Believe me. I have been honest about who I am and what I want."

"You have not. I am *not* some country girl easily fooled."

"I do not think you are." He stood resolute, like an innocent man. But how could he be? He looked so sad. "The day I walked away from my father's ultimatums and my mother's social scheming, I stopped being their son. I am my own man. Nothing is going to change that."

"It doesn't matter to me." He couldn't change the truth. She'd thought she had meant more to him than that. She'd been imagining that when he gazed upon her, the world vanished and all that remained was his infinite love for her. She'd thought that when he'd pledged his intentions, it was because she made him whole. That their love was the kind of a rare shining blessing bestowed sparingly in this world.

But she was not so special to him. Whatever caring he felt for her, it could not measure up to what she had imagined. He had been passing time, that was all, a rich man's harmless flirtations.

"My maternal grandmother was poor, but when we were in need she shared what she had with us." How sincere he looked, striving so hard to win back her regard. With another story, no less, one meant to tear down her defenses and overturn good sense. "What I told you was true. My father's investments improved and we moved back into our house, but I never forgot—"

"Please, not another tale," she interrupted. "You will say anything to salvage your self-opinion. When you leave tomorrow, you will not take my heart with you."

"But I love you."

"You love me?" She marched through the barn doors and into the yard, rocks crunching beneath her shoes, the cheerful shafts of sunlight threatening to steal her from his sight. His beautiful Meredith. Why couldn't she see his feelings?

"I think I fell in love the first moment I set eyes on you. You had a streak of mud on your cheek and you were standing in the middle of the road." *Please remember that moment,* he begged, the instant in time when their lives changed.

Her anger melted away, leaving a moment of pure longing that made her so sad that his soul could bleed. The wind gusted, bringing a few stray blossoms from the flowering apple trees. Soft pink petals rained down on her, clinging to her tendrils and the slope of her skirt. Being near to her brought more hidden places within him alive. Nothing could stop his love for her.

The future rolled out before him like the prairie unspooling in every direction. He saw the year to come of courting the prettiest schoolteacher west of the Mississippi, his engagement ring shining on her slender hand. There would be a little wedding with wildflowers and Meredith radiant in any gown she wanted. He could picture their comfortable home and plenty of fertile land close to whichever town her teaching job had taken them. Horses grazing behind whiteboard fences, fruit ripening in the orchard and Meredith cradling their baby in her arms.

Never had he seen his future so clearly. Never had he wanted something so much.

"I remember thinking you were trouble on horseback." She stared down at her sewing hoop as if searching for a solution. Finding none there, she gave him one last appraisal. Her longing had vanished, but the sadness remained. She hiked up her skirts as if ready to flee. "I should have paid better attention to my first impressions."

"You loved me once. You said so. You can love me again." It was the only hope he had.

"No. I cannot. This is goodbye, Shane Connelly." She could not hide her sorrow as she hurried up the walkway, taking with her the best dream he'd ever had.

For what felt like the eight hundredth time, she blinked furiously until her vision cleared. It took a few attempts until the blurred colors of her quilt block took shape again. The purple stood out brighter than all the others, a reminder of everything she needed to forget.

Just put him behind you, Meredith. She willed every thought, every image, every memory of Shane from her mind and concentrated on poking the needle through the fabric, feeling the contact of the tip against her thimble. She pulled the thread through in a muted rasp that echoed in every corner of her bedroom. She'd never felt empty like this, as if hollowed out of all feeling. She was as spent as if she'd run a hundred miles without rest.

Footsteps bounded down the hall, light and bouncy and cheerful. Minnie skidded to a stop in the open doorway, bits of leaves in her hair and shavings of bark on her dress.

"Whatcha doin'?" Minnie tromped in and bounced onto the edge of the bed.

"Stitching a block." She placed her needle again. "Have you been playing in your tree house?"

"Yes, but it wasn't any fun today, so I came in." Minnie sighed dramatically. "Aren't you going to ask why?"

"No, because it has to do with the man I refuse to think about, so you will just have to tell me about something else." She only had to hold her composure for a few more hours. Once the house was dark and she was in bed, she could cry if she wanted to. No one would know. She tugged her thread gently, tightening the stitch. "Judging by the delicious smells wafting up here from the kitchen, you succeeded in talking Cook into baking a chicken pie for supper."

"I asked her to make more molasses cookies for Shane, so he could take some with him." Her bottom lip wobbled. "I know you don't want to hear his name, but I'm sad he's leaving. He was so nice to me."

"He *was* nice to you." She couldn't refute that. Meredith pinned her needle into the fabric and set the hoop aside. The window seat creaked slightly as she stood. She brushed stray curls out of her sister's blue eyes filling with tears. "Who wouldn't be charmed by you, sweetheart?"

"There's no one like him. Just no one." Fourteen was a tough age, still so very much a child. Minnie swiped her eyes to keep the tears from falling. "I thought he was going to stay a long time and train all our horses."

"He was never going to stay for long, and I think Mama's interference made their stay much shorter." She eased onto the bed beside her sister and drew her close. "Sadie said that one day when we were at school, Mama went outside and told Braden and Shane all the qualities she expected to see in a Worthington horse. They were to be dignified in all respects. No biting or running away with their drivers. Sadie kept track of the clock. The lecture went on for over an hour."

"That's because Papa was really hurt by a horse once, remember?"

"Yes, I remember. God spared him, but Mama has never forgot it." She wanted Minnie to see this was for the best. Maybe it would bring back Minnie's smile. "I think it's easier for the horsemen if they move on to a quieter place."

"Do you think Shane will miss us?"

"It would be impossible not to miss you, dear one." She squeezed her sister tight, treasuring her like the precious gift she was. "Now shouldn't you be getting ready for supper? If Mama sees the leaves in your hair, she's not going to be happy."

"I have leaves in my hair?" This seemed to be news to Minnie.

"What do you expect when you climb around in trees like a monkey?" Meredith gave Minnie a final hug.

"I'm not a monkey. Tilly, did you hear what she called me?"

"I heard." A tray rattled as Tilly swept into the room. "Look what I brought. Supper. I talked Mama into letting us have a picnic up here. She's feeling under the weather."

"Disappointment, I expect." Meredith grabbed her comb off the bureau. "Knowing Mama, she already had the wedding planned and the invitations composed."

"She's taken it hard, it's true." Tilly set the tray on the bed, scooting it carefully into the center of the mattress. "Meredith, how are you doing?"

"It is not a mortal blow. It just feels like one." She took the comb to Minnie's hair. "I will survive, so there's no need to talk about it again. There, the leaves are out. Minnie, do you want to say grace?"

"I love saying it!" Minnie busily settled in front of the tray, crossed her legs, settled her skirts and steepled her hands. "Hurry. I've thought up a good one."

Over the top of her head, Meredith shared a smile with Tilly. Having them here was the best balm she could ask for. She settled onto the feather mattress, careful not to tip the tray and jostle the juice glasses, and settled beside Minnie on the duvet cover. Tilly did the same on the other side, and together they bowed their heads, folded their hands. Minnie cleared her throat.

"Dear God," she began primly. "Please bless this food we are about to eat and especially please bless Shane because he's leaving and Meredith and me are gonna miss him. I think Meredith will miss him more, so please help her to be a teacher so she won't be so sad. Amen."

"Amen." Meredith opened her eyes only to find they were blurry again. "That was sweet, Minnie."

"You said a very good prayer." Tilly reached over to hug Minnie with one arm, Meredith with another, sisters not only by blood but of the heart.

Chapter Seventeen

It had been a rough and sleepless night as Shane halted Hobo and dismounted on the lawn outside the Worthington home. Dawn hinted at the horizon, turning the darkness to gradients of shadow, allowing him to make out the trunk of the maple and the branches beneath Meredith's window. His boots scraped against the bark and the leaves shivered as he pulled himself up limb by limb into the arms of the tree. His pulse drummed frantically against his rib cage, pounding in his throat and making him halfway dizzy.

"That's a female for you," Braden had said last night when they'd shared supper at the table in the bunkhouse. "Contrary. Not one of them make a lick of sense. They rip your heart out as easily as a basting seam in a dress they're sewin' on. It's why I'm a bachelor at thirty-five and proud of it."

He could see why permanent bachelorhood would be tempting. A lizard skittled out of his way and out of sight as he heaved onto the final limb and rose carefully to a standing position. The last thing he wanted was to wake the entire house with a crash and a boom and be caught in a crumpled heap on the ground outside Meredith's bedroom. Her parents weren't likely to be understanding. The bough beneath his soles groaned with his weight as he caught hold of the lip of the windowsill.

Being this near to her calmed him. The curtains were closed, but she was behind the glass, beyond the fall of muslin, close enough that he could wake her with a few words. The comfort of knowing she was close invited memories he could not stop—Meredith's laughter, Meredith's dimples, the fall of her hair in the sunlight. The way she filled him with love overflowing.

Please watch over her, Father. He set the small jewel box he'd bought in town. There. It was done. He ought to climb down and meet Braden outside the kitchen, because Sadie was packing them meals for the road, but he lingered. This would be the closest he would ever be to Meredith again.

"Psst. Connelly." Braden rode into sight below, saddle packs loaded. "Time to go."

The hardest step was the first. He tore himself away, ignoring the cruel pain. The next step down the tree was easier to stand. He swung off the lowest branch and hit the ground, leaves rustling, his heart bleeding. He could not endure looking back. The grass crunched beneath his feet, an owl gave the final hoot of the night, serenading him as he swung up into the saddle.

Goodbye, Meredith. He gathered Hobo's reins in wooden hands. Every bit of him went numb as he pressed his heels to the gelding's side and rode away from the only woman he would ever love.

Meredith woke with a start and the strangest sensation she was not alone. Dawn had yet to chase the darkness from her room as she threw back the covers, put her feet on the floor and followed the tides of her heart to the window. The muslin curtains whispered against her fingertips, soft cotton fluttering against her cheek as she drew them open. The faintest pre-dawn glow shone in the east, illuminating the underbellies of clouds and casting the view in silhouette. The maple shivered in the soft breezes and the faint *clip-clop* of steeled horse shoes chimed above the birdsong from the fields.

Shane. Her hand flew to the window, the glass cool against her palms as she searched the small section of the driveway visible from her room. Nothing moved in the shadows of the road and she waited, knees knocking. Need riveted her in place, and she could not move. She was driven by the need to see him one more time, the wish to memorize what she could of him and the longing to turn back time. If only she could relive the past knowing what she knew now. Maybe she could have kept her affections casual and her eyes wide open.

Maybe. Then again, perhaps she had been fated to fall in love with him. She feared God had led her to Shane for some reason she could not guess. She had made a mess of it. She couldn't have stopped herself from seeing the good in him—there was so much good. If only the man he had pretended to be was the real Shane Connelly. Maybe then their story would have had a different outcome.

A shadow moved on the distant driveway. Two riders on horseback! Her gaze fixed on the one nearest to her, his familiar wide shoulders set, tall in the saddle, and her feelings soared. For a single moment she forgot their differences. Affection rushed through her stronger than any force, diminishing her anger and betrayal. Love clung stubbornly, like roots to the earth, refusing to let go.

Time would do that, she told herself. There would come a day when he would be a vague memory. If time was kind, then she would forget every detail about him—his dimpled smile, his easy humor, the feel of his hand cradling hers, even his name. A lump rose in her throat as he rode out of her sight, disappearing down the road, gone to her forever. Still she yearned for him like winter missed spring and she almost didn't see the small jewel box glinting in the first light of dawn.

Heart pounding, she opened the window. The warm sun on her face felt out of place on this morning of loss, the scenery of the green grasses and trees and the merry splashes of purple and yellow flowers discordant. Those colors grew into blurs as she blinked hard to clear her vision and lifted the trinket from the sill.

What had he left her? Trembling, she opened the lid. Inside the exquisite box of ivory lay a piece of gold jewelry. The telltale ticking told her it was no locket, but a timepiece. Something every teacher needed.

She was not the sort of girl who cried over a man, but tears fell anyway, one by one, pieces of her soul she could not hold back.

"Meredith!" Minnie's voice came as if from a mile away instead of next to her on the buggy seat. "Meredith? We're here."

At school. She felt fuzzy, as if she were looking at the world through a mirror, that it was only a reflection of little substance. She gathered her bag and lunch and didn't bother to wait for the new driver to help her down. He was a gangly boy from Angelina's grade who'd had to drop out of school to help earn a living for his family. Nice enough, but she could not stand to have him help her. It would only be another reminder of Shane.

"Meredith!" Kate called as she climbed out of her father's buggy. "Can you believe it? Two more days of school and then we're done. We're free."

"Unbelievable." It didn't seem real—not the morning,

not the fact that Shane's departure was a rip in the fabric of her life that left everything in tatters, and surely not the fact that her school days would end. She'd been dreaming about the day, hoping and planning for it, yet now it struck her like a falling anvil. She would no longer see her dearest friends every day.

"Bye, Pa!" Kate called out cheerfully, waving as her father drove off, horse and buggy joining the busy traffic on the road. "I studied and studied last night and I'm ready for the tests today."

"Tests?" Her schoolwork had completely flown out of her mind.

"Arithmetic and history." Kate fell in stride beside her. A boy ran across their path, chasing a red ball. Little children's squeals of delight pealed until someone yelled, "Tag! You're it!"

"Meredith, are you all right? You seem distracted. It wouldn't have anything to do with a handsome black-haired, blue-eyed man?"

"I wish it didn't." Dimly she realized they were climbing the stairs clomping into the vestibule. She plopped her lunch pail on the shelf along with all the others and her feet felt leaden as she continued on into the schoolroom.

"...Mama sent a telegram straightaway to our dear friends the Kellans..." Narcissa informed her group at the front of the room, talking loudly enough for her voice to carry. "They are very close friends to the senator and his wife, you know—"

"Ignore her," Kate advised on the way to their desks. "She's eaten up with jealousy because Shane wouldn't give her the time of day."

"He's gone." The statement came flat and, emotionally, as hollow-sounding as she felt.

"Who's gone?" Lila looked up from her history text.

Concentration furrowed her brow and she tossed a lock of brown curls out of her eyes.

"Shane." The starch went out of her knees and she collapsed into her seat. His manly image silhouetted by the dawn tormented her. He'd ridden away and now there was no mending what had happened between them.

Not that she wanted it, not that it could be. Not after what he'd done. But she could not seem to help the tiny thread of wishing within her that would not break.

"You mean he left?" Kate slipped into her desk, her bag thudding against her desktop. "Just like that? After spending lunch with you yesterday?"

"Like a *courting* man?" Scarlet emphasized, walking up to their group. "Everyone saw it, Meredith. He's in love with you."

"It was not love." Love did not masquerade as something else. She fumbled with her books. Her fingers did not seem to work properly. The texts tumbled and slid over the desk, falling onto Scarlet's side.

"How can you say that?" Scarlet gently pushed the books back.

"Even I saw it." Ruby, two desks behind, left her seat to join the discussion. "And I'm an official objective observer. I hardly know you all, but I recognize true affection when I see it. The way that man looked at you." Ruby paused and placed her hand to her throat. "It was like a dream come true. I would give anything to have a good man look at me like that."

"So would I," Earlee chimed in breathlessly, cheeks rosy from her long walk to school. "Perhaps you could write to him. He could court you through letters. It would be so romantic."

"It's not going to happen." She swallowed hard, determined to keep her feelings buried. She was perfectly able to manage a tiny disappointment in love. And if a voice inside her argued it was no small affection she felt, then she simply did not have to listen to it. She slipped out of her cardigan and draped it over the back of her seat. "Earlee, you're right, it would make a nice story, but Shane is gone. Please, let's not mention him again."

"I'm so sorry you were hurt," Ruby, as sweet as spun sugar, emphasized. "I've heard the best way to get over one beau is to find another. I noticed Lorenzo looking this way."

"He's wondering where Fiona is," Lila informed her. "He's always been sweet on her."

"And we've all been sweet on him," Kate spoke up, earning a bit of light laughter. "Oh, there's Fiona now."

While her friends greeted the latecomer, who looked a bit windblown from her horse ride, Scarlet leaned close and squeezed Meredith's hand.

"I'm sorry, too," she whispered. "I prayed for the two of you."

"Some prayers are not meant to be answered." It didn't make her sad. Really. She was determined to control her feelings. She would make it true. Shane was gone and that was the way it should be.

Even if a little voice within her wanted to argue.

"...in spite of the fact he rode that awful horse, the one with all the scars—" Narcissa's words rose above the growing hubbub in the classroom "—*I* recognized him."

I never noticed Hobo's scars, she realized. She'd been so intent on the man, she'd been blind to the horse, the one beaten with a whip on a wintry road until Shane had come along and saved him.

Don't be a fool, Meredith. Keep control of your feelings.

She carefully removed her sewing from her book bag, doing her best to listen to Fiona's tale of her morning, of how close she was getting to Ian's grandmother and that it was hard to believe come Sunday she would finally be his wife.

"And he can move into the house and you won't miss him so much," Earlee said.

"I do. He's away so much, I hardly get to see him. He's lucky to have a job at the mill, but it's hard being apart. I didn't know it was possible to love someone so much there's no room to breathe. That's how full of love you are." Fiona blushed, a little shy.

"No one deserves it more." Meredith swallowed hard against overwhelming emotions—a mix of gratitude for her friend's happiness, a rush of loss of her own, the enduring bond of friendship that she treasured so much. She set down her sewing and twisted around to make eye contact with everyone, hoping they could read the meaning behind the question she asked. "On Saturday?"

"Yes," Lila agreed, catching her eye.

"Absolutely," Scarlet chimed in.

"I can have Pa swing by and pick her up," Kate volunteered.

"It's agreed?" Earlee asked.

"Agreed," Fiona finished as they all turned to Ruby, who looked confused by what was going on. "Would you like to join our sewing circle? We meet every week in the afternoon."

"I'm not a very good sewer." Ruby looked crushed.

"The friendship is the important part of the gathering." Meredith spoke from the heart, with love for the friends who had once welcomed her into their midst and with admiration for the young women they had all grown to be. "It's one of the greatest blessings of my life. Join us. We would love to have you."

"We could give you sewing tips," Lila encouraged.

"And you wouldn't have to sew. I often bring my embroidery," Kate offered.

"And I tat or crochet," Scarlet added. "I would teach you to do it. It's easy."

"And I am really good at sewing dresses," Earlee chimed in. "I'm always making something for one of my six little sisters. I could give you tips, too."

"Please say you will come," Fiona urged, her dark ringlet curls framing her face.

Ruby nodded, overwhelmed at being included.

Miss Lambert rang her handbell, calling for students to take their desks and quiet down. Because it was time to break apart, they settled back into their seats, opened their books and prepared for the day—one of the last days they would all be schoolgirls together. As Meredith gently placed her quilt blocks and squares back into her bag, she braced herself for the pain of seeing the purple color that reminded her of Shane. There were other colors, ones her friends had helped her choose in the mercantile. She heard again the conversations she'd shared with her friends and with her sisters as she'd sewed each square.

Life was like a patchwork quilt, she realized, seemingly haphazard pieces thrown together, but there was a great grand order to the colorful squares and a beauty that defied all, for it was stitched together with love.

"Meredith!" Scarlet's sharp whisper penetrated her thoughts. "Miss Lambert is calling us. Time for our arithmetic exam. The last one ever."

All things came to an end, she thought. It was the sweetness of the time that mattered for it made memories to cherish. She stowed her sewing into her bag, dropped it under her desk and trailed her friends to the front of the room where their teacher waited.

The sun was past its zenith before they stopped along the trail for lunch. The prairie rolled endless behind them, but the Rocky Mountains in the far distance flanked them.

Up ahead hovered the promise of hills and, beyond, a mountain pass.

Shane dismounted, leading Hobo straight to the small creek gurgling beneath the shade of cottonwoods. The cool felt good, the breeze off the water better. While his horse drank he swept off his hat and stood a moment. Every mile behind them had been a torment, knowing it was taking him farther away from his Meredith.

She would have found the box by now. Was she wearing it, thinking of him? Or was she too proud? Too wounded? Judging by the sun, she might be chatting with her friends in the schoolyard, sewing away on her quilt patches. Simply from picturing her dappled with sun filled him with sweet agony, wanting the woman he could not have. She'd said goodbye, turned her back and walked away.

"Looks like pork loin sandwiches." Braden tossed him a wrapped bundle. "Whatever cons there were working for the Worthingtons, the meals were some of the best I've had anywhere."

"Are you sorry we left?" He unwrapped the sandwich and took a bite.

"I'm sorry I didn't leave sooner. I'd forgotten how controlling a woman can be." Braden shook his head, digging into his meal. "There's nothing like being a bachelor. It's a better option considering."

Shane unhooked his canteen from his saddle and twisted the cap. It wasn't that long ago he had agreed with his boss. Getting out of an engagement that was more duty than choice had left him with a bad taste for marriage. That was before he knew what real love felt like and how it could transform a man. He swigged the lukewarm water, swallowing every last drop. His love for her didn't stop like a match quickly blown out but remained burning as if there were no force strong enough to stop it.

If I'd had more time with her, he thought, taking another bite of his sandwich. Maybe he could have made her understand. Picturing how angry she had been with him, how resolute, cast him in doubt. She thought he'd deceived her with his tales, but it was not true. There had been no lies, just the values he had learned along the way.

"We'll fill up the canteens here and ride as far as we can," Braden said around a mouthful. "Don't want to waste any time. We'll stop and set up camp around nightfall."

"Good plan." Going forward was the only sensible solution. He'd come too far to quit on Braden and his own ambition for the future. But nothing about his future felt right without Meredith in it.

He wedged the last bite of the sandwich into his mouth, knelt to fill his canteen in the fresh running water, and offered Hobo a molasses cookie from his pack. How could he go on? It was impossible, considering an unbreakable bond to Meredith held him back.

Chapter Eighteen

"See you tomorrow!" Fiona called from the saddled bay Clydesdale, who had been tied all day long with other horses on the shady side of the schoolhouse. Flannigan, eager to stretch his legs, tugged politely at his bit and Fiona laughed. "I'd like to stay and chat longer, but this guy has a mind of his own."

"Goodbye!" Meredith called out alongside her remaining friends. Kate had already taken off with her father, heading for their homestead far west of town. Ruby was expected home to help with the farm work, so she'd already taken off at a fast walk heading east.

"Meredith!" Minnie hung out of the buggy, waving wildly. "We're waiting for you!"

"Take Maisie home first and then come back for me." The last thing she wanted to do was to rush straight home. Too many reminders were there, aside from the fact that she wasn't sure she could face her mother's depression. Shane's leaving would be sure to hit her hard.

"Are you regretting sending him away?" Lila asked, as they fell in step together. Scarlet joined them, followed by Earlee, catching up with them breathlessly.

Meredith didn't want to answer, but she felt the abiding affection of her friends and there was no safer place to admit the truth. "Regret? Yes. But I don't see any other solution. He's not right for me. He's not the man of my dreams."

"He seemed dreamy to me," Lila commented. "Really decent and solid. Not caught up in himself."

"I got the feeling he really cared about others," Scarlet agreed.

"And the way he looked upon you, Meredith," Earlee started.

"No! No more." She rolled her eyes. She loved her friends, but her heart could only take so much. "How about a change of subject?"

"I have one." Lila grinned. "There's someone waving at you. Isn't that the superintendent?"

Meredith stopped in her tracks. Sure enough, Mr. Olaff was crossing the street, an envelope in hand. She could think of only one reason why he would look her up.

"Ooh. Do you think he has a job for you?" Lila gripped her arm.

"Maybe it's the school you wanted." Scarlet grabbed her other arm.

"I've prayed so hard for you, Meredith." Earlee hopped up and down with excitement. "I have a feeling my prayers are about to be answered."

"Miss Worthington, good afternoon." Mr. Olaff tipped his hat cordially. He was a grandfatherly gentleman with a friendly smile and a likable manner. "Your letter of application has been at the top of our list for some time, and with your perfect score on the teaching exam, I am happy to offer you this."

"A school?" she croaked, not daring to hope but knowing it was true all along. She stared at the envelope he held out to her, importantly thick.

"It's a contract for three months' teaching at the Upriver School," Mr. Olaff said kindly. "June, July and August. I'm assuming you are interested?"

"Interested? I'm completely overcome." There was her dream, just like that, finally arrived. She took the thick packet gingerly, half expecting it to evaporate and disappear. "Thank you, Mr. Olaff. I would love that school."

"Then you take your contract home, read it carefully and bring it back to me by Friday. I'll let the folks know they have a fine teacher for the summer." With a tip of his hat and a wink, Mr. Olaff headed back to his office next to the bakery.

"Meredith!" Lila's grip tightened with bruising strength.

"You did it!" Scarlet squealed.

"Congratulations!" Earlee clapped with delight.

"You're officially a teacher!" Lila jumped with excitement, and suddenly they were all doing it, hopping as giddily as eight-year-olds. "But what about Earlee? Didn't you get a school?"

"I haven't put in my application yet," Earlee explained. "There's too much work at home with the animals and garden and the crops. I can't leave my sister Beatrice to handle it all. When the harvest is in, then I can think about teaching."

"And I'm not going to do anything," Scarlet bemoaned as they hesitated on the corner, about to go their separate ways. "I have no plans. Maybe I should get some."

"I'll be cutting fabric at the counter at my parents' store. Probably for eternity." Lila winked. "Unless Lorenzo changes his mind about me and sweeps me off my feet."

"I'm sure there are great romances ahead for all of us," Earlee declared, her sunshine hope infectious. "Lila, you need a handsome man of mystery to come new to town to sweep you off your feet."

"At least it would counter the endless boredom in the mercantile," Lila teased. "Speaking of which, my stepmother will be watching the clock and wondering why I'm not there to help out. See you all tomorrow!"

"Bye." Scarlet took a step in the opposite direction. "My ma is waiting, too. See you in the morning."

"See you." Meredith, alone with Earlee, wasn't surprised that her friend was gazing down the street where the flag was waving. "Are you hoping there's a letter at the post office?"

"You know I am." She squinted against the glare and adjusted her slouching sunbonnet's brim. "Did you want to talk about what really happened with Shane? You're obviously holding a lot inside."

"Talking about it won't help, but thanks." For a moment, she looked so sad it nearly brought tears to Earlee's eyes. She swallowed hard, wishing to high heaven her friend was not in too much pain. Meredith turned over the envelope in her hand. "This means I have to tell Mama and Papa."

"Do you think they will forbid you to teach?"

"It would crush me if they did." Meredith might have the prettiest dresses of any girl at school and she had the finest things, but she had sorrows, too.

"You know where I am if you need to talk." Earlee wrapped her arms around her friend, giving her a caring hug. "Come by any time. It's chaos at my house, but you will always be welcome. I'm here to listen."

"You are a treasure, Earlee."

"No, I'm no one special at all." She loved Meredith for thinking so. "Did you want to come with me to the post office?"

"Sure. I've got a few more minutes until Minnie swings back by for me."

"Great." It was nice to have company.

"So, are you going to tell me about him?" Meredith asked. "You haven't mentioned your interest in front of the others, so I haven't said anything. The curiosity is killing me."

"It's nothing like what you and Shane have." She blushed. "It's just a one-sided thing. I'm the one who cares."

"That can be rough. We've both agreed matters of the heart are confusing and complicated."

"And painful." The pain of not knowing, the pain of hoping against hope, the pain of being what she feared was too plain and too average for love. Then there were the constant demands of having a big family whose needs had to be met. What man wanted to put up with that? "Oh, look, there's Minnie. She's caught up to you."

"She can wait for me for a few minutes, if you need to talk."

"No, go on. You have to face your mother sometime. May as well get it over with." She gave Meredith another hug, this time for encouragement. She was grateful for the interruption because she was afraid Meredith would guess about her feelings for Finn. He'd been all she could think about all day, wondering if there would be a letter from him today and if he had been thinking of her.

Her stomach was a jumble of nerves when she stepped into the post office and asked for their mail.

"Nothing for your family," the postmaster commented across the counter.

Nothing? Again?

"Thank you anyway." She pushed away, feeling the first drop of disappointment fall and another. She had been waiting and waiting for a letter. She had to accept the fact none was coming.

It wasn't as if she were in love with him, just a harmless crush. She set her chin, blindly retracing her steps to the door. She knew full well Finn McKaslin did not feel that way for her. So why did the sun dim as she stepped onto the boardwalk? Why did her disappointment feel more like sorrow?

He's all wrong for you, she told herself. *He's four years older, he's in prison and even if he wasn't, he would not be the kind of man your parents would ever approve of.*

But he had so much goodness in him. She hated the possibility that all his goodness might be lost. She'd hoped she could make a difference. It was her Christian duty.

That was what she told herself. And it was all truth. But there was a deeper truth she could not hide from. She had secretly hoped he had been charmed by her letter and would fall in love with her. Foolish and unrealistic, she knew, but a tiny part of her had hoped anyway.

She hated to think that Meredith felt this way, too, crushed and hurting. It was what happened when the fairy tale did not come true. With a sigh, she hiked the strap of her book bag higher on her shoulder and set off down the boardwalk. She had better get moving. She still had Ma's medicine to fetch before heading home.

Every plod of Sweetie's hoofs on the road home reminded Meredith of the man who was missing. It wasn't Shane who sat silent in the seat in front of her, guiding the horse home. It wasn't Shane who drew to a halt in front of the house and held out his hand to help her down. The shadowed depths of the barn did not hide him from her sight. She could not listen for the pad of his step on the walkway or hope for a glimpse of him through the windows as she went about her afternoon. Not even the envelope she clutched in her hand could drag her thoughts from what she had lost.

He was false, she reminded herself. He was not what he'd seemed. But none of that could diminish her grief.

"I'm gonna see if Cook has any cookies to spare." Minnie dropped her things with a plop on the entry table. "Want some?"

"Not today, cutie." She pushed the dark feelings down and set her things by the front door. "You go on."

"Molasses cookies are my new favorite." Minnie bounced away, skirts flouncing, china knickknacks tinkling on their glass shelves as she skipped by.

"Wilhelmina!" Mama's voice traveled through the reaches of the house. "How many times do I have to tell you? A lady does not run around like a herd of stampeding cattle."

"I'm not running." Minnie bounded through the dining room and out of sight. "I'm skipping."

Poor Mama, working so hard to make ladies out of them, but it was an uphill battle. Meredith eyed the path to the kitchen, where sanctuary awaited her along with a cup of milk and a plate of cookies, but she was a young woman and nearly a high-school graduate. She would behave as one. Clutching her contract, she went in search of her mother.

"Meredith, do come in." In the sun-filled library, Mama looked up from the pages of her book. "The ladies of the club chose Mark Twain for our next meeting, but he's entirely too outrageous. Hardly proper at all. I don't know what the world is coming to."

"It is a wonder," Meredith quipped, slipping into the overstuffed chair opposite her mother. Sunlight poured through the windows and winked in the pond outside, where ducks gathered and quacked, pleased that the trainers had gone from the nearby corral. Did everything have to remind her of Shane? She briefly squeezed her eyes shut, praying to forget him.

"Do you have a headache, my dear girl?" Mama slapped her book closed and dropped it with a thud onto an end table. "I'll have Sadie made a compress and some soothing tea."

"I'm troubled, Mama. That is all." No poultice was going to help with that. She toyed with the edge of the envelope, gathering her courage. "Mr. Olaff offered me a teaching position today."

"And I assume you did not turn him down on the spot?"

"No, this is the employment contract." She ignored the horror on her mother's face and tried to see the concern there. At least Shane had been right about that. She was blessed to have parents who fought so hard to protect her. "I'm asking for your blessing, Mama."

"I simply cannot give it. A daughter of mine working? It's nonsense. You have everything you need right here." She drew herself up, a general in charge of the battle she had resolved to win. "I forbid it. What will Leticia Bell say? Or the Wolfs? Or the Davises? It is not seemly. A young lady does not hire herself out like a teamster's horse for wages. I refuse to allow it."

"Mama, don't you see? I need your approval." She set the envelope aside and took her mother's hand. "I'm no longer a little girl. I'm all grown up. You've done your job."

"It's not done until you are suitably married, young lady." Mama's grip strengthened, holding on, her chin up, her tone nearly shrill, clinging so very tightly to what was past.

Falling in love with Shane had changed her. She could see that now. She understood something she'd never been able to fathom in her mother's overprotective, rigid ways. How very much Mama treasured being a mother, raising her little girls and all the happy times they'd shared. How hard it must be to let that go, as time demands by rolling forward, changing little girls to young women.

"You need to allow me to do this, Mama." She did not bother to hide the abiding affection she had and always would have for her mother. "It's time to let me take the love and the lessons you have given me and make my own way. I promise you, wherever I go it will always lead me back to you."

"I do not think I can bear it." Her mother's lower lip trembled, a rare show of emotion. "You will stay right here where I can take care of you. I demand it."

"I promise to come home for Sunday dinner as often as I can." Her vision blurred. Those pesky tears had returned. She blinked hard, but they fell anyway, one by one rolling down her cheek. "I love you, Mama."

"I love you, my precious Meredith." A single tear betrayed her. "Whatever will I do without you? We will need to get you a sensible horse, one that will not shy at the slightest thing. Perhaps you should take my Miss Bradshaw, she is a very respectable mare. We shall have your father order you your own buggy straight away."

"Thank you." Her throat closed, overwhelmed with gratitude and emotions too powerful to dare speak of.

"I just wish you had more traditional ambitions." Her mother sniffled, swiped at her eyes and sat up straight, in control again. "Are you sure there is no way you can forgive the Connelly boy?"

"You can't help yourself, can you?" Meredith ignored the cannon blast of grief at the sound of Shane's name, fighting not to let it show. "You only liked him when you found out about his family."

"Yes, because that's when I knew he was good enough for my girl."

"Because he is rich." She did not know *that* man—the wealthy senator's son from Virginia. Her gaze drifted to the window and the empty corral beyond. When she thought of Shane, she remembered his dependable goodness, the gentle notes of his baritone, the kind way he treated all manner of animals and people. She loved the country boy who'd won her heart. She missed him with all the depth of her being.

"You decided Mr. Connelly was *not* good enough because he was rich." Mama didn't bother to hide her smile as she reached for her book. "You might think I'm prejudiced, but you are, too, my dear."

"I am not," she denied, too fast and too vehemently.

"Then there's always Lorenzo Davis," her mother suggested.

What if Shane was more like her than she'd imagined, and his stories and his confessions were true? What if the pieces he had left out of the stories he'd told her had nothing to do with rebellion against his controlling family and everything to do with finding his own path? Just as he'd said. He may come from an influential family, but he did not rely on that influence.

It was his social position that had upset her. The notion that he was a rich man, not a man who trained horses. That he would want a life in society and a wife to go with it, and not a girl who loved the country and wanted to teach small children to read. She had been the one. She had misjudged Shane, and there was no one to blame but herself. Ashamed, she opened the envelope and removed her contract. The carefully scribed pages offered her one dream, but she had lost another—the best one of all.

I have been honest about who I am and what I want. Shane's words came back to her, words she refused to believe were sincere at the time. *I am my own man. Nothing is going to change that.*

She could see the truth. She'd been so afraid of getting hurt, she had closed her heart to him. Now he was gone. There was no way to fix the mistake she'd made. Her grief darkened and deepened, as if to steal all the sunlight and warmth from the summery day—from every summer day to come.

She rose from the chair, clutching her contract and left the room. There was no spring in her step, no joy in her heart. She feared there would never be again.

Chapter Nineteen

"I hate that this party has to end." Meredith gave Fiona a final hug, looking so beautiful in her white muslin gown, simple but sweet. "It was such a beautiful wedding, I doubt any of us could top it."

"It was nothing fancy." Fiona's dark curls bounced as she shook her head, a vision of loveliness, lustrous with happiness. "Just Ian's grandmother and my best friends. Everyone who matters to me."

"It was our honor to have witnessed it." Meredith meant every word. Reverend Hadly had performed the ceremony after the Sunday service, and they'd had a small luncheon party at the little rental, where Ian and Fiona were to make their home together. It was simple to imagine the newlyweds' laughter filling the house like summer breezes.

"You are now a wife." It was Lila's turn to hug Fiona next. "Remember you used to tell us this day would never happen?"

"I do. I vowed never to marry and look at me, I'm the first one of us to be a bride." Fiona hugged Lila back. "Thank you all for being there with me today. As if marrying Ian wasn't enough, having my best friends with me made it a day I will cherish always."

"I wonder who will be the next of us to marry?" Scarlet asked, arms out. She drew Fiona into a quick hug.

"It will be Lila," Earlee guessed. It was her turn to embrace the new bride.

"Yes. Lila will be tallying up the purchases of all the men who come into the mercantile," Kate agreed. "She is bound to catch someone's eye."

"While I'm stuck on the farm all summer. There will be no romance for me." Earlee didn't seem to mind her fate in life, caring for her brothers and sisters and her ill mother. "I do, however, need to live vicariously through all of you."

"I need to do that, too," Ruby announced, hugging Fiona in turn. "I'll be out on the homestead all summer, just me, the pigs and the chickens."

"And I'll be up in the woods where there are no handsome men, just homely ones." Kate rolled her eyes. "Why can't lumberjacks be cute?"

"There must be a law against it," Meredith quipped, leading the way toward the awaiting horses and her new buggy. "Only horsemen seem to be handsome."

"And Lorenzo," Scarlet pointed out.

Lorenzo. Meredith untethered Miss Bradshaw from the hitching post. She could only pray that her mother would not start trying to fix her up with Lorenzo. There was only one man who could fill the void in her soul, only one who was her perfect match and her beloved in every way.

"Goodbye!" Ruby called out from the back of an old bay gelding. The horse plodded off in the direction of the open prairie.

"I'll see you in church next week!" Kate slid onto the seat of a homemade cart and gathered her mustang's reins.

"Goodbye!" Meredith called out as she directed Miss Bradshaw down the driveway. On the seat beside her, Earlee, Lila and Scarlet leaned over the sides to wave at Fiona, arm in arm with her husband.

"She is a beautiful bride." Lila sighed wistfully. "Doesn't she look so happy?"

"Exultant." Meredith caught one last sight of the couple. What a picture they made. Ian brushed a curl from Fiona's eyes, carefully hooking it behind her ear. The act was more loving and tender than Meredith had ever seen. "They are going to live happily-ever-after beyond all doubt."

"I think so, too," Scarlet agreed.

"Me, too," Earlee chimed in.

"Me, three," Lila added.

Soon they were in town, Lila left in front of her family's store. Scarlet was next, dropped off in front of her home on Third Street. Earlee climbed out at the first crossroads south of town, leaving Meredith alone with a cheery wave. Miss Bradshaw kept her sensible pace as a runaway cow bolted into sight before dashing off into another field. A jackrabbit bursting out of the grasses did not so much as make the mare blink. Meredith wasn't sure when the musical clanking began to accompany the horse's gait until Miss Bradshaw drew up short and tossed her head, clearly deciding it was not prudent to go any farther.

"What's the matter, girl?" Meredith set the brake before clinging out to investigate. Puffs of dust rose up with each step. Temperate winds played with the hem of her skirt as she swished over to the mare.

Not one to withhold her opinion, Miss Bradshaw lifted her back left hoof and gave it a shake to emphasize the problem. A shoe had come quite loose and dangled by all but one little nail.

"Good afternoon, miss." A rumbling baritone startled her from behind. "Looks like you have a problem."

No, it couldn't be. She went icy-cold at the shocking

idea. *I'm making it up,* she thought. *I want to see him so desperately, I'm imagining the sound of his voice.* She fisted her hands, doing her best to stay calm. It could not possibly be him. She had spurned him and sent him away. A man would not come back after such rejection.

"Looks like your horse threw a shoe. I can take care of that, miss. No problem." He strolled to her side. His shadow tumbled over her, tall and as substantial as the man.

Shane. She opened her mouth, but nothing happened. No words, not a sound, not even air. Her entire mind erased, as if she had forgotten the English language. She stared, captivated by him—his steadfastness, his determination, his love for her shining in the bluest eyes she had ever seen.

He towered beside her, mighty, rugged and trail-dusty. Her horseman with a black Stetson shading his face, as real as could be. What did this mean? All the terrible things she'd said, the way she'd spurned him and the assumptions she'd made horrified her now. Surely he had not come back for her, could he? Everything inside her yearned for him to say those words.

She knew it could not be true. No doubt he had returned to Angel Falls for another reason. She had her chance, and she had failed him.

"It won't be the first time I've assisted a pretty country miss on this road." He knuckled back his hat, revealing the striking planes of his face. No dimples, no smile, no hint of softness gentled the hard unforgiving contours. Was he remembering, too, the moment they'd first met? Instant awareness had crashed through her hard enough to wobble her knees.

"This will only take a moment." As if he had no recollection of that day, as if she were a stranger he did not

know, he approached the horse. The low notes of his baritone made the horse swivel her ears, eager to tune in. He
laid a reassuring hand on the mare's flank. "Good to see
you again, Miss Bradshaw. I hope you've been well."

The mare gave a very proper, distinguished nicker and
shook her hind hoof impatiently. Clearly she did not appreciate having to wait for a solution to her problem.

"Shane, what are you doing here? Why have you come?"
The words came out more strained than she intended. The
wind caught them, stealing them away. She watched the
impeccable line of his shoulders stiffen.

"Had a few loose ends to tie up." He sounded strained,
too. He knelt, took a pair of pliers from his back denim
pocket and gently cradled Miss Bradshaw's hoof.

"What loose ends? I wasn't aware you knew that many
people in town."

"I don't." He gave the nail a twist and removed the
horseshoe. "I got as far as Great Falls before I had to turn
back."

"What about your job?"

"I quit." He lowered the mare's hoof gently to the
ground. He rose to his full height and patted her on the
neck. "There you go, Miss Bradshaw. You are a good girl."

As if that were irrefutable, the mare nodded with great
dignity.

"You quit? The job you were so devoted to?" A gold
curl tumbled from beneath her sunbonnet, bouncing along
the edge of her face, making him remember all the times
he'd used it as an excuse to touch her.

"It was time for me to move on." He braced his feet,
steeled his resolve. It wasn't easy to face her. She hadn't
given him one hint he had a chance with her. With the way
she glared at him over this piece of news, it made him leery
about offering his heart to her again.

"I suppose it's time to go back to your predetermined life." Her chin shot up a notch. All strength, his Meredith, and spirit. He saw her spirit as clearly as the road at his feet, as the grasses dancing in the wind, as the vulnerability in her gray-blue eyes.

"That's right. Back to you." He strolled toward her, palms sweating, pulse racing as if he'd been fighting a mountain lion. Oh, but it felt good to gaze upon her. To see again the roses in her cheeks, the dear little cleft in her chin, her beauty that sustained him. This was the moment of truth. He could not lose her. He did not know how to win her back. He'd come all this way, given up his apprenticeship, rehearsing what he would say to her with every passing mile.

None of it came to mind. Practiced phrases couldn't help him. Only one thing could.

"Meredith, please forgive me." He put aside his pride, because she was more important. He opened the door to the places within him he liked to keep under lock and key. "I was wrong. I should have told you the whole truth. My only excuse is that you bamboozle me."

"So, it's my fault?"

"Absolutely, darlin'." She had no notion the power she held over him. A man didn't stand a chance. "The first time I set eyes on you, it was like being kicked in the chest by a Clydesdale."

"It was?" Hope, silent but not mute, lit her eyes.

It touched his soul. Hope. She was hopeful. Maybe all was not lost after all. He swallowed hard, encouraged. "I wasn't looking for anything serious. I fought my feelings for you nearly the entire way. But something happened to me when I first gazed upon you. I've never been the same, Meredith. You've changed me, and I can't go on without you."

"But the things I said." She lifted her face to him, raw pain twisting her voice, out of place on this day of bright sunshine and beauty. She took a shaky breath, as if in the worst kind of pain. "I didn't realize until you were gone what I had done to you."

"You did nothing so bad." Everything within him ached to caress the furrow from her forehead, to kiss away her every sorrow. His feet pulled him forward, close enough to see the threads of green and gold in her stormy eyes, to see the silken texture of her creamy skin and the most precious gift he had ever been given—her love revealed.

"I sent you away. I wouldn't believe in you, the man you are." She hiked her chin higher, like a drowning woman going under for the last time. "I didn't forgive you when you asked me, and now it's too late."

"When we got to Great Falls, I told Braden that was as far as I could go. Not one more step. I had to go back." He reached out to brush an errant curl from her face. The caress of his fingertips against her forehead was the sweetest wish. "I had left my heart behind and I couldn't go on without it. Without you."

"Without me? Then it's not too late?" This had to be a dream too wonderful to be true. Her senses filled with him and only him—the scent of dust on his shirt, the warmth of his sun-browned hand, his loving kindness too incredible to believe.

"Too late? No, not as long as you take me back." He folded the lock of hair behind her ear and he did not move away. There in the middle of the road for any passersby to see, he cradled her face as if to cherish every detail, as if he could not look at her enough. "I owe you the truth. We can't go on if I don't."

"What truth?" Her mind had gone fuzzy again. Emotions more powerful than any she'd ever known lifted through her, as if to raise her feet from the ground.

"The things I didn't tell you." He had never seemed stronger than he did with his armor off, his defenses down, vulnerable. "I should have let you closer. I should have let you in. Then there would have been no doubt."

"Hearing the truth from Narcissa did come as a shock."

"I noticed," he drawled in his easygoing manner, but there was nothing easygoing about the steel in his voice, the certainty, the commitment. "The time I lived with my grandmother was the first I'd known of real love. When my father's fortunes reversed and we went back to our lives, I went back to loneliness and impossible expectations and family duty. I went back to friends who had rejected me years before and I could never really trust again. My parents' way of life of manipulation and self-interest left me unable to believe in anyone. Until I met you."

Beneath her palm, she felt his heart beating true.

If it is a dream, Father, please don't let me awaken. Let me stay right here with this man forever. She curled her fingers into his shirt. He was real beneath her fingertips, soft muslin and iron muscle and sun-hot warmth. She had missed him as if he'd been gone a century. She drank in the things she cherished most about him—his dependability, his integrity, his good character.

"I love you, Meredith." He'd said the words before, but this time with a force great enough to bind her to him forever. "I need to know if there is a chance you can ever love me again."

He had to ask? Couldn't he see it? Amazement swirled through her. His hand cradling her face trembled ever so slightly, a betrayal of his fear. She leaned into his touch, savoring the beauty of being held by him.

"There is a chance." She smiled, happiness rushing in. "A very good chance."

"How good?" A tinge of amusement hinted in the corners of his mouth. His heartbeat beneath her fingers slowed.

"One hundred percent." New dreams flashed into her mind, as perfect as could be. She saw a home full of cheer and laughter and calico curtains fluttering at the windows. Rescued horses grazed peacefully in green fields. Their children played happily in the front yard. Dreams only Shane could give her. Shane, towering before her like a gift from heaven, the greatest treasure of all.

"I love you," she confessed. "I love you with all I have."

"As I love you." He leaned closer, impossibly closer, until their breaths mingled. His gaze arrowed to her mouth and her lips tingled sweetly. He did not lean in for a kiss. "I was on my way to ask about a job."

"A job?"

"I hear someone by the name of Worthington is looking for a horse trainer. Figured he might give me a chance. I'd like to be gainfully employed when I ask for your hand in marriage."

"You're proposing to me?"

"Not yet, but I will when the time is right." His chuckle became a kiss, a tender brush of his lips to hers. His kiss was gentle and reverent and fairy-tale perfect.

Overwhelmed, she stepped back, but she could not let go of his shirt, let go of him. She was grateful to God for bringing them together. Love was an entirely new territory, but she had faith that God would see them through.

"C'mon." Shane took her hand. "Let's get you home."

"You know what this means, don't you?" She hardly needed his help into the buggy. Bliss filled her, made her lighter than air. "We have a chance to live happily-ever-after."

"A chance? No, darlin'. There's no chance. It's a certainty. I promise you that."

The sun chose that moment to brighten, as if they were not alone. Birdsong crescendoed, and their melodies carried on a loving wind. The green growing grasses, daisies blooming in the fields, the sky as blue as dreams. Never had the world been so beautiful. Never had she felt so whole. The pieces of her life were coming together, the pattern so beautiful that it hurt the eye to see. She remembered to take a moment to thank God for His gifts before she scooted over on the buggy seat to let Shane take the reins.

* * * * *

CALICO BRIDE

For the Lord seeth not as man seeth;
for man looketh on the outward appearance,
but the Lord looketh on the heart.
—*1 Samuel 16:7*

Chapter One

Angel Falls, Montana Territory
July 1884

"Thank you, Mrs. Olaff." Lila Lawson closed the cash drawer. "Please come again."

"Of course I will. How can I resist? You have such a pretty display of summer fabrics." The kindly elderly woman hugged her brown-paper-wrapped package. "Once I sew this up, I am coming back for that beautiful lawn. You promise not to sell it all until then?"

"My word of honor." She intended to snip fifteen yards of the delicate fawn-colored material off its bolt and hold it beneath the counter. It was her prerogative as the shopkeeper's daughter and it was the least she could do for Mrs. Olaff, who was a loyal, longtime customer.

The front door swung shut with a jingle of the bell hanging over the doorway and she was alone in the mercantile full of pleasantly displayed merchandise. Again. She glanced out at the street. Why couldn't life be more like a dime novel? On the other side of the perfectly spotless windows—she had cleaned them to a shine this morning—a parade of people, horses and wagons, fancy buggies and humble, handmade carts hurried by. Everyone was going somewhere, doing something and it seemed as if the merry sunshine called her name. The whole world was out there and excitement could be waiting around every corner.

She retraced her steps to the fabric counter at the far end of the store, the tap of her shoes echoing against the high ceiling. The sharp briny scent of the pickle barrel seemed to follow her as she circled around the edge of the counter. Her skirts swished and rustled in the silence.

How about a little excitement, Lord, please? Just a little diversion, something to break the monotony.

She picked up her pen, dunked the tip into the ink bottle and resumed her letter to one of her best friends, Meredith, now a teacher at a small summer school north of town.

Dear Meredith,
Dull. That's my life in a single word. Ever since we graduated not a single exciting thing has happened. Lorenzo Davis hasn't stepped foot inside the store. I would even welcome a visit from Luken Pawel to break the monotony. But everyone from school is busy with new jobs like you, or on their family farms like Earlee and Ruby. I miss you all. Not only that, I'm bored. Did I mention it?

Lila chuckled to herself, imagining Meredith would do the same when she read the letter—if she wasn't completely bored by its dull contents. Not that Lila didn't appreciate her blessings, because she thanked the Lord every day for them.

She had a comfortable life, a wonderful father, a sister she loved and friends she cherished. Plus, all the fabric she could want to sew. The bolts surrounded her in dignified rows of blacks, browns and grays, cheerful calicos and lively ginghams. Being around the fabrics perked her up, the bright spot in a long day's shift of standing on her feet.

"Lila!" a discontented woman's voice called from the door behind the long front counter.

That would be her stepmother.

"Don't tell me you are standing around again?" Eunice Lawson pounded into the doorway, her round face pursed with annoyance. "Can't I take one afternoon off to have tea with my friends without the store falling apart?"

"No."

"No, what?" Eunice waited, sour disapproval wafting through the air to compete with the pickle brine.

"No, *Ma.*" The single word was like an arrow to her heart. Her mother had died when she was fourteen and having to call the woman her pa had remarried by the same designation hurt in more ways than one.

"Be a good girl and be helpful. I left a list to keep you busy all afternoon." Eunice tossed what she probably thought was an encouraging smile before storming out of sight.

Oh, joy. Why couldn't she be allowed to sit quietly and sew during the quiet moments in the store, as Eunice did or the hired lady who came on Saturdays? Lila blew out a sigh, listened to her stepmother's footsteps knell up into the second story and went in search of the list. She found it tacked on the wall behind the cash drawer and frowned at the first item.

Move pickled herring barrel and scrub floor beneath.

At least that would break the monotony. She tapped over to the little supply closet and gathered the essentials she would need.

This wasn't the excitement I was hoping for, Lord. How did the saying go? Be careful what you pray for. Amused, she dumped water from the pitcher into the bottom of a pail. It wasn't as if she had been terribly careful or specific in her prayer, had she? So she didn't intend to complain about the outcome. She grabbed a bar of soap from the closet shelf and made a beeline for the fish barrels.

Try to love your work, Lila, she told herself. Some days she did. Other days, not as much. She set down the bucket and put her shoulder into the first barrel, took a deep breath, tried not to breathe in the fishy smell and gave it a shove. Why couldn't her life be more like a book? She feared her life might always be placid and humdrum, the way it was today. Since she had already read every volume in last month's shipment of dime novels she was out of reading material and her thirst for adventure went unsatisfied.

As she grabbed the mop, a loud, shocking series of rapid pops erupted from the street, noisy enough to echo in the store. The smooth wooden handle tumbled from her hands and the mop hit the floor with a *whack*.

Was that gunfire? She whirled toward the window where the orderly pace of the afternoon had turned into a frantic blur. Horses reared, women ran into the nearest shops and buggies sped by, all heading away from the center of town. Cries rang out as another series of bullets fired.

What was going on? She found herself being drawn toward the door. Angel Falls was a quiet town full of honest and hardworking folk and very little trouble, until recently. Last summer, a train had been robbed just east of town and only one of the men responsible, Finn McKaslin, had been caught. Crime had grown since. She had heard of a few reticule snatchings, several horse thefts and two shops had been broken into. But gunfire had never rang on the streets before.

Was it coming from the bank? She opened the door and poked her head out just enough to see down the empty boardwalk. Many blocks away saddled horses ringed the front door of the bank while two men stood guard with Winchesters at the ready.

A bank robbery! Panic licked through her, shaking her from head to toe. Shots fired again from the bank. Were the people inside afraid? Hurt? She thought of Meredith's father who owned the bank and she gripped the edge of the door for support. *Watch over them, Father. Please keep everyone safe.*

The institution's ornate front doors swung open and a handful of men dashed out, their faces covered with bandanas, rifles clutched in hand. There was something menacing, defiant and cruel about them as they mounted up and gazed around the empty streets. She gulped hard, watching a very tall, very thin man hop onto his jet-black horse.

A sensible young lady would look away. A smart young lady would duck for cover, but this was better than any dime novel. Riveted, she watched as the bank door burst open and a man dashed out, rifle raised. He got one shot off before fire erupted. He fell on the steps and didn't move.

Her jaw dropped. Her heart stopped beating. Was he dead? Her knees gave out and she clung harder to the door, rattling the overhead bell. *Lord, let him be all right.* The outlaws didn't care. They beat their horses with the ends of their reins, shouting harshly. The animals bolted, galloping full-out down the street. They were coming her way!

Danger. She slammed the door shut. Her limbs felt like pulled taffy as she clamored behind the solid wood counter. She gripped the wooden edge with clammy fingers, her knees buckling. Horse hooves drummed closer, the beat of steeled shoes against the ground rattled the windowsills. Men shouted, guns fired, glass tinkled and something zinged to a stop in the counter in front of her.

A bullet? As her knees gave out completely and she sank down onto her heels safely behind the counter, she caught one last glimpse of the robbers speeding past, spurs glinting in the sunshine. A bank robbery wasn't the kind of excitement she had wanted. She swiped at her damp bangs with one shaky hand. Somehow she was sitting on the floor. It was not exactly the way a heroine in a dime novel would handle danger.

The door rattled open and a bell chimed. No other sound blew in on the still air. Not a single clomp of a horse's hoof, not a drum of shoes on the boardwalk. It was as if the entire town was holding its breath, afraid the outlaws would return, afraid it was not safe. Her pulse hammered like war drums. Was anyone there? Or had she not shut the door properly and it blew open?

She took in a deep breath, willed the trembling from her knees and pushed upright. Still a little wobbly, but she was not afraid. This was her first taste of adventure. Surely if there was ever a next time she would do better. She had grown up protected and sheltered and for that she was grateful, but she liked to think she had a courageous spirit. She smoothed her skirts and studied the store. The door stood open. No one was there. Right away she noticed the odd distortion in one of the glass panes. There was a little round hole just like a bullet would make.

A bullet. Her heartbeat skipped again. She skirted the counter to take a better look and she saw a man sprawled on his back on the floor in front of the open door with a blood stain blossoming on his white muslin shirt.

"M-miss?" he croaked in a baritone that sounded as if he were out of breath, as if he were a heavy smoker. The tin badge on his chest glinted as it caught a ray of sunshine. "You wouldn't happen to carry bandages, would you? I would like to buy a few."

"A few?" He was joking, right? What he needed was medical attention. She lifted the hem of her skirts and dashed to his side, heart pounding, knees shaking, her breath rattling between her ribs. Blood spread across his snowy shirt like a bottle of ink spilling. She knelt down and she reached to help him, but what did she do? She'd never seen an injury like this before. "You are going to need a great deal more than a couple bandages."

"I'm being optimistic," he panted between winces of pain.

Optimistic? He looked as though he was he going to die. The hard planked floor bit into her knees as she bounded into action. His rugged face turned ashen. He looked familiar. "You're the new deputy."

"Guilty." He wheezed in another sputtering bite of air. Muscles worked in his impressively square jaw, the sort of jaw a hero in a book might have. Dark brown, almost unruly hair framed a face so rugged and handsome it could have been carved out of stone. "Burke Hannigan. You're Lawson's oldest daughter."

"Yes, I'm Lila. You look a bit worse for the wear, Deputy Hannigan." From a shelf she snatched a stack of soft flannel squares, cut for baby diapers, and retraced her steps. "It looks as if you ran into a bullet out on the street."

"I've done worse and lived."

"You shouldn't be so cavalier. Look how fast you're bleeding." The crimson stain had grown larger and brighter, taking over his entire shirtfront. Her hands trembled as she plucked a piece of material from the stack and folded it into fourths. "It was brave of you to try and stop the bank robbers."

"But I didn't succeed. I couldn't run fast enough." He gritted his teeth, obviously as pained by that as by his wound.

His chest wound, she realized as she laid the cloth directly above the obvious bullet hole in his shirt. "Better luck next time."

"I didn't know a woman like you believed in luck." He winced when she applied pressure.

"It's just an expression, as I'm not sure you are the kind of man God would help." Maybe this wasn't the time for humor, but the wounded deputy laughed, sputtering with each deep rumble and, horribly, she felt the warm surge of blood against her palm intensify. "Perhaps you should lie back and stay quiet."

"If I wanted a woman to tell me what to do, I would have married one." He reached for a second piece of cloth and folded it, his bloodied fingers leaving marks on the flannel. Sweat broke out on his forehead at the effort. His chiseled mouth tugged down in the corners, making his hard face appear almost harsh, but his deep blue eyes radiated thankfulness and a depth of feeling that only a man with real heart could give. "I just need to catch my breath, and then I can go."

"You aren't going anywhere, Deputy." He definitely could have stepped off the pages of one of her beloved novels. The alpha hero, rugged and brave, tough enough to take a bullet to the chest and still want to right wrongs and capture villains. Very hard not to like that. "I'm going to fetch the doctor."

"I don't need a doctor." He clenched his teeth. A tendon jumped along his jawline. He was hard muscle and solid bone beneath the flat of her hand. His heart beat oddly fast and heavily, as if something were indeed wrong. He gasped in a breath, stuck the cloth on his other side and applied pressure.

He'd been hit by two bullets? Maybe she was a little in shock, too, since she hadn't noticed. When she plucked another cloth off the stack and added it to the one beneath her palm, her hand was coated red.

"You must have real bandages in this store—" He stopped to pant and wheeze. More blood oozed between her fingers. He wrestled with each breath. "Fetch them. I can patch. Myself. Up."

"Even most men would have enough common sense to lie in the street where they fell." She added another cloth to the pile. Light chestnut wisps fell down from her braided cornet to frame her face. "You are going nowhere, Deputy."

"We shall. See about that." He gasped. If his head would stop spinning, he would be all right. It was probably from the blood loss. That was easy to fix with a bandage. "I just need to catch. My. Breath."

"That looks like it might take you a while." She pressed him down by the shoulder until he was flat on the floor again. "To do so would be at your great peril, and I am not going to let anything happen to you. You collapsed on my shift and that makes me responsible for you."

"I had to get a bossy store clerk." He considered it a good sign that he could quip. "I can't lay here."

"You already are." Her soft alto brooked no argument. She was a willowy, petite young lady with big sea-green eyes and a perfectly dainty oval face. She had delicately carved features, high striking cheekbones, a softly chiseled jaw and a nose gently sloping and cute as a button. Lila Lawson's rosebud mouth pursed. "Don't sit up until this bleeding stops. No, don't even think about it."

"It's a. Free country. I can. Think what. I want." He figured as long as he had some sass, he wasn't knocking on death's door. Yet. It would take more than a few bullets to stop his mission, but in truth he was feeling a little woozy.

A little help here, Lord. Just a tad. He sent the prayer up, hoping the Good Lord would see fit to hear him.

"It's a free country, yes, but you are in my family's store, which means it's my store." She added another diaper to the pile on his chest, her hands wet with his life's blood. Compassion lurked in the depths of her eyes, green threaded with sky-blue. The most beautiful eyes he'd ever seen. "Can I trust you to lay here? I want to shout up the stairs. Someone has to fetch the doctor and I know if I leave you alone in this store to do it, you will drag yourself out the door on your hands and knees."

"Not sure. About. The. Hands." Being as he couldn't much feel them. He felt as if he were drowning, like the time he was held under the surface of the Yellowstone River when Kid Billings had taken objection to being arrested. He'd come near to dying that day. It felt a lot like he was feeling now. Boy, the pain was sure getting worse. "Maybe. I'll. Rest. A. Spell."

"Good decision." Her smile softly curved the innocent corners of her sweet mouth, a mouth obviously made for smiling. She leaped to her feet. "Don't you die on me."

That was starting to be his worry, too. His throat tightened. He hated to have it end like this. He hadn't done nearly enough with his life. There were promises to keep and a mission to finish. He watched Lila's pink calico skirts swirl out of sight and listened to the light *tap, tap* of her shoes on the boards. His vision began to darken at the edges. Regrets hit him. If he died right now, would he have done enough to earn his salvation?

He didn't know. He listened to the faint murmur of Lila's voice, the dim patter of shoes growing close. A shiver shook him so hard his teeth rattled. Iciness gripped him although it was the middle of July, the day hotter than a roaring stove top. He hadn't shaken this hard since he'd been caught in the teeth of a North Dakota blizzard chasing Wildcat Willy all the way to the Canadian border.

"My sister is running to fetch Dr. Frost." Lila returned, her lovely face a perfect picture of concern. She really was very comely. His chest tightened gazing up at her, feeling cold sweat bead on his forehead and roll off his neck. Her soft hand lighted against his cheekbone. "You are making me worry, Deputy, and I want you to stop it."

"Sorry." He gritted his teeth together so they wouldn't chatter. He looked like a weakling in front of her, shaking and trembling and sweating. Not to mention the bleeding. If he could will himself well, he would. She leaned away from him for a moment, leaving his sight only to bob back in again. Something warm and scratchy covered him. A wool blanket.

"That should help." Serene in the midst of crisis, she added another diaper to the pile on his chest and pressed painfully down. "You, sir, are the most troublesome customer I've had yet today."

"I try to stand out." He gasped, hating the weakness and that he was showing pain. "Don't like being. Second fiddle."

"You're one of *those* men." She rolled her eyes for emphasis, lightening the mood, trying to distract him from the blood staining the blanket. So much blood. "First you're too tough to let a bullet wound stop you, and now you need to be the center of attention."

"Trouble." He sputtered out the word.

"You very much are. My stepmother is going to insist we bill you for this." She hoped he didn't notice she was shaking as hard as he was.

"Put it. On my. Account."

"You don't have an account." He was knocking on death's door and he hadn't lost his sense of humor. Tenderness gripped her. She liked this man, and he was dying right before her eyes. She could do nothing but watch. "If you want to start one, we will need a letter of recommendation from another merchant where you have an account and a letter from your employer to verify your job."

"Will do. Right away."

Lord, let him be all right. Don't let him die.

Footsteps pounded on the boardwalk outside, distinctive taps and the faint jangle that made Burke Hannigan's eyes turn dark, his every muscle grew taut and he launched a few inches off the floor, only to cough, sputter blood and collapse back onto the wood planks. It didn't sound like the doctor. Dr. Samuel Frost didn't wear spurs.

"You have to lie still." She grabbed another fold of fabric to hold over the wound. "I've decided not to let you die, so you will simply have to comply."

Sadness darkened his blue eyes. He shifted slightly beneath the blanket, breathing faster as the footsteps pounded closer. Someone hollered a door or two down the boardwalk, the sound carried clearly through the open door.

"Hannigan? Where are you?" His boots struck like hammers, his spurs rang with menace. "Don't tell me you're dead because that would make my day."

What a horrible man. It could only be the town's sheriff. How he was voted into office remained a mystery for more than half the good citizens of Angel Falls. A shiver trickled down her spine and spilled ice into her veins. He was coming their way.

"Take this." Deputy Burke Hannigan's whisper vibrated with pain. His compelling gaze latched onto hers, his plea going soul deep. "Hide it. Promise?"

Something pressed into the palm of her hand and she didn't look at it. With a nod of agreement, she automatically slipped it into her skirt pocket as boot heels and spurs struck the boards outside the threshold. A shadow fell across her, and when she looked up Sheriff Dobbs swaggered through the doorway as if he owned the place. She felt Burke stiffen beneath her fingertips as his every muscle tensed.

"So, you're not dead after all, Hannigan." The sheriff scowled. "But the day ain't over yet."

Chapter Two

Dobbs. Burke's mouth soured at the sight of the snake. No, thinking of the sheriff as a snake did a disservice to reptiles everywhere. He blinked hard against the fiery pain scorching him, rasped in a breath and locked gazes with the villain. He did not blink. He'd learned long ago to never show weakness to a bad man.

"It takes more—than an outlaw—to stop me." He bit out the words as if the double bullet holes weren't affecting him one bit. "Don't give away—my job—just yet."

"I'll put up a post. I was plannin' on it anyway." Footsteps struck the floor with a bully's force, the only power left a man with no heart and a black soul. "You're a lightweight. Never should have given you the job."

Lightweight? Burke didn't let the insult bother him. He was a good half foot taller than Dobbs. He knew what Dobbs was. He had gotten a good eyeful working for him the past few months. "I'll prove myself."

"I doubt it, boy." Dobbs lifted his upper lip in a sneer.

Burke's vision blurred. That couldn't be a good sign. Reality wavered around him like a mirage. From the blood loss no doubt. His teeth clacked together like a train's iron wheels on a track. Pain consumed him like flame. He was fading fast. Lila's pretty face hovered over him but her image blurred, too. He caught a pinch of concern, a fluff of cinnamon-brown curls and sweetness. So much sweetness. The pressure of her hands felt distant on his wounds. The world slowly began to melt away.

Keep the badge hidden, he wanted to tell her. *Keep your promise to me.* But the words would not come and he couldn't say them in front of Dobbs anyway.

"Looks like I ought to put you out of your misery like a downed horse." Dobbs bit out with a hint of laughter.

"What a horrible thing to joke about." Lila's gentle alto held a note of dismay. "Step away from him. I don't need your brand of help."

"Just tellin' the truth, gal. Life is hard. You ought to toughen up and accept it."

Easy to feel Lila's outrage and distress. Her emotions seemed to vibrate through her gentle touch. She was all he could see—every other bit of his surroundings had gone. She was a smudge of creamy skin, rich brown curls and pink calico, and he clung to her image, remembering her sweet beauty and rosebud smile.

"Ignore. Him." He coughed out the words.

"I intend to. Hold on, Deputy." She ignored everything but him. Voices murmuring at the doorway, the strike of her stepmother's shoes on the stairs and the scary amount of blood soaking her hands and her dress. "Don't you leave."

"Won't." The one word cost him. His eyes drifted shut but the hint of a smile touched the pale corners of his lips.

"Deputy?" Her heart crashed to a stop. "Burke?"

"That's life, missy." The sheriff scoffed. "No sense tearin' up about it. First you live, then you die."

Her faith taught to turn the other cheek, so she ignored him. She collapsed back on her heels, shaking.

Tears scalded the backs of her eyes. Was Burke dead? She couldn't tell if he was breathing. She laid two trembling fingers against the side of his throat. Nothing. Nothing at all.

Wait. The tiniest flutter pulsed against her fingertip. He lived. Relief rocketed through her. Now that she was a little more calm, she could see the barely noticeable rise and fall of his chest. He was holding on, just as she'd begged him to.

"Stand aside, Dobbs." Dr. Sam Frost's terse demand betrayed his tension. Were the wounds mortal? Worry crept around her heart and cinched tight.

Please, let the deputy be all right. She rolled back the crimson hem of the blanket for the doctor, who was already kneeling and reaching into his medical bag. He worked quickly, pulling out his stethoscope and leaning in to listen. Two deputies pushed into the room. There was no disguising the doctor's concern as he straightened.

"Lila, you need to leave the room now." The doctor tore apart the deputy's shirt. Buttons flew and hit the floor with ping sounds.

"No, I'm staying." She braced herself but nothing could prepare her for the sight of Burke's chest. Two seeping wounds tore into his flesh, marring his perfect physique.

"Lila! Get away from that man." Eunice tromped around the corner of the counter. "He has no shirt."

"But the doctor might need help." She swallowed hard, feeling woozy at the sight of ruined flesh and bone. Sympathy pains cut deep into her. She hated feeling so helpless. "I have to do something."

"You will avert your eyes and come with me, young lady." Eunice grabbed an elbow and Lila was wrenched to her feet. All around her movement and flurry and voices drummed dimly in her head.

"On three," the doctor ordered and along with other men lifted the unconscious deputy onto the front counter.

"What do you think you are doing?" Eunice demanded. "We conduct business in this establishment. How will we serve our customers?"

"Mrs. Lawson, human life takes a higher priority." Dr. Frost appeared pained, hardly paying her any attention as he poured a solution from a brown bottle onto the separate wounds. "I need better light. Lila, find me some lanterns. I need to operate."

"Someone had better reimburse us for our lost profits," Eunice announced, although it didn't appear as if anyone were listening.

Lanterns. They had a whole shelf of lighting needs. Lila twisted away from her stepmother's grip and dashed down the aisle. Her fingers felt wooden as she opened a can of kerosene and poured it into the first lamp she grabbed.

"He's not gonna make it, Doc," Dobbs commented. "Don't think the sheriff's office is gonna pick up your bill when he dies."

"I'm not worried about the money." Dr. Frost sounded busy and annoyed, although she couldn't see him because of the shelving and the way her stepmother stood like a barricade between her and Burke Hannigan's bare chest.

"I'll take that." Tight-lipped, Eunice twisted the lantern from Lila's grip. "Fill another, but that is all. We can't spare anymore expense than two lanterns."

"Does the deputy have family in the area?" the doctor asked, strained as he lighted a match to his scalpel to sterilize it. "No? Any next of kin?"

"He didn't list a soul on his application." Dobbs's spurs clanked against the planks as he headed toward the door. "No one cares if he dies. I'm leaving. Good luck, Doc. You'll need it."

Lila wondered if Burke could hear what was going on around him, if he was touched by the sheriff's callous disregard for human life. She felt dirtied by the words, as if they had somehow brushed against her soul and she was glad when the door slammed shut. She set the can on the shelf; the lamp's reservoir was full. She ran with it toward the deputy. Blood streamed out of wounds the doctor investigated.

"One didn't go too deep. Hit a rib." As if that was good fortune, Dr. Frost dropped a bullet into a pan with a *clink*.

"Go upstairs, Lila." The hard set of Eunice's round face held a warning. She took the lamp. "Go. No argument."

"But—" She had a thousand arguments but she bit her tongue. Disobeying her stepmother would only upset Pa. That was the last thing she wanted. As hard as it was, she forced her feet to carry her across the room and toward the door to upstairs. When she looked back, she couldn't see anything of Burke but his thick dark hair, tousled as if he'd just run his fingers through it. What happened next was God's will and so it was to God she prayed as she took the stairs one at a time with Eunice on her heels.

"Nothing so terrible has ever happened here before." Lark huddled in the corner at the kitchen table with fearful eyes. "All those gunshots. Do you think they will come back? Oh, do you think we are in danger?"

"Not likely." Lila used her most confident voice to reassure her little sister. She shut the kitchen door behind her, making sure to listen for Eunice's footsteps, which were heading into the parlor. "If you're worried, I can stay with you for a bit."

"Yes, I would like that." The girl tossed a cinnamon-brown braid over her shoulder—a shade matching Lila's—and sighed with great relief. She was a sweetheart, the identical copy of their mother. "You know Eunice. She told me not to be silly."

"She means well." She went straight to the washbasin.

"But she isn't Ma." Lark nibbled on the edge of a sugar cookie. "Do you reckon she's right? That this town will become lawless and we will have to sell the store and move? I don't want to leave the store."

"I can't see our settled town going to rack and ruin easily, not if Eunice has anything to do with it." She rinsed the blood off her hands. Burke's blood. "Everything will be fine, just you wait and see."

"What about the deputy? Is he really going to die like Eunice said?"

"No." Her stomach twisted up tight as she remembered the flash of his deeply blue eyes. Sadness gripped her as she grabbed the bar of soap and lathered her hands. "We're going to take good care of him so that he lives."

"Isn't his family going to take care of him?" Lark put down her cookie, no longer hungry.

"The sheriff said he doesn't have any family." That was even sadder. If Burke passed away, no one would care and no one would mourn him. She set down the soap and rinsed in the basin.

"He has to have someone somewhere." Lark wrinkled her freckled nose. "Everybody has family."

"I don't know. Who knows if Dobbs is right?" She grabbed a towel and dried her hands. Lark was right. How did someone get to be all alone? Everyone came from somewhere, even a handsome deputy with a killer smile.

"Oh, I know!" Lark bounded off her cushioned chair and dropped to her knees next to the paper box by the stove. She rattled through the folded newspapers. "You are talking about the new deputy, right? That's what Eunice said when she told you to stay up here away from him."

"Yes." Lila swallowed her resentment, remembering Eunice's parting admonishment. "Why?"

"I remember reading something. Let me see." She plucked out a paper and leafed through it. "Here it is. Burke Hannigan."

"That's him." A spark of interest thrilled through her like joy on a sunny day. She gripped the back of the chair, stopping herself from thundering around the table and snatching the newsprint from her sister. She was merely curious, that was all, wondering about the injured stranger. "What does it say?"

"'The town of Angel Falls welcomes new deputy Burke Hannigan. He hails from Miota Hollow near Miles City, where he worked as a deputy before the town burned to the ground in a grass fire.'" Lark paused to comment. "Oh, that's too bad. I read about that early this spring. It doesn't say he has family."

"Then the sheriff was right." Did she sound casual? She sure hoped so. As she hung up the towel, her pulse drummed in her ears, making it hard to hear as Lark bowed her head and continued to read.

"'He's a bachelor and this reporter has surmised he is not willing to settle down, so be that a warning to you ladies who might be interested in catching our new deputy's eye.'" Lark stopped again. "There is no mention of any relatives, so he really must be alone. How sad."

"Yes." She thought of him in the room below, stretched out on the front counter. Her palms went clammy and her knees weak. He didn't look strong enough to survive surgery. He'd lost so much blood already.

"'He is, however, skilled with a six-shooter,'" Lark read on. "'According to Sheriff Dobbs, he received a perfect score on the marksman part of his interview.' That's all it says about him." Lark folded the newsprint with a rattle and tossed it back into the box. "I wonder what happened to him? Why is he all alone?"

"We may never know." She remembered the deputy's sense of humor as he stubbornly denied the seriousness of his wounds. A ribbon of tenderness wrapped around her. He may have no one to care, but he had her. No one should be alone.

"Girls?" Eunice poked her head around the door. "Bring out more cookies. My friends will be staying longer than usual. No sense going out on those streets until we are certain all is safe."

"We're not safe?" Lark's eyes widened.

"The robbers rode away," Lila pointed out, wanting to reassure her little sister. "Nothing is going to happen. We'll bring the cookies."

"That's my good girls." Eunice let the door swing shut. Her steps tapped away and the faint murmur of lady's voices rose and fell like music.

"I've said a prayer for the deputy." Lark neatly scooped cookies off the rack and onto the platter. The tangy scent of molasses filled the air.

"I have, too." Lila leaned close to help and something in her pocket made a muted thunk against the counter. The badge. She'd completely forgotten about it. Why had he given it to her? She remembered the glinting tin star, which had been pinned to his shirt. She didn't remember watching him remove it. How odd.

"I'll take these in," Lark volunteered, seizing the platter and whisking away from the counter. "If Eunice sees you, she will find some other chore to keep you busy."

"Thank you." She had the best sister. She waited until the door had swung shut before she plucked the badge out of her pocket. It wasn't in the shape of a star. It wasn't made out of tin. It was a heavier metal in the shape of a shield.

This wasn't what he'd been wearing pinned to his chest. She squinted at it, her heart hammering. Streaks of blood coated the emblem and obscured the raised words ringing the symbol. A few steps took her to the washbasin. She dropped the badge in and reached for the soap. Two rubs and the badge shone in the sunlight slanting through the kitchen window.

Montana Territorial Range Rider, she read. The words made a banner above the rifle and horse symbol. Lila's knees went out and she collapsed into a nearby chair.

Burke was a Range Rider, a territorial lawman who answered directly to the governor. The organization was the highest arm of the law in the land. What was he doing in Angel Falls? Why was he wearing a deputy's badge on his shirt? She dried the shield with the hem of her skirt, remembering the plea in his eyes when he had pressed it into her hand. *Hide it. Promise?* he'd asked.

The door swung open. "Lila, it's the doctor."

Her stomach fell to her knees. She slipped the badge into her other skirt pocket and pushed shakily to her feet. What if it was bad news? What if Burke hadn't made it? Icy trembles spilled into her veins as she padded on wooden feet. She stumbled to the door, where the doctor spoke to Eunice.

"Deputy Hannigan is stable for now." Dr. Frost's quiet announcement made the air whoosh from Lila's lungs. Burke was alive. She gripped the edge of the door frame. Relief tripped through her.

"Although he is gravely weak." He spoke in low tones, so his words wouldn't carry to the trio of matrons seated in the parlor. That didn't stop the ladies from leaning on the edges of their seats, keen to listen in. "He is far too injured to move right now."

"What are you saying, Doctor?" Dismay wrinkled Eunice's nose. "Are you saying he has to stay here?"

"Yes. Until I'm sure his bleeding has fully stopped it is too risky to move him. He could die."

"His life is important," Lila spoke up, her voice scratchy. She was aware of the weight of the badge in her pocket as she stepped forward. "He must stay."

"Not here, he can't." The woman drew herself up to full height and set her jaw. "What would people say?"

Lila grimaced. She knew how Eunice could be. Eunice always got her way. Now what did she do to help? What should she say? She could not reveal Burke's secret, but neither could she fail to protect him.

"That hardly matters, ma'am." The doctor frowned. Genuine concern drew lines into his face. He had married recently, and love had polished away the distance and stoicism that always used to define him. "The deputy's life comes first."

"I am a practical woman, Doctor." Eunice planted her hands on her plump hips and leveled the medicine man with a look that would have undoubtedly stymied the bank robbers into retreat if she had been standing in line at the bank. "There is my husband's business to consider. Can you imagine anyone wanting to shop here with a dying man on display? They would all run down the street to our competition."

A touch of inspiration struck her. Lila straightened her spine and squared her shoulders. "He stays here. He's a servant of our town and he was injured in the line of duty. If you make the doctor move him and he dies, word will get out and it could hurt Pa's business. It could put a stain on our family reputation."

"I had not considered that." Eunice's indignation faltered. Her forehead crinkled as she pondered this new angle.

"I'll fetch some men to move him," the doctor said with quiet authority. "You will need to ready a bed for him. And, Lila? You likely saved his life."

"I did?" She shrugged, aware that Burke was still critically wounded. "I didn't do much."

"You kept a cool head in a crisis and you applied pressure to the wounds. You did a good job. I'm sure the deputy will be grateful."

"I just want him to recover." She swallowed, pleased to know she had made some small difference to the man with the bluest eyes she'd ever seen. "I read what to do in a novel."

"Then you had better just keep on reading." The doctor winked as he backtracked to the stairs. "Never know what useful things you will learn next."

"That's all you need, a reason to keep reading." Eunice shook her head as she returned to her friends. "Go fix up a pallet for that deputy in the storeroom. He's not staying upstairs in our home. When you are done there, you can clean up after him. I fear the floor will never be the same."

Nor will I, Lila thought. She grabbed Lark by the hand and ran to the linen cabinet. She intended to make Burke as comfortable as possible.

Chapter Three

The store was silent. Only one man stood vigil next to the front counter, where Burke lay as if already in death's clutches, his face white as the muslin sheet covering him. A terrible aching seized Lila as she drew nearer. He was a substantial man, dwarfing the entire counter, and yet he appeared vulnerable. Close to death. She braced her fingertips against the counter, her throat dry.

"It's good of your family to take him in." A junior deputy, Jed Black, cleared emotion from his throat and nodded toward the stairs. "Do you have a bed ready for him?"

"No. My stepmother thinks it best he stay down here." She knew how uncharitable it sounded. She crept closer, careful not to step on a squeaky floorboard although she suspected a loud sudden noise would not wake him.

The man was a powerful force, even in sleep. When she brushed her fingertips on top of his hand, his skin felt cool. Shadows bruised the angles of his face, the rest remained bloodless. His chest rose slightly, still breathing.

Lord, let it stay that way.

"You will feel better in no time," she assured him in a whisper. If only she could will strength and life into him like the heat from her touch.

"Lila!" Lark's voice echoed faintly in the stairwell. "Help!"

She tried to turn away, but it was as if a magnetic force held her in place. Tears seared her eyes when she remembered his striking blue eyes and the depth of feeling she'd seen in them, the unyielding determination not to give in to the weakness of his injuries and the strength of his character she'd sensed in their conversation. A strange honeyed sweetness swirled through her, feeling strangely like respect. It was not fair so strong a man could be this fragile. She walked backward, unable to take her gaze from him.

"Lila!" Her sister's call was muffled by the feather topper she clutched. The thick bundle of encased feather down blocked most of the girl from sight. "I found it. But I'm stuck."

"You're stepping on a corner of it. Don't move." She rushed up to scoop the half tumbling bundle and together they carried it down the last of the steps. "Thanks for finding this. I know it couldn't have been easy."

"Eunice doesn't know. I waited until she was in the kitchen getting more tea for her friends." Lark paused to glance over her shoulder. Her eyes widened with sadness. "He doesn't look as if he will be all right."

"Come." She tugged on the topper, knowing what her sister saw. Sadness gripped her. This wasn't the kind of excitement she had in mind when she'd prayed for a break in the monotony, either.

If only she could rewind time, so the deputy with the soulful blue eyes and wry smile could be whole again. But not even God would turn back time, for it marched forward, each moment giving way to the next without mercy. She shuffled into the storeroom and together they dropped the topper on the wooden pallet. A light dusting of white flour puffed upward, residue from the heavy bags she had just finished moving.

"This doesn't look too comfortable." Lark swiped brown curls from her face. "If I were hurt, I wouldn't want to lie down there."

"Don't worry, I will make it nice for him. The topper will help." She grabbed a corner and shook. The scent of mothballs wafted upward along with another puff of flour dust. When she folded it in half, the thick down made a fairly comfortable mattress. "See how I moved the pickle barrel over for a little nightstand?"

"The lamp looks homey." Lark bobbed to fetch the folded sheets from the top of the stack of fifty-pound flour sacks. "I'm going to run up and get some pillows. I'll be right back!"

She darted out of sight, hurrying earnestly, only wanting to help. Lila shook out the bottom sheet, and warm feelings of the best kind filled her up. She loved her sister.

In the store, the front door opened with a jangle of the overhead bell and heavy boots clamored across the plank boards. She tucked in a corner before whirling to peer around the doorway. The doctor had returned. The tension dug into his face and she spun away so she couldn't hear his words. She knew what the medical man was going to say. Burke was worsening.

Cast Your care upon him, Father. She shook out a top sheet, dread quaking through her.

"On three, boys." The doctor counted down, with a heave she could hear them lift the unconscious man from the front counter. Hesitant footsteps told her they carried him gingerly, careful not to jostle him.

She worked quickly to tuck in the last corner just as the men huffed and puffed in her direction. She flattened against the wall so they could squeeze by and deposit him on the makeshift bed. She'd never seen anyone so pale and still alive. Burke lay on his back, his dark hair tousled, his powerful physique motionless. She remembered his laughter—how promising and rich the sound—and his insistence that he was fine even as his life's blood streamed out of him. He was a good man, she was sure, and a good man should not die.

"What chance does he got, Doc?" Jed Black hitched up his gun belt.

"He's strong and he's young. He has that going for him." Dr. Frost appeared grim, as if he were digging for hope. "I will do my best."

"Appreciate that." Jed tipped his hat. "He hired on a bit ago, but he has helped me out of a jam a few times. He doesn't deserve two bullets to the chest."

"No one does," the doctor agreed. "Thanks for helping."

The men shuffled out mumbling their goodbyes, and the sunshine tumbling through the small window felt like shadow. An unbearable sorrow claimed her for this man she did not know.

She wanted to know him. In her favorite novels, the hero always lived. He fought bad guys, faced perils, doled out justice and lived to fight another day. Maybe a quiet, boring existence wasn't so bad after all. She was safe, she was happy, healthy and whole. Not everyone could say the same.

"Lila, if you could fetch me a chair, I would appreciate it." The doctor knelt to lay his fingertips against Burke's wrist, feeling for his pulse. "It's going to be a long day. My guess, an even longer night."

"Of course." She tore herself away, hurrying to fetch what the doctor needed, but the responsibility she carried for Burke remained, a link to him she could not explain.

Burke was hot—sweating hot. His skin burned. ̄ beaded on his forehead. A rivulet trickled do̶ of his neck, under his collar and down his s̶ felt like a desert floor, the air too swe̶

His nightclothes stuck to his damp skin, smoking in places where the fabric burned through. The pain was nothing as he felt his older sister's arms clamp around him, holding him captive and keeping him from racing into the burning shanty. Tears mingled with sweat and grit from the smoke.

"Lemme go!" he yelled, frantic, watching the orange tongues of flame rise from the kitchen window and gobble up the roofline. "Mama! Papa!"

"We can't help 'em." Ginna's tears dripped on the top of his head. Her sobs shook him, but she didn't let go. "We'll get all burned up more."

His throat was too dry to speak. The fierce heat from the fire seemed to evaporate his tears. He watched the window just like Papa said, but no one came.

"I'll get your mama and be right out," their father had promised, handing Burke through the open window and into his sister's arms. He could still hear his pa's voice in his head. "Ginna, take him into the fields and keep him there. Don't come near this house no matter what happens. You do what I tell you. Do you understand?"

"Yes, Papa." Six-year-old Ginna had sounded so brave and her bravery remained as she sat down in the soft carpet of growing wheat, taking him with her. Her iron hold did not relent. "We have to do what Papa said. We have to stay away from the fire."

"But it's burnin' 'em up!" He choked out sob after sob watching the fire shoot up into the sky. Terror and grief tore through him, trapped in his soul. The heat became unbearable and the fire consumed him. It melted the ground at his feet and burned away the memory like the dream it was, leaving him in bed gasping for the surface of consciousness like a drowning man.

"It's all right." A cold cloth covered his forehead. A gentle touch brushed the side of his face. He was still drowning, but at least he could draw in air. Lila's next words came from farther away and were not directed to him. "Does he have a fever?"

"Yes, and it's getting worse," a man's voice answered, one he dimly recognized. Not the sheriff. At least he could be relieved at that. "Ice is on its way. Fetch me some tarps. I'll need to ice him down."

"I'll hurry." Her soothing touch vanished, her sweet presence faded. The pad of her shoes and the rustle of her skirts became silence and he was drowning again, pulled back into nightmares that were not dreams at all.

"Let go, Ginna!" The fire had grown like a monster in the night. "Lemme go!"

"No. I c-can't." Sobs choked her and rocked the both of them. Overhead thunder rumbled. The hot wind gusted and stirred a whirl of red-hot ashes into the air. The roof collapsed with a mighty crack. Flames and burning debris shot up into the blackness.

"Mama." He whispered the word, knowing his mother would not be coming for him. His father would not be following her or sweeping him into his big strong arms ever again. "Papa."

Ginna finally let him go, her raw hands sliding away from his middle as she slumped sideways into the bed of wheat, overcome by tears. He stumbled onto his knees as rain began to fall in hard drops that hit the ground like hail.

Nobody came. The night ticked away, the dawn drew color on the eastern horizon and the sun rose. Finally Ginna took his hand and said kindly, the good big sister that she was, "We must go find the neighbors."

His feet felt heavy. The heat of the fire stayed with him both on his skin and in his heart. The midsummer morning was soon scorching and sweat dripped off his forehead. The sun blazed like a white-hot fire in the sky. Such a long, sad walk. Two miles away, the Dunlaps' shanty came into sight. Mrs. Dunlap glanced up from watering her garden, dropped her bucket and came running. Ginna's hand slid out of his and that was the last time he saw his sister. In this dream that was his past, he searched for her long and hard. But she was gone and he was alone.

Until a faint cold penetrated the nightmare. He heard a woman's gentle alto reading to him, her words so faint he could not distinguish them but he clung to the sound. He no longer felt lost and forgotten. For as long he could hear her voice, he was not alone.

"Lila, it is past your bedtime."

She stopped reading, marked the place on the page with her thumb and squinted through the half dark with tired eyes at her father standing in the doorway. "Can I stay up late, just this once?"

"It's not good for your health, child." Pa padded into the fall of the lamplight. He was a robust man, although some vital part of him had never recovered after her mother's death. "No, you must come to bed."

"But, Pa, I want to stay and help."

"The doctor is here." He pinched the bridge of his nose. "The deputy will be in good hands. If anything changes, I'm sure Doc Frost will let us know. Come, now. Your stepmother is very concerned about your reputation."

"As you said, the doctor is here, as well." She was loath to put down her book. She glanced at the man on the pallet and felt tethered to him in a way she didn't understand. She needed to help him. "I'm in the middle of a scene. At least let me finish the part where the Range Rider is backed into a canyon and out of bullets. Please?"

"You'll have to dangle for a bit, I'm afraid." Pa held out one hand. "Perhaps you can sneak in here when no one is looking tomorrow and read the rest of the scene for the deputy. Not that he can probably hear you."

"He can." Reluctantly, she shut the book's cover. The lamplight caressed the man on the pallet, who was fighting a fever, sweat sluicing down his face and dampening his dark hair. Earlier, when she had rejoined the doctor after the supper dishes were done, Burke had been restless, tossing and turning. After two hours of reading, her throat may be scratchy but he was resting calmly.

"I promise not to leave his side." Dr. Frost withdrew his stethoscope from his medical bag, which sat at his feet. "His fever is the main concern. If it hasn't broken by morning..."

A lump formed in her throat, making it impossible to answer. Sadly, she pushed off the stool and backed away from the foot of the pallet. Would he die in the night? She resisted the urge to smooth his tangled hair and dry the sweat beading on his granite face.

"Lila, you're dawdling." Pa stood in the hallway, waiting to close the door. "The deputy is not your responsibility."

"It feels as if he is." It took effort to force her shoes to carry her across the threshold. She took one last glance over her shoulder, surely not the last time she would see him. He lay motionless as if only a shell, but she remembered his smile and his humor. She reluctantly placed one shoe on the bottom stair. She could not explain why with each step she took up the staircase, she left a piece of herself behind.

"Pray for him," Pa advised as he closed the door tight behind her. "It's all any of us can do for him now. He's in God's hands."

"Will you pray for him, too?"

"I already have many times. I hate seeing this happen to anyone so young."

"How do you know anything about him?" She clutched her book. He was just like the hero in her favorite series of novels. Maybe that explained the quick, innocent spark of her interest in him. "He hasn't been in the store, has he?"

"Not that I remember. A while back he stopped to help me when a spoke broke on the delivery wagon." Pa ambled into the fall of light from the upstairs lamps. "At least a few of the town's other deputies would have kept on going, but he dismounted, moseyed up and took over the repair. Expert at it, too. Had the spoke jury-rigged together and back in place in half the time I had been wrestling with it."

Not only an expert marksman but he excelled at wagon repair. Burke was definitely an interesting man. Lila crept down the hallway, where light spilled from the room she shared with Lark. "He struck me as the type of man who would stop and help someone in need."

"He never wanted so much as a thanks in return. I tried buying him lunch, inviting him to a home-cooked meal, but he wouldn't have it. He keeps to himself, that one." Pa lightly tweaked Lila's nose. "You get some rest, my dear. You worked hard to help the doctor today. You showed compassion your mother would be proud of."

"Thanks, Pa." She didn't know how to explain that she'd felt drawn, as if she had no other choice. That wasn't the same as compassion, more like duty and responsibility. She felt inadequate as her father padded toward the parlor where Eunice awaited him. Eunice put down her needlework to speak to him in low tones. Lila turned away, dragging her feet down the hall. Heaviness weighed on her, exhaustion that turned her bones to lead.

"Is he any better?" Lark popped into her doorway.

"No. His fever is severe." She bit her tongue to keep from telling how concerned the doctor had been. The shadows deepened in the hallway like living things seizing her.

She could not give in to hopelessness. "I was going to pray for him again. Will you join me?"

"Yes." Lark locked her arm in Lila's and they ambled into the bedroom together.

"We surrender their spirits to the Lord." The minister's words lifted on the hot summer wind that stirred the grasses next to the open three graves.

Burke clasped his hands behind his back, bowed his head forward and squeezed his eyes shut. The images of those coffins sitting in the graves remained etched on the back of his lids. He was so sad no tears would come.

"They are in a much better place, little boy." Mrs. Dunlap rested a heavy hand on his shoulder. "Do not be sad. Think how happy they are in Heaven."

Her words did not comfort him. The sun blazed as if it were the house fire burning him up, too. He wished for Ginna's arms holding him tight around his middle. He wished for Pa's rumbling voice when he told a bedtime story and the comfort of Ma's gentle fingertips as she would clean away a swipe of dirt from his face. He wanted them back. More than anything, he wanted them back.

"Ashes to ashes, dust to dust," the minister went on, talking about things Burke did not understand.

He did not want to understand. He wiped sweat from his forehead with his sleeve. He'd never been so hot. Feelings bunched in his throat, as sharp as knives. The grief burned him up from the inside, the way the fire had burned the house. He wanted to be in Heaven, too. That's were Pa was and Ginna. He wanted his Ma. But dirt shoveled down on the coffins and he was alone.

"You are a good boy. Not a single tear." Mrs. Dunlap patted him on the top of his head. "Good, she's here. Do you see that nice lady?"

He didn't want to look, but he did. He tugged at his buttoned collar because the air was suffocating him. A lady in a black dress climbed down from a buckboard. Her hair was pulled back so tight it stretched her face. Not a speck of dust rising up from her footsteps on the street dared to settle on her skirt. She walked like a soldier, like someone who did not like little boys.

"Is this him?" She had a rough voice, like the wood Pa had split to make the kitchen table before he sanded it. "Is this the orphan?"

He did not know what an orphan was.

"Yes, poor thing." Mrs. Dunlap gave him a little push between the shoulder blades. "We would offer to keep him but we've raised our own. At our age, it would be too much."

"I understand. He's not your obligation." Stern lines kept the black dressed lady's mouth from hardly moving when she talked. "He looks small for his age."

"He took a bad case of diphtheria last year. I remember his mother feared losing him."

"The scrawny ones have a hard time being adopted." The frown lines dug deeper on either side of her mouth. "Come along, boy. I don't want any nonsense from you."

"No, ma'am." He glanced over his shoulder but Mrs. Dunlap simply nodded as if he were to go with this stranger. The minister clapped him on the shoulder and walked away. Everyone left except for the man with the shovel tossing dirt into Ma's grave.

Blistering heat scalded his eyes and felt likely to peel away his flesh. He took one step with the black dressed lady and all light faded from the sky, all color from the earth. There was only darkness as he died inside. No longer his ma's little boy, his pa's only son, his sister's baby brother, he was nothing at all.

Chapter Four

The morning felt unnaturally quiet as Lila splashed in the washbasin in the corner of the bedroom. Maybe it was the early hour, that's what she tried to tell herself as foreboding trembled through her. Outside the curtained window, no birds sang, no shadows moved, even the wind held its breath as if waiting. She knew, because she'd peeked between the closed curtains. Clouds stood ominous in the sky, heavy like black wool and pressing on the air.

"Lila!" Lark punched her pillow and groggily yawned. "What time is it?"

"It's daylight." She dropped her toothbrush into the holder, gave a final glance in the mirror, fluffed her bangs with her fingers and spun on her heels. "Don't worry, I'm done. Just be glad you're not old enough to work in the store yet."

"I wish, but Eunice doesn't trust me to." Lark yawned again, hauled the covers over her head and muttered incomprehensibly. She didn't move, drifting back to her dreams.

Lila quietly closed the door, her skirts rustling as she tiptoed down the hallway. The house was silent, the kitchen dark, the cookstove unlit. Looked like the coast was clear.

Eunice wasn't up yet to thwart her morning mission. She intended to check on Burke and nothing would stop her. Not even the terrible tight sick feeling digging deep into her stomach.

She was afraid for him. She had lain awake half the night listening for any sound that might hint to her how the deputy was doing. The doctor did not leave, no one came to assist him and the downstairs remained silent as she descended the stairs. She avoided the squeaky spots and pushed through the door into the store.

Dr. Frost stood at the front counter, rolling down his shirtsleeves, his medical bag on the floor beside him. Exhaustion lined his grim face and his shoulders slumped as if with defeat. Had Burke died? Her knees gave out and she clutched the door. Cold horror breezed though her, leaving her unable to speak.

"Lila. Good." The doctor reached for his bag. "I've got another patient to check on. Will you stay with the deputy?"

"You mean he's alive?" The words rasped out of her tight throat and her dry mouth.

"His fever broke an hour ago. The worst is over."

Thank You, Lord. Her knees felt firmer. "He lost so much blood. He will recover, won't he?"

"He's otherwise healthy and in his prime. I don't see why not." The doctor managed a small smile. "I have other patients to tend to. I won't be long. Keep watch over him, Lila, will you?"

"With my life." Her attention rolled back to Burke. She couldn't help it. Her fingers tingled as if unable to forget the memory of touching him. It was an odd sensation that was part lovely and part sweet.

The front door opened with the chime of the bell, but her attention was on the storeroom. Faint light filtered into the small hallway from the single window. A thin muslin curtain did its best to hold back the sun, but large streaks spilled onto the floor and the pickle barrels and onto the pallet. The deputy lay on his back, the sheet to his chin, breathing normally in sleep. She'd never seen a more welcome sight.

"Lila, what are you doing down here on your own with a man?" Eunice's scolding echoed in the store. Her skirts snapped as she stalked closer. "Do you have no common sense?"

"The doctor asked me to keep an eye on him." She hurried into the hall, praying her stepmother would not wake him. "He's improved. Isn't that a blessing?"

"The blessing would be having him out of this building. That is what I'm praying for." Eunice tapped her foot impatiently. "There is no chaperone here. No one to safeguard you."

"I don't need a chaperone. I don't need safeguarding." It wasn't easy keeping her frustration out of her tone. Eunice was a practical woman, something her father appreciated very much. She loved Pa and arguing with his wife would only upset him. Lila sighed. "I have work to do down here before I can open the store."

"I suppose Lark can help me in the kitchen." Eunice's gaze narrowed as if she were trying to ferret out the truth. "You will stay an appropriate distance from him, and I will come down to check on you. Don't think I won't. I won't have anyone in this town saying I didn't handle this situation properly."

"Yes'm." She thought of Pa and how it would hurt him if she was anything less than respectful to her stepmother. She bit her lip to keep silent. She thought of all the good Eunice did—kept the house, fussed over Lark, made sure the business ran smoothly. She was a great comfort to Pa's life.

"I don't want you going into the room. Do you hear me? Don't you step foot beyond the threshold as long as you are alone with him. I need your word, Lila."

"You have it." She pushed aside the misery threatening to take over.

"This is for your own good, you'll see." Pleased, Eunice smiled and patted Lila's cheek. "I'll have Lark bring down your breakfast. Don't forget about the herring barrel. I want this floor spotless before a single customer arrives."

There was no way to avoid the fish barrel. Lila sighed and went in search of the mop. She found it on the floor right where she'd left it yesterday afternoon. The sudsy water had to be changed and that would lead her to the back door. Eunice said she couldn't go inside the room so she kept her toes on this side of the threshold.

Shadows hid him. The lamp's wick was out and the muted light from the window fell across his chest but couldn't reach his face. She bit back her frustration. She needed to see him. Maybe it was her sense of responsibility returning. Yes, that had to be it. She was a very responsible sort. She had also given her word to the doctor she would watch over him. His breathing remained regular and his slumber deep. If she had the wish to lay her hand across his forehead to make sure the fever was truly gone for good, she did not take a step forward. She'd made a promise to her stepmother.

It took all her strength to tear away from the doorway. She had a floor to scrub clean, barrels to move and the front section of boardwalk to sweep. That would keep her busy and perhaps take her mind off the man.

It did not.

Burke came to consciousness slowly. First there was only shadow and a distant pain that constricted his breathing. As he surfaced, he was aware of a muslin sheet beneath him and over him, the softness of a feather pillow, the scent of pickles, herring and something he couldn't quite recognize. Cinnamon, maybe? His mind remained foggy and it took effort to try to open his eyes.

Where was he? He struggled to force his eyelids apart. Sunlight spilled through a nearby window and exploded like dynamite in his skull. He ignored the discomfort but he couldn't see much through the glare. Shelves full of canned goods, cartons and stacks of bulky sacks. He heard the scrape of a chair nearby and in the distance the muffled rattle of a wagon passing by on a street, no, a narrow alley, judging by the echoing clip-clop of a horse's hooves. He was somewhere in town. Pain radiated through him. He was hurt. His mind remained foggy. What had happened?

It was the dreams he remembered. The red ashes raining down from the sky, the flash of lightning in the storm, the dirt tumbling into his mother's grave. He could still feel Ginna's arms around him, although he hadn't been that boy in twenty years. He tried to lift his head and a sharp-edged blade of pain sliced through the dullness in his foggy brain. He exhaled sharply. Laudanum. He'd been under its effects before. This wasn't the first time he'd been shot in the line of duty.

"Burke?" He recognized the voice, soft like a melody, as gentle as a hymn, as arresting as a sonnet. Skirts rustled and a chair scraped closer this time. "Good morning, Deputy. Can you hear me?"

Lila. He remembered her. She hovered over him, burnished with the blazing light. Her green-blue eyes studied him and he could read the concern. For him. His heart thumped. It had been a long time since anyone had bothered with concern for him. He licked his lips and found them cracked. His tongue felt like sand. He tried to speak but no sound came. Just pain.

"You must be thirsty." She slipped from his view. All light bled from the room. The tap of her shoes, the rustle of her petticoats and the drip of water told him she was not far away, but he could not summon the strength to turn his head so much as an inch to find her.

Vulnerable. Defenseless. He didn't like being either. He was alone in the world, he had to keep his guards up. His pulse kicked, galloping frantically. It all came back to him. The assignment, arriving in town, holding back when he saw Cheever riding shotgun with Slim's gang. That didn't stop Cheever from shooting him. The outlaw must be still mad over his pa's death.

"Here you are." She returned, coming between him and the blinding sunshine and touched a tin cup to his lips. "Drink slowly. You can have only a few sips at a time."

The cold water wet his lips and rolled across his tongue. He swallowed, wanting to grab the cup from her and drain it dry to the last drop, but he could not summon the strength to lift his arms.

"If you keep that down, I will give you a few sips more." Cinnamon-brown braids tumbled over her shoulder and curly gossamer wisps framed her soft oval face. She had high cheekbones and a dainty nose, long dark lashes and a full rosebud mouth made for smiling or, he suspected, singing hymns in the church choir.

He'd never seen anyone so beautiful. He waited while she turned away to put down the cup, hating that she had moved out of his sight again. This wasn't like him. He knew better than to get tangled up with a woman like her.

"The doctor ran out to check on another patient and to get a bite of lunch." She returned and folded the edge of the sheet lying across his chest. Her feather-soft touch soothed him, but he could not accept it. He could not get used to it. Unaware, she gave the edge of the sheet a final pat and straightened up. She reached for something, a book, as it turned out, a paperback serial. "I was reading to you while you slept. I hope you don't mind. Dr. Frost said it might help you to hear a friendly voice."

He swallowed painfully. Air rattled in his throat and didn't sit right in his lungs. When he opened his mouth a rattle came out and not the question he needed to ask.

"Are you uncomfortable?" Concern animated her eyes, kindness resonated in her voice. Lovely crinkles tucked the porcelain smooth skin of her forehead as she set down her book. She glanced at her watch pin. "I'm afraid you can't have more laudanum for at least forty minutes more."

Frustration clawed through him. He didn't want something to cloud his judgment. What he wanted was to get back on his feet. He tried to move but nothing happened. Not a muscle flickered. The effort of trying to speak left him dizzy and nauseated. He was as weak as a kitten. He drew in a wheeze of air and listened to the oxygen rattle in his throat. He couldn't just lie around. He had a report to make. He had to be sure she kept his secret.

"Badge?" He choked on the word. It came out garbled and more of a cough than a word. White-hot pain hit him like the sharpened edge of an ax and he squeezed his eyes against the blow.

"It's upstairs tucked in my hope chest." Her skirts rustled, her petticoats whispered and the stool groaned as she shifted her weight. He forced his eyes to open wider, fighting waves of pain as she whispered, "No one will think to look for anything there. Don't worry, Marshal."

He gulped, nearly blacking out.

"Don't worry. I will keep your secret." Her rosebud lips parted into an intriguing smile as she leaned in. "I'm very good with confidences. If there's anything you need, you let me know."

"Up." That came out more as a wheeze than a word.

She shook her head. "Sorry, not even your strength of will can do that. The doctor said you are not to move an inch, not until he's sure your stitches will hold. One of the bullets lodged close to your heart and nicked a lung. Very serious."

He swallowed, fighting the adrenaline coursing through him as he thought about being stuck flat on his back. He'd wanted to be a territorial lawman since he'd been five and a trio of them had rode into town. He could still feel the frayed edges of wood against his fingers as he'd clung to the fence in the orphanage yard watching the impressive men on their powerful horses riding straight and tall in the saddle, a symbol of justice and might.

"You have caused some excitement in town." She grabbed her book to mark the page with a length of purple ribbon. "Everyone is talking about the new deputy who drew so fast, not a single person on the street saw more than a blur and your gun firing. Too bad you didn't hit anyone."

"No." A sick guilty feeling sank into his stomach. How did he tell someone as obviously good and wholesome as Lila what he really was? If she knew what he was capable of, she would never speak to him again.

"And the newspaper said you were an expert aim, so that must be a great embarrassment to you." She clutched her book with both hands.

"Yes."

"Whenever anyone talks about the infamous bank robbery, everyone will remember the quick draw and the bad aim." She shifted on the chair. "The holdup is all any of the customers talked about all morning. Apparently it was some famous outlaw gang."

"I know."

"I suppose you would. All those wanted posters tacked all over the sheriff's office." A bell faintly jingled from the other room and her chair scraped as she hopped to her feet. She set her book on the cushion. "That's a customer. I've got to go. Don't worry, I'll be back."

He didn't answer. He didn't look as if he could, poor man. The effort of waking had paled him even more. Her shoes dragged on the floor as she tripped down the hall. His gaze was like a magnet on her back trying to pull her back. Eunice had a ladies' aid meeting at the church, so there was no one to wait on the customer. She had to go.

"Lila, there you are." One of her best friends, Earlee Mills, smiled from behind the fabric counter at the far end of the store. In tow was her little brother, Edward, who pushed at a loose tooth as he studied the button display, held captive by one hand. Earlee didn't look inclined to let him go. "I heard all about the excitement. Are you all right? I saw the bullet hole right through the front window."

"It went into the counter, but all is well. I was providentially behind the counter instead of in front of it at the time." She flung her arms wide and gave Earlee a quick hug. "Oh, it's good to see you. I've missed you, all of you, so much."

"It's only been four days since church. We all saw each other then. And we have our sewing circle this week." Earlee looked sweet in a handed down blue calico dress that perfectly matched her eyes. Her hair tumbled down from her sunbonnet in golden ringlets. "Edward, remember what I told you?"

"Don't touch a thing," he repeated, pulling his fingers back just in time from a button made in the shape of a dog.

"My fault. I shouldn't have let go of you." Earlee rolled her eyes, good-natured as always and caught hold of her brother once again. "I just finished writing a letter to Meredith. That's where we're headed. The post office."

"Oh, I meant to stop by there yesterday but then all the excitement happened. At least I have something thrilling to write about. Meredith will keel over from shock, as my life is so boring." She paused, gathering up the words to tell the news about Burke, but they didn't seem to want to come.

"No, *my* life is boring," Earlee teased. "You can trade with me if you want. I'm stuck out on the farm and you are here in town, where all the action is."

"Action? Yesterday was the only action I've seen yet. Remember, if you trade lives with me, then you have to deal with Eunice."

"Oh, point taken. Think I'll keep the one I have."

"I knew you would say that." Laughing, Lila stepped behind the counter. "Did you come to get that trim you were hoping for?"

"No, I wish." Earlee glanced wistfully at the glass beneath the wooden countertop, where spools sat lined up in a long row of delicate laces, beautiful silk ribbons and colorful rickrack. "Ma needs another bottle of tonic. Her heart is troubling her again."

"I'm sorry she's ailing." Earlee's ma had suffered a severe case of small pox which had left her in a weakened state ever since. As the oldest girl, the responsibility of the children and the housework fell on Earlee's slim shoulders. Lila wished Earlee's situation could be easier. She bopped over to the medicine cabinet behind the cash drawer and sorted through the many bottles. "I'm keeping her in prayer."

"That would be a help. Thank you." Earlee cleared her

throat and attempted to be stern—and failed. "Edward, what did I just tell you?"

"I'm sorry, Earlee. I can't help it. My finger just did it all on its own. Honest." The little boy didn't look very worried about getting punished. "There's a real bullet in here."

"Stop touching it." Earlee shook her head and tugged her brother away from temptation. "Did you hear Chance Bell got winged by a bullet? It went right through the wall of the hardware store. Someone else was shot right on the bank step. One of the bank's guards. Word is that he was winged in the leg and will be all right. Ma got word through her church group to pray for the deputy who got shot twice in the chest."

"He's here." She lowered her voice, wondering if Burke could hear her or if he'd drifted back into a healing sleep. "In the storeroom."

"Here?" Earlee's eyes widened as she opened her reticule and plucked out a fifty cent piece. "Is it the really attractive deputy? The newest one? He's even more handsome than Lorenzo Davis."

"I didn't think that was even possible until I saw Burke." She blushed, glad to take the coin and make change in the drawer. It gave her something to focus on so she could pretend to herself she wasn't blushing.

"Burke?" Earlee arched one dainty eyebrow. "You're on a first-name basis with him?"

"I am. I tended to his wounds after he stumbled into the store." She dropped a dime, a nickel and two pennies onto Earlee's palm. "Don't look at me like that. I had a responsibility."

"You like him."

"He's too old for me." Twenty-four to her eighteen. Six years was a lot. He was the manliest man she'd ever met, but in a good way. A mighty way. He was just like the Range

Rider in her favorite novel series, but she couldn't tell Earlee that. "He will be strong enough to be moved soon, because Eunice is not going to let him stay here a second longer than he has to. Then I'll never see him again."

"You *do* like him." Earlee tucked away the money and gave her brother what passed for a scowl but fell far short. Edward lifted his forefinger off the wrapped butterscotch candy in the candy barrel. "What about Lorenzo?"

"Maybe I'll give up on Lorenzo." Lila ripped off a length of brown paper.

"But you've been in love with him since you were eight years old. That's a long time."

"Oh, he's never going to fall for me. I thought maybe after he forgave Fiona for ignoring him and falling in love with Ian, that he might turn his eye to me. But he's never going to, or he would have done so." That hurt, but it wasn't a surprise, either. "Things don't always work out the way you wish."

"What made you change your mind? Is it this new man? The deputy?" Earlee laid a gentle hand on her brother's shoulder.

"No." She didn't want to say anything until she was sure, but she'd spotted Lorenzo in church last Sunday watching a certain young lady with a wistful look, and that lady wasn't her or Earlee. She tied the package neatly with a string and handed it over. "I'm going to hold out for a dime-novel hero."

"Oh, I just finished reading the last book you lent me." Earlee tucked the bottle inside her reticule. "The Ranger Rider hero is utterly too-too."

"He always saves the day and he's a really good man down deep, no matter what." Fine, so she was thinking about Burke. How could she not? "I can't wait to see what comes on the train today. I'm expecting a new batch of books."

"Exciting. I can't wait, either." Earlee's smile faded as she kindly nudged her little brother away from the candy. He gazed at it with such longing. Treats like candy were not common in the Mills' house. Earlee clearly hesitated, worrying her bottom lip. "How many pieces for a penny?"

"A dozen." It was six candies, but Earlee was family to her. "Edward, did you want to pick out the pieces?"

"Really, Lila? Oh, I would!" Not expecting such a privilege, he hopped up and down with excitement. "Can I have a butterscotch one?"

"Absolutely." Lila grabbed a little striped paper bag meant just for candy and circled around the counter. "Here you go. Make your choice."

"Ma likes the peppermint balls." He bent his head to fish one of the cheerfully striped candies from the mix. "And Ramona does, too."

It took a while for Edward to pick just the right piece for everyone in his family. A customer came in and Lila waited on Lanna Wolf, who was in need of a new packet of needles. After wrapping the packet and adding the sale to the Wolf's account, Lila gave Edward an extra butterscotch candy for the road, hugged Earlee goodbye, refused the penny and dashed to the storeroom. Her patient lay asleep, a powerful man in spite of his wounds, a hint of natural color returning to his face.

Thank You, Lord, she prayed, grateful he was improving. Heroes should always recover to fight for justice another day. The door jingled, drawing her attention. It was the glass repairman come to replace the damaged pane in the front window.

Chapter Five

Earlee Mills couldn't stop her hands from shaking as she plopped onto the bench outside the post office and stared at the letter, just to make sure she hadn't imagined it. It was definitely real. She ran her fingertip over the stark hand-writing that spelled out her name. Finally, after months of waiting and believing he had given up caring about her, Finn McKaslin had sent a letter.

"Earlee." Edward popped the butterscotch out of his mouth and held it by two sticky fingers. "Can we go home now?"

"Just one minute." She tipped the letter so he couldn't make out the return address. She didn't want anyone to know about Finn. A lot of people's opinions of him had changed ever since he'd been convicted of robbing a train last summer, but she had always carried a torch for the youngest McKaslin brother. She knew he was a good man down deep. Even good men made mistakes. "Why don't you watch the horses go by for two more minutes?"

"I'm hot. I want to play in the creek." Edward gave a gap-toothed grin, which always worked on Ma.

Earlee felt her strength weakening. It wasn't easy to say

no to that cute freckled face. "I said two minutes. Is that really very long? Then we will be on our way."

"Okay." He popped the candy back into his mouth, wiped his sticky fingers on his trouser leg and turned toward the street. Fortunately a matched team of glossy black horses paraded by drawing a fashionable buggy with gleaming red wheels, which absorbed all of the boy's attention. "One day I'm gonna own me a buggy and horses like that."

"Yes, you will." She tugged a hairpin out of her coiled up braids and slit the envelope neatly open. Her fingers felt wooden and she stabbed herself in the scalp when she slipped it back into her hair. For months she'd had to accept that Finn wasn't interested in her. And why would he be? Fairy tales didn't happen to girls like her. She had to be realistic. He had only ever been in need of a pen friend, someone to help ease his loneliness.

There was a single sheet of paper and a short note in his masculine script.

Hello, Earlee,
It's been a while since I got your letter. Honestly, I didn't know if I should write you back. It's something that's been bothering me the whole time and I may as well get it off my chest. I'm being selfish writing you and looking forward to your letters. I am lonely here and unhappy, but maybe you shouldn't spend your time writing to a convict like me. That's what I am. I've come to accept it. After spending a month in solitary confinement or the pit, as we call it here, I can't be in denial any longer.

He was in a pit? Earlee tore her eyes from the letter, feeling as if she'd been struck. How horrible for him. A pleasant puff of warm breeze fanned over her face and

stirred her bangs. She was free. She had never given it
much pause before. Beauty surrounded her, bright blue sky,
dazzling sunshine and the colorful excitement of the town
street. The scent of the bakery wafted down the boardwalk,
horses strutted by, and she could go anywhere if she had
a mind to. Edward clomped over and dropped onto the
bench beside her.

"Can we go now?" he begged.

"It hasn't been a full two minutes." She tweaked his
nose gently to make him grin. The candy was tucked in the
corner of his mouth and made him look a little chipmunk.
"But I suppose I can walk and read at the same time, if you
promise to warn me before I walk into a hitching post."

"I'm good at watching for stuff!" Edward bounded onto
his feet, his boots thumping on the planks. "Hurry, Earlee!"

"I'm coming." She pushed off the bench and followed
her little brother down the boardwalk. Her attention drifted
back to Finn's letter.

> *I appreciated your description of town life and life
> on your farm. Your writing made me forget where
> I was for a few moments. That's a gift I'm grateful
> for but don't write me again.*
> *Goodbye,*
> *Finn.*

"Earlee!" Edward grabbed her elbow.

She glanced up and skidded to a stop just in time. A
teamster's loaded wagon and double team rumbled by. She
wobbled on the edge of the boardwalk, heart pounding.

Finn had said goodbye. He didn't want her to write anymore. Crushing disappointment settled like an anvil on her
chest. She remembered him as he'd been in their school
days, although he was several classes ahead of her. His

dark hair tousled by the breeze, his good-natured grin, his easygoing friendly manner that made every girl in school swoon just a little.

"We can go now." Edward tugged her forward, shaking his head disapprovingly. "Girls."

"Boys." She ruffled his hair affectionately. She tucked away Finn's letter. That was the end of that. He didn't want her as a pen friend. If this were a story she was penning, the correspondence between the hero and the heroine would be the catalyst for a great romance, one of rare love and infinite tenderness, the kind of love that would last for all time.

But real life was not like a novel. She sighed and tugged another hairpin from her topknot. She had one more letter to open. She withdrew Meredith's envelope from her pocket and carefully unfolded it, trusting Edward to keep her from tripping as she bent her head to read.

Lila plunged her hands into the warm soapy water and grabbed one of the wet garments from the bottom of the tub. A hot puff of air breezed down the alley behind the store and across her face. She thought of the deputy asleep on the other side of the wall just feet away. She could picture him perfectly. There was something incredibly decent about Burke Hannigan. Definitely hero quality.

Lord, please save him. I believe he is worth it. She wrung the excess water from his shirt and scrubbed it on the washboard for a third time, although it did no good. The bloodstain had set. What was a Range Rider doing in Angel Falls? There were few more respected or awe-inspiring professions in all of Montana Territory—at least not in her opinion. And to think he had walked right into the store and into her life. She shook out the sudsy garment and leaned over the washboard again.

A faint ring of spurs sounded alien against the background noise of traffic over on the main street and the voices murmuring from the open windows of the neighboring buildings.

"'Afternoon, missy." The warmth seemed to fade from the breeze as a shadow fell to a stop over her washtub. Sheriff Dobbs gazed down at her with his thumbs in his trouser pockets, dressed all in black, his tin star on his chest. "Is Deputy Hannigan still breathin'? Or was I right? He looked nearly dead the last time I saw him."

"His fever broke in the night, but he is still very weak."

"Then he's alive?" The sheriff seemed amused by that.

"He most certainly is." She shivered, even in the blazing heat of the day. She had never felt more aware of being alone. No one was in the alley. No dogs roaming, no kids playing kickball or chase or tag, not even persnickety Mr. Grummel from next door and his cantankerous donkey. She set her chin, determined not to be intimidated. "The doctor is sitting with Deputy Hannigan. Would you like me to fetch him for you?"

"Doc Frost is here? No, I don't like doctors." The sheriff rocked back on his heels, considering this information. He stared down the alley as if his thoughts, whatever they were, consumed him. "I came to get what belongs to the sheriff's office. Hannigan's things."

"You mean his clothes?"

"And anything you might have found in the pockets. Any papers, maybe his badge."

"His b-badge?" She lost her grip on the shirt. It tumbled out of her hands and plopped with a splash into the sudsy water.

"I don't want that to fall into the wrong hands." He tried to smile, but it fell short and looked more like a sneer.

"Of course." She shook off her hands, water dropping

into the dust as she reached into her pocket. The five-point deputy's star glinted dully in the evening light as she held it on her palm. She'd removed it from his shirt a few moments before.

"That's fine, young lady." He covered her hand with his, his touch lingered a tad too long.

Lila's stomach turned. She jerked back, her pulse thumping like a scared rabbit in her ears. Dobbs turned away, spurs singing. He stopped to look the building up and down, studying the entrance and windows before moseying on his way.

Her pulse roared through her veins and she tremored with the force of it. This was more excitement than she felt comfortable with. At least Burke's secret was still safe. She'd kept her word to him. Relieved, she dunked the clean garment in the rinse water and plunged out the soap bubbles.

She could still see the sheriff taking his time ambling down the alley. Why was Burke working as a town deputy? The question crept into her thoughts as she wrung out his shirt and caught sight of one of the bullet holes. If he was a Range Rider, shouldn't he be out riding the range, hunting down outlaws and protecting trains? Or was he conducting an investigation right here in town?

"Howdy, Lila." Mr. Grummel called out from his cart as he drove by. "Eunice has you doing laundry again?"

"It's the deputy's clothes."

"Ah, that's good work you do. That poor man. Oy." Mr. Grummel pulled back on his reins and his donkey ignored him, stepping forward in brazen disobedience. "It's a wonder the bank hasn't been robbed before this. All these villains running loose. I don't know what's wrong with the world. It wasn't like that in my day. Stop, you stubborn donkey."

Mrs. Grummel poked her head out of the next door. "Albert, is that you? Did you pick up the package from the depot like I asked you to?"

His answer was drowned out by the squeal of the Bellamy kids from across the way. Three little boys, a dog and a ball tumbled into the alley, their calls, shouts and barks echoing against the buildings like a thunderstorm. The donkey brayed in protest.

A perfectly normal afternoon. Lila hopped up the steps to the small porch, where she clipped Burke's shirt to the small clothesline. Over the sights and sounds of kickball and the Grummels' conversation, she upended the washtubs neatly and stowed them on the porch, amazed that the afternoon could still feel so normal when she no longer felt exactly safe. That feeling did not fade until long after the sheriff was gone from her sight.

"How is the deputy?" The tray rattled as Lark set it on the edge of the counter.

"Better but still weak." Lila tallied up the last of Cora Sims's purchases. The tangy comfort of chicken broth steamed into the air. "Lark, you are a dear."

"Since Eunice is still at her meeting, I thought I would bring it down and save you a few steps." Lark sidled up and stole the pencil. "Go, take care of him. I can manage this."

"But Eunice—"

"What she doesn't know won't hurt her." Lark grinned as if she knew full well how hard it was for her big sister to say no to her.

It wasn't fair, but she loved her little sister too much to argue. "Let me finish up at the fabric counter. Miss Sims is still deciding."

"I can do it." Lark rolled her eyes.

Lila went around the shelves to the corner of the store where Cora Sims fingered the new shipment of calicos.

"I love a nice cheerful calico. I'm making new curtains for my sitting room."

"This would be very lovely." Lila hefted the bolt off the rack. The cotton was fine quality and soft to the touch. She breathed in the starchy, cottony smell as she set the fabric on the cutting counter. A few tugs of the material and in unrolled with a *thump, thump*. She admired the dark blue sprays sprigged on the light yellow background. "These will be very cheerful with the sun shining through a window."

"Exactly what I thought. I need twenty yards, please." Cora glanced over her shoulder to check on her adopted daughter, Holly. "I heard there was a bit of excitement in your store yesterday."

"So, you've heard all about Deputy Hannigan?" She gave a few more big tugs on the fabric and measured it against the ruler tacked to the counter, one long yard after another. "Word travels fast."

"I hear the deputy was a hero. He was running to the scene, spotted the robber getting away and drew his gun." Cora shook her head. "I'm not sure what violent thing will happen next. Not six months ago I was nearly assaulted on the street."

"And your reticule was stolen. I remember." Lila smoothed the cotton carefully and took out the scissors, which were snatched from her hand.

"Go on," Lark sang sweetly as she pushed up to the counter. "Miss Sims, if I remember, the sheriff hardly did a thing to that man."

"If it hadn't been for the bounty on his head, I wouldn't have gotten any justice. Rafe, my fiancé, was enraged." Cora waved her fingers in a friendly goodbye. "Take good care of our deputy, Lila. Don't look so surprised. I can smell that delicious broth from here."

"Does everyone know?" she asked as she wove through the store.

"That you're sweet on the man? Probably." Cora's answer sounded amused.

"I'm not sweet on him. Not really. It's my duty to take care of him. I take my responsibilities very seriously." She gripped the tray and went up on tiptoe to give Lark one last glance. It appeared as if she were doing fine folding up the cut fabric and chatting with Cora. No need to worry, and Lark was right. What Eunice didn't know wouldn't hurt. Eunice did not see Lark as capable, but how else was the girl to prove she was able to run the store?

Burke stirred, lifting his head an inch off his pillow as she neared. Had he been waiting for her? Her heart skipped a beat in hope, but she had to be practical. He had probably heard her footsteps and smelled the chicken broth she'd made for him. He was hungry, not interested in her personally.

"You're awake again." She slipped the tray on the barrel that served as a nightstand. "You look better."

"I feel better. Still can't get up off this pillow, though."

It was good to see a hint of the man she'd first met with humor twinkling in his striking blue eyes and dimples bracketing his lean, masculine mouth. A smile tugged into the corners. She wasn't fooled. "Have you been trying to get up on your own, while I wasn't here?"

"Guilty. If I had succeeded, I would be halfway home by now, although it might have caused a stir." He paused to catch his breath. "I don't know where my clothes went."

"Your trousers are drying on the clothesline, but I'm afraid your shirt needs more work to save it."

"Maybe I could buy one from you. I saw a display of ready-made shirts in the store."

"We'll talk price once you are strong enough to stand. Until then, you are my prisoner, Deputy." She grasped the paper packet carefully so as not to spill the laudanum. "Open up."

"I knew this was coming, too." He made a face before taking the packet from her and dumping the acrid white powder onto his tongue. He seized the glass she offered and swallowed fast, but apparently not speedy enough to wash away the taste. "Bitter," he gasped, when he handed over the empty cup.

"This should help." She gave him a buttered slice of bread. His sun-browned fingers brushed hers and a jolt of sunshine spread through her as peaceful as a summer's morning. She tried to keep her gaze from noticing his ruggedly handsome and chiseled features overly much.

"Thanks." He chewed slowly, watching as she filled a spoon with the good broth. He swallowed. "Do you play nursemaid often?"

"I have some practice with it." She hoped he couldn't see the truth. She tried to tuck her emotions away and keep them out of sight. "I have a little sister, you know. Younger siblings are pesky, always needing tender love and care."

"I was the younger sibling, and something tells me you don't mind taking care of your sister so much."

"I wouldn't trade her for anything." She couldn't explain why her hand wasn't steady as she arrowed the spoon at his mouth. She grabbed the cloth napkin to hold it beneath the spoon, where a droplet of broth fell onto it. "How many older brothers and sisters do you have?"

"None."

"None?" Her frown wrinkled with confusion. But hadn't he just said he was the youngest? How could that be unless… Then realization dawned. She recognized the unspoken sorrow in his heart. She knew exactly what that loss was like. "I'm sorry."

"I had an older sister." He winced as if the pain were an old one but had never fully healed. He sipped the broth from the spoon and took his time swallowing.

"You don't have to tell me." She knew how difficult it was to talk about her ma's passing. "I understand."

"I was four years old when our house caught fire in the middle of the night." His gaze caressed her like a touch, lingering on her face. He seemed able to read her secrets written there. "A stray ember from the cookstove may have started the fire. I never really knew. All I remember is startling awake, choking on black smoke. The kitchen was roaring and glowing as if a fiery monster had been let loose in it."

"You had to have been terrified." She filled the spoon carefully, her hand steadier.

"I was. Ginna's bunk was across from mine and the fire was burning her nightgown. I couldn't see her because of the flames and the smoke. Pa took her out first, walking through the fire without thought for himself. Ma was there, too, but she couldn't make it to me. I remember her screaming in pain and telling my father to get me out first before her. So I was handed through the window to my sister and my life was spared in exchange for my parents'."

She didn't know what to say. She bowed her head, thankful at least one life had been saved in such a tragedy, although she wished there had been more. "I lost one parent to small pox. I cannot fathom losing two."

"Ginna took me into the wheat field and held me to keep me from running back into the house. She was seriously burned, it turned out fatally, but she never let go. She never complained about her own injuries. She had to have been in agony, but she walked me to the neighbor's house miles away and only when I was safe did she collapse."

"She loved you. That's a big sister's job." She remembered how curious she'd been about Burke and unsatisfied with the newspaper reporter's lack of information about him. She felt shamed, prying where only sadness dwelled. "Here, you must eat. You need to rebuild your strength."

He said nothing more as he sipped the broth from the spoon she held. Four years old. She remembered when Lark was that age, cute as a button and impossibly innocent. What an incomprehensible loss for a child so young. "Did you have other family to turn to?"

"No, I did not." His granite jaw tensed. "None that I know of, anyway."

"What happened to you afterward?" She refilled the spoon, concentrating on the task.

"It's not something I talk about often." He leaned back into the pillows, exhausted. "But I want you to know."

"You have been through enough with the fever and gunshot wounds." Concern shimmered in the swirls of green and blue of her irises when she shook her head. "No, you must not strain yourself more."

"I'm all right." His throat tightened. It had been so long since someone had been truly concerned for him. "I spent the next three years at an orphanage until I was hired out to work for room and board in the local fields for nine months out of the year."

"No one adopted you?"

No one had wanted him but he couldn't say the words, not to her. He didn't want her to think less of him. The wounds of that time had become fuzzy. He remembered the people in charge of the orphanage tried to do their best but were overwhelmed and underfunded. The families who had hired him had not been particularly kind to the small children working their fields. The boy he'd been, despairing and alone, had learned to cope. He took another sip of broth. "I came to like being on my own, and I like it now. No ties. Life is simpler this way."

"I suppose some men might agree with you." She appeared surprised at his answer and he wondered why. He wished he knew what she was thinking. "You are a lone wolf type, I suppose."

"That's me." He grinned so she wouldn't guess it wasn't by choice. "I don't settle down. Now it's your turn. Tell me about your mother."

"My ma was a lovely woman." The spoon wobbled, spilling broth onto the napkin. "Whoopsy-daisy. I am all thumbs today."

"You miss her still." He knew what that was like, yearning for those who were gone. "You tended her when she was sick."

"I did. Until the very end." The edge of the spoon bumped against his upper lip, spilling hot broth onto his chin.

"Good going, Lila." She rolled her eyes and leaned close to swipe the wet from his face. The tiny butterfly strokes of the cloth were the gentlest thing he'd known in two decades. She leaned back, folding the napkin. "Sorry about that. I get emotional about it even when I try not to be."

"It happens." He shrugged, forgetting about his injuries until the movement tugged at the torn flesh and cracked bone. He wheezed against the pain, pretending all that hurt him was the physical.

"Sometimes I think it would be easier if I never cared for anyone again." She refilled the spoon. Less unsteady this time. He slurped in the warm, tasty broth and felt stronger for it.

"That has been my conclusion," he confessed, swallowing. "Although you don't seem the type to live that way."

"I'm not. It might be easier to keep my heart safe, but I don't want to go through life with nothing to show for it. Loving someone and being loved is the only real living. Anything else is just existing, just passing time and I don't want to have to explain to God at the end of my life why I wasted all the opportunities He gave me to be loving." She dipped the spoon into the bowl, pausing thoughtfully. "If God is love, then I believe that is what we are all called to do."

"I've heard that argument before." He had a different calling and a path God had set him on. Burke envied the man who would win Lila's heart one day, who would have the right to brush those cinnamon-brown wisps from her eyes and kiss her innocent rosebud mouth. To protect her and cherish her and grow old with her in the security God meant true love to be.

Sharp, heavy footsteps pounded closer like the strike of a hammer on nails. Lila gasped, sat ramrod straight and spilled a spoonful of broth on her flowered skirt. The store owner's wife filled the doorway with flounced skirts and disapproval.

"Lila May Lawson, what are you up to?"

Chapter Six

"Eunice! I mean, Ma." Lila gulped, dismay twisting her gorgeous face as she rose from the chair. The chair scraped harshly against the wood floor. Broth sloshed over the rim of the bowl and hit his sheet with a few fragrant drops. "The doctor told me to look after him."

"There is no chaperone, and do my eyes deceive me or is Lark running the store? You left a *child* in charge of the mercantile?" The pleasantly plump woman turned most unpleasant as she snatched the bowl from Lila. "I have serious doubts about your judgment, young lady. Now back to work. I want the entire store dusted. You are to send Lark upstairs to work on her needlepoint. And don't look at me like that, or I will have a talk with your father."

"Pa?" She winced and bowed her head. "There's no need to tell Pa about this. I was only trying to do what was right."

"I will be the judge of that." Eunice Lawson marched out of sight, herding Lila ahead of her and did not look back.

Burke swallowed, wishing he could have more of the soup and hoping Lila didn't get into trouble over helping him. She'd gone out of her way to care for him and few people had done that over the years.

He leaned back into the pillow and closed his eyes, hurting more than usual. Maybe he shouldn't have spoken of the past. It was gone. Nothing, not even God, could change it and it stirred up all sorts of longing for things he'd lost and could never find again.

After what he'd done in his life, no decent woman—no good, kind and gentle woman—was going to be able to love him.

He tried not to listen to the muffled boom of Eunice Lawson's unforgiving voice through the board walls, his sympathy for Lila growing. He didn't wait long for the strike of shoes on the boards or the charge of displeasure in the air as Eunice returned.

"I will not have the town whispering with rumors and speculation behind my back." Eunice towered over him, hands on her broad hips. "All it takes is one hint of unpleasant gossip and customers stop coming in the front door. This store is my husband's livelihood and I will not jeopardize it."

"No, ma'am. I understand." He felt ages old and tired. He felt every sore and stained spot in his soul.

"I know what you are." Her gaze narrowed as if she could see those stains hidden within him. "You are a grown man, twenty-five, twenty-six years old."

"Twenty-four, ma'am." His stomach coiled tight. He knew where this conversation headed. Only one outcome stared him in the face. Sadness crept in at the thought.

"I see how you look at the girl. She is far too young for you, mister. It is time for you to go." The woman turned on her heel and did not look back. "I'll have the sheriff make other arrangements."

"No, please." He struggled onto his elbows. The room

spun. Sick dizziness swirled in his skull. "Have Jed Black take me to my boardinghouse."

"So long as you are gone today." She hesitated at the door, distaste curling her upper lip. "I see what you are, and I don't want you in this establishment an hour longer."

He collapsed onto the pillow, breathless, in pain of the type that laudanum could not ease. He stared at the ceiling, wanting to strain to hear the faint pad of Lila's footsteps in the next room or the comforting sound of her dulcet alto. But that was unwise. Eunice Lawson wasn't entirely wrong. He did feel something for Lila—what it was he didn't exactly know, but it would be best left unexamined.

He squeezed his eyes shut against the fall of sunshine through the window. He preferred the dark, he told himself, willing it to be true.

What was Eunice planning to do? Anxious, Lila carefully folded up the delicate fawn-colored lawn she'd cut off the bolt to hold for Mrs. Olaff, keeping an eye on the front door where Eunice had barreled through a few moments ago. She might be back any moment, so Lila quickly tore off a length of brown paper and wrapped the fabric.

"I don't understand why I can't run the store." Lark sighed, disappointed, as she cut off a length of white string. "It was for a few minutes. I was doing fine. I didn't make a mistake adding up the purchases or anything."

"You are very good at arithmetic," Lila encouraged. Anger beat like drumrolls at her temples but she did not wish for it to show. It would only upset Lark more. "Eunice will come to see that and then you will have my fate."

"I love the mercantile." Lark sidled close to wrap the string about the bundle and tied it up in a bow. "I can feel Ma here just like when I was little and I used to cling to her skirts when she was helping customers."

"I know." It was why she loved the fabric counter. Her mother had stood measuring calico by the yards and chatting with customers, who were her friends. Those who knew Lorraine Lawson instantly became her dear friend. She had loved everyone. Lila plucked up the package and hid it safely on the shelf behind a bulky ordering catalogue. Eunice did not have the same outlook on the family business. Lila put away the scissors. "I always feel close to Ma when I'm standing right here."

"I'm as old as you were when you started working here after school." Lark fingered an edge of yellow gingham. "Maybe if I can help out every day, Eunice could afford to start paying you."

"I doubt that will happen." She shouldered the fawn-colored bolt of material back to its place on the lower shelf.

The door swung open with a whoosh and the bell overhead rang jarringly. Eunice swept in, her shoes striking the floorboards like bullets. Silent fury reverberated from her as she focused her stern glare on Lila.

Oh, no. Her stomach dropped. She gripped the edge of the fabric shelf.

"I don't want one word from you." Eunice charged ahead, and the door whooshed open again. Two grim-faced deputies trailed in her wake. Jed Black glanced across the store, lifted his shoulders in a shrug as if to say there was nothing he could do. The deputies followed Eunice into the storeroom. Would her stepmother truly do something so uncaring?

"Eunice!" She rushed around the buttons display and past the cubicles of yarn. "We were only talking, Eunice."

The strike of her stepmother's heels on the floor did not pause. Oh, why did Pa have to be out on deliveries when this happened? Surely he could talk reason to his wife. Lila ran as fast as she dared, her skirts twisting and hampering her as she dashed into the hallway. Eunice stood with her hands on her hips and her chin set, watching the two deputies each lift one end of the pallet, but she could not see Burke. The men blocked her view of him.

She skidded to a halt. "You can't take him."

"Can't? Young lady, I can do whatever I want. The deputy goes."

"At least wait for the doctor to come back from his rounds." She went up on tiptoe, straining to see any glimpse of Burke. She saw the bumps of his feet beneath the gray blanket, but that was all. "What if he starts bleeding again?"

"That is not my lookout." Eunice did not care. This man's life did not matter to her. "Back up, girl, make room. Think of this as your own fault."

Cool fear crept beneath Lila's skin and slithered there. She fell back, stumbling until her spine hit the wall, seeing the truth in her stepmother's eyes. How could Eunice be this cold? Lila bit her bottom lip. There was nothing she could do but watch the deputies shuffle by carrying their still burden.

She watched him go by. He'd turned ashen again. The jostling must be hurting him greatly. Her chest twisted in sympathy. If only there was something she could do, some way to help him. His dark blue gaze latched onto hers. For a brief moment the closeness forged between them returned. She read his resignation before he looked past her, breaking the connection between them. Distance settled and he could have been a stranger.

That was the way of a man who wanted no ties, she realized. He was friendly enough and very charming and he had shared with her a piece of himself, but leaving was easy. Ends were expected. He had never been the one getting attached.

She was. A little piece of her heart broke as the bell over

the door jingled like a musical goodbye and he was gone from her sight. Maybe forever.

"I don't know how you could do this. Even you." Lila pushed away from the wall, tears stinging her eyes. She was too old to cry; she felt shameful at the burning she could not stop. She blinked hard, trying to will it away. What if something happened to Burke? Who would take care of him? Who could make sure he was safe and comfortable and fed? And why couldn't she stop caring about a man who did not want any ties?

"You had best set the storeroom to rights and tally up every item from the store we used on that man. He will pay the bill, or else." Eunice's set chin eased a tad. "I know you are angry with me, child, but this is for your own good."

"I am eighteen and I can decide that for myself." She stumbled down the hall, doing her best not to imagine Burke being carried through the streets of town. She grabbed an empty crate and gently placed one lamp into it to be cleaned up later and sold at a steep discount, used. Fury boiled beneath the surface, and she did her best not to let it control her. But it wasn't easy.

"It may not seem like it, but I am doing my best for you, your sister and your father." Eunice sounded strained, perhaps a little wounded, as she hesitated in the doorway. "I do not expect you to understand. That man is no good. Mark my words."

"You have a habit of judging people." A lamp shade rattled as she lifted the second lamp and settled it next to the first one. "It doesn't mean you are right."

"I am looking out for this family. I would have thought you would appreciate it." Eunice turned on her heels, pounded down the hall and disappeared into the store.

Lila closed her eyes. A verse from Ephesians flashed into her thoughts. *And be kind to one another, tender-*

*hearted and forgiving one another, even as God in Christ
forgave you.* She took the words into her heart. *Lord, help
me to think kindly of Eunice. Help me to handle things the
right way.*

That didn't stop her heart from breaking. She gathered
up her skirts and settled onto the edge of the chair, gazing down on the bare spot where Burke had lain. The half-
eaten bowl of broth sat on the small table. The dime novel
she'd read to him was on the lower shelf.

Burke may be gone, but her sense of responsibility to
him remained. She tucked the book into her pocket and
stood, clear on what she needed to do.

Nausea roiled through him like motion sickness. Burke
stared at the whitewashed walls of his room at the boardinghouse, listening to the tick of the clock he couldn't see
and hearing the sounds from the open window he could
not get up to close. On the street below, men called out,
horses clomped by and wagons rattled over the ruts in the
road. Dust wafted in along with the hot air and the even
hotter sun.

Hours had passed, judging by the process of the patch
of sunshine marching across the foot of his bed. The straw
tick was a vast improvement over the hard pallet he'd been
resting on at the mercantile, but being alone was not. He
grimaced, mad at himself. All it took was a small bit of a
woman's kindness and he missed it. What was wrong with
him? He was tougher than that. He didn't need anyone.

What he needed was a drink of water. He tried again to
lift his head off the pillow, but the dizzy sickness rocked
through him. Sweat broke out on his forehead and he collapsed the few inches onto his pillow. His tongue had
turned to sand, the inside of his mouth to sandpaper and
thirst had become a pain he could no longer ignore.

Be tougher, he told himself. Be strong. He could handle this on his own. If he rested a little more, then he could move enough to grab the dipper from the pail Jed had left by the bed.

Footsteps thudded up the stairway. A slow, heavy gait. He tried not to let hope leap into his chest. Jed had promised to come by and check on him. Not that he needed any help, but he wouldn't turn down a full dipper of cool water, either. Then he heard a silvery sound along with the footsteps.

Spurs. They rang like bells as the door squeaked open. Burke squeezed his eyes shut, gathering his strength and wondering if he had enough should he require it. His firearm was on the bureau top, too far away to do any good. He willed his heart rate to slow. He had to trust that God wouldn't send him on a mission he couldn't win.

As long as his cover wasn't blown, that is. As long as the sheriff wasn't questioning who he pretended to be, and then maybe he had a chance. He opened his eyes, aware that Dobbs watched him from inside the doorway.

"Look what the cat dragged in." The sheriff smirked. Not a whit of sympathy softened his cold gaze. Not an ounce of humanity gave life to his stony face. "I hear you got kicked out of Lawsons'. Where is your protector, now, boy?"

"Don't need one." His voiced sounded scratchy and dry.

"That's what you think." Dobbs moseyed up close. "I've been watching you for a while. I haven't made my mind up yet."

"You aren't the only one." The friction of the words in his throat made him cough. The cough drove sharp strikes of pain through his chest. Reeling, he swallowed hard. He couldn't lift his head. He hated being defenseless and weak.

Dobbs laughed, a short burst of mean. "I didn't know what to make of you. Almost didn't hire you, but when I saw you draw I thought I knew what you were."

"What's that?" His gaze slid to the right top drawer of the bureau. Five, maybe six steps away. How would he ever get that far if he should need to? He didn't dare try to lift his head from the pillow. He would conserve what little energy he had should he need it. "Who do you think I am?"

"I've been keepin' a close eye on you." Dobbs kicked the bed frame.

The shock of movement ricocheted through him like a blow. Burke clenched his teeth, determined not to let it show. Nausea gripped his stomach. His head spun slowly.

Dobbs knelt down to check under the bed and pulled out an empty satchel. He opened it and felt for anything that might be hidden in the lining. "You might be useful to me. No lawman has the kind of speed and accuracy you have. Only a man who lives and dies by his gun. A man who knows the way the world really works."

He tossed the satchel beneath the bed and stood. He opened the top left bureau drawer and pawed through the socks and handkerchiefs folded there. "When you went and missed Slim's gang not by an inch but by a mile, I knew I was right. You clearly weren't trying to stop them."

"No, I wasn't." When he'd spotted Slim's gang and his old nemesis, Cheever, his instinct had been to shoot. But he'd caught sight of Dobbs down the street, standing with his .45 holstered and his arms crossed on his chest, watching the show, and he'd realized there was more to his investigation than he'd first thought. Dobbs either knew about the robbery before it happened, or didn't mind that it did. Just in time, he swung his gun away and plugged two shots into the hitching post.

"You want to look good, be the big man in town. I see it,

but I'm top dog around here. Don't you forget your place." Dobbs slammed the drawer shut and opened the adjacent one. He moved aside the folded shirts and studied the .45. "Well, I guess there are no surprises. I'll be talking to you again soon."

Footsteps tapped gently in the hallway. Dobbs stilled, tilting his head to listen to the unmistakable rustle of a woman's petticoats.

"Burke?" A knock rapped on the door frame, and he recognized Lila's voice. "I was told by the owner to come on up—" She fell silent. He could see the hem of her pretty blue calico dress enter the room and pause. "Oh, what are you doing here, Sheriff?"

"Nothing." The laughter crept back into Dobbs's voice as he backed away from the dresser. "Just checking up on the deputy. Guess I'll keep him around for a while after all, as long as he knows his place."

Spurs chimed with every angry strike of his boots. The door smacked shut, and he was gone. Burke listened to his retreating footsteps and tension drained out of him, leaving him weaker than before. Glad that was over.

"Why does the sheriff treat you like that?" A chair scraped against the wood planks and came to a rest at his bedside.

"He's establishing dominance. It's what bullies do."

"Are you all right?" Her skirts whispered as she settled into the chair beside him.

The thoroughly feminine sound comforted him and he opened his eyes. "I'm fine."

The basket she carried made a quiet thud as it came to rest near her feet. She was a vision in light blue sprigged cotton. Gazing upon her made his injuries ache less and the shadows inside him fade. Gratitude overwhelmed him when she lifted the dipper from the pail. Inviting droplets splashed from the ladle as she leaned in, bringing it closer.

Bless her. The refreshing wetness tumbled over his cracked lips and he slurped it in. Cool water sluiced across his sandy tongue, chasing away the grittiness and trickling down his throat. The agony that had been his thirst began to recede when he took another long swallow.

He shouldn't be glad to see her. His spirit shouldn't be rejoicing that she was near. He couldn't help it. Her presence was like that cool drink of water.

"I'm tougher than I look." He watched her while she refilled the dipper. Soft cinnamon-brown wisps had come loose from her braid to frame her oval face and caress her porcelain skin.

"Will he guess who you really are?" Distress drew tiny crinkles around her green-blue eyes.

"That's not your worry, Lila." His heart could stop at her lovely innocence, if he let it. "Your stepmother isn't going to like that you're here with me."

"My stepmother doesn't need to know. I'm eighteen. I'm capable of making my own decisions." She brought the dipper to his lips again and tipped it.

He drank, grateful for the water and for her as his nurse-maid.

"What did Eunice say to you?" she asked.

"Your stepmother was only looking out for you." He let his head drop back into the pillows. Now, if only the room would quit spinning.

"She said something hurtful to you, didn't she?" The dipper clunked lightly into the pail. "She had no right to say whatever it was."

"She had every right. I never said she was wrong." He felt awkward with her here, when he didn't think she ought to be. He may as well get it over with. Sooner or later Lila would start doubting and wondering, seeing the bad that had been there all along. The bad he couldn't pray away. "I'm no good for you, Lila."

"I don't know. You seem all right to me." Her forehead crinkled adorably. She appeared a little confused by his comments but her sweet smile remained on her soft red lips. She lifted the lid of the basket she'd brought. The scents of chicken soup and buttermilk biscuits filled the air.

"I went to all the trouble of cooking for you." Dishes rattled as she uncovered them. "At least wait until you are done eating before you reject me."

"I'm not rejecting you. I'm warning you."

"Is this about the 'no ties' speech you gave me?" She carefully filled a spoon with broth. "Because I heard it. I'm not going to fall in love with you, Burke. Honestly, my heart is already taken."

"By who?"

"That's none of your business."

The spoon brushed his bottom lip and he sipped from it. The soup was hot and bracing and good. Just what his body needed. He couldn't send her away if he wanted to. He needed her and she knew it. Bless her for knowing it, bless her for coming. He had no one else.

"At least give me a hint." He swallowed, waiting for the next spoonful.

"It's not a real man so much as the idea of one." She carefully tipped the spoon against his mouth. "When my pa met my ma, he said it was true love at first sight. They were the other's best friend, missing half, soul mate. Pa said he couldn't breathe until she breathed, too."

"They were happy." He sounded surprised, as if anyone married could be.

"No, they weren't merely happy. They were joyous. That's what I want. I want a man who can be the other half to my soul, who knows my heart better than I know it myself and who is the champion of my dreams." She set the spoon in the bowl and reached for the plate of biscuits. "As you can see, that man isn't you."

"Yes. I fall far short."

"So rest easy, Deputy. I'm not setting my bonnet for you." She broke apart a buttered half of crumbly buttermilk goodness and set it on his tongue. "You are safe from the likes of me."

"Unless you lower your standards."

"I'm not interested in lowering them *that* far." She teased gently, because laughter was easier than admitting the truth. "And if no woman will ever claim your heart, I can't think I would ever be a danger to you. Unless you are not as tough as you claim."

"I'm tougher."

"Then I don't see any reason why we can't be friends." She spooned up more soup. "You seem to need one, Burke. At least until you are on your feet again."

"I suppose I can suffer through your friendship for that length of time."

"Good." She saw the glint of emotion in his midnight-blue gaze and the truth behind his words he could not admit to.

Neither could she.

Chapter Seven

Earlee couldn't get Finn's letter out of her mind. She padded through the grass, squinted into the early-morning sun and adjusted the buckets she packed. The grass felt soft beneath her bare feet and cool. The last vestiges of dawn painted the eastern horizon a faint pink. She breathed in the freshness of the grass, renewed by the night, and the hint of wild roses blooming hidden among the grasses. She savored the wide-open feeling of the prairie. She had to enjoy being outside while she could. Come September, she would be shut inside a schoolroom, if she could find a job, that is. She had a few more applications to fill out and mail.

"Good morning, Bessie." She set down the pail of fresh cold well water in front of the milk cow. Big brown eyes sparkled their appreciation and the Guernsey held out her soft brown head for a pet. Earlee obliged her with lots of strokes. "You are such a good girl. I brought you some grain, too. I know how much you like it."

In a show of affection, Bessie rubbed her poll against Earlee's skirt before diving into the grain bucket. That left only one bucket, empty, which she circled around and set beneath Bessie's full udder. She knelt to begin milking and leaned her cheek against Bessie's warm, soft side. Milk zinged into the tin pail and her mind wandered.

I'm being selfish writing you and looking forward to your letters, Finn had written. Selfish. That's how he saw it? Now that the initial devastation of his rejection had begun to fade, she could think about his words more clearly. *Maybe you shouldn't spend your time writing to a convict like me.*

Did he really think she would have begun corresponding with him if she thought it was a bad way to spend her time? It wasn't that long ago, before Finn fell in with a bad crowd, that he'd stopped to give her family a ride. He had cheerfully handed up each of the younger children into the wagon bed. He'd been kind to her sisters and brothers and respectful of Ma.

That's why she'd become smitten with him in the first place. He'd talked to her as if she were nobility and held out his hand to help her onto the wagon seat. A flash of recognition sparked in her heart when they touched. Kind was the true nature of the man, and she'd never forgotten it. Even when he'd been arrested for masterminding a train robbery, she hadn't believed it of him. He'd made the bad mistake of committing a serious crime, but to mastermind it?

"Earlee? Whatcha doin'?" Edward broke into her thoughts, his bare feet pounding through the grass. "Can I help?"

"Bessie's picket pin needs to be moved."

"I can do it!" Edward dashed off eagerly.

Bessie lifted her head from the grain bucket and mooed after the boy, apparently needing a pet from him, too.

With a smile, her thoughts returned to analyzing Finn's letter. *Your writing made me forget where I was for a few moments.* He may not want her to write him again, but he'd enjoyed her letters. He was rejecting her out of concern for her. He wasn't selfish; he cared for her.

"Earlee! Edward!" Ma called from the back doorstep. "Breakfast."

"Coming." Perfect timing. She squeezed the last of the milk into the pail and waved to her mother.

Ma waved back and disappeared into the house. Poor Ma. This morning was a good one for her. She was up and assisting Beatrice with the kitchen work, but she tired easily. Ma was so delicate. There was no way she could ever discuss this situation with her.

So, did she send him another letter? Or did she do as Finn asked? She didn't know what to do. He'd clearly penned, *don't write me again*. She gave Bessie a pat on the flank and grabbed the bucket.

"I'll be back in a bit, good girl," she told the cow and carried the heavy milk pail toward the house. Edward finished moving the picket pin and came running after her.

In the wash of early-morning sunshine, Lila knelt before the penny candy barrel and opened the little striped paper sack. "What kind do you want?" she asked the children.

"The lemon ones." Little James McKaslin didn't hesitate. "That's my favorite."

"Then we had better get a lot of those. I'll pick all the best pieces." She counted out a half dozen of the biggest lemon drops and plopped them into the bag. She loved this part of her job. "What would you like, Daisy?"

The platinum blonde little girl pondered for a moment. "The striped ones, please."

"Good choice. Those are my favorite, too." She dropped an equal amount of peppermint balls into the little bag and handed it over. The children bent over their candy, each politely taking one piece before handing the paper bag to their mother to keep for them.

"Thank you, Lila." Joanna McKaslin hugged the wrapped bundle of fabric and notions. "What time do you think your father will be by with the rest of my order?"

"Probably sometime around three." Lila leaned against the counter. "We've been busy this morning, so Pa has a lot of deliveries today. Will that be too late?"

"Not at all. I'll keep an eye out for him." Joanna opened the door and watched over her children as they padded onto the boardwalk. The sounds from the street swirled in with the dusty breeze. The ring of harnesses, the rumble of voices and the clop of horseshoes rang like pleasant music as Joanna waved goodbye and closed the door.

"You spend too much time with the customers." Eunice looked up from the ledger open on the long front counter. "This isn't a social event, it's a business. Look at all the dust those people let in."

"There's no reason not to like Mrs. McKaslin." Lila headed straight to the fabric counter to put away the bolts she'd taken down and cut for Joanna. "She's a good customer and a nice lady."

"She lived with that man before she married him." Eunice snapped the ledger shut. "I don't want a woman like that in this store."

"She *lived* next door to him. That's different than living with him." Lila did not believe Joanna was the type of lady who would do anything improper. "They are married now, so it's really not our business."

"We run a fine establishment. Our customers need to trust they will not be uncomfortable in this store." Eunice cared very much about profits. "The midmorning lull has died. Why don't you go out back and finish hanging the laundry?"

"I'll be happy to." She had been up early scrubbing the household garments, towels and sheets on the washboard and had made better progress than Eunice knew. Gladly, she shouldered the heavy bolt of candy-pink calico onto its shelf and hefted another light lavender one.

As she was setting the final bolt of light blue sprigged into place, the door chimed and Narcissa Bell paraded in with her mother. Definitely time to leave.

"Good morning, Mrs. Bell!" Eunice sailed across the store, her tone falsely bright. "Whatever can I do for you?"

Lila ignored the sneering look Narcissa sent her way and turned her back. She would never forget what Narcissa had done to try to break up Meredith and her beloved fiancé. Shane had managed to keep Meredith's heart, but it was no thanks to their archenemy. Nor would she forget the names Narcissa always called Ruby. Lila was all too happy to trip out the back door.

The sun was bright on the porch as she overturned the washtubs. Next door, Mrs. Grummel was hanging up petticoats on the clothesline strung between her porch posts.

"Pretty morning, ain't it?" the older woman asked as she clipped the last waistband. "I see you've been to your washing early to beat the heat of the morning, too. It's likely to be a hot one. Don't tell me you have another load to do."

"No. I have a break from the store." Lila extricated the basket from behind the washtub and kept it level as she hopped down the steps.

"You poor girl. If I had to work for Eunice, I would find myself another job. Take care not to get overheated." Mrs. Grummel grabbed her clothespin bag and disappeared inside her building.

Another job. That had never crossed her mind. She hurried down the alleyway, going as fast as she dared without jostling the basket. She had never pictured working anywhere else but in Pa's store, where he and Ma had once been so happy. She swallowed the lump in her throat, stepped onto the boardwalk and dodged shoppers on their way to Main Street. The train rumbled on its tracks a few blocks over, black smoke rising above the storefronts like a billowing snake. Horses stood at the hitching posts jingling their bits and watching her scurry by.

Tiny airy tingles filled her at the thought of seeing Burke again. She wondered how he'd fared through the night with no one to tend him. She crossed the street, dodged a horse-drawn milk wagon and dashed down the boardwalk on Prairie Lane. The boardinghouse was quiet. A cleaning woman mopped the floor and didn't look up as Lila headed for the stairs.

Surely the doctor would have checked on him, she thought, as she tapped her knuckles on his door. He wouldn't have been left all alone.

No answer. Should she come back later? But what if he was in need of help? He could have succumbed to a fever again and could not answer the door. Boldly, she grasped the brass knob and turned. The door squeaked open and she peered in, seeing only a small slice of the room. There was no motion or no sound from within as she poked her head in farther.

"Burke?"

The smallest groan. Concern propelled her forward to see the man grinning at her. He was sitting up!

"I was hoping that was you." Whiskers stubbled the rock-hard angle of his jaw. "The doc just left. He said I'm doing better than expected. Probably because of your superior chicken soup."

"And don't forget the biscuits." Relief made her knees shake as she glided toward him. Her gaze roamed over him hungrily taking in the important details—his improved color, the faint flush of health in his cheeks, his bright eyes. She sank onto the chair beside him. "I'm so glad. I have been praying very hard."

"For me?"

"You were the one injured, right? Of course it was for you. My sister did, too." She set her basket on her knees. "Have you had breakfast?"

"Mildred, the owner, brought me tea and toast this morning." He adjusted his pillows and leaned into them, still sitting. His dark tousled hair made him look rakish. With his shadowed jaw, he could easily be mistaken for a dangerous outlaw. "Really early this morning, as it turned out, so I'm starving."

"Good. I predict you will make a full recovery." She pulled out one wrapped item after another. "I made you two sandwiches when Eunice wasn't looking. Egg sandwiches, since I was making breakfast at the time. Do you mind?"

"Mind? It smells great." He looked eagerly at the bundle. It was good to see him improved. She sent a thankful prayer Heavenward and handed him one wrapped sandwich. His fingers brushed hers as he took it.

Just ignore the skittles of awareness tingling inside your heart from that touch, she told herself. Ignore it and she could pretend it didn't happen. She straightened her shoulders and uncorked a small jug of cool tea. "I'm leaving you some cookies my sister made yesterday. An apple. A bowl of baked beans and some slices of ham. Here's another jug full of chicken soup."

"Lila, thank you. I can't believe you did this." He took a big bite of his sandwich.

"I couldn't let you starve."

"I appreciate that." He swallowed and chased it down

with a gulp of cool tea. The liquid trailed down to his stomach. Good. "What does Eunice say about you being here?"

"Nothing, as she thinks I'm doing the rest of the laundry on the porch, but I got up extra early to do it. She's busy impressing Mrs. Bell, so she won't notice I'm gone for at least five more minutes."

"I'm a bad influence on you."

"Yes, it's all your fault for getting shot." A dimple cut into her right cheek. "You could have chosen another store to stumble into."

"Yes, but the barbershop next door didn't look as if it had bandages. I intended to patch myself up and keep trailing the bad guys."

"The ones you didn't shoot on purpose?"

"Well, yes. I wanted to make sure they didn't try to gun down an innocent citizen on the street on their way out of town." He didn't figure she could understand the reason he felt strongly about protecting others. If she knew the truth, she would bolt off the chair and sprint out the door.

"Proof you are one of the good guys." She gazed at him with admiration shining in the swirl of her green-blue eyes.

"I'm not so good." The old shame remained, regardless of how hard he tried to push it aside. "I'm just doing my job."

"You are very dedicated."

"It's what I'm called to do." It was more complicated than that, but he didn't elaborate. Frustration ate at him because Lila shouldn't be here looking after him. He wasn't her lookout, he wasn't her concern.

"See what I brought?" She pulled a book out of the basket, the edges of the cover dog-eared from wear. "I was reading this to you when you were unconscious. I thought you might want something to pass the time while you are recuperating."

"I appreciate it, but it won't be long until I'm on my feet again."

"Yes, I know. You are invincible." She tapped the book before setting it on his bedside table. "Just like any passable Western hero."

"Passable?" He held back a chuckle. Lila could make him forget who he was and make him believe in the man he could be. He felt different when he was with her.

"Sure. I don't think you can compare to the hero in the book. He's really amazing."

"He's fiction." He squinted at the book. It was the same one she'd read to him. Did he admit it was his favorite series, too? "Fiction can't compare to the real thing."

"Too bad I haven't met the real thing."

"You will know him when you see him." He laughed. His healing wounds vibrated with pain but it didn't stop him. That's what she did to him, she made his world brighter. "You're leaving so soon?"

"I'll be back with your supper whenever I can slip away. You won't be rid of me easily."

"Did you hear me complain?" His throat filled with words of gratitude he did not feel comfortable saying. He bit back anger at himself because he didn't want to rely her. He didn't want to depend on anyone. "Tomorrow I intend to be up and about to forage for myself."

"Maybe I will come anyway. Someone has to watch over you, Deputy. You have agreed to be my friend and there's no getting out of it."

"I've been in sticky situations before and have gotten out of them," he quipped.

"Yes, but not with me." She lingered by his bedside for a moment, as refreshing as a summer's morning with her lustrous hair, green calico dress and her mouth as sweet as a strawberry. Her fingertips brushed his rough jaw and cheek, the slightest of touches, the briefest of contacts but the magnitude shocked him all the way to his soul.

"Be safe, Deputy." She swirled away with a whisper of petticoats and grace, taking all the sunlight with her.

He sat as if in darkness, his sandwich in hand, listening to her faint footfalls grow fainter. He no longer felt alone.

Laundry fluttered on the clothesline as she opened the mercantile's back door and hopped into the dim hallway. Seeing him briefly wasn't enough. She missed him. She didn't want to admit it, but she did.

"I am taking a break." Eunice slapped shut the account book and wiped the pen point on the wiper. "I expect you to run the store."

"Fine."

"Do *not* leave Lark in charge." Eunice corked the ink bottle with a pointed glare.

"I won't." She wanted to get along with her stepmother, she really did. "Go upstairs and relax. It's been a busy morning. I'll take care of everything."

"Fine." Eunice pushed away from the counter, her skirts billowing, and disappeared upstairs.

"Can I take a break, too?" Lark peered through the shelving, a little pale and tired-looking.

"Go ahead. I will take over the restocking—" The door-bell interrupted her with a harsh jangle as the door flew open and banged violently against the door catch. Pa stood in the threshold, his clothes torn, his hat missing, his hair standing on end. Blood ran down one side of his face and stained his shirt and sleeve.

"Pa!" She watched in horror as her father staggered. She caught his arm as Lark scrambled to grab the other. A blur of motion on the street outside was a horse and buck-board dashing down the street. "What happened to you?"

"I'm all right." He leaned on them heavily, struggling to catch his breath. Blood streamed down the left side of his face. A purple-red bruise marred the skin of his left eye, which had swelled alarmingly. The lid could barely open. Wet blood marked his off-center nose and his bottom lip, torn and puffy. "Thad is fetching the doc. I just need to sit down."

"Sit down? You need to lie down." She couldn't believe her eyes. "Let's get you upstairs."

"I don't need pampering, girls." He extricated his arms from their clutches, a strong man determined to walk on his own. "I'm no weakling."

"No, of course not, Pa." Shock washed through her as she slowed her pace to match his. The door to upstairs seemed a mile away. Her poor father. Had the horses bolted? Had he taken a spill off the wagon?

Whatever had gone wrong, her father needed prayer. *Lord, please help him. Please take care of my father.* She tried not to imagine terrible things—a dangerous head injury, for instance.

"Pa, you didn't tell us what happened," Lark said, her face pinched with concern.

"I'm not sure you girls ought to know." He huffed heavily, as if angry. "It can be a rough world out there, and today I ran into some roughness."

"What do you mean, Pa?" Lila opened the door for him while Lark hovered in the background, her hands steepled anxiously.

"Some men jumped me." Anger made his voice harsh, something she had never heard in her life. He grasped the handrail and pulled himself up one step at a time.

"Jumped you? You mean they beat you up?" Lila couldn't believe it. How could anyone want to attack her father?

"Some men with bandanas masking their faces rode out of a gulley flashing their rifles. They told me to get down and hand over my horses and wagon." He became angrier with each step he took, panting with the intensity of his fury. "I had about ten rifles aimed at me, so I had to climb down and surrender the wagon. I didn't have any choice."

Shock trembled through her. Armed men had pointed their guns at her father? Anything could have happened. Anything. "I'm so glad you did as they asked, Pa."

"Me, too," Lark chimed in as she trailed them up the stairs. "Were they horse thieves?"

"They weren't after just the horses. They wanted the wagon, the deliveries. Everything." His wedding ring was gone, even his boots.

"Arthur!" Eunice spotted them and came running, horror stark on her face. "What happened? Lark, hurry and fetch the doctor. Lila, bring him right here onto the sofa. Oh, my poor Arthur."

"I'm all right." He wasn't a man used to attention. "Frost is on his way."

As if to prove it, a knock rapped impatiently on the door below. Without waiting for an answer, boots thudded on the stairs, echoing in the stairwell. Lila helped her father to the sofa. He looked broken, somehow, as if the attack had taken something from his soul. Her eyes stung, and anger at the thieves pounded crazily in her chest. She stepped aside to make room for the doctor.

"Thad said it was urgent." Samuel Frost set his medical bag on the floor in front of the couch. "Arthur, what did you go and do?"

"Trouble found me." More blood streamed from the gash on his head.

"I'll say, but it doesn't look too bad. I say you got off lucky, considering. Lila, fetch me some water. Lark, I'll need clean cloths and bandages. Eunice, prepare the bed. Arthur is going to need some rest when I'm through with him."

Relief shook through her, making it difficult to walk but she made it to the kitchen. She skirted the table, grabbed the water pail. Pa would be okay. That's what mattered. That's what she had to focus on. Except for the fact that her stomach rumbled with fury. What gave thieves the right to hurt innocent people, especially her pa?

Cowards, that's what they were. Ten armed men jumping one unarmed man. Doing what amused them, taking what they wanted. Her jaw clamped shut so tight, her teeth hurt. It wasn't right. It shouldn't be allowed. This time the sheriff would have to do something. If not, she knew Burke would.

"The lawlessness in this town." Eunice marched down the short hallway, muttering to herself. "I've just about had enough of it."

For once, she and Eunice were in total agreement. She set the bucket down by the doctor's side.

"Thank you, Lila." Samuel Frost took a stack of towels and bandages from Lark and dunked the corner of a cloth into the water. "First, I need to clean away this blood and see what we're dealing with. Arthur, how is your eyesight? Do you have double vision?"

"I wish I didn't."

"Any dizziness? Nausea?"

"Yes on both counts. They struck me hard, Doc. With the butt of a Winchester."

Lila briefly shut her eyes, wincing against the thought of anyone treating her father like that. She gently nudged her sister down the stairs and closed the door tightly behind them.

"Why would someone do that to Pa?" Lark whispered

shakily. The enormous space of the store echoed around them ominously. The sunshine no longer felt friendly. The world no longer felt kind.

"I don't know what makes some people behave meanly." She wished she did. She thought of Burke. A week ago his wound had seemed extraordinary, the violence of the bank robbers an anomaly. What was happening to their town? Now Pa was injured. Her dear pa.

The front door chimed and two identical little girls, the Frost twins, tromped in like a whirlwind, followed by Molly, their new stepmother.

"You stay and help them," Lark whispered, too distraught to face anyone. "I'll get more water."

She hugged her sister, wishing she knew what to do to reassure her. Wishing she knew how to reassure herself.

"I'm sorry your pa is hurt," Penelope said.

"Real sorry," Prudence added. "But our pa is a real good doctor."

"Yep, he can make him lots better," Penelope finished.

"I'm sure of it." Lila couldn't help being enchanted by the girls. They both had identical black braids and golden-hazel eyes and fine-boned porcelain faces. One twin wore a green calico dress with a matching sunbonnet while the other wore blue. "What can I get you today?"

"We were about to take Samuel to lunch when Thad McKaslin came rushing into the office. Apparently he came across your father in the road," Molly Frost explained as she laid a gentle hand on each girl's shoulder. "I promised the girls a few pieces of candy to tide them over until their father is done."

"It will be my treat." Grateful for something useful to do, she grabbed a striped paper sack from behind the counter. "What would you girls like?"

"Cinnamon!"

"Butterscotch!"

Unable to resist the double level of cuteness, Lila knelt at the barrel and dug through the candy for the best pieces of each. "How about you, Molly?"

"Just one peppermint. I insist on paying you."

"Your penny is no good here." She dropped a few peppermint balls into the sack and handed it to the closest girl. "I was going to close the store for a bit, but you are welcome to stay in here. Or there's a bench on the back porch if you two want a little fresh air and shade."

"I may steer the girls and their soon-to-be sticky fingers away from your merchandise. Thank you." Molly's gentle smile was lovely as she led her beloved stepdaughters to the back of the store.

Lila went to turn the sign from open to closed and a familiar shadow filled the doorway, tall, wide-shouldered and as awesome as a dream.

Burke. She blinked. Surely she was imagining him. He could not be here, he could not be real.

"I heard what happened." He pushed through the door, substantial flesh and bone. He did not look well. All color had drained from his face. He swayed a little on his feet but didn't topple. Breathing heavily, he planted one palm against the edge of the counter and leaned on it, obviously willing himself to stay standing.

He had come. But why? And how? "You shouldn't be up. You shouldn't be here."

"How is your father?" Concern layered the rich tones of his voice, emotion that softened the hard lines of his face and his whiskered jaw.

"He's been beaten. The doctor is with him now." Whatever it took, she could not give in to the need for comfort—for his comfort. She must not think about laying her cheek against the dependable plane of his chest. She must not wish to be enfolded safely in his strong, sheltering arms.

"Who did it?"

"He didn't say." A tiny hiccup escaped. It was a hiccup and not a sob. "This is peaceable country. I don't understand why armed men would hurt him and rob him."

"Things change and there are some folks that don't need a reason to do harm." Burke caught her hand with his, and sorrow lived there. "I promise I will do what I can to help your father."

"I know." The anger within her didn't abate, but her worries did. "Thank you. It's not right. Someone who would hurt someone else for gain is the worst sort of person."

"I agree." He gently tugged her close. His fingers curled at her nape and into her upswept hair. Nice. Soothing. Gently, he drew her against his chest and she didn't resist. She rested her cheek against his shirt and sighed when his mighty arms folded around her.

Safe. Sheltered in his arms with his jaw brushing the crown of her head, she felt safe. Drinking in his solace, she relaxed into him, listened to the reliable beat of his heart and held on tight.

Chapter Eight

You should not be holding her, Burke thought, but could he let her go? Not a chance. An emotion suspiciously like tenderness took root. She felt light and fragile in his arms. He breathed in her sweet lilac scent and listened to the quiet whisper of her breathing. He couldn't remember holding anyone since the last time his sister had held him in the wheat field. Lonely places within him ached with a razor-blade sharpness that cut him to the marrow.

He didn't deserve to hold her but he could not stop. The silken gossamer of her hair caught on his unshaven jaw and tickled his skin. The light press of her cheek to his chest tore him up. He swallowed hard, not believing he could be holding anyone so fine. That anyone so fine would want to be held by him.

Footsteps rang faintly through the store. Heavy, measured thumps. Sounded like the doctor's gait. Reluctant, Burke lifted his cheek away from her hair. When he wanted to comfort her, he had to straighten and put on his stony defenses. His fingers remained at the base of her neck and his other hand remained twined with hers. He could come to like being closer to her. Their gazes met and the dazzling wonder of her green-blue eyes filled with amazing light. Regard for him shone there undeniable and true.

He was not worthy of it. The right thing to do would be to step away and pretend he hadn't noticed her feelings for him. An honorable man would save her from the certain heartache he would bring her. A noble man would not yearn for her caring. When she stepped quietly out of his arms and unlaced her fingers from his, the bond of caring remained between them. Distance did not stop it. He wanted to gather her back in his arms and draw her to his chest. To one more time drink in the incredible and rare closeness of holding her.

It took all the honor he possessed to let her walk away.

"Dr. Frost." She hurried toward the medical man, her calico skirts swirled around her. She clutched the edge of the counter. "How is Pa?"

"I stitched up the gash in his scalp. I'm concerned about the blow he took to his skull." Dr. Frost snapped his medical bag shut. "For now, it doesn't seem serious, but if his symptoms don't improve or grow worse, send for me immediately."

"Absolutely." Her teeth dug into her bottom lip, worrying it.

Burke longed to draw her back into his arms to comfort her, but she'd moved several yards away. He wasn't sure he should try to walk with the store spinning so wildly. He let his eyes drift shut, fighting the dizziness he didn't want to admit to. *Lord, keep me standing upright. Lila needs help.*

"Deputy, I thought I told you to stay in bed." The doctor didn't sound too astonished to find him on his feet. "You won't heal right if you don't take care of yourself."

"I'm fine, Doc." He kept his eyes closed, not concerned with his own welfare. It mattered little.

The back door slapped open. Footsteps clattered, ringing in the quiet store. "Pa! Pa!" little girl voices called. "We've been waiting for you *forever!*"

"What are my girls doing here?" The doctor laughed, sounding happily surprised.

"Waiting for you," one high-noted voice informed him.

"And we're gettin' hungry," an identical voice added.

Should he risk it? he wondered. Bravely he opened one eye. The room had stopped spinning so he opened the other to see twins girls hanging on to both of the doctor's shirtsleeves. Both were cute as buttons in their braids and calico dresses.

"Thank you, Lila. We will be keeping Arthur in prayer." A kindly blonde woman waited in the bright fall of light through the open back door. When her gaze landed on her husband, she gentled. Love lit her softly, the way happy endings come in a fairy tale.

The twins dragged their father toward her and the family left together, their voices drifting after them as they discussed what to order at the diner and not to forget slices of apple pie for dessert.

Love had happened to other people. Not him. For him, love was something to lose, something that had failed to protect him from the world's harshness. He had no call for that kind of weakness in his life. So he was at a loss to explain why the echoes of the happy family lingered in his mind and why he pushed off the wall to settle his hands on Lila's shoulders.

He liked being near to her. He breathed in the faint scent of soap in her hair and the lilac sweetness that wrapped around his heart. The need to comfort her roared through him with a fury that shook his bones, violent and consuming and yet infinitely tender.

"I will find the men who hurt your father," he vowed.

He brushed one fingertip over a lock of hair curling at her nape.

"You are a good man, Burke." She swirled to face him, lifting her chin so she could look him in the eye. Admiration softened the dear contours of her face. Caring polished her delicate features and made her impossibly more beautiful to him.

An answering caring threatened to rise up, but he caught it in time. What was he doing? Who did he think he was? He couldn't feel this way for Lila. He ought to move away from her, but he couldn't. His thumb traced the dainty cut of her chin, marveling at the satin softness of her skin. His gaze slid to her soft, rosebud mouth and deeper emotions left him weak.

Step away, Hannigan, he told himself. Don't think it. You don't even have the right to dream of kissing her.

Sharp, heavy footsteps rang in the stairwell. "Lila? I need you." Eunice's irritation sharpened her words and rang down the stairs and into the store with impressive force. *"Now."*

"I'm coming," she promised, but she didn't move away. She didn't break the connection of his touch. She had to feel this, too. Was she as vulnerable as he?

"I need to help with my pa's care, now that the doctor has gone." She didn't need to explain. He already knew she had to go. Was she lingering just to stay close to him?

He did not have the right to hope for that, too.

"Tell me. What can I do for you?" he asked with honest concern.

"You can try taking care of yourself for a change." She laid the flat of her hand against his jaw. "Go back to bed. Rest."

"No. Me? I'm fine."

"You can hardly stand up." The rough, masculine texture felt wonderful against her palm. He was substantial and tough and he'd come to comfort her. He'd vowed to find whoever did this to her pa. Impossible not to like him even more. "I worry about you, Burke."

"No need." His baritone rumbled gruffly, as if he were too tough to need a mere woman's concern, but she wasn't fooled. Something hid deeper in his voice, something she could not hear, only feel.

She knew no one had truly worried over him in a long, long time. She was glad to be the one who did. In truth, she could not stop it. An endless supply of caring welled up from within her and she knew better than to examine it. If she were falling in love with anyone, then it could not be with Burke Hannigan. He had made that perfectly clear.

That didn't mean she couldn't take care of him. "Why don't you sit down? I'll drive you to the boardinghouse."

"Sure, but weren't your horses and wagon stolen?"

"We have another team. Driving horses for the family buggy, and Pa keeps a second wagon in case the first needs repairs." She looped her arm through his. She held her anger at the thieves and her caring for Burke in check. "Don't look at me like that. I'm a very good driver."

"I've seen a lot of women drivers, and experience has taught me to expect the worst." Humor looked good on him.

Too good. She had to be practical, businesslike and casual. She had to act as if she wasn't remembering how he'd held her in his arms. As if she couldn't remember in the least the joyous comfort of being enfolded against his chest.

She pointed to the back door. "There's a comfortable bench on the porch. It's shady this time of day and a nice place to relax. Go sit."

"What did I tell you when we met? I don't like bossy

women." He probably thought he could divert her with his incredible handsomeness and humor.

Not going to work. "Life is full of hardship and take-charge women. How sad for you."

"At least I'm getting a little sympathy," he quipped. "It might help my spinning head."

"Sit, and don't even think about getting up." She couldn't resist taking his arm and steering him in the correct direction. "Promise me you will rest?"

"I make no promises. Go to your father. You will worry less when you see him all patched up and looking better." He brushed the curls from her eyes but he didn't move to the back door.

She couldn't force her feet toward the stairs. She was anchored to him like a ship to the shore. Time halted, the demands of life melted away until there was only the kindness luminous in his midnight-blue eyes and the synchrony of their hearts.

"Lila!" Eunice called, her annoyance echoing down the stairwell like a thunderclap. "Do not make me call for you again."

"Go." He withdrew first. It was like being torn apart. His features pinched as if he were in agony, too. His tender silence said what words did not.

Her heart rolled over, touched beyond measure. The silence of true feeling remained with her as she shuffled forward, loath to leave the man she would not, could not love.

"I don't know what to do about the deliveries." Pa sat up, his frustration palpable as Eunice rushed to plump his pillows. His wounds didn't look nearly as serious with the blood cleansed from his face, his nose straightened and his gash stitched. He appeared almost like his old self. "Our customers have been so good to us. I don't want to leave them without their groceries for supper."

"It is a worry," Eunice agreed. "Lie back, Arthur. You are going to follow the doctor's orders if I have to force you to do it."

"All right, Eunice." Pa patted his wife's hand, patient as always. The doctor was right. Pa wasn't badly injured. In a few days, he would almost be as good as new. "I wasn't thinking of taking the wagon out myself, but someone has to."

"I can." This was her chance to help her father. He'd had a very bad day. The last thing he should worry about was losing business, after losing his horses, wagon and merchandise. Lila took the tray Lark carried into the room. "I know how to drive, and it wouldn't take me long to redo the morning's orders and to pack up the afternoon deliveries."

"That's not going to happen." Eunice jerked the tray from her, still terribly upset and trying hard to please Pa. It must be difficult being the second wife, the necessary and convenient woman a bereaving widower had married when he hadn't loved her. Lila settled on the foot of the bed.

"No." Pa's eyebrows furrowed together. "I won't have it. Those bandits are still out there."

"We could hire someone." Eunice set the tray on the bedside table with a clatter. "I hate to have such an expense, but you are right, Arthur. We can't disappoint our customers. We don't want to lose their business."

"Which is why I should go." She leaned against the foot post. "Let me, Pa. Please?"

"I'm not sure." He rubbed his forehead, as if he had a raging headache and thinking was difficult.

"Then at least let me do the deliveries in town." She used to ride along with him when she was a little girl. "I know how it's done. Nothing will happen to me with so many people out and about on the streets."

"I don't like my daughter doing a man's work." He relaxed into his pillows. His black eye, bandaged nose and puffy lip made him look bedraggled, but he was still his patient self. He thought a moment and nodded, a sign he was about to relent. "What do you think, Eunice?"

"Who will run the store? I can't leave your side, Arthur. The doctor said you have a concussion and need to be watched. I won't risk your health."

"Lark can do it." Lila spoke fast before her father could frown and her stepmother could object. "She's never made a mistake so far when she's helped in the store. If she feels overwhelmed or needs help, then she can call up to you, Eunice. Otherwise, you will have to hire someone or close the store. Neither is good for profits."

She waited breathlessly, praying a one word prayer. *Please, please, please.* She hoped the Lord was listening. She wanted to do this for her father. To take one burden off his mind.

"Yes, if Lark would like to." Pa held up one hand when Eunice protested. "It's only for an afternoon."

The rapid sound of thuds came from the kitchen down the hall. Lila could imagine Lark hopping up and down with glee. She must have been able to overhear the conversation.

"Thank you, Pa. You won't regret it." Lila launched forward to carefully kiss his cheek. She did not want to jar his poor head, since he had to be in more pain than he was admitting. "I'll start filling the orders."

"Tell your sister to run and tell one of the Dane brothers to bring the spare wagon and our buggy team by." Pa managed a one-sided grin. "Lila, you are quite a young woman. It's good to know I can count on you."

"It's good to be counted on." She squeezed his hand before she left. Lark waited for her in the hallway, skipping in place with joy.

"I'll run to the livery straightaway." She hurriedly tied the strings of her sunbonnet. "I promise I won't let Pa down. He's counting on me, too."

"Yes, he is." She opened the door for her little sister. Her not-so-little sister, these days. Lark stood tall and slender, looking ladylike as she remembered not to run down the stairs. Halfway down she slowed and walked gracefully, so like their ma it put a lump in Lila's throat.

Now that one wounded man was tended to, there was another one to deal with. While her little sister went out the front door, Lila trailed out the back. She pushed open the screen door and poked her head around the door frame. Was he still there? The sight of Burke sitting with his eyes closed surprised her. He was snoozing. She resisted the urge to remove his hat, lie him down on the bench and find a pillow for his head. Doing those things would wake him, and he looked like a man who needed a nap.

What had it cost him to climb out of bed? He was barely strong enough to sit up, and yet he'd walked here to comfort her, regardless of the pain he had to be in. He'd done that for her.

Don't read too much into it, she warned herself. She spun on her heels and quietly closed the screen door. Maybe Burke would do the same for anyone he knew. Maybe he was simply being a good friend. He *was* a Range Rider, after all, a man of exemplary honor.

The instant she waltzed into the storeroom, she spotted one of the new crates that had just come in on the morning train, the top off, showing a handful of titles from their latest book order. She let her fingertips rest on the spine of one volume of her favorite series. She had already plucked her copy of the newest installment and it was waiting for her upstairs on her nightstand. The character in the books would definitely push himself beyond all limits just to be helpful. But it seemed to her in comparison that Burke's caring toward her went beyond an employee's devotion to his job.

Didn't she just tell herself not to read too much into his actions? The man had an impossible hold on her, but one thing was sure. He was a very, very good man.

She grabbed an empty crate and filled the first order, humming.

He'd just turned fifteen at the start of summer. In the hot evening sun, Burke situated the old gun against his shoulder and ignored the sting of the morning's beating that had broken the skin on his back. He concentrated on lining up the notch on the barrel with the five-inch piece of scrap two-by-four sitting on top of the stump.

"How long are you gonna stay with them folks?" Olly talked around a plug of tobacco.

"You mean the farmer and his wife? 'Til the end of the harvest." Harvest felt like a long time away.

"Do you like stayin' with 'em?"

"No, but I've stayed with worse. Much worse." Burke let the kiss of the late-July breeze ruffle his hair and tug at his battered hat brim. It waved through the seed-heavy tips of the wild grasses and sent daisies to nodding as he let out a breath, fastened his gaze on his target and squeezed the trigger. The old rifle let out a ringing blast and a burst of fire. The lead bullet thudded into the wood and set it flying into the grass. Bull's-eye. He shrugged. "Got nowhere else to go but the orphanage. If I go back now, they'll just find me some other farm to work."

"You ought to strike out on your own." Olly spat juice

into the grass as he chased down the chunk of wood. He held it up in the air. "Dead center. Don't no one shoots like you do."

"It's not like it can do me any good." He stood the rifle upright on its butt and poured gunpowder down the barrel—just enough, not too much. "It's not like I can earn a living at it."

"Sure you can."

"Me? No. I wish." The plug of tobacco Olly had given him soured his mouth and made his stomach sick-feeling. It was hard talking around a wad stuck into his cheek, so he spit the whole thing into the grass, hoping his buddy wouldn't notice. They'd met at the swimming hole back in April, where Burke had come to wash off the grime from long days of sowing oats, wheat and corn. They'd been fast friends ever since in what little spare time Burke had. He gave the barrel a shake and a tap.

"My pa does." Olly set another chunk of wood on the stump. He carried his polished Winchester carelessly, as if he was used to packing a firearm, a man of the world.

"Is he some kind of gunslinger?" Burke fed a bullet into the muzzle and used the ramrod to push it deep into the barrel.

"You could say that." Olly kicked at daisies and sent their heads flying into the grass as he made his way back from the stump. "See if you can shoot that one dead center."

The chunk was smaller, maybe three inches. A challenge. "You're on." Burke raised the hammer, slid a cap over the hollow pin. He settled the rifle against his shoulder and carefully sited.

A rattle of a wagon bouncing over road ruts startled him awake. Burke blinked. The bright memory of the dream broke apart and faded like smoke as one of the brothers who ran the livery stable pulled a pretty pair of quick-stepping bays to a stop.

"Whoa, there." Walton Dane climbed down. "Deputy, you have been the talk of the town, at least until today. Now poor Arthur is. A shame what's happening to a peaceful place like this. Some say it's the railroad's fault."

"Others might say it's man's fault." Burke tried to boost himself off the bench seat, but nothing happened. He swept off his hat, rested his back against the cool brick wall and breathed in enough air to make his head stop swimming. "Doing wrong is a man's choice."

"We didn't used to see many men like that in these parts." Walton paraded onto the porch. "Now we've got 'em on the town's payroll."

Hard to miss the venom in Dane's words. He tried to stand again and he made it off the bench. He broke out in a weak, cold sweat.

"You had better watch yourself, Deputy." Dane yanked open the screen door. "Folks are hoppin' mad about the sheriff. One day they just might run him out of town. That might go for you, too."

"No one is running me anywhere." He hated the physical weakness trembling through him when he needed to be strong. He had a job to do, a sheriff to stop.

"We'll see." Dane shouldered through the door, leaving behind an air of disdain that was hard to ignore.

Folks were starting to think he was in league with the sheriff. He couldn't let it bother him. He wouldn't be a good Rider if he didn't. He did his best to ignore the pain slicing through his ribs, maneuvered forward and made it to the screen door.

"Coming through!" Lila sang in her dulcet alto, three crates stacked high in her arms. She peered over the top of a small bag of flour. "Go wait for me in the wagon. I'm taking you home, mister."

"Is that so?" He manhandled the crates from her so smoothly, she didn't have time to protest. Too bad his wounds didn't have time to hurt. Humor made the pain matter less. "Remember, I don't take orders from a woman."

"You must be getting used to it by now. Give me back my crates."

"Not a chance, sweetheart." The light drained from his eyes as he took the first step off the porch. It hurt so much. He stumbled into the alley blindly and gave thanks when his vision cleared. He hoped Lila couldn't see his knees shake or hear the groan of keen-edged pain he did his best to bite back. So far so good. He wasn't bleeding or lying on the ground, so he gathered every scrap of willpower he possessed and hefted the crates up into the wagon bed and lost his eyesight again.

"Move aside, Deputy." Dane returned, carrying a stack of six and plopped the boxes down like they weighed nothing at all. "Lila, do you want a hand up? I'll get the rest of the orders."

"I can climb up myself, thanks." She waltzed up next to him in the shade of the wagon, her presence restoring his vision and easing his pain. She tied her sunbonnet ribbons into a bow beneath her chin. "Time to get you home, Deputy."

"Home? No. I'm staying with you." The need to protect her rose up fiercely within him, greater than any pain and mightier than any weakness. "I intend to keep you safe."

"Unnecessary. I'm perfectly safe if I stay in town."

"You never know what might befall you." He grabbed hold of the side of the wagon to keep steady. "It's better to be safe than sorry."

"What if I'm a risk-taker? What if I like to let the winds blow where they may?" She swung up onto the wagon seat before he could help her.

Sunshine slanted into his eyes and outlined her with blazing gold, and against the bold blue sky she could have been a dream he had wished into his life. Emotion choked him as he followed her shakily onto the seat. "That's risky talk for a fabric counter clerk. I think you need me."

"I need you?" She tugged up the brim of her sunbonnet. The sage-green color brought out the luster of her bright hair and the compelling green in her irises. She arched one slender eyebrow. "You are entirely wrong, Deputy. It's you who needs me. I fed you, remember?"

"I do. I'm grateful. You are a good cook." His throat felt doubly thick. The words sounded clumsy as he reached for the reins.

"I saw that wince. Burke, I don't want you to strain yourself. You could have died from your wounds." Her hand settled lightly on his arm. All humor faded as she searched his face. Honest caring radiated from her, the most beautiful thing he'd ever known.

All he wanted was to have her gaze upon him with caring and kindness for the rest of his days. If he could have her, then he would cherish her with all the might he possessed.

He could never be worthy. He waited for Dane to latch the tailgate before he snapped the reins. "I'm too tough to die."

"That's your opinion. I have a different one. Since it's a free country, I'm going to keep it. You won't change my mind."

"If only I were strong enough to try." He did his best not to fall off the seat. He had a hard time focusing on the alley ahead. He kept the horses walking slow and hoped his dizziness would fade. "I can be stubborn, too. I'm going to do my job. You won't stop me."

"Your job? Driving my father's delivery wagon is your job?"

"Close enough. While I'm laid up and no use to the town, I may as well spend my time protecting ladies and their wagons when I can." He hoped she could not guess why his voice sounded strained or why he could not look at her as he chirruped to the horses to keep them walking.

"Yes, I'm glad you can make yourself useful," she said lightly. "As long as you don't fall off the wagon seat."

"I'm getting the swing of driving while dizzy."

"There ought to be a law about that."

"I'll be sure and take it up with the sheriff."

The back stoops and windows of the alleys passed in a blur. He was able to focus enough to see a donkey pulling a cart turn off Main and head in their direction.

"Lila!" Mr. Grummel called as he approached. "I heard about your father. Oy. At least you have the deputy beauing you. Smart girl."

"It's nothing like that, Mr. Grummel!" Lila explained, but the older man held up his hand to wave off her words, chuckling. She frowned. "Some people leap to the oddest conclusions."

"That they do." He eased the horses to a halt at the intersection. When Lila smiled up at him, it made him forget about the past, leaving only the here and now where there was no reason he couldn't care about her, no reason they couldn't be more than friends.

Chapter Nine

❧

"I'm sorry this is so late." Lila handed over the last crate on the daily order. The prairie winds pleasantly swirled her skirts and ruffled the tendrils that had worked their way out of her braided up-knot.

"I'm surprised you were able to make it at all." Joanna McKaslin took the crate gladly. "After my husband heard what happened to your father, he planned on driving into town tomorrow to fetch the order. Is it safe for you to be driving on the roads alone?"

"I'm not alone." For the thirteenth time that afternoon she gestured toward the wagon seat where Burke sat holding the reins. The breeze ruffled the ends of his dark hair. Dressed in black, his face shaded by the dark brim of his Stetson, he could have been any woman's dream come true. Not that she was dreaming.

Fine, she was dreaming, but only a little bit.

"He insisted on coming along with me. Since I couldn't get rid of him, I decided to make the out-of-town deliveries, too," she explained, praying she wasn't blushing.

"Deputy Hannigan." Joanna smiled her approval. "I don't pay any attention what some folks have been saying about him. I'll never forget how he stopped to help us in town last month. James had been stung by a bee and the deputy went to the trouble of asking the clerk in the nearest shop to make a poultice for him to take the pain away. That man has a kind heart."

"Yes, he does." He also had a stalwart spirit—or a stubborn one, depending on how you wanted to look at it. He'd insisted on driving through town, patiently negotiating traffic and residential streets although he looked ready to tumble off the seat. Would he admit he was in pain?

Never. She watched him like a hawk, but she'd only caught the tiniest grimace twice. He'd blithely talked her into the out-of-town deliveries, since he was armed and he didn't figure any robbers would want to raise trouble with the town's deputy. He sat powerfully, as if not a thing was wrong with him, but she knew better.

"Have a nice evening, Joanna."

"You, too, Lila. My family is keeping your father in prayer."

"Thank you so much." She crossed the shady covered porch and hopped onto the sun-blasted pathway flanked by flowers blooming merrily in boarder beds. Bees buzzed and the distant sound of children's laughter came from somewhere behind the house.

Burke held out his hand to help her into the wagon. Maybe he did look a little better. The fresh air may have done him some good. She plopped onto the seat next to him and arranged her skirts. The dappled shade overhead was refreshing. She could not admit to herself it might be the company.

"That was the last delivery." He snapped the reins. "The next stop, home?"

"Are you anxious to be rid of me?" She tugged at her sunbonnet as the matched bays plodded forward. The wagon rattled and lumbered along the dusty driveway toward the country road, bouncing her on the seat. She pushed her bonnet off her head and let it dangle by the strings down her back. The breeze fanned her face and her hair. Much better.

"Yes, I am anxious to be rid of you, but you already know that." Humor hooked the corner of his mouth, betraying his real feelings. "I'm a lone wolf. Spending an entire afternoon with a lady is more than I can do."

"You need toughening up, Deputy." She knelt down to unbutton her right shoe. "Maybe I can help you with that."

"Do I look like I need help?" The hook of his grin widened. "I'm too tough for that."

"Good, because your afternoon with me is not over yet." She loosened her shoelaces.

"What does that mean? That was the last stop."

"I packed a few snacks when I was crating the orders." She slid her foot out of her shoe. Her summer weight stocking felt too hot, so she shucked it off. "Why don't you take the next right when we hit the road to town?"

"Are you going to leave that off? Because if you are, I don't think it's decent that I see your bare feet. Your stepmother might come after me with a broom."

"It's just my feet, and besides, didn't you just say you were tough?"

"There's tough and then there's stupid. Put your shoe back on."

"No, I'm dying in this heat. The thermometer at the bank said it was ninety-five when we were in town last. It's gotten much hotter since." She bent to undo her other shoe. She didn't list the reasons why she was so uncomfortable. Her corset bound her tightly, a layer of clothing she could not take off. Her petticoats were the lightest cotton, but also added to her discomfort. Did her feet have to be hot, too? "Just don't look."

"I'll try to restrain myself." He chuckled as he reined the horses onto the main stretch of road, desolate and dusty this time of day. "But if your stepmother finds out, I'm blaming you."

"Much better." She tugged off her other shoe and wiggled her toes. "Turn right up there. It's not a driveway, but the wagon won't tip over."

"You've been here before?"

"It's the best spot to wade the river in the entire county."

Tall grasses gave glimpses of old wagon tracks as they danced and swayed. He urged the horses off the road and onto the bumpy ground. The wagon wheels lurched over clumps of bunch grass as the horses picked up their gait. Rich shade beckoned beneath the arching rustle of old cottonwoods and the lush grass looked invitingly cool. The music of the river sang above all the other sounds. Sunshine on water glinted with promise.

It was hard to believe strife could happen anywhere in the world with beauty like this, hard to believe Slim's gang and Cheever lurked in this peaceful prairie valley. He knew they were probably behind the attack on Lila's father. They hadn't gotten away with a lot of money from the bank, and they had to eat. The delivery wagon was full of groceries and supplies. His promise to her weighed heavily on him. He would catch Slim and Cheever. Arthur Lawson deserved justice.

Lila hopped from the seat, not bothering to wait for his assistance. He suspected his tough act hadn't fooled her nearly enough. She knew he was in pain. She was a dear sight as she landed with her bare feet crunching in the grass. She reached up, arms slim and elegant and plucked the pins out of her hair. The coil of her long braid came loose and slid down her back. She tossed her head innocently, lifting her face to take in the kiss of the cooler wind off the river's surface. Her thick lashes brushed her ivory skin as she closed her eyes briefly, savoring the sensation of the wind.

His pulse tumbled. He lost the ability to think. He forgot how to breathe. Never had there been a more arresting sight. He memorized the moment, the curve of her cheek, the faint smile on her lips and how alive she was, crowned by the sunny sky and surrounded by daisies. One day far in the future he would want to remember this moment, remember her.

He stumbled down and tied the horses, unable to look away. He laid his hand on the grip of his .45 tucked in the waistband at his back. The trouble had happened far out of town, nowhere near here, but he could keep her safe. In a blink, he would lay down his life to protect her, his Lila, as sweet as the wildflowers brushing at her skirts.

"This way." She circled around a thistle flower where a big honey bee drank and skirted in the other direction to avoid the crown of a gopher hole. A jackrabbit darted through the foliage, terrified by the invader in a calico dress. Across the span of the river a doe lifted her head from grazing to stare at them warily.

"Divine." She sank both feet into the clear water, holding her skirt safely out of the water with both hands. "Oh, it's so cool. You have to feel this."

"I haven't gone wading since I was fifteen years old." The summer his life had gone from miserable to worse. The summer he'd grown up in a hurry. He'd lost more than his innocence that year, things he'd never been able to get back. "Kids play in the river."

"Don't you dare call me a kid." She flicked one long braid behind her shoulder and lifted her skirts higher. The snowy white lace edging her petticoats flashed against the silvery water's surface. "You are far too much of a stick-in-the-mud for your own good. Always playing the hero."

"Hero? Hardly. Maybe I'm the villain. You just don't know it." It was the truth and he held his breath. What would she say? Would she believe him?

"A villain? I don't think so."

Maybe she couldn't see it now, but she would. He sank onto a nearby boulder at the grassy edge. Eventually she would be able to see the real man he was. He couldn't hide it forever.

"I know what you are, Burke Hannigan." Water sparkled around her. She marched toward him, splashing rainbow droplets with every step. "You are in danger of suffering heat sickness. A little fun isn't going to hurt you."

"It might. You never know. I'm not used to frivolity."

"Yes, but something tells me you aren't opposed to it." She knelt at his feet and untied his boots. "At least give it a try. Since you are on leave from work, what else do you have to do?"

"Riding shotgun with you isn't as easy as a man might guess." He resisted the syrupy feelings gathering deep inside. "I can untie my own boots."

"Let me do it." She tugged on the second pair of laces and they fell free. "I don't want you to bend over too far and tear your stitches."

"My stitches are fine."

"I know." Mesmerizing tendrils tumbled forward to shield her face. Her affection warmed the air like summer and it made forgotten seeds take root within him. An answering affection he had no right to took root along with wishes he had no chance at.

She tugged off his boots and then his socks. He should stop her but he couldn't. He could not turn down her care and her closeness. When she rolled up his trousers to his knees with ladylike tugs on the fabric, he did his best to hold back his heart. He truly did. It fell anyway.

She cared for him. It was not right, it would not last, but for this moment he could not reject it. He needed it more than air to breathe, more than any sustenance. When she offered her hand to help him up, it was more that she offered. More that he accepted.

"You have gone gray again." She slid her arm around his back, as if to support some of his weight.

She probably had no notion what that meant to him, how she stole a piece of him. He didn't need to lean on her, he was too proud and independent to do it now that he was back on his feet, but he loved her for it. He loved her.

"The rocks are a little slippery and the water is—"

"Cold," he supplied, startled by the icy bite of the current. The wetness sluiced over his toes and lapped around his ankles. The gray stone river rocks bit into his soles, but she was right. He cooled down ten degrees. He grabbed the brim of his hat and tossed it into the grass.

"There's a boulder over there." She pulled him upstream into the tug of the current. Silt clouded upward like dust with every footstep. "I'll get you sitting down and then I'll fetch the treats from the wagon."

"You have been spending too much time with your stepmother." He grabbed hold of her braid and tugged, gently, before draping his arm around her shoulder. Not to lean on her, but to draw her close to his side. Being with her was nicer than anything he'd ever known. "You are not in charge here."

"Oh, and you are?" She planted her feet, forgot about her skirts and they dropped into the rushing water. Not that she noticed. "Because you are the man, I suppose?"

"Why? You act like that's the wrong answer. Of course I'm in charge because I'm the man."

"I can't believe my ears." Mirth made her eyes twinkle like emeralds. "The hero in the Range Rider books would never say something like that."

"I'm no hero," he protested lightly.

"But you have your passable moments. This isn't one of them. I think I've discovered the reason why you are a lone wolf. No one woman would have you."

"Yes. You've stumbled on the truth." His foot slipped on a stone, and he was glad she was there to steady him. He hated the weakness that left him shaky as he eased onto the sunny rock. Water gurgled around him and to his left the river spanned wide and dangerous. But here, in the dappled shade of the cottonwoods with both the horses and the country road in sight, Lila was safe. He could relax and let his guards slide down. "No woman has ever wanted me."

"I'm not at all surprised." She towered above him, blocking the sun, lithe and willowy and full of life and beauty. "The article in the newspaper warned you were not about to be caught by any lady in this town. Pete, who owns the paper, wasn't kidding."

"I get that everywhere I go. If there's a town newspaper they want to know if I'm single and willing." He raked a hand through his hair.

"But you're too much of a lone wolf." She waded away from him, her skirt hem floating in the water. "Haven't you been tempted even once?"

"Once." The truth rolled out, impossible to stop.

"Ooh, now I have to know more." She bounded up the bank, her alto bobbing on the breezes. "What was her name?"

"Sorry, but that's on a need-to-know basis."

"And don't I need to know?" She swirled through the daisies and went up on tiptoe to lug a few items from beneath the wagon seat. "I'm curious about the woman who could bring down your defenses."

"She is quite amazing." He leaned forward to dip his finger into the cold water. "I have never met anyone like her before."

"Do tell. I'm listening." She splashed into the glinting water, startling a dragonfly hovering nearby. Her skirts billowed around her as the current tugged and flowed. "Did she steal your heart?"

"As close as anyone has ever come," he confessed.

"Not that you would release it completely, ever really let anyone in." With a small basket hooked over one arm, she dipped the water bottle into the rippling water, filling it. "Or did you?"

"If anyone could, it would be her." He didn't feel comfortable saying more. No one's kindness could mean as much to him as Lila's had. His throat tightened with the feelings he could not speak. They remained wedged beneath his Adam's apple, a lump he could not budge.

"What was she like?" She handed him the small jug, deliciously cold from the water.

"She is pure caring." The deeper reaches of his consciousness could still remember the lilting softness of her voice reaching him through the fever and nightmares. For a time, she'd been his anchor, the only one he'd known in his adult life. "She has brown hair, but no ordinary brown. It has layers of color. Cinnamon. Auburn. Russet. Ginger. Chestnut."

"She was beautiful."

"To me, she's the most beautiful of women." The lump in his throat expanded, straining his words, making it hard to speak. "She has eyes that are the color of a northern sea, an eddy of ocean green and stormy blue sky that can make even a man like me dream."

"I have brown hair. I have green-and-blue eyes." She narrowed her gaze at him and plucked open the basket. Fresh strawberries spilled out of an ironware bowl and tumbled over onto a neighboring stack of sugar cookies. "You aren't being serious."

"How do you know?" He grinned, hiding his heart because she would not believe him. He didn't blame her. A sweetheart like her would not be interested in a man who had made bad choices in his life. Some choices could not be reversed, some acts could never be redeemed. The river's whisper and the melody of larks and Lila's sunny presence kept him in the light, away from the past.

"Have a strawberry. They were brought into the store fresh this morning." She held the basket out to him, refusing to stop taking care of him.

"I've told you a secret." He plucked a ripe berry from the bowl. "Now it's your turn."

"You didn't tell me a secret. I think you were playing a joke on me. Not a mean joke, but you managed to avoid my question quite nicely."

He pushed off the boulder, ignoring the protest of his healing wounds and the rush in his head from standing too quickly. "I answered your question the best I could. No one in twenty years has been as close to me as you."

"Oh." She gave her braid a toss, lifting her chin so that her gaze met his. Whatever she felt remained shielded and the saucy uplift in the corners of her mouth gave no clue. "Is that only because you were shot and couldn't escape me?"

"Yes, that's exactly the reason why. The only reason why." He held the berry to her lips. "Ladies first."

"Surely you had friends growing up?" She took the strawberry from him and popped it into her mouth.

"For a time in the orphanage, but it was difficult. The

other children were always coming or going and the lucky few were adopted. I was hired out to a different place every year."

"No friends." She set the basket down on the boulder. "I can't imagine what that must have been like. My friends, the seven of us, have mostly been together since we were very young. They have been my pillars. When I lost my mother, they helped see me through."

"I'm glad you have them." He pulled her into his arms.

She rested her cheek against his sun-warmed shirt and her soul stilled. She listened to the steady beat of his heart as his iron-strong arms wrapped around her. Complete peace. Total bliss. Feelings filled her that were purely romantic, as poetic as if they had come straight off the pages of a novel. Not even Earlee, who was gifted with paper and pen, could have written a scene more moving than the joy she felt in Burke's arms.

And he was alone. He had no one, except for her. She breathed in the sunshine and soap scent of his shirt and let her eyes drift shut. "Who did you have to see you through? Wasn't there anyone you could turn to?"

"No one." His cheek caressed her forehead with one tender stroke, then two before he drew away and released her. "You will have to do."

His shadow fell across her, engulfing her, cutting off all light from the sun above. She could not stop her feelings from rising up buoyant to the surface. Unspoken affection darkened his gaze that was so deep she could see past his defenses. She could hear what words could not give meaning to.

"Thank you for everything you've done for me." His baritone dipped, tiered with feeling. He cradled her jaw with his calloused hands. No man could be gentler. "You saved my life when I was shot."

"I applied bandages and pressure." She couldn't help leaning her cheek against the rough pads of his fingers. The well of emotion she felt for him deepened fathom by fathom. "It was nothing."

"You read to me. You put cold compresses to my forehead." He leaned a wisp closer so that she could see the lighter blue flecks in his irises and each individual whisker stubble. "You stayed with me every time I felt most alone."

"I don't have much else to do." Her humor fell short.

He did not smile. He did not chuckle. "Tomorrow when your pa returns to his delivery driving, make sure he takes a gun with him. It would be best if he didn't go alone. It would be worth the cost to hire someone."

"I'll tell him." She felt cold, although the sun blazed and baked through her cotton dress. "You are going back to work tomorrow, aren't you?"

"I have a job to do." He leaned his forehead gently against hers. The contact was more poignant than a kiss. She could feel his regrets. She knew he was preparing to tell her goodbye. He cleared his throat. "I won't forget what you did for me, Lila. I will never forget."

"You think this is the end, that we won't have the chance to see one another again?" She could feel tension move through him. "I thought we were friends."

"We're not friends." He nudged her jaw, tilting her face to his. His lips slanted inches above hers and hovered for a fraction of a second. Then his mouth brushed over hers with a light, feathering kiss. A kiss so sweet it brought tears to her eyes. A kiss that stilled her soul.

When he broke away, he stared out at the horizon for a moment, as if warring with his internal thoughts. He did not move but held on to her for a few minutes more. She recognized the wish moving through his heart because the same wish moved through hers.

"No, we are not friends," she agreed. It was a good thing she wasn't falling in love with him because that kiss alone could have made her tumble irrevocably, inexorably. "I think we will always be a good deal more."

She swirled away from him to pluck a cookie from the basket, wishing he was a settling-down kind of man. Tucking away her tender feelings, she splashed through the water and kicked up a cool spray.

He chuckled, not quick enough in his weakened state to dodge it, but his good-natured laughter rang above the merry birdsong and burned itself into her memory, a sound she still could hear hours later long after the sun had set and darkness fell.

As she sat in her room finishing her letter to Meredith, she remembered Burke's booming laughter and his kiss, her first kiss.

Now that was definitely like something out of a book. She dipped her pen into the bottle, tapped off the excess ink and continued writing with a smile on her face and in her heart.

Chapter Ten

"My pa is looking to hire another gun." In dream, Olly dropped a pinecone on the top of the stump.

They were target practicing again in the stuffy heat of a muggy August evening, his only free time off from field-work and chores around the farm. Burke set the gun on its butt. He pulled the last bullet from the leather pouch tied to his belt. Tonight he needed to melt more lead.

"It's a real job. You interested?" Olly swung his sleek Winchester by the barrel as he strode through the grass, crushing daisies beneath his boots.

"Interested? Sure." Burke sited carefully. "But I can't walk away from my fieldwork just for one day's work. The farmer would tan my hide and there's no one to stop him from hitting me. If he kicked me out, I'd have to go back to the orphanage."

"It's not work for only one night, stupid." Olly spat a stream of tobacco and laughed with a mature confidence. He was grown up for his years. They might be the same age, but Olly was older somehow. Rough language slid easily off his tongue, and he knew a lot of the world. "This is a legitimate job offer."

"With pay?" Burke squeezed the trigger, the flash bang

of the long rifle knocked him back a foot but the pinecone shattered into a hundred pieces. Perfect hit.

"Pay, room and board. Long term. It's gun work. You would be providing security for my pa." Olly leaned his Winchester against the rough bark of a skinny pine and untied his pack. "You would stay with us. Pa would pay you a dollar a day."

"A whole dollar?" That was thirty dollars a month. Over three hundred a year. He would be rich. He put down his gun, raked a hand through his hair and tried to imagine having so much money.

He could buy a fine driving team and maybe a shiny buggy to go with it. Or he could buy his own land, maybe it wouldn't be a big place, but he didn't need much. A little shanty with a roof and a cookstove, maybe his own milk cow. His own horse and buggy, his own house. Maybe he could save up enough to go back to school. He had the notion of becoming a Range Rider one day, and he figured he needed a lot of schooling for that.

Excitement jumped in his belly, and he felt hungry for those dreams. Desperate to have them.

"I've never seen anyone shoot the way you can." Olly pulled out a silver flask. "That's talent. Real talent."

"It's just shooting." He shrugged. It came easily to him, as simple as breathing. His talent didn't seem like anything special, but if it could get him out of the farmer's house and earn him money, he wasn't going to argue. His back was still scabbed and tender from his last beating. "You are serious? Thirty dollars a month?"

"As serious as a judge." Olly uncapped the flask and the strong scent of alcohol carried on the wind. Whiskey, Burke knew because the farmer drank it. Olly handed over the alcohol. "All you have to do is keep a sharp eye out and make sure Pa and his men stay safe. Are you in?"

"Yeah. Why not? Anything is better than what I've got." He took the whiskey, feeling good about his decision. He would sneak back to the farmer's house, pack up his clothes and bedroll and he would be free. A man on his own. He lifted the flask and coughed when the burning whiskey hit his tongue. It tasted the way kerosene smelled, but he choked it down. He was a man now and he was in control of his own destiny.

Burke woke with a start, blinked away the dream and sat straight up in bed with the taste of betrayal on his tongue. The sun was bright, traffic sounds clattered through the open window to echo in his rented room. He'd slept longer than he'd intended, judging by the slant of the sun on the floor. He pushed off the covers, ignored the trembling weakness when he stood and the pain in his chest when he moved and poured water from the pitcher into the washbasin.

His hand was steady enough this morning to shave. As he scraped at his whiskers with the sharp edge of his razor, he realized he hadn't trusted another living soul since that first taste of whiskey with Olly. The mistakes of his past stood in his way and he couldn't be the man Lila needed. If he could have just one prayer answered, then that would be it.

He set his razor on the rim of the basin and splashed water over his face. Yesterday's happiness clung to him. He couldn't remember having a better day. He hadn't been that happy in ages. He grabbed the towel off the bar and dried off. But yesterday's sparkling moment of happiness didn't belong in his life.

He got dressed. He bit back a groan of pain as he slipped into a white shirt. He buttoned up, trying to stop the musical lilt of her laughter rising up in his memory. She'd refused to believe he was a villain. She was wrong.

If God was merciful, He would never let Lila know the truth. Burke tugged on his trousers, sat down to put on his boots and bowed his head instead. *She isn't in Your plan for me, this I know, but keep her protected. Find for her the man who can make her happy beyond imagining.*

He reached for his belt and holster. The man who stared back at him in the mirror radiated hard, cold purpose. The besotted fellow who laughed in the river yesterday had gone and was no more. Burke pinned on his tin star. Work waited for him. He buckled on his holster. Work was his life. It was the only thing that could redeem him. Today was the day he made Dobbs and everyone else see the man he used to be. He hated that Lila would see it, too.

"I didn't make a single mistake tallying the sales yesterday, did I?" Lark asked anxiously as she peered around the edge of the shelf she was dusting. "I double-checked every total."

"You did it perfectly." Lila swiped away the figures on her slate with a rag. "Not a penny off, and you remembered every sale price. Eunice will have to admit you can handle the store on your own now."

"I want to be like Ma." Lark went back to stocking. Hidden behind the aisle of pots and pans, the honesty of her hopes rang as clear as a bell. "Maybe it can be the two of us running this store one day. It can be the happy place it once was when Ma was alive."

"It's a good plan." So easy to remember those happy days when their mother rushed around this space, humming to herself as she restocked or did the books or cleaned, tossing loving looks to Pa all the while.

That was the kind of love she longed to find. She refused to let her thoughts spiral back to yesterday afternoon. Do not think about his kiss, she warned herself as she snapped open the accounts receivable ledger.

The door swooshed, the bell sang merrily and her dear friend Kate Schmidt waltzed in with her sleek dark hair tamed by a ladylike knot. "How is your pa?"

"He's at the sheriff's office filing a report." Lila circled the counter to hug her friend. Burke rolled into her mind. Pa was probably talking with him right now.

"It's a shame he has to do that. I don't suppose Dobbs will do anything." Kate headed straight for the far end of the store.

"Burke will look after him. I know he will take care of Pa." Lila slipped behind the fabric counter. "A man like him, why he could even get our horses back."

"I hope so." Kate shook her head. "First the bank and now this. Pa isn't going to let me drive alone anymore, at least until those men are caught. He came with me. He's over at the feed store."

"I know how you love to drive." Kate lived far west of town in the foothills of the Rocky Mountain range and now that she had her own horse, she was always out in the cute little cart her father had made her. Lila knelt to retrieve the colorful flosses she'd saved for her friend. "Does this mean you won't be coming tomorrow?"

"No, I'll be there, although I won't be able to stay as long as usual." Kate ran her fingertips over the beautiful threads. "Oh, these are perfect. Just what I wanted."

"I slipped them in as a special order, but Eunice hasn't found out yet." Lila tore off a length of brown paper to wrap the pretty flosses in. "Is this for a new project?"

"Always." Kate loved to cross-stitch. "You'll be able to see it tomorrow. Ma has a few things she wants me to pick up while I'm here. Oh, Lila, look."

They turned together to the front windows. On the

boardwalk across the street a tall, lanky young man with very nice shoulders marched along with great purpose.

"Lorenzo." Kate sighed. "I am always going to have a crush on him. He's dreamy."

"I suppose."

"You *suppose?* You were always sighing right along with me. Something is wrong." Kate didn't take her gaze off the man as he stopped to chat with a shopkeeper out sweeping his walk. "You can't be feeling well, Lila. Maybe you should have Eunice check you for a fever."

Lila bit her lip. How did she begin to describe her association with Burke? The closeness, the kiss, the laughter and then the feeling of goodbye? She couldn't fight the suspicion that she wouldn't see him again.

"My dear sister has chosen someone else!" Lark popped up to comment. "She's in love with the new deputy."

"Lark!" How could her own sister betray her like that? "It's not love. I'm not like that with him." She bit her lip. Did what she just say make any sense? She didn't think so. "I mean, it's not like that with him. I'm not in love with him."

"No, you are calm as could be talking about him." Kate's mouth quirked up at the corners, as if fighting a smile. Across the street Lorenzo nodded goodbye to his friend and continued on, stalking out of sight. Kate sighed. "Maybe he has replaced Lorenzo in your affections?"

"I've decided to give no man my affection." She couldn't say more or that when Burke's work in Angel Falls was done, he would leave town forever. She grabbed a basket from the stack by the door and handed it over. Pa stormed into sight on the boardwalk, shoved open the door with a clatter and pounded into the store.

"Pa!" She'd never seen him glowing red with anger.

His battered eye had swollen shut, the skin a shocking purple-black.

"I'm fed up." His puffy lip twisted with rage. "Forgive me, girls, but that sheriff burns me. I can't remember the last time I've been this furious."

He slammed his fist into the counter, vehemence heaving through him. Lila jumped. Lark gasped. Kate stared wide-eyed as he took a deep, calming breath.

"Papa." She laid her hand on his forearm. "What happened?"

"Dobbs, that's what. He refuses to investigate." Pa gentled his voice, regaining control. "He says it happened outside of town, so it's not his job."

"I'm not surprised." Everyone she knew had a complaint about Dobbs. "Why don't we find Burke? I know he cares. He can make this right."

"Hannigan? Ha!" Pa spit out the word and jerked his arm away. "He was the worst. Standing around in the sheriff's office, a newcomer to town, questioning me on what happened."

"He has to do that if he is going to investigate." She ached for her poor father as he pressed the heel of his hand to his forehead and accidentally bumped the stitches marching along his hairline.

He winced. "That wasn't what he was doing, Lila. I know you are a good girl and you don't know the ways of the world. Eunice and I have seen that you don't, but believe me when I say the deputy was less than helpful."

That made no sense at all. She remembered the bliss of Burke's kiss and this concern about her father. "Did he try and tell you that you shouldn't go on your deliveries alone until he catches the thieves?"

"No. In fact, he questioned that it even happened at all. Can you imagine? He called me a liar to my face." He flushed with anger again and he pushed away, marching through the store. His hurt and indignation knelled in the hard strike of his boots. "You are never to talk to that man again, Lila. If he comes in this store, no one waits on him. Understand? You send him away. And don't forget to account for the supplies he used while he was here. I've decided to agree with Eunice and to bill him after all."

The door closed behind him with a bang, leaving them alone. Eunice's muffled voice of concern murmured through the ceiling above. Lila stared in disbelief at the closed door, not able to understand exactly what had happened. Burke wouldn't have been cruel to her father. He wouldn't have been disrespectful. Something was wrong.

"I've never seen Papa so angry," Lark whispered, worried again.

"It makes no sense." Simply thinking of him made her stronger. She knew he would make things right. "Pa must have misunderstood."

"He seemed fairly sure about what happened." Kate plucked a box of canning lids off the shelf. "I hate to say it, Lila, but if what he said about the deputy is true, you need to be careful. He might be cut from the same cloth as the sheriff."

"Impossible." Tenderness filled her as she hefted a five-pound sack of white sugar from a shelf for Kate. "I know him better than you do. He isn't anything like Dobbs."

"I pray that you're right," Kate said in her gentle way. "Looks can be deceiving."

"I'm not deceived." She thought of the badge still tucked away in her hope chest. She remembered how Burke had driven the wagon so she could make her deliveries although he was still in pain. His honor, his goodness and the tenderness of his kiss assured her. Burke would never do anything wrong.

If only she could speak to him, she knew she could make everything right. Her father's ultimatum kept her from leaving Lark in charge of the store and going straight to him. She would not disobey her pa.

She realized Kate had quietly gone about her shopping and carried a partially full basket to the front counter. Lila opened the sales book to a new page.

"Burke is one of the good guys," she assured her friend.

Kate nodded as if she wanted to believe it but didn't.

"That was a good touch, Hannigan." Dobbs moseyed over to the bar.

The saloon was quiet this time of day and stuffy with the stale odors from the night before. Dank cigar smoke and spilled whiskey tainted the air as he sidled up on a stool. The barkeep nodded to Dobbs and hurried over with a bottle and two shot glasses, which he filled.

"Good to see you, Sheriff. Deputy." The barkeep nodded, set the bottle on the counter and backed away warily.

Warily. That was interesting. Burke had to wonder why. He made a mental note to talk to the man after hours when Dobbs wouldn't be around. He waited for the sheriff to reach for his glass first.

"Accusing Lawson of stealing his own horses and goods for the attention." Dobbs rasped out a grating chuckle. He downed the whiskey in one swallow. "You should have seen the look on his weak face. That storekeeper is getting on my last nerve."

"I can see why." The glass felt cool as he dragged it on the bar in front of him. He was no longer a fifteen-year-old boy impressed by whiskey. He let it sit. "You told Arthur to get out of your sight and he went."

"Spooked like a scared jackrabbit." Dobbs upended the bottle and poured another generous shot. "Got no backbone. None of 'em do. How about you, Roger? Do you got a spine?"

The barkeep startled. Tension crept into his jawline.

"That's what I thought." The sheriff barked out another harsh chuckle. "Chickens. I got no respect for 'em."

Dobbs was busy gulping his whiskey, so he didn't notice how Burke pressed his lips tight against the glass so none of the liquid did more than wet his upper lip when he tipped it.

"You've got me wondering who took the horses." He set the glass down.

"Why do you think I would know?" Dobbs plunked down the bottle. "Do you know what I think, Hannigan?"

"I'm curious." He ran his finger around the rim of the glass.

"I think you play the good guy when it suits you, but you're as black as sin underneath." The sheriff knocked back another double shot. "I caught up with a few friends of mine the other day. One of them says he knows you."

His pulse kicked up a notch. He didn't let it show. "Cheever?"

"Guess I know why you didn't shoot him that day in the street." Dobbs knocked back another shot, emptying the glass. "It ain't nice to shoot a friend."

"True." His mouth soured as time rolled back. Memories he would rather stay forgotten surged into his thoughts, filling his head with images he could not stop and blotted out the present. The past came alive as the scent of the whiskey on the bar mixed with the scent from the bottle on the hot August evening. In the Cheever cabin, fifteen-year-old Burke had tossed his bedroll and mended satchel on the floor. Dust clouded upward and he coughed.

"This your friend?" Old Man Cheever reeked of cigar smoke and whiskey. He had a grizzled, unkempt appearance. His untrimmed mustache and beard gave him a wild look, or maybe that was the dead gleam in his eyes.

"Pa, this is Burke." Olly spat out a stream of tobacco juice on the floor. "He's the best shot I ever saw."

"That so? I hear you need a job, boy." When he grinned, four teeth were missing as if he'd taken a hard fist to the mouth. One tooth had a jagged, broken look to it. "I'll give you a dollar a day, the first month up front."

"Really?" He hadn't expected that. Thirty whole dollars. He stared in amazement as Olly's father reached into his pocket and pulled out a thick fold of paper money. He'd never seen so many greenbacks in his life.

"Hold out your hand." Mr. Cheever laid a twenty-dollar bill on it and a ten. "There you are. Thirty dollars. What kind of gun you got?"

"A long rifle. I picked it up for painting an old lady's house on my time off five weeks ago. I haven't had it long." He stared at the money. He was rich. And there was more to come. He could earn it. Think how that would improve his life. No more beatings. No more farmers who couldn't care less about him. "I could get better. I just need to practice more."

"Boy, you aren't seeing the larger picture here. No way am I letting you do security work with a gun that's no better than garbage. Here's a Winchester. Brand-new." Olly's pa shoved the fold of money into his shirt pocket and grabbed a rifle among many leaning against the wall by the open door. "This is yours."

"I can't afford it. Yet."

"It's my gift to you. Welcome to the gang." He tossed it over. "You hungry? Did you get something to eat?"

"Not enough." His stomach rumbled at the mention of food, but he couldn't take his eyes off the rifle. The black barrel was sleek and shiny, not a scratch on it. The stock was polished walnut and smooth as silk. He ran his hands over the gleaming wood and glossy steel. He'd never owned anything so nice.

"There's some rabbit stew and corn bread left from supper." Olly held out a plate. "Eat until you're full. There's plenty."

Burke had been hungry for so long. He'd been fed, but he hadn't been fed until he was full. The farmer had called second helpings an indulgence, but Burke figured the man and his wife were cheap. They didn't want to spend a penny more than they had to to feed him. Unable to let go of the rifle, he tucked it in the crook of his arm and grabbed the plate. On it was a thick chunk of buttered corn bread and a full bowl of steaming stew. His stomach growled and he ate standing up, shoveling spoonful after spoonful into his mouth.

"You've got a home now, boy," Old Man Cheever said. "You've got a place to belong. Don't you worry."

Burke swallowed hard, stopping the memory before it could carry him any further into the past to a place he could not bear to recall. He pushed away from the bar. "Cheever is my oldest friend. His old man gave me my first Winchester."

"So he told me." Dobbs hopped down from the stool, not bothering to pay. "He also said you went missing one night after a heist."

"Missing? Things went south, and I got left behind." Burke hopped off the stool, bitterness darkening him. "I was shot. Too injured to move."

"They thought you were dead." Dobbs pushed through the swinging doors into the blaring heat. Dust swirled in the air, stirred by a strong wind and traffic on the side street. "Imagine their surprise to see you alive with a tin star on your chest."

"A man's got to make a living." He could feel the sheriff's quandary. If he pushed too hard to make the man believe him, then it might backfire. He had to sound casual. "I spent a stretch of time in prison. They commuted the term when I convinced them I was reformed."

"God bless parole." Dobbs chuckled.

"I keep my nose clean most of the time." He shrugged as he took his time moseying down the boardwalk. "Now and then an opportunity comes along to help out an old friend or a new one."

"To think at one time I feared you might be too squeaky clean to be of any use. Glad I was wrong." Dobbs slapped him on the back.

Pain shot through his chest as his wounds protested. Burke covered his groan with a barking laugh. "Me, squeaky clean?"

"I thought you might be investigating me, boy." Dobbs appeared relaxed about that now. "I haven't been able to stop all the complaints against me. I know a man or two who wrote to the governor's office."

"There's a whiner in every crowd."

"You just gotta know how to silence 'em." Dobbs's gaze narrowed.

Burke's guts cinched. He figured the sheriff still had his suspicions, but at least he'd made a step in the right direction. A buttery blur on the boardwalk across the street caught his attention.

Lila. She handed over a small sack of flour out to her father, who was waiting on the wagon seat, with the wind swirling her skirts and trying to steal tendrils from her braids. The sunshine dimmed as she swiveled and saw him stopped in the middle of the boardwalk, with Dobbs patting his shoulder again.

"I'm gonna trust you, boy." The sheriff growled. "If you cross me, I'll make you sorry you was ever born."

Burke nodded, his throat too tight to speak for Lila's face wreathed with confusion and emotions he was too far away to read, but he could feel.

Did she know he hated what he'd said to her father? Surely she could piece together that he was investigating Dobbs. And why was he upset about it? He had to let her go. He'd been able to fool himself yesterday thinking he could ignore the past, but today was a new day. The past was alive and littered with things no one could forgive.

"Looks like a storm's blowin' in." Dobbs marched on a few paces. "C'mon, boy. Don't go moonin' after that calico. She's out of your league."

He couldn't argue with that. He drank in one long last look before he strode away, knowing she watched him the whole length of the street.

Chapter Eleven

"Ian's grandmother is such a dear," Fiona McPherson stitched on the gingham tablecloth she was hemming. "I'm so glad she lives with us. She is a blessing to my life."

"A new husband, a new grandmother." Lila paused with her needle in midair. They were tucked on Scarlet's roomy porch where the wind rattled the leaves shading the Fisher family home on the quiet end of Third Street. "You finally have the family you deserve."

"I am blessed." Fiona sighed, the dear that she was, her dark curls framing her heart-shaped face. Her wedding ring glinted in the light. "These past months being married to Ian have been the happiest I've ever known."

"It shows." Kate smiled as she poked her needle through the fabric stretched across her embroidery hoop. "I'm praying each coming year of your marriage is more joyous than the last."

"Me, too," Ruby chimed in as she worked loose a knot in her thread. "You and Ian seem made for each other."

"A fairy tale come true," Earlee agreed as she pinned a section of a skirt she was cutting down for her sister. "Speaking of fairy-tale loves, has anyone heard from Meredith lately?"

"No," Lila admitted. "I got sidetracked and only finished a letter to her on my way here."

"I wonder what sidetracked her," Ruby said, not so innocently. "Or should I ask, who?"

"The handsome new deputy." Scarlet's crochet hook stilled. "I saw them driving through town together."

"Burke was helping me with my deliveries." Lila's face heated. She had to be shining like a strawberry, which made her remember how he'd handed her a berry when they had been at the river together. He'd practically fed it to her, and then his kiss... She blushed harder.

"Somehow I don't think he was only helping her." Ruby tossed a light blond braid over her shoulder, sweet as could be. "I think he was beauing her."

"Maybe there will be another engagement soon," Earlee speculated. "First Fiona, then Meredith. Are you next, Lila?"

"Hardly, as my father has forbidden me to see Burke." There was more, but she wasn't ready to talk about it or to dim their merry gathering with unhappy talk.

"Burke, is it?" Fiona plucked a pin from her work and dropped it into her pin box. Her needle flashed as she worked. "You and the deputy are on a first-name basis. That's a good sign. You're being awfully quiet, Kate."

"I've got my floss in a twist." Kate bent over her hoop, fiddling with the beautiful blue floss.

"Does anyone else notice how red Lila is turning?" Earlee squinted as she threaded her needle.

"Why are you forbidden to see the deputy?" Ruby asked as she went back to stitching a patch on her father's work shirt. "Doesn't your pa approve of him?"

"Is it because he's older than you?" Scarlet stopped counting her stitches to ask.

Lila studied her friends' curious faces, all glowing with expectant happiness for her. They had the wrong idea, all but Kate. Worry dug fine crinkles into Kate's brow. Her friend would never admit it but she didn't approve of Burke. She knew how it looked. She was confused by his behavior, too.

"There's no engagement in our future." She may as well nip those hopes in the bud before her dear friends started planning an engagement party. "I only just met him and besides, he's not the settling-down type."

"That's what I think, too," Kate spoke up in her gentle, caring manner. Her shoulders relaxed a fraction, as if she had been more than worried. "I'm sure he's nice enough, but a man like that has a past."

"Ooh, it's like an adventure novel," Earlee spoke up, delighted. "The rugged, dangerous hero breezes into town and captures the heroine's heart."

"But then he rides out of town after all wrongs are righted," Lila finished. "I read the same stories."

"Because you lend me your books," Earlee quipped.

"Those kinds of stories don't end in marriage," Lila pointed out, quite practically. No one might guess how much it hurt to admit. When he was gone, the tenderness of his embrace and the beauty of his kiss would stay with her always. "I'm not in love with him and I won't fall in love with him. We're just friends."

"That's how it started with Ian and me," Fiona pointed out sweetly.

"And remember Meredith and Shane?" Earlee added. "Do you see a pattern, Lila?"

"I see a bunch of romantics on this porch." She rolled her eyes and went back to basting the tucks in the waistband of the calico apron she was sewing. Another item for her hope chest, which was getting quite full. She noticed Kate hadn't said anything more but had bent her head over her work. "Kate and I spotted Lorenzo in town yesterday."

"Lorenzo." Scarlet sighed. "I've caught brief glimpses of him in church this summer, but that's all. How is he going to fall in love with me if he never gets the chance to see me?"

"Or me?" Kate joined the conversation quietly.

"I know he's not about to fall for me." Ruby sighed, too. "I don't think he even knows my name."

"You might be surprised," Lila spoke up, remembering catching Lorenzo Davis watching Ruby a while ago. "After all, someone has to end up with him. He'll get married eventually."

"Maybe when he has stopped pining for Fiona," Scarlet speculated. "Fiona, you broke his heart."

"I didn't mean to. I was never interested in him. I was never interested in anyone." She laughed, a musical happy sound, proof that her life had transformed from sadness to joy. "Remember how I wasn't going to marry anyone? I was going to move far away so I would never have to see my parents again."

"You didn't have to move so far to escape them, and we're glad." Lila reached out and covered Fiona's hand with her own. Understanding between all of them settled silently, a lifelong love of friendship that God had blessed them with. A blessing she would never take for granted.

"Who wants some lemonade?" Scarlet asked, setting down her crocheting. "I made sugar cookies to go along with it."

"Me!" Fiona and Kate called out.

"Me!" Earlee, Scarlet and Ruby chorused together.

"I'll help you," Lila offered and secured her needle in the pinned seam. At least the conversation had safely turned away from Burke. She hoped it would stay that way. With the secret memory of his kiss to smile over, she followed Scarlet into the house.

* * *

Something in the vicinity of his chest tugged hard, like a lasso tightening. Burke didn't have to turn down the street to know Lila was near. The sight of her captivated him, left him unable to think, much less breathe. She strolled along the boardwalk swinging a woven sewing basket. Carefree and lovely in a light yellow cotton gown, she was as breathtaking as a sun dawning. Her simple bonnet tied with a matching yellow ribbon hid most of her cinnamon-brown locks except for the unruly bouncy curls that framed the graceful curve of her face.

Softer emotions threatened him. He clamped his jaw. Maybe he would turn back around on his patrol so she wouldn't spot him. The taint of his past clung to him as he headed in the other direction past the feed store. It would be best to keep away from her. It would be doing her a kindness.

"You're not foolin' me one bit." A strapping man in a muslin shirt and denims pushed out of the store's front door. Devin Winters's hands fisted in what appeared to be anger. "I heard what you did to Arthur."

"I didn't do a thing." He planted his feet and resisted the urge to check over his shoulder to see if Lila was in hearing range. "You are misinformed."

"Hardly." Disdain soured Mr. Winters's face. "Arthur doesn't lie and he didn't beat himself in the head. You know that as well as I do."

"I was merely making on observation is all." The back of his neck tingled. That always happened when Lila was near. Her presence tugged at his soul in a way he could not deny. He swallowed hard and faced the shopkeeper. "Have you had any problems lately? Anything stolen? Is there something I can help you with?"

"Nothing I would want to talk to you about. If my

wagon needs a repaired spoke or my horse throws a shoe, I'll give a holler." Scorn laced his words as he turned and went back into his shop.

Burke hardly noticed. Horses and their drivers, teamsters and their wagons and pedestrians on the boardwalks hurried by, yet he saw nothing but Lila. Her skirt snapped with her gait. The low melody of her voice rose and fell as she talked quietly with her friend. Above all the noises on the street, hers was the only thing he could hear, the only sound that kept him riveted. Air stalled in his chest as he watched her tap along the opposite boardwalk, growing smaller with distance.

Utter sweetness. Her kiss had been just as pure as she was. The memory of being with her and splashing together in the cool river refreshed his dusty soul. He wished he could call out her name, cross the street and have the pleasure of talking with her, the way a courting man would. But he could never court her. Love whispered through him and he kept his boots rooted to the planks of the boardwalk. He did not call out her name. He did not rush across the street.

Who knew a man like him could love anyone?

As though hearing his silent question, she chose that moment to glance over her shoulder. Time stood still. Nothing moved and no one else existed but the two of them. Their gazes caught and held. Wholesome longing filled him up. Was she feeling this, too?

She broke away before he could tell. She swirled down the street, swinging her basket and talking with her friend. Had nothing passed between them? He hung his head. The pain burrowing into his chest was no longer a physical one.

"Those strawberries look too good to pass up." Cora Sims, the good customer that she was, set her full basket on the counter. "I must have at least a half quart."

"I'll let you pick your own." Lila gestured toward the counter. "Go on back and take which container you would like."

"Thank you kindly." Cora efficiently circled around the counter, probably used to doing so a dozen or more times a day in her dress shop. "You wouldn't happen to know anyone looking for a job, would you?"

"Not outright." Lila opened the sales book, inked her pen and lifted the first item out of the top of Cora's basket. "I could ask my friends just to be sure. Why, do you know of an opening?"

"I plan on hiring a store manager to assist me when I get married next month." Cora chose one of the little buckets of strawberries and wove around to the front of the counter. In the back of the store, Eunice cleared her throat in protest and a bolt of fabric hit the cutting counter exceptionally hard. Cora gracefully pretended not to notice. "I want to start someone now to train them. Ideally, I would like to hire you, but I know that's impossible."

Across the store, the bolt of fabric hit the counter with another hard *thump, thump*.

"Can you imagine? My parents would forbid it." She tallied another purchase with a fast scratch of her pen. "I'm afraid I am in this store for life."

"As you ought to be," Cora agreed warmly. "But if you have a friend just like you, I would hire her in an instant. It comes with generous pay and a room, as the renter in the upstairs apartment above my store just moved out. I still plan to work at the shop, just not long hours. I would give whoever I hired a lot of say in how she did her job."

"Sounds wonderful to me." Realizing she had spoken without thinking, Lila blushed. She wondered what Eunice would thump around on the counter next. "Will this be on your account?"

"Please." Cora waited politely while Lila wrapped up her purchases and handed over the pail of strawberries.

"Have a nice evening," she wished and followed Cora to the door. She opened it for her. Hot humid dusty air breezed in as Cora stepped out. Since it was the end of the business day, Lila cheerfully turned the lock and flipped the sign in the window around to Closed.

"What do you think you are up to, young lady?" Eunice's terse tone reverberated against the walls of the empty store. Her heels tapped a staccato rhythm, drawing closer. "You are not in charge of this store, Lila. You are given rules to follow for a reason."

"I know." She added Cora's total in her head, double-checked it and scribbled it down in the ledger.

"Then explain this," Eunice demanded.

A thick fold of fawn-colored fabric landed on the counter in front of her. The material she'd saved for Mrs. Olaff.

"How many times do I have to tell you? Every yardage of material that is cut has to be paid for immediately." Eunice held her hands out helplessly. "This is not your store, Lila, as much as you would like it to be. Which customer do we bill?"

"I will take care of it." She tore off a length of wrapping paper. "I will take it over to Mrs. Olaff this evening."

"And you will explain to her the policy again. That woman thinks she can have her way just because her husband is the superintendent of the county schools. She is not above having to pay for her purchases."

"I was trying to do her a favor." She carefully wrapped the beautiful fabric and tied it with white string. Immediately, she regretted her words.

"Your allegiance must be to this business, Lila."

Help me to show compassion, Lord. She thought of all the kind things her stepmother did for Pa. She thought of how Eunice had taken charge of the household when she and Lark had struggled with it after Ma's passing. Eunice had straightened out the chaos the store had been in, for Pa had gone through a hard grieving period. No one was perfect, and Eunice gave the family her best.

The back door opened and boots strode in the hallway. Pa strode in, sweeping off his hat to fan himself, a little dusty from his afternoon on the country roads. "It was a relief to have the Pawal boy ride with me. He's a strapping kid. The two of us didn't have a lick of trouble."

Time had passed so quickly. She was no longer the little girl helping her mother in the store, just as she was no longer the schoolgirl helping out after school.

Pa stopped in his tracks. "Is something wrong?"

"No, I was just apologizing for making a mistake." Lila plucked the package from the counter. "Eunice, I won't go against your rules again."

"Thank you." Eunice lifted her chin with great dignity. "Supper will be on the table in one hour. Don't be late."

"I won't." Lila unlocked the door and bolted outside. Pa didn't look upset as he scratched his head, bumped into his stitches and winced. She watched him for a moment through the glass. His swollen lip had gone down, but his black eye had become a sickly swirl of yellow and green. He had asked her to get along with Eunice long ago and it was a promise she must keep somehow. Lost in thought, she turned around and nearly crashed into someone walking by.

"Lila?" A familiar deep-noted voice rose with surprise. "Are you all right?"

"Sure, but I would be better off looking where I was going." She took a step and watched Burke hesitate before his confident stride slowed to match hers. She thought of how he had treated her father. It hurt that he hadn't made things right.

"I see you have a last-minute delivery." He gestured toward the thick fold of material clutched in the crook of her arm.

"Oh, the package." She had forgotten about it. Seeing him again jarred her. The kiss, the closeness and how he'd treated Pa. She felt awkward. "My work is never done. What about yours?"

"It's ongoing and never-ending, although my deputy shift is over and I'm headed home." He stood straight and strong, his wounds all but forgotten.

Pure stubborn male will, she suspected. "Home? Isn't the boardinghouse temporary?"

"My room, then." He shrugged. "I haven't had a permanent home for a long time."

She shouldn't be talking with Burke. Too late she remembered her father's ultimatum. How did she tell Burke about it? They reached the end of the block and stepped onto the cross street together. Plumes of dust kicked up beneath their shoes. "What about Miota Hollow? The newspaper said you were from there."

"Part of my cover story. I'm from a little town east of the Montana and Dakota border." He walked along like a perfect gentleman in a leather vest, crisp white shirt and black trousers. He appeared nothing like the renegade who had guarded her on her delivery route. Nothing like the man who had kissed her with infinite tenderness. This Burke could have been a polite stranger. His tone dropped, so that only she could hear his admission. "I call Helena home, for the little time I spend there. I keep a room in a boardinghouse to come back to."

"Another rented room?"

"I told you. I don't let anything tie me down. Even a

rented room is a little too permanent for me." A note of sadness rang in his tone. For a moment, his casual manner slid away, revealing the man beneath.

She wondered about the sadness. What would it be like to always roam from town to town and assignment to assignment? He formed friendships only to leave them. It had to be lonely.

Remembering her promise to her father, she put her sympathy for him aside and her caring. She could be casual, too. She could pretend there had been no kiss with this man who wanted no ties, this man who hadn't helped her father. She cleared her throat, hoping to sound breezy. "Today I'm a little envious of your no-ties philosophy."

"Why's that?" He sounded distant again, remote. Back to business.

They stepped onto the boardwalk together. She flicked a braid over her shoulder. "Eunice."

"Ah, the stepmother." Understanding softened the harsh edge of his voice. "That isn't a surprise."

"No. I'm sorry, but you will be receiving a bill in the mail."

"For the supplies I used over my stay at the store. I expected as much." He nodded in grim acceptance. "I guess I didn't need a letter of credit from another store and a job reference after all."

"You made such an impression, more than any letter could." Humor deepened the green and blue swirl of her eyes.

"I wonder if your stepmother would consider a new career," he quipped. "I could hire her to deal with the really scary outlaws."

"No banks in the territory would ever be robbed again." Her gentle retort made them laugh together, the merriment rising above the quieter sounds of the street. It was after five, most of the shops had closed up. The streets were nearly quiet. The boardwalk stretched two more blocks, empty except for a merchant far down at the end sweeping his part of the walk.

"I'm sorry for what I did to your father." He blurted out the apology on the dying wisps of her laughter. He fisted his hands in frustration and remorse. "I wanted to back up Dobbs. Make him see I had a dark side."

"Oh, that makes sense." The unhappiness returned. She sighed, clutching her package more tightly. "You really hurt Pa. He felt betrayed and humiliated."

"I know how that feels, and I hated doing it to Arthur." He refused to hang his head, but the past whispered reminders of the man he used to be. The man he would always be. Burke began to believe he could never escape it. That no amount of sacrifice and service would ever free him from his guilt or his penance.

"When this is all over and before I leave town, I'll explain everything to him. I'll apologize." He wanted her to know that he intended to do the right thing. "Arthur doesn't need to go through life thinking he deserved to be treated badly, after your family took me in."

"That would mean a lot." They had reached the block's end and she drew to a stop. "He thought well of you before. He talked highly of your wagon repairing skills."

"I've had a lot of practice. This isn't the first time I've come to town posing as a new deputy." He brushed an errant curl from her cheek. The warmth of the afternoon they'd spent together crept into his cold soul. He'd never known sweetness like her. "I need my badge back. I should have gotten it before now, but Dobbs has searched my room twice by my guess. I think it's safe to take it back."

"What if he searches you next?"

"Is that a bit of worry I hear?" His hand lingered against

the satin of her ivory cheek and the silk of her hair. Soft feelings weakened him. He didn't want to love her, but he did. *Lord, help me.*

"Worry, oh, no. Curiosity, yes," she quipped.

"I don't believe you for a second." He could read the truth in her eyes, the same truth he was trying to avoid. Feelings came into being, sometimes no matter how hard one tried to ward against them. His love for her wasn't something he could express or act on but it lived lasting and steadfast, the strongest emotion he had ever known. He swallowed hard, hoping his affection did not show. "I worry for you, which is why I need my badge back. It's why I can't see you anymore."

"And I can't see you." She laid her fingertips over his, gently increasing the contact of his hand against the gentle curve of her face. "Pa has forbidden it and I cannot go against it."

"I wish…" It was one sentence he could not complete. A roil of emotions too many to name twisted up inside him. He was not a free man or a redeemed man. If he was, then he would never leave her side. He could fight for her, provide for her, protect her in all ways. Commitment fired up in him all-consuming.

Help me to walk away from her. He did not have the strength on his own. He had to do what was right for her. He swallowed hard, taking a moment to cherish the soft fall of sunlight burnishing her hair and the brush of it against her cheek. Her green-blue gaze met his with the same tender feelings that rooted in his soul.

For one moment filled with longing, he saw the future he could not have with her. He envisioned their little house in town and coming home to her as his wife. Supper would be on the table and a cooing baby in a bassinet. He wanted it so sorely he could almost feel her arms wrapping around his neck tight to welcome him. His entire being yearned for the beautiful dream of a life spent with her.

A dream he could never have. The past choked him. It was time to part paths from her but he could not walk away. Not yet. Her soft rosebud lips softened slightly, as if she wished for another kiss. He wanted nothing more than the sweetness of brushing her lips with his, but he could not allow it. He could not stay on this perilous path. He had to get off it. He had to end it. He tilted her head gently and pressed a chaste kiss to her forehead.

Her disappointment rolled through him. He was disappointed, too. He hadn't meant to fall in love with her, but he was in control of his decisions. He would do the right thing.

"Leave the badge behind the stack of washtubs on your porch right before dark." He gave her flyaway tendrils on final nudge so he could admire the color of her eyes one last time. "It's been nice knowing you, Lila."

"The honor has been entirely mine." She blinked hard and in that moment love blazed brightly in her gaze. For one precious moment it shone unmistakable. He wanted to watch forever, to feel the connection of being cared for, but it could not last. She tucked her feelings away and left, tapping down the side street with her package to deliver and taking the last of the sunshine with her.

Chapter Twelve

It was right before nightfall. Dusk was made darker by the black storm clouds blotting out the stars and stretching as far as Lila could see out her bedroom window. Humid, uncomfortable heaving wind gusts exploded through the screen, scattering Lark's drawings as she lay on her stomach on her bed and ruffled the pages of the open book on the nightstand.

"Whatcha doing?" Lark asked, her pencil rasping against parchment.

"I think a storm is on its way." Distant lightning crackled along twisting cloud bellies, illuminating them with a purplish glow. "I need to bring in the bench cushions."

Lark mumbled something, her pencil darkening a portion of the page as she worked. Lila left her sister to her sketching, listened in the hallway for her parents' voices rumbling softly from the parlor as Eunice read something aloud to Pa, probably from the church magazine she was so fond of. Seizing the opportunity, she quietly opened the door and tiptoed down the stairs. The weight in her pocket pulled on her conscience as she padded through the dark, echoing store.

She'd had to speak to Burke to tell him goodbye. She

had to speak to him to tell him she couldn't speak to him. Technically, that wasn't breaking her promise to Pa, but it felt wrong. She unlocked the back door, careful to open it slowly enough so the hinges would not squeak.

The instant she stepped outside, the muggy air closed around her like a damp blanket. She eased across the dark porch, groping. Her eyes took a moment to adjust to the inky darkness. Noises echoed eerily between buildings as she plucked the cushions from the bench and tossed them inside. She felt like a heroine in the new Range Rider novel she was reading, caught in the dark of night in an echoing alley with only shadows to guide her. She even felt watched, too, as if she weren't exactly alone.

Burke had dominated her thoughts all evening long. Having to end things with him distressed her. She missed him already. She missed knowing she could never laugh with him, walk down the street at his side or look forward to another wagon ride with him holding the reins.

I'm sure this is Your will, Father. Her prayer felt small against the angry stretch of the bruised sky above and the silence settling in the alley. *Please help direct my heart. I know I should not love him.*

A gust of wind knocked over something on Mrs. Grummel's porch. What sounded like a tin watering can rolled with uneven metallic thuds and then clunked to a stop. With the wind kicking up, a storm was definitely on its way. She knelt by the stacked washtubs. A strange shadowy flutter in the dark at the metal rim caught her attention. She reached behind the stack. Something was hidden there!

Sunflowers. She pulled the bouquet gingerly from behind the relative shelter of the tub. The wildflowers were furled up for the night, their delicate yellow petals the exact shade of her dress. Burke. Why had he done it? She reached quickly into her pocket and seized the badge. Out of the corner of her eye she saw a movement in the inky darkness.

Burke. She couldn't see him, but she knew. His presence changed the night, changed her. She tucked his badge where the flowers had been and straightened. Affection that no storm or hardship or ultimatum could diminish burned inside her. She could not stop it. Maybe nothing could. It wasn't smart and there was no way a relationship could work out between them, but she wished. She hoped.

Across the alley, a shadow parted from the others and took distinct shape. She recognized the assertive tilt of his Stetson, the mountain-wide shoulders, the strength in his tall muscular frame. It was too dark to distinguish his features but she could feel his kindness like a candle in the night, a single flame burning brightly. He raised one hand in both hello and goodbye, and she raised hers, too. The gulf between them was wide. The space between their hearts was not. Still feeling the faint tingle of his earlier kiss to her forehead, she walked backward to the door.

Precious seconds ticked by and she wished she could make time stop, but the wind gusted with a sudden icy chill. The sky overhead broke apart in a blinding flash of white-tailed lightning. Thunder crashed so loud it drowned out the sudden clamor of hailstones pummeling the ground.

He rejoined with the shadows. She backed through the door. They were apart again, but strangely not separated by heart at all.

Burke ducked out of the hail into the Steiner Saloon. As thunder cannoned overhead and ice stones hailed on the roof with a deafening clatter, he wove around empty tables and couldn't forget Lila. He tried to. She stayed front and center in his thoughts, the willowy shadow on the back porch clutching a spray of sunflowers. He knew she cared for him. He had felt the existence of her affection as surely as if she'd said the words aloud.

"What'll it be?" the barkeep asked, shining a tumbler with a hand towel. Dobbs had called him Roger. "Whiskey?"

"Not tonight." He sidled up to the bar and pulled out a stool. He wasn't a drinking man. "I came to talk to you."

"To me?" Roger's towel stilled. He carefully set the tumbler on the bar. The dim lamplight could not hide the tic in the bartender's jaw. "So now you're doing Dobbs's dirty work?"

Dirty work? Burke settled on the stool and leaned his forearms against the edge of the bar. "What if I were?"

"Tell him I don't have it all, but I can get it by the end of the week." Roger tossed his towel on the bar, distaste curling his upper lip. "No need to say it. I know Dobbs will be mad, but it's his own fault. I told him when he threatened me there wasn't a whole lot to spare. Wait right there."

"Threatened you?" How about that. He'd stumbled onto his best piece of hard evidence yet after two months of subtly asking questions around town. Burke shook his head. God never failed. God always led him exactly where he was meant to be. He glanced around the saloon, taking in the half dozen tables, beaten up chairs, the floor clean but scarred by cigarette butts, matches and one too many brawls. He'd been in many saloons like this over the years and the memories tortured him.

Lightning flashed, starkly illuminating the room around him with a brief blinding whiteness. Time reeled, taking him backward in time to the glare of the lantern shining in his face. Memory seized him and he was fifteen-years-old again.

"Here's where you sit lookout." Old Man Cheever blew out the wick, and the sudden change to blackness pressed upon Burke's eyes. "You protect us. That's all you gotta do, boy. Just follow Olly's lead."

"I'll show him the ropes, Pa." Olly spoke up with importance. Experience puffed up like pride in his voice. "Don't worry. We've got your back."

"That's my boy." He disappeared in the thousand shadows and shades of the night. When he spoke again, his voice came as if disembodied. "That's the sign. Rifles ready. Here she comes."

"Now the fun starts, Burke." Olly stretched out on the rocky high ground and dropped the pail of ammunition between them. "Get yourself a good view of the road below."

"I see it." Excitement quivered through him as he lay belly down. A rock jabbed his ribs and he swept it away, impatient to get his polished new rifle positioned. He lined up the site with the dark roadway below.

No one came or went. There was no sign of Mr. Cheever or his other employees. He wondered what they were moving that needed security. It was too late at night and there weren't enough men to move cattle. Maybe it was gold. This was mining country. Maybe Mr. Cheever had a lot of nuggets to move. That would explain why he was so secretive.

A faint drumming of hooves and the rattle of rigging rose above the sounds of the plains. Six horses broke into sight pulling a small stagecoach. Two men sat on the seat, one with the reins, the second with a rifle.

Thunder cracked in his ear. Burke jumped, realizing Olly had taken a shot. Adrenaline hammered through his blood, making his own gun shake. He watched with horror as the rifleman on the seat below slumped sideways and fell bonelessly off the side of the stage.

"You killed him!" Hoarse with terror, his words carried no more sound than a whisper. "You just…killed him."

"Looks like it." Olly beamed. "I hit him square in the chest. Pa'll be real proud of me."

Burke gulped. He hardly paid attention to the chaos below. On horseback Mr. Cheever rode firing at the driver.

"Take him down," Olly shouted in his ear. "I left him for you."

"I c-can't." He tossed the gun at his so-called friend, sick over the weapon he'd been fawning over not an hour earlier.

"You have to." Olly tossed it back. He picked up his Winchester long enough to site and fire. "Awww, winged him," he said, disappointed.

Range Riders who had been protecting the stage surged forward, their badges glinting faintly in the moonshine.

"Shoot, dummy!" Olly hollered. Peppering gunfire exploded through the night.

A peal of thunder rattled overhead, shaking the rafters, drawing Burke back to the present. He blinked, startled to realize he was sitting in the bar in Angel Falls.

"This is all I got." Roger slapped a thick envelope on the bar. "Tell that—" He paled. "Dobbs. What are you doin' here?"

"I came for my money and not a moment too soon." Dobbs took the closest stool. "Hannigan, you weren't helpin' yourself to what was mine, now were you, boy?"

"No, Roger thought I was working for you, and I guess I am." Burke swallowed hard, but the bitterness of the past remained thick on his tongue. At least Lila was out of his thoughts where she belonged, where he wanted.

Where she would remain.

Morning rain pattered on the boardwalks and puddled in the street to make mud. Lila lifted her skirts to the tops of her polished black shoes and crossed the intersection carefully. Her soles squished in the mud but not a drop landed on her pink calico. A horse splashed through the wet and muck.

"Lila," a familiar rumbling voice called out.

She knew who the rider was before he spoke. She stepped safely onto the boardwalk on the other side of the street and whirled. A Stetson shaded Burke's face. He sat astride a stunning black mustang. Silhouetted against the dark sky and silver rain, he could have ridden right out of the story she'd been reading.

"I can't speak to you." She hated the distance between them. No smile softened his features, as if he hated it, too. "I'm sorry."

"Then we won't talk." Burke reined his horse over, swaying slightly in the saddle, his posture and command that of an accomplished horseman. She didn't see how anyone could look at him and merely see a deputy. She saw nobility, honor, might. He could not hide who he was, not from her.

"Don't say a word," he orderly gently. "Ever since I decided to stay away from you, I keep running into you. This morning I saddled up to ride out of town and you are the first person I come across. It's either bad luck or Providence."

Providence, she decided. At least that was what she hoped.

"I'm following a couple leads on my day off." He glanced casually up and down the street. No one was out in the humid heat where the threat of lightning kept most folks close to home. "The sheriff is sleeping off his bender from last night, so I thought it was a good time."

She nodded, wishing she could speak. Seeing him strengthened the well of affection rising up within her.

Burke leaned to lay his gloved hand tenderly against the curve of her face.

They needed no words. She could feel the love in his touch. Respectful and sincere, it traveled as if on a current from his heart to hers. Could he feel the same from her? Did he know? She wanted to hold back, she wanted to be sensible but her love for him overpowered reason. All she wanted, all she could ever want, was him.

It was not meant to be. She pressed her cheek against his palm. What if this was her only chance at true love? What if the one man who matched her soul was Burke? He would leave and take her only chance for happily-ever-after with him. And then what? She thought of all she would regret if she continued down this path. She thought of the rest of her life alone and unmarried, running the store with Eunice and how all she would have of Burke would be his memory.

Tears stung behind her eyes but did not fall. She wouldn't allow them to. Bourne away on emotion, she covered Burke's hand with both of hers and drew it to her lips. She kissed his knuckles, nerves needling at her boldness. Could he feel what she could not say?

"Me, too." His midnight eyes darkened to a stormy black, but tenderness shone in him as he bent his head to kiss her lips. No kiss could ever be more loving or respectful. She clung to him, wishing the moment could last forever. On tiptoe, she wrapped her arms around his neck and held on but she could not stop the moment from ending. She fell back on her heels, Burke straightened and his saddle creaked.

"I wish." The tenderness of his gaze deepened. A muscle jumped along his jawline. Regret lined his face as he tipped his hat to her. "I just wish."

The wind gusted, driving rain into her face and blurring

her vision as he rode away, a lone rider dressed in black, outlined by the storm. She swiped at her eyes, the pesky rain, so full of pure love her ribs ached from the pressure against them.

Maybe there was a way, she thought. *Let there be a way,* she prayed.

"Lila!" a friendly voice called out, as dear as could be. Shoes drummed on the slick boardwalk. "Wait for me!"

"Earlee." She gave her face a final swipe drying away the last of the rain—not tears. She was too strong for that. She firmed her chin and genuine joy smiled through her at the sight of her friend hurrying closer. "What are you doing out in this weather? It's a long walk from your family's farm."

"Pa let me take Hilda." She gestured to the swaybacked, gray-muzzled mare hitched to a cart tethered in front of the druggist's storefront. That could only mean one thing.

"How is your ma?"

"It's a struggle for her." Earlee looked miserable, as if she hated being helpless to help her mother get well. "She is determined to hold on, and we're all glad to have her with us."

"I pray for her every night." Lila wrapped her friend in a comforting hug. When she stepped back, Burke was merely a small dark smudge against the long stretch of road. She missed him already. "Do you have some time or do you have to rush right back?"

"I have time and a list of errands to run." Earlee linked her arm in Lila's. "Where are you headed?"

"To the post office. I have the monthly bills to mail." She patted her skirt pockets. "How about you?"

"I need to check the mail, too." Earlee's golden blond curls bounced as she walked. "I saw something interesting on the way here."

"You did? Ooh, tell me."

"I saw a friend of mine kissing this incredibly handsome deputy right in the middle of the street."

"Earlee!" Lila turned beet-red. "Were you watching?"

"I tried to look away, honest I did. But I couldn't believe my eyes. Does this mean he is courting you?"

"Burke?" she sputtered. "No. Definitely not. He's not exactly the marrying type."

"It looked like it to me." Earlee couldn't contain her delight. "He does have that dangerous thing about him. Dark, handsome, oozing charm. I see why you're in love with him."

"I'm not—" She led the way around the corner. The rain drove against them, making her squint. "Maybe it's time to confess it out loud. I am in love with him. Oh, Earlee, what am I going to do?"

"Maybe he loves you enough to change his mind about settling down. Never underestimate the power of love." She thought of her own dilemma and Finn's letter that kept haunting her mind, his goodbye she could not forget. "Deputy Hannigan seems like a nice guy. I know what folks are saying about him. I've heard the stories about your father and he's spending more time with the sheriff after hours."

"He's not like Dobbs. He's a good man," Lila insisted. Sincerity defined her, pinching her eyes and tensing her from head to toe. It was as if she could will it to be true.

"I know what it is like to see the good in a man others think are bad." She swallowed hard. Did she share her secret and her heartache? "You see the good in him."

"There is so much good. I'm certain of it." Conviction gave power to her words. "I can't say how I know, but I do. Eunice thinks he's a terrible man. Pa has forbidden me to talk with him. They won't understand and there is nothing I can do to make them."

"I know how you feel." She thought of Finn so far away, incarcerated and suffering. By his own fault, she knew, but it was hard not to remember the kind young man he'd once been. She cared for him. She did not want to, but she did. "I've been corresponding with someone my parents would not approve of if they knew."

"Corresponding?" Lila appeared shocked. "I know nothing about this."

"I've kept it quiet. I'm not ready for everyone to know." She stopped beneath the land office's awning, where the slap of rain did not reach them. "There is a lot of good in the man, but I'm afraid all anyone would see is the bad and they wouldn't approve."

"It isn't as if you can tell your heart what to do." Understanding softened Lila's tone. "Even when you know it's impossible, your affections remain."

"Exactly." Earlee thought of Finn's life of labor and hardship. He was paying the price for his crime. It would be a shame if the laughing, good young man she'd once known died in that place. Maybe her letters would help to keep the goodness inside him alive.

A relationship between them would be impossible. He had a long sentence and he had never shown her anything beyond platonic respect, but her love for him could make a difference. Wasn't that what her faith taught? That love could give light to the darkest of places where even hope dared not grow? And where love could shine, then hope could follow.

She could hear the letter she intended to write to him unfolding in her head. She would tell him of funny stories from the farm, because there were so many, tales meant to make him laugh. She could give Finn a reason to laugh and remember the man he used to be. It was the right thing to do.

"Isn't that Cora Sims's store?" Lila skidded to a halt in front of the town's nicest dress shop. "You wouldn't happen to be looking for a job, would you, Earlee?"

"I am, actually. I have a few applications for teaching jobs to mail. That's one reason I came to town." The fall was fast approaching. There would be harvest time on the farm, canning and preserving and the cellar to fill and then she intended to teach. Her family could desperately use the income. "I have my teacher's certificate, remember? Why do you ask?"

"I have to speak with Cora first, then I'll tell you. Come in out of the rain and wait while I do?" She phrased it as a question with a desperate silent plea.

"Sure. I love to look at all the pretty gowns she has on display," she agreed, thinking of the verse from Psalms her mother had read to her this morning, as she did every morning. *Wait on the Lord; be of good courage, and He shall strengthen your heart.*

It's true, she thought, God's timing was impeccable. Her burden lightened, she trailed Lila into the store.

Chapter Thirteen

"Eunice, is Pa back from his deliveries yet?" Lila peeked around the storeroom door where her stepmother sat in a chair marking the new shipment of buttonhooks against the invoice tacked on a clipboard.

"No. He's a bit late and I'm worried." Eunice's chin went up. "I heard you practically give away the penny candy to the Worthington girls. They are a wealthy family. They can afford to pay."

"They are good customers and Meredith's sisters." The bell sang above the door in one soft note, as if someone had opened it gently.

"I don't care who they are." Eunice set down her pencil. "I do not want to have this discussion again."

"Fine." She'd been worrying over her decision all morning. The noon hour had been busy. A break in the rain had sent customers flocking into the store eager to get their shopping done without being rained on. She may as well ask the one question weighing on her mind while the store was quiet again. "Is there any chance you will ever pay me a wage?"

"A wage? Whatever do you need that for?" Eunice picked up her pencil and made a mark on her clipboard.

"You have everything you need right here. Your father provides for you."

"Yes, but I am requesting a wage." She knew it was a losing battle, but she had to ask. She had grown up in this store. She did not want to leave. "Please. It would not have to be much."

"Your father relies on me to keep this store running at a profit." Eunice looked at her as if she'd sprouted two heads. "I can't imagine you would want to interfere with your father's income."

"No, I certainly would not." The bell jingled once and was still. A second customer? This was not the time to discuss the issue further.

"That's a good girl. Don't forget to keep the floor clean. Customers are dragging in all kinds of wet and mud." Eunice turned her back, absorbed in counting the merchandise.

This was the way it had to be, she realized. The store echoed around her. No customers roamed the aisles or selected purchases off the shelves. Odd, considering she'd heard the door.

A bouquet of sunflowers lay on the front counter. Raindrops dampened their satiny pedals like dew. She ran a fingertip over one closed bud and smiled. A shadow fell across the window. Burke stood on the boardwalk, hands on his hips, boots braced powerfully. The impact of his dark blue stare speared through the glass and it was as if they stood side by side. She felt the brush of his kiss to her forehead, the comfort of his hand against her cheek.

Just one chance, she found herself praying. *Just one.*

Burke lifted his hand in a slow wave. She missed him even before he strode from her sight. The need to hear his voice tore through her with a terrifying power. She wanted to rip open the door and run after him. To be close enough to see the lighter blue flecks among the midnight-blue and the hint of a day's growth on his granite jaw. She wanted every minute she could find with him. Overwhelmed, she gripped the counter where his flowers lay, hurting so much she could not breathe.

The back door rasped open and Pa's voice rumbled low in the hallway as he spoke with his wife. Lila curled her free hand around the green stems to give her courage.

"Was that the deputy I forbade you to see?" Pa asked, his tone low and ominously quiet. His footsteps stopped behind her.

"You said I couldn't *talk* with him." Lila clutched the flowers, drew her spine up straight and faced her father.

"It was what I meant, and you know that. Daughter, I am disappointed in you." Hurt pinched in the deep crinkles in his face. He looked smaller, more vulnerable than she'd ever seen him, even after the death of her mother.

"Please allow me to talk to him." She wished she could tell him why. "I want to see him."

"He brought you those flowers? He's courting you?" Pa looked horrified.

"No, not courting. He is more than a friend, less than a beau." She loved her father. She did not want to hurt him. "You were young once. Surely you can guess how I feel."

"He's a bad man, Lila. The way he treated me." He shook his head. Only the faintest wisps of color marked his eye. The thin scab on his lip was the only visual sign of the beating he'd suffered. His hat hid his stitches. "He's spending a lot of time with Dobbs. He's one of those charming men who are friendly until they have lured you in close or have no use for you. You need to stay away from him."

"I can no longer do that." The door from upstairs inched open and Lila saw her sister listening in, perhaps sensing what was to come. "I've been offered a job and I've decided to take it. It comes with lodgings, so I will be moving out, as well. This is my formal notice."

"You can't mean that. You can't walk out on your responsibilities here because of a disagreement over a man, a man who isn't good for you." Pa's jaw tensed. His color flushed. "Lila, you will not take that job."

"It's for the best," she insisted, although the move would not be easy. Eunice came out to see what was going on. Her stepmother looked as displeased as Pa. Lila had to be honest. "I'm not happy here. I love this store. I love you, Pa, and I respect everything you are trying to do here, Eunice, but our differences can't be solved. I hope you can understand in time."

"Lila, you can't go," Pa pleaded.

"It's time for me to move out. I'm not happy about it, either." She stopped to brush a kiss to his cheek. "If I don't do this now, then I'm afraid life is going to pass me by."

It was time to grow up. Her parents would understand eventually. She spun away, already going through her possessions and how best to pack them. On the stairs she stopped to give her sister a hug. "Now it's your turn."

"He's not the kind of man who will marry you," Eunice called out from the base of the stairs, her pronouncement echoing against the ceiling like thunder.

"He's not why I'm doing this."

She had always lived in these rooms. The parlor sat quiet, everything in its place. She remembered being a little girl running around the couch to show Ma the pretty bow she'd tied in her rag doll's hair. She could hear the echo of Lark's toddling footsteps and Ma's musical alto as she lavished praise and gave both daughter and doll a kiss on the cheek.

Nothing stayed the same. Life rolled forward inexorably like a wave in the ocean too mighty to stop. If she did not show courage now and seize this opportunity Cora had given her, there may not be another. She may spend her days wishing she'd had the courage to follow where God's wave would have taken her, sitting in the mercantile always wondering what if. If she was going to be the heroine of her own life, then she needed to make a change.

Fiona was married. Meredith was engaged and teaching school. Her friends had followed their dreams. Now it was her chance to live hers.

Burke strode out of the alley after a productive day. He'd left Lucky, his mustang, bedded down in a warm corner stall at the livery. With the evidence written down in his back pocket he had enough for a territorial judge to issue a warrant. All he had to do was telegraph his superiors in Helena. He whistled as he marched down the street. When he looked up, he couldn't believe his eyes.

Across the way, Lila struggled with a heavy crate in her arms. All thoughts of work flew right out of his head. He bolted out into the muddy street and the rain, which had returned with the thunderheads. "Hey, pretty lady. Where are you going with that box?"

"Wouldn't you like to know? It's good to see you." Sorrow dimmed the wattage of her smile. "Thank you for the flowers. Again."

"Do you know what they mean?" He took the crate from her, surprised at how heavy it was. Her father should have given her the wagon if she had this large of a delivery. "Sunflowers always move to face the sun. That is what you do to me, heart and soul, make me move to face you."

The admission cost him, so he said nothing more. He studied her out of the corner of his eye, pretending he wasn't. He shouldn't be giving her flowers or carrying her delivery. He wanted to keep his distance, but he didn't like being apart from her. "Maybe next time I should go for something fancier."

"No, I rather like the sunflowers." She blushed shyly, a light pink color traced across her nose and cheeks.

In the silence between them, hope beat crazily in his chest. She turned down the cross street and he matched her pace, taking the outside edge of the boardwalk so she could walk beneath the shelter of the striped awnings and jutting roofs crowning each store front.

"You're speaking to me." He broke the stillness between them.

"Yes. My father isn't pleased, but as I no longer live under his roof he can't forbid me to." She watched him through the long curl of her lashes.

"Wait. You don't live above the store?" He skidded to a halt. "You moved out?"

"Moving." She pulled a key ring from her skirt pocket. "Here we are. Would you mind carrying that up for me? It's really heavy."

"Yes, as it is full of books." He caught the door she held open with his elbow, so she could slip up the stairs first. The enclosed landing made a tight turn and kept rising. Another door whispered open and he stood in a pleasant room with polished floorboards and white plastered walls. A green length of calico covered a sofa with neat tucks. A length of yellow cloth draped a round table at the other end, near to a small cookstove in the corner.

"Welcome to my home." She gestured toward a built-in row of shelves near the door. "The furniture came with the rooms and is worse for the wear, but I can spruce things up. I will have it cozy in no time."

"It already is." He set down the box. "Why did you move out?"

"I stayed at the mercantile because it was a family business. It was expected. But in truth, Eunice and I do not see eye to eye and we never will. It will always be her store to manage, since that's the way Pa wants it. It's her right as his wife." She knelt to fish a book out of the box and slip it onto a shelf. "I've been staying there because it was easy, because I can still remember my mother in that store and because I was afraid to make a change. I would have to stand up to my parents, face their displeasure and be on my own."

"You aren't alone." He set a book on the shelf, his arm brushed hers. "You have family. You have friends. You have me."

"I know." She couldn't resist turning toward him. "I have been praying for God to fix my mundane life, and I wonder just how long He has being trying to do that. But would I budge off the fabric counter stool? And if I did, I didn't go far. I was the problem in my life. I can see that now. I was waiting for it to come to me. I think you might just be God's last ditch effort to get me to figure this all out."

"Me?" He chuckled, shaking his head. Shadows deepened around him like twilight. "I don't think God would use me for good."

"Too late." She knew the truth. "You stumbled in bleeding and almost dying. You were the answer to my prayers, although I'm sorry you were shot."

"Thanks, I think." Then he took the book from her hands and set it carelessly on the shelf. Moving in, moving closer, as ominous as the dark clouds visible through the window behind him.

"I wouldn't have discovered who I really was without you." She splayed her palm against his chest. The reliable thud of his heartbeat made her smile. Sturdy and stalwart, that beat. Just like the man.

"You give me too much credit." Sadness weighed in his

voice, dropping it a note lower. "I'm a bad influence on you. Everyone says so."

"Eunice. My father, sure. But they don't know about the other badge you carry." She loved the man. She wished she could step back into denial where it was safe. Where as long as she didn't love him, she wouldn't get hurt. It was too late for safety. "Although you could be right. I quit my job. Moved out of my father's house. Who knows what I might do next."

"It's not a joke, Lila." Although the curves of his mouth threatened to hook upward. "They aren't wrong. If all goes well, I leave next week."

"So soon?" She swallowed hard to hide the wince of pain. It slashed through her like a saber. Maybe if she sat very still, the agony would stop.

"Yes. I have what I've come for." An apology marked his features. He could not mask his infinite caring. "I wish I could stay."

"I do, too." Her affections wobbled on the edge. She held on to them tightly, afraid of where they would take her. "You could stay now. For supper. I could fix something."

"No, let me. I will be right back." He cradled her chin in his hand. His face became stone, his gaze remote and he tore away from her with a grimace he could not hide. Sorrow cloaked him. "We have this time. Let's make the most of it."

His abiding strength shone through as he tipped his hat. He turned crisply, striding away like a Western hero straight out of her dreams. He was her dream, she realized. Everything she had ever wanted in a man, everything she prized, everything she loved.

She must not let her heart fall any further for him or she would never get it back. She listened to the door click shut and his boots ringing down the stairs, growing more distant until there was only silence.

* * *

What are you doing, Burke? he kept asking himself that question as he dogged down the boardwalk in the rain. The delicious scents from the meal the diner had packed up for him permeated the air, undeniable proof of what he was about to do. He was beauing Lila. He shouldn't be anywhere near her, but he was acting like a courting man.

I know I don't have that right, Lord. He wanted God to know he was perfectly clear on what he deserved and what he didn't. He wasn't making assumptions. His boots splashed through a puddle on a low place in the planks and he shifted the box he carried so he could see his way better. He'd been honest to Lila about having to leave, but he felt as if he were doing something wrong. That was usually a sure sign that he was.

He was being selfish. He wanted time with her. For once he wanted to know what it was like to be loved. It had been a lifetime since he'd felt accepted, since someone had looked at him as if he were somebody in their view. *Forgive me for wanting that, Father. I am not strong enough to stay away from her.*

Thunder grumbled, rumbling as if in answer. He wasn't a man who could forgive himself for that weakness. He wanted to see her gaze up at him with love quietly alight in her eyes. He wanted to walk into her rooms and feel as if his existence mattered to her. She chased away the loneliness which had trailed him since he was four. Being with her made the sorrow of the past twenty years vanish.

"I saw you from the window." The door swung open. Lila's skirts snapped in the fierce winds. "It's raining so hard, you're drenched. Hurry in."

"Another storm is on the way." He shook off what water he could like a dog, which made her laugh. He thought of the lucky man who would have the privilege of listening to her soft, musical laughter, the man who would be able to take her as his wife. Terrible jealousy rolled through him mixed with complete despair. He didn't dare ask God to let him be that man. They both knew it couldn't happen. The Lord would never allow it.

"That smells good. Did you go to Dolly's?" She led the way up the stairs, lithe and graceful. She spun at the landing and closed the upstairs door after him. Cool air blew through the windows and snapped white curtains. Rain beat on the roof with wet fury as he surrendered the food carton to her.

"She makes the best fried chicken." He managed to speak past the lump gathering like a fist behind his sternum. "I got something else, too."

"Let me see." She dug through the packaging and came up with a book. "Oh, you bought it! I was going to give you my copy after I was through."

"I figured this way we could read it together after supper."

"You have the best ideas, Deputy." The lamplight shining from the table's center revealed her completely. She felt open to him, unguarded spirit and emotions. He was vulnerable to her in a way that frightened.

No barriers stood between them. There was no past and no worries about the future. Nothing but the present moment with her gentle regard and his ardent devotion. He swallowed hard, taking a step forward. He could not stop. His future would be barren without her, but he would be satisfied with this moment to hold in his memory forever. He would always see her like this, polished by lamplight, wholesome beauty and calico innocence with raindrops drying on her long cinnamon-brown braids.

Lightning scored his eyes and flashed like gunpowder. Lila jumped, twisting toward the window where thunder boomed in answer, rattling the glass panes. The liquid hammering of the rain had changed tunes. Hail fell like snow and hit like steel.

"Let's eat in front of the window and watch the storm." She handed him a plate. "I love to watch the lightning."

"Whatever you want." He did not take the plate but unwrapped the bundle of fried chicken for her. "I'm happy as long as I'm with you."

"My feelings exactly." She filled her plate with chicken and buttermilk biscuits, hashed potatoes and buttery green beans. She left the thick wedges of cherry pie for later. "You aren't like the Rider in the books, are you? He has a woman fall in love with him in every town he rides into."

"I've never had a way with the ladies." He grabbed the other plate from the table and dropped two drumsticks on it. "Truth is, you're the only one I let close to me and that was because I was shot and bleeding. I was too weak to ward you off."

"Yes, I had you at a disadvantage. What was a man to do?"

"Exactly. I was unable to use my typical woman-repelling powers on you in my injured state."

"Your unconscious state, as you were asleep most of the time you stayed with us." She grabbed a cup of cool water and settled in front of the large window seat. The wind blowing in brought welcome coolness. The hail fell at a slant away from opened glass. "I'm not sure I believe you. Surely you have left a broken heart behind, at least a time or two."

"Never." He eased down beside her, sitting straight, his shoulders braced, his jaw set. "There has not been anyone but you. I've tried to stay away from you. I couldn't."

"I tried, too." She squeezed her eyes briefly shut. She

did not want him to see how much his admission mattered to her, although she feared he already knew.

"I love you, Lila." No man in the world could be more gentle as Burke when his calloused hands cradled her jaw. He gazed at her with reverence she could not measure but her heart responded to.

Don't fall deeper, she told herself desperately trying to keep from being forever lost in his eyes and in his soul. But it was no use. He leaned in slow and deliberate. His mouth claimed hers with a kiss that became a wish. A wish for a future. A wish for forever. A wish their time together would not end. Her heart was no longer hers.

When she broke away, she was not the same woman she'd been. She was stronger, better. What she felt for Burke was an infinite devotion that words could not define.

"I love you, too," she whispered, the admission too small for the greatness she felt within.

He nodded, as if he understood, as if the greatness was within him, as well. He took her hands in his, linking their fingers, their hearts forever one. He bowed his head to begin the blessing. Perhaps Heaven leaned in a little closer to listen.

Chapter Fourteen

"Lila!" Lark sailed into Cora's shop with a chime of the over-the-door bell and exuberance. "It's strange to see you behind a different counter."

"It's strange to be here, but nice." Definitely nice. Her first morning at her new job had gone smoothly. Cora was a joy to work for and she'd been so pleased with Lila's performance that she'd left to run errands. Lila glanced at the only customer in the store who was industriously matching ribbons and buttons to a sample of delicate pink lawn and didn't yet look as if she required help.

Glad to have a few moments to chat with her sister, Lila skirted the counter, swished around a table displaying the newest velvets and wrapped Lark in a hug. "I've missed you."

"Are you terribly sure you like it here? Eunice is making me clean beneath the fish barrels." Lark wrinkled her nose.

"You said you wanted more responsibilities." Lila had a hard time letting go of her dear sister. "I've shared your pain, so I won't belittle it. Eunice can be a tough taskmaster."

"I think she misses you, too." Lark clasped her hands

behind her back and studied a beautiful polonaise and poplin dress tailored with overskirts, tucks and imported lace.

"I'm sure she does miss how well I did all the cleaning," Lila quipped.

"Ma had to do it, so I will, too." Lark squared her little shoulders, petite and sweet and sparkling. "I came to see if you want to go to the bakery with me. It is your lunchtime yet?"

"Cora will be back in a few minutes. Wait here a moment, okay?" She caught her customer looking up. "Is there something I can get for you, Mrs. Fisher?"

"Yes, dear." Scarlet's mother, a stately woman dressed in the finest bonnet, tailored gown and imported slippers gestured to her in a kindly way. "I am ready with my choices. Cora has promised to have this frock finished for my daughter by week's end. You will remind her, won't you?"

"I'll be happy to, although I knew she was working on it this morning."

"Excellent."

She felt in her element among the pretty fabrics as she slid behind the display counter to write down the rest of Mrs. Fisher's order. "The mother-of-pearl buttons are a lovely choice. They match the silk ribbon perfectly. This will complement Stella's complexion."

"You are all growing up so quickly." Mrs. Fisher sighed, helpless to keep time from turning. "It was only yesterday you were all five years old, I'm sure of it."

"My pa says the same thing." She took the samples and double-checked them against what she'd written down. "Say hello to Scarlet for me."

"I will, dear."

"Have a nice day." She tucked the information into the top of the order book, where Cora would be sure to see it. The doorbell chimed, humid air breezed in and voices erupted on the boardwalk. Cora, back from her errands, chatted amicably with Mrs. Fisher.

"You look happy," Lark observed. "I'm glad you're here, even if I miss you."

"I'm glad, too, even if I miss you." She tweaked her little sister's nose. This felt right being reliant on herself, forging her own path through life. It seemed so much time had passed since she'd prayed for a little excitement, and God had answered her generously. There would be so much to learn here and so much to do. It would be a whole new adventure managing this pretty store.

"Whew, it's almost pleasant out there. Not too hot at all." Cora breezed in with an arm full of packages. "It's your turn, Lila. Be sure and take the entire hour."

She grabbed her reticule and led the way through the store. The clean windows sparkled, she'd washed them for Cora earlier in the morning, and something caught her eye. A tall, scarecrow-lean man rode a black horse through town. His wide-brimmed hat shaded his face. His clothes were nondescript, a brown shirt, black trousers and boots, but she'd seen him somewhere before. The back of her neck tingled at the memory.

"C'mon, Lark." Fear beat like a hummingbird's wings behind her ribs as she hauled her little sister onto the boardwalk. Shoppers littered the way ahead. Horses and wagons provided obstacles that hid the lone rider from sight. The sun glared in her eyes and reflected blindingly off store windows as she tugged Lark after her.

"Hey! Lila. The bakery is that way." Lark pointed across the street.

"Hurry." She'd lost sight of the rider and horse. She perched on the street corner on tiptoe straining to see beyond Emmett Sims's teamster's wagon. Nothing. No sign of him. She'd lost him.

"What's wrong?" Lark's forehead furrowed. "You're completely pale."

"Come with me. Don't ask why. Just come." She squeezed her sister's hand in reassurance, checked for traffic, waved to Mr. Grummel driving by grumbling to his donkey and led the way across the street.

Last night's storm kept dust from the air and mud in the wagon ruts, which squished beneath her shoes. She smelled fried chicken from Dolly's Diner as she towed Lark down the intersecting street to the sheriff's office. What if Burke wasn't in? What if Dobbs was there alone?

She was strong enough to handle that man. She steeled her spine and forced her feet to carry her forward. The door was open to the breeze and angry voices rumbled inside.

"I don't care. I say it is your jurisdiction." Lorenzo Davis stabbed his forefinger with angry jabs in the sheriff's direction. "You are the only law around these parts. You had better do something."

"Don't tell me what to do, boy, unless you want to end up with more trouble." Dobbs laid his hand on the grip of his holstered Colt. "Is that what you want?"

"I want you to find whoever stole my cattle. One hundred head missing. My father shot in the leg. Fencing bashed and broken." Lorenzo swept off his hat and slapped it against the edge of Dobbs's desk. "My family pays taxes to this town and this county. I expect you to find my cattle."

"Ain't gonna happen." Dobbs stood. "What do you think, Hannigan?"

"I think you're looking for some sympathy, Davis. There's no proof your cattle are missing." Burke strolled into sight. His attention faltered when he spotted her. His eyes shielded and he laid his hand on his holstered gun, just as Dobbs did.

"Proof?" Lorenzo fumed, disdain for the men dripping in his voice. "Do you know what I think? You are behind the crimes happening around here, Sheriff. Deputy, you ought to be ashamed of yourself."

A muscle jumped in Burke's jaw, his only reaction as Lorenzo stalked off, hat in hand. Fury darkened his eyes and he looked mature, no longer the schoolboy she'd once had a crush on but like the powerful rancher he was always destined to be. He nodded at her. "Lila."

"Lorenzo." She stepped aside to let him pass. The sweetness of her crush on him had faded to nothing, because she knew now that's all she had ever felt for him. Admiration, an innocent adoration, but it had no depth or no potential for any. It was like a leaf blowing on a wind compared to the anchoring, iron effect Burke had on her as he approached.

"What a surprise to see you here. Hi, Lark," he added. "What are you two fine ladies doing in this end of town?"

"I don't know," Lark spoke up. "Lila wouldn't tell me as she dragged me here."

His chuckle was the music of her dreams. "I was just about to come look you up, Lila. Wondered if you wanted to spend another evening with me."

"Yes." She felt the sheriff's gaze, not exactly a curious or a comfortable one. Uneasy, she grabbed Burke by the wrist. "We were just about to go to the bakery. Come walk with us."

"I'll lock up, boy," Dobbs called out, not ashamed at listening in. "Go on with your gal. I've got things to do."

"Thanks, Dobbs." Burke joined her on the boardwalk. A gust of cool air ruffled her bangs bringing back memories of the evening spent in her sitting room. They had watched the storm roll in. A dazzling display of lightning snaked across a velvety black sky, accompanied by a symphony of thunder and hail. Afterward, they had sat in companionable silence curled up on the sofa, he at one end and she at the other reading.

Peace filled her at the memory. She laid her hand on his wide shoulder, went up on tiptoe and whispered what she had seen in his ear. His eyes went black. Tension hopped along his rocklike jaw. An emotion strangely like sorrow pulled at the corners of his hard mouth.

"I'll take care of it," he promised. He caressed curls away from her cheek, his touch light and unnecessary, but it was the connection he needed. She needed it, too. The power of his emotions coursed through her, a current with no end. His sadness touched her. She didn't know why.

"Keep a watch for him whenever you can. Take notes if you see him again. Maybe even if you see anything out of the ordinary. Would you report it to me?" His thumb grazed her chin. Tenderness mixed with the sadness. "I'm gonna have to turn down lunch with you."

"I understand." She laid a hand on his chest, one final connection to him, the man she loved, before she tugged Lark with her. They left him standing on the busy boardwalk, a motionless shadow, a man alone.

Hold until the unit arrives on train tomorrow. Stop. The warrant had come through on the sheriff. Burke read the telegram in the shadow of Lucky's stall. His black gelding snorted, clamped his velvety lips around the bottom of the page and jerked.

"Sorry, this isn't for you, buddy." He leaned against the wall where cracks of sunlight filtered between the gaps of the boards and lit up the page. *Want to get Slim's gang also. Stop. Wait for instructions.*

"Looks like our time here is nearly done." Misery cut through him. He'd never minded moving on. The drifting nature of his work suited him. No ties, no loss, no permanence. He could go like the wind, never stopping too long to really think about what he couldn't have in life or how much he wanted it.

How much he wanted her. Lila. In all his wanderings he'd never met a woman who made him wish he could put down roots, tie up his heart and live a real life. To have a home, a wife to love, a family of his own.

All things he could lose. All things he could not keep.

It's a moot point, Hannigan. He scrubbed a patch of straw away with his boot, lit a match and set it to the folded telegram. The flame caught and licked greedy, devouring the paper. Lucky nickered in his throat, not fond of fire of any type, but he'd seen this before.

"Easy, boy," Burke assured him as he knelt, letting the embers of the page tumble onto the exposed earth. When the flame approached his finger, he let it fall. A few more moments and his orders were nothing but smoking ash. He ground it out well with his boot heel, made sure all embers were out and buried in the dirt.

Lucky snorted loudly in relief. He spotted Burke grab the currycomb and nodded his approval.

"Got to get you looking your best for our dinner with Lila." His time with her would be coming to an end. He grimaced, hating how much it hurt to think of leaving her. It was for the best. She didn't know his real story. She didn't know the man he'd been.

He fit his hand into the leather strap of the comb and began to brush Lucky's flank. The horse stilled, he stroked the metal teeth of the comb along the grain of the mustang's soft black coat. The past floated to the surface, memories he could no longer hold back.

"Shoot, dummy!" Olly hollered over the *crack, crack* of gunfire booming through the night. "Pa could get shot while you're being a big chicken."

"I'm no chicken." Horror unfolded below. A Range Rider rocked back in his saddle, blood blossoming on his shirt. The moonshine captured him perfectly as he collapsed backward onto his horse's rump, still firing. One of Cheever's men shouted in agony, a victim of that last bullet, before the powerful-looking man with a square jaw and integrity radiating from him tumbled off his horse and fell lifeless to the ground.

"Shoot, or else!" Old Man Cheever shouted his threat and raised the hairs on the back of Burke's neck, where the muzzle of a rifle pressed. "Shoot or I shoot you."

"I can't." He watched in horror as another Rider fell, badge glinting dully in the moonlight. He lay with eyes open in surprise, mouth twisted as if with determination, but the life had gone from him, slipped away in an act of cold-blooded violence.

Nausea twisted his stomach at the carnage below. The driver and his gunman, dead. Two of Cheever's men, dead. Three Range Riders, dead. Air chocked in his throat. Terror clawed wildly in his chest. Gunfire flashed in the draw below. There was one Rider left and Burke knew without asking what Olly's pa would make him do.

"Hold yer fire, boys!" The old man hollered to his men. "Let the kid make his first kill."

"No," Burke choked. Sickness bubbled in his stomach. The acrid taste of it soured his mouth. "I won't."

"You will." The barrel dug into the flesh behind his right ear and below his skull. "Pick up your gun. *Pick it up.*"

The hair on his scalp prickled and tried to stand straight up. He'd never heard a threat like that, so menacing and terrifying. His hands shook. He picked up the polished, brand-new Winchester. It felt cold in his hands.

"Take aim." The gun boring into the flesh between his neck and skull gouged deeper. "It's you or him, boy. You decide. Now, *aim*."

Burke swallowed hard. He didn't want to die. Numbness crept through him until his finger couldn't feel the trigger. His sight blurred as he lined up the shot with the lawman's chest. The Rider took advantage of the ceasefire and, caught without cover, turned to face him with gun raised. He didn't fire.

"Don't do it, son." A warm, steady voice. A plea in calm eyes. "I can help you."

"There's no hope for this pup." The old man laughed. "No one is gonna help you but me, boy. Don't listen to a lawman's lies." He spat.

He knew Cheever was right. No one cared, no one would help him. He also knew that the outlaw wouldn't, either. He was alone, like always. He would always be alone. The hope for anything more was gone.

He couldn't shoot. His finger didn't move and he didn't want it to. Maybe he was going to die anyway, and he wasn't going to have to explain to God, if there was one, that his last act had been to gun down an innocent man.

"Shoot." The old man's hand closed over his in an instant. Fast as lightning, Cheever's forefinger pressed his against the trigger. There was no stopping the inevitable.

No! Burke's soul cried out in horror. In the fragment of the second it took the rifle to fire, he shifted the barrel hoping to miss the heart. The shot deafened him, the gun's butt kicked hard against his shoulder and the Rider fell.

"He's down!" one of the gang called out victoriously below. "Good job, kid."

Revulsion twisted through him. The Winchester tumbled from his hands. He never wanted to touch that rifle again. Vaguely he was aware of men stepping out from behind rocks and tree trunks, applauding before heaving open the coach's doors. Olly's pa stood up and stuffed a plug of chew into his cheek. "That wasn't so bad, was it, boy? You're a wanted man now. There ain't no goin' back. Decent folks won't want you near them. You are no good. You are a marked man."

The Rider he'd shot lay like a lump at the side of the road. He'd tried to miss his heart but it looked as if he'd failed. Shock rattled him. Disgusted at what he'd done, he rolled over on his side and retched. He'd taken a life. His soul bled, torn apart, and he swiped sweat from his face. Realized too late it was tears.

"You did good, Burke." Olly slapped him on the back. "I hesitated with the first one, too."

Old Man Cheever spat out a stream of tobacco juice. "The second one is easier."

It had been. Burke hung his head, the near decade-old rip in his soul smarting. Lucky reached around to dig his teeth in Burke's shirt.

"Sorry, buddy." He returned to grooming, the rhythmic motion calming, but nothing had been able to erase the stain on his conscience. He'd been young, he'd been vulnerable and he'd been forced to do it. Every shot he'd taken with that Winchester had been with a rifle at his back or a gun pointed to a hostage's head, but he'd done it all the same. At the time he had believed Cheever was right. That no one would want him, there would never be a normal life for him. But now he wanted it, Heaven knew he did.

What was he doing beauing Lila? He knelt to curry down Lucky's front legs and belly. By not telling her about his past, it was as good as deceiving her.

I know what to do, Lord. He straightened and switched

the comb for a brush. *I just don't want to do it. I don't want to end things with her, not yet.*

The horse in the neighboring stall nickered. Down the aisle another horse answered. He brushed Lucky's forelock and tail. It didn't matter what he wanted. It was time to do what was right.

When he was done, he gave Lucky a pat and set aside the brush. He wouldn't think about losing her. He wouldn't allow himself to imagine the loving light fading from her beautiful green-blue eyes when she looked at him. If he did, then he couldn't get through it. He'd chased felons through treacherous mountain passes in the dead of winter. He'd tracked soulless outlaws in the heat of summer through the badlands with no sleep and a single canteen of water. He'd been shot, dragged from a horse, survived fistfights, gang fights and his past, but he wasn't tough enough to face losing her.

One step at a time, Hannigan. He blew out a breath, grabbed Lucky's lead and guided him down the aisle. The oldest Dane brother didn't hurry looking up from his forge.

"Got the buggy in back," was all he said with a cold drip of disdain before jamming a horseshoe into the fire with a big pair of tongs.

While Burke hitched up Lucky, he kept his mind on his job. He'd done some good in this town. Because of what he'd tracked down on Dobbs, an innocent man in the territorial prison would go free and another would receive a lighter sentence. Roger, who had been threatened into giving part ownership of his bar to Dobbs, would no longer live in fear. Lila's father might get his wagon and horses returned. Lorenzo Davis might get some of his cattle back. There were more long-term wrongs that Burke wasn't able to track down the evidence for, but his boss was aware of them. Once Dobbs was indicted, more folks would feel safe enough to speak up.

He buckled the last of the rigging and hopped into the buggy. Lucky lifted his head, feeling the bit, his ears pricked and swiveling, eager for the command to go. When Burke released the brake and chirruped, the mustang stretched out into a snappy walk, glad to be out and about in the wind and sun. The sky was a clear robin's-egg blue, although white thunderheads gathered in the south. The last of yesterday's storm had evaporated from the streets as he reined Lucky down Second.

Jed Black, his fellow deputy just starting his evening shift, didn't tip his hat as he patrolled the boardwalk. Their friendship had been strained recently. Burke tried not to let that bother him as he adjusted his hat to cut the sun, but it did. It always did. One would think he had been on the outside looking in for so long, he would get used to it. He hadn't.

He drove past the feed store. Devin Winters was out sweeping in front of his shop. The shopkeeper took one hand off his broom to shake his fist in anger. There was no mistaking the contempt on the man's face. No doubt the story about Lorenzo's experience in the sheriff's office had gotten around town by now, another story added onto the others. To them he was showing himself to be a bad seed, just like the sheriff, and they weren't all that wrong. He tightened his grip on the reins, steeled his spine and prepared himself for what he had to do.

Chapter Fifteen

It was like being in one of her favorite novels, Lila decided as she turned the sign over in the front window. Her official first day as a store manager had successfully ended and her unofficial job as Burke's assistant was still going strong. She kept an eagle eye on the street as she grabbed the dry mop and began to clean the day's dust from the polished oak floor. The skirts of the nearby display rustled as she guided the mop beneath the table.

She noticed Scarlet's sage-green straw bonnet out of the dozen others crowning the heads of women hurrying about the last of their errands. She unlocked the door and swung it open just as Scarlet swirled to a stop beneath the shop's swinging sign.

"I had to come see!" She tugged at her bonnet ribbons as she waltzed in. "Ma said you were doing a spectacular job, and she's right. You look as if you belong here."

"I feel that way." She eased the door shut and whirled her mop into the corner. "No pickled herring barrel to clean. No Eunice. I can sew or read if all my other work is done between customers."

"That's nice." Scarlet gestured toward the small front counter, where a paperback novel sat, pages ruffled. "You look happy, Lila. I'm glad for you. You have no notion how much I've been praying for you."

"And I for you." Her dear, dear friend. What would she be without Scarlet and the rest of the gang? She had grown up with them as her closest friends and they were a big part of who she was. She was a better woman because of them. The Lord had blessed her greatly that first day in Sunday school when they had met as small children and again the day Meredith first came to school. And finally, when Ruby joined them. "There have been so many changes lately, it feels like ages since we were all together."

"I think we should meet in your new rooms for our next sewing circle gathering." Scarlet stopped to admire the display of rich velvets in a dozen different colors. "I have enough lace made for a hat. Ma was right about this fabric. It would be perfect for brim lining."

"You have a new project to start on and I—" She glanced toward the window. A lone horse and driver pranced down the street, but it wasn't the bank robber. Her heart skipped because it was Burke.

"You're in love with him, aren't you? You don't have to say it. I can see that you are." Scarlet studied the ends of her bonnet's ribbons. "I think he's a bad man and I'm worried for you."

"He's not bad. He's a good man. One of the best." She watched the black mustang stride closer and then Burke on the buggy seat, holding the reins. Dressed in black, he appeared as dangerous as a bandit. A five-o'clock shadow darkened his angled jaw and his capable hands drew the horse to a stop at the hitching post. Dangerous, yes, but how could anyone not see the integrity radiating from him? "You don't know him as I do, but if you did I'm sure you would agree."

"Everyone has some good in them. That's not in question." Scarlet turned to watch Burke hop down from the seat. "It's a matter of the bad. I don't think a man like that is good for any girl."

Scarlet's heart-shaped face pinched in a perfect picture of loving concern. Her soft red locks floated with the hot puff of wind as she opened the door. "Don't be mad at me," she begged.

"I'm not. I love you, Scarlet." She was beginning to see what love really was. An action, not an ideal. A concern for others instead of one's self. Standing for what was right, regardless of how hard that may be.

Burke's boots tromped on the boards. Her soul turned to him. She was helpless to stop it. He walked in larger than life, her very own hero.

"I should go." Scarlet squeezed her arm gently as if in a plea. Her skirts rustled as she wove around Burke without saying hello to him. In time, she told herself, Scarlet would understand. One day everyone would know the Burke she esteemed.

"I'm almost done. Two more seconds." She gripped the mop, guided it along the far wall and back again. "There. Now I can go."

He didn't smile. The lines of his face were harsh and his midnight stare remote. Tension corded the tendons in his powerful neck.

"Is everything all right?" She stowed the mop in the little closet by the counter, withdrew her bonnet and closed the narrow door. "You look as if you had a difficult afternoon."

"Nothing I can't handle." His attempt to smile failed.

She could feel his pain in the stillness. She thought of what Scarlet had said and what others had to believe about him. The story of Lorenzo's cattle had spread like wildfire through town.

"You don't have to handle it alone." She touched his shoulder. Beneath her fingertips, he was as strong as a mountain and felt just as distant. "You have me."

A tick pulsed along his whisker-rough jaw. His gaze pinched, poignant. He looked like a man waging an inner battle. As if he could not allow himself to believe her.

Trust me, she pleaded. She wanted to be what he needed, his shelter in a storm, a soft place to fall, a love he could always believe in.

"You undo me," he choked, wrapped a hand around her nape and drew her against his chest. There, she breathed in the soap scent of his clean shirt and savored the sweetness of his embrace.

Don't let this end, Lord. She squeezed her eyes shut, holding him tight, holding on with prayer. *Don't let me lose him. Let him love me enough to stay.*

Burke pressed a kiss to her forehead. His reserve evaporated and he held her tight for one revealing moment before he broke away.

"I have a picnic place picked out. Let me show you." He offered her his arm and she accepted it. Hearts beating in synchrony, they headed outside. She locked the door and they drove off in the buggy together.

Winds stirred the grasses in a rustling song as Burke reined Lucky to a stop. The mustang lifted his nose to smell the meadow full of nodding flowers, chirping birds and cool dappled shade from the orchard trees. The fragrance of ripening apples and plums mingled with the summery aromas of sun-warmed grasses and the first blackberries ripening in heaping falls over what used to be a livestock fence.

"The old Holbrook place." On the seat beside him, Lila bounded to her feet. The pale pink calico dress she wore, sprigged with pale blue and yellow flowers and adorned with silk ribbons, dainty lace and pearl buttons made her belong in this meadow dotted with small blue buds, yellow sunflowers and wild roses. "I haven't been here in ages."

"Did you know the family?" He hopped down and reached up to catch her. The sunlight bronzed her as he lifted her, dear in his arms, and set her gently on the ground. Her sweetness filled him and became a part of him.

"No one knows the family." Daisies waved at her ankles as she grabbed the rolled blanket beneath the wagon seat. "There were children about my age, but they never attended school. One day they moved away. Some folks said there was a tragedy. Another said financial hardship. But the property was never sold, no one came to tend it. It's sat here forgotten for as long as I can remember."

"A mystery." It was a mystery how he would ever end things. He hefted the basket and the jug while larks sang and a gopher popped out of his hole to watch them curiously. "You've been here before?"

"As kids, we would come to pick the fruit and eat the berries." She strolled among the wildflowers, her skirts fluttering in the breeze. "Scarlet would climb high into the trees to get the best fruit. She was fearless. Heights didn't scare her. I'm not sure if anything does. We would stand at the fence nibbling on apples or plums and dream about our lives to come."

"What did you dream?" He set down his load and took the blanket from her. Gave it a snap.

"Isn't that a little personal?"

"You're blushing." The edges of the blanket fluttered in the wind.

"I was thirteen." She caught one edge and they both walked backward, drew the blanket tight and lowered it to the ground. "And yes, I'm blushing."

"I'm curious. Now I have to know." The breeze tried stealing the edges of the blanket, but he anchored it with the jug of lemonade and a nearby rock before striding over to help Lila anchor her corners.

"Let's just say it involved a fairy-tale ending and leave it at that." She kept her foot on the blanket corner and stretched, trying to reach a rock.

"I hear those kind of endings are popular with you ladies." He hefted up the rock and set it in the appropriate corner. When he straightened, his shadow fell over her. She gazed up at him with tenderness.

Tenderness.

"Everyone deserves a happy ending." She searched him, as if she could look into his soul. No one had gotten closer in decades. Her caring felt as sustaining and as tangible to him as the sun blazing down.

"Not everyone." The words ripped past his constricted throat. Could she see the scars that had never healed? The wrongs he'd committed?

"Yes, everyone who believes in Him. *And we know that all things work together for good to those who love God.*" Her treasured answer proved she could not see into the darkest reaches, where his secrets lurked. Her love gentled him, shining in her eyes, smiling on her lips, whispering without words from her heart.

He wanted to believe. He wished for nothing more than to be able to slip off his past like a shirt he no longer wanted and simply let go. But the wrongs he'd done were a part of him, something he could not shed.

He wanted to be a part of her world, where goodness reigned and life could be wholesome and safe. Where wildflowers fluttered in a prairie breeze and dreams really could come true.

Not his dreams. He could not be in her life. Before he

could gather the words, she spun away, taking his heart with her.

"I kept a close eye on the street," she said as she knelt to pluck a wild rose from its stem. "As close of an eye as I could while I worked. I may have missed a few things, but I still saw enough to make a list. Want to see it?"

"Sure." The word came out rough. The pressure in his throat increased. He tried to swallow but couldn't.

"I had the best time." With the rose in one hand, she pulled a piece of parchment out of her pocket with the other and handed it to him. "I saw two different men wearing spurs. Spurs aren't common around here. Dobbs wears them, and a few other men in town, but I didn't recognize these men. I wrote down their descriptions as best I could."

"This is great, Lila. The Pinkertons should know about you." The details she'd scribbled down could have described a lot of men, but they also fit exactly two wanted men he knew rode with Slim's gang. One of them could have been Cheever. They must have been dressed to blend in with the ranchers and working folk, doing reconnaissance for a future job.

Not going to happen, he thought, remembering the telegram he'd burned. Tomorrow reinforcements would come, they would arrest Dobbs, round up Slim's gang and stop the violent crime plaguing this little corner of the territory.

"It was like being an adventure-novel heroine." She plucked a sunflower, the stem snapping crisply. "You must feel like this every day."

"Most days the work is mundane, but now and then a mission gives me a few high points." He tucked her note into his pocket. "Meeting you has been one of them."

"Your eyes are sad."

"I suppose they are." All of him was sad, down to the soul. The flowers in her hand drew his attention. The sunflower's satin yellow petals opened to the light just as his heart was open to her. If she could see his sorrow, then she could see more. "Do you know how I feel about leaving?"

"I do. I'm going to miss you." Her words quivered, as if she were fighting emotion she did not want revealed.

To him, all was revealed. He swallowed hard against the lump rising higher, the tangle of emotions he did not dare feel. He was loved. Lila loved him. Her devotion shone through when she gazed up at him, looking at him as if he were somebody to her, somebody ten feet tall, her beginning and her end. He was her beloved, and she was his.

A dream he could not keep.

He could not dwell on the day to come when he would tie his belongings to the back of his saddle, ride Lucky away from town and never look back. If he stayed in this moment, if he made it last as long as possible then he could hold on to Lila.

"I fear this is our last evening together." She came into his arms just as he reached out to draw her closer. "That's why you seemed remote earlier. You were going to tell me tonight."

"Yes." His arms folded around her. "I just learned the news."

"We always knew you would go." She laid her cheek against his chest. The slight coarseness of his muslin shirt felt comforting. "You don't form any lasting ties."

"I'm not a settling-down kind of man."

"That is too bad." She fought the grief threatening to consume her. If she kept her tone light, he would never know how deeply she'd fallen for him. She'd tumbled so far there was no coming back. "If you were that kind of man, then we could have stayed in touch. Exchange letters. Form a long-distance friendship."

"That would have been nice." His muscles tensed. Tendons corded. His voice sounded strained. "It would be better for me if we ended things the way they are. Then what we feel right now can be a memory marred by nothing, the best one I've ever had."

"Or me." She squeezed her eyes shut, not ready to let this end. Tears balled in her throat but she wouldn't let them rise.

Please don't go, she silently pleaded, *don't let this end.* As if he felt the same, he clung to her. She listened to the drum of his heart, thudding in time with hers, and felt the rise and fall of his chest, as they breathed in the same rhythm. They were so similar, and like harmony and melody they were not quite complete unless they were together.

Burke stiffened a second before she heard the crackle of a boot in the grass and the metallic click of a Colt's hammer cocking. She realized the birds had silenced, the gopher had disappeared. The back of her neck tingled and iciness snaked down her spine.

"You are going to have to excuse us for interrupting, missy." Dobbs. His sardonic, mean-edged tone made her knees weaken. "We are in need of your beau."

"Why do you have a gun drawn on me?" Burke's noble baritone held no hint of fear. "What's up, Sheriff? Is there some kind of trouble?"

"It turns out there is."

Dobbs wasn't alone. She recognized the squat little man with the bar mustache she'd described in her paper to Burke. His rifle was aimed directly at her.

She gulped. She'd never looked down the barrel of a Winchester before. Little stars danced before her eyes. A loud drum rushed in her ears like a freight train heading her way and drown out Burke's words. She felt the vibration in his chest as he spoke, about what she did not know.

Another man stood behind the cover of the buggy, his long-nosed .45 drawn, gleaming in the sun. She didn't recognize him. He was brawny, unshaven, his stubble as black as the unkempt fall of his hair. He wore a red bandana at his throat, a bright splash of color against his black clothes. His cold hard glare made her shiver. The man's gun pointed at Burke's back. Did Burke know? How did she tell him? His grip had tightened on her, so she couldn't move. His every muscle tensed like those of a bear ready to spring.

"It turns out the assistant clerk at the depot is a friend of mine." Dobbs crunched through the grasses, crushing daisies and sunflowers beneath his boots. "Lucky for me, old Harold didn't feel well and went home early or I never would have heard about your telegram."

"Then I guess we have a problem." Burke rolled her out of his grasp and drew with one smooth motion so fast it was a blur. The momentum sent her stumbling onto the ground. The flowers fell from her hand but not her belief in him.

The outlaws circling them responded. Hammers thumbed back, rifles ratcheted, gunmen took deliberate aim as Dobbs swung his arm a few inches in Lila's direction. "It's your call, Marshal. Do we shoot her now or will you put down your weapon?"

"Let her go." He kept his gun trained dead center on Dobbs's chest.

"Sorry, can't do it." The sheriff didn't answer. The voice came behind him, a voice straight out of his nightmares. "If I remember, Burke, you need incentive to make the right shots. Some things never change."

"Olly." He wasn't surprised. Kid Cheever had grown up, wide-shouldered, tall, rangy and he'd finally acquired his father's cold, dead eyes.

"I thought for sure I'd finished you off that day in town."

Olly spat out a stream of juice, the plug of tobacco distorting one cheek. "You are a hard man to kill."

"You ought to know. You've tried twice. Twice you have left me to die in the street." He pushed aside the memories of the year spent in the gang, the arguments, his attempts to escape and then the hopelessness when he realized escaping wouldn't matter. He was a criminal, an outlaw, and what was done couldn't be forgotten. "You've been busy robbing trains and banks. What were you doing bothering with a delivery wagon and cattle?"

"Got to eat, and that bank job was a bust. There wasn't much in the tills and the vault was locked. We have to make a living somehow." Cheever cocked his gun and aimed it at Lila, who sat where she had fallen, her big green-blue eyes as round as saucers. Two guns were trained on her now. "It turns out I need a good sniper for my next job. What, didn't you tell the lady what you used to do?"

"Don't, Olly." Burke lowered his gun. He would rather be blasted away than to lose Lila this way. "Just let her go, and I'll do whatever you want."

"You'll do what I want anyhow." Greed and power glittered in soulless eyes. "There's a payroll I want to get my hands on, and tonight is the night."

"You don't want to do this." Burke didn't flinch when Cheever took the gun from his hand. Unarmed and defenseless he tried to think of how to stop the inevitable from happening.

"Sure I do." He laughed at that. "Your little lady doesn't know you were once the most hunted gunman in the Dakotas, does she? Or that last I checked you were still wanted for murder in Wyoming?"

No, please, no. Burke squeezed his eyes shut for one long moment. He was a courageous man, but he lacked the bravery to face her. He knew what he would see. Revulsion. Disgust. Horror.

"Oh, guess I ruined the surprise." Cheever spat again. "Dobbs, get her up and tie her good. Burke, don't forget. Her life depends on you."

He hung his head. She would hate him for the lies. She would hate him for what he'd been and because that part of him would always be inside him. Everything that mattered to him was lost. Surely this could not be in God's plan, but he figured God owed him nothing. God had guided him this far but maybe no further. Perhaps finally all accounts would be settled. God might be through with him, and his impossible quest for penance would be over.

Olly wasn't going to let him live. It was Lila he had to save and that was the reason why he held out his arms for one of Cheever's lackeys to tie his wrists.

Chapter Sixteen

Night had fallen hours ago, so it had to be near midnight. Lila watched the narrow patch of the sky. From her place on the floor of the buggy and the thick trees blocking the Heavens, she couldn't see much but she knew they were far west of town. The buggy bounced and jostled on sloping roads, unlike the relatively flat lanes on the prairie. The brief glimpse of a mountain peak, close enough to touch, confirmed her suspicions. They were far from Angel Falls, far from anywhere.

The outlaw's words kept spinning through her mind. *Your little lady doesn't know you were once the most hunted gunman in the Dakotas, does she? Or that last I checked you were still wanted for murder in Wyoming?*

Burke hadn't denied it. He'd stood with his powerful shoulders braced, his chin raised radiating integrity like the Range Rider she'd believed him to be. But a gunman? A murderer? No, she couldn't imagine it. Not the man who'd held her with infinite tenderness, who had treated her with immeasurable gentleness. She wouldn't believe it. The outlaw, the one Burke had called Olly, was lying.

"Here we are." Dobbs sawed back on the reins and the

buggy rocked to a halt. The mustang's hooves pounded in protest in the dirt.

"Easy on the bit, Dobbs," Burke barked out, harsh and with authority like the tough lawman he was. "Don't hurt the horse."

"A bleeding heart. That's a weakness, boy." Dobbs kicked the brake, tossed down his reins and leather whispered in a strange sliding rasp. Lila couldn't guess the sound until she heard a handgun cock. Dobbs had drawn his weapon. "Even when you had me fooled, you couldn't stop helping folks. You gotta learn the way of the world and I'm about to give you a good lesson. People are only good for one thing, using to get what you want."

"Dobbs, take the gun off her. I've agreed to cooperate." Frustration punched in his words.

"Maybe you've got more lessons to learn. Such as you don't cross me." The threat hung in the sultry air.

What was happening? She couldn't see Burke. She couldn't see Dobbs, only the deep shadows of the dashboard. Bridles jangled, horses sidestepped and boots thudded on hard-packed ground. Before she could protest beefy hands wrapped around her forearms and hauled her out of the buggy. Her elbow rammed into the frame. Her knee struck the step. She fell on her knees to the ground. She couldn't see anything. The forest was too dark. She could not see the men who held her.

"Git up," a disembodied voice spat. "I want ter watch ya walk."

"She's got a real nice walk," another voice, edged with threat, said with a laugh.

Her stomach twisted. What was going to happen to her? The safety of town, of her family and friends was several hours' drive away. No one knew she was here.

"Leave her be." Burke's fury darkened his face and

twisted his jaw, apparent even in the shadows. "You hurt her and nothing can make me help you. Nothing."

"There's always something that works." Enough scattered starlight filtered through the old-growth trees to faintly glow on the steel of the sheriff's .45. The muzzle nosed against Burke's temple. "Take him, boys."

Terror for Burke coursed through her. Vaguely she realized she was being half dragged through the thick shadows of the trees toward an abandoned claim shanty. The moss-covered roof tilted at an angle, as if it were in the process of falling down. A hitching post in the far corner was not. Its thick round logs sank deep in the ground and rose taller than a man's head. The crossbar, waist-high, looked capable of holding the strongest ox.

Without warning, the men holding her let go. She was grateful for the release of their warm, clammy hands, but she hit the ground hard enough to rattle her teeth and knock the wind out of her. Pain slammed through ribs and she rolled to her side, trying to catch her breath. Her lungs gasped, her throat spasmed, tears swam in her eyes. Suddenly her lungs relaxed, she drew in air and swiped the dampness from her cheeks just in time to be dragged along the ground by her wrists and dropped in front of the hitching post.

She wasn't alone. Burke stood, back to the post, ankles apart, a chain gleaming in the darkness. Blood trickled from the corner of his mouth. His hat was gone, his shirt torn. He was hurt.

"Burke." His name escaped her lips, raw with fear for him and herself.

He didn't acknowledge her. Not a muscle flickered as he towered overhead, iron-strong and defiant and invincible. The man he'd called Olly tied his hands behind him and bound him to the pole.

"Your turn next." Olly's silky tenor held a note of darkness. She shivered as his fingertips trailed the cut of her jaw and lingered on her vulnerable neck. "You are a pretty piece of calico."

"Cheever," Burke growled a warning that didn't sound at all like the tender man she'd fallen in love with. Menace grated in his tone.

As if hit, Olly removed his hand.

Roughly her wrists were bound behind her back and tied to the pole next to Burke's boots. Being tied up wasn't exactly comfortable. The rope burned the delicate skin of her wrists and dug so tightly it felt as if her bones were about to break. Her shoulders screamed with agony.

Dizzy with discomfort, she drew in fresh air in deep gasps and listened to chains binding her to the post rattle and clink. She recognized the *snick* of a padlock closing. Burke stood above her, as silent at the pine pole they were bound to.

"Hope you're comfortable." Done binding them, the outlaw rose. A sneer that was part amusement and part hatred twisted his shadowed face. He spat a spray of tobacco juice that landed in the darkness. "There was only one chain in the wagon we commandeered, but at least this way you can say your goodbyes to your lady friend. You have time. We ride in an hour."

That sounded terribly final. Lila leaned back, expecting to find the pole and found Burke's calf and knee instead. She looked up at him but saw only his shirt and the underside of his jaw, clenched so tight she could make out the delineation of tensed muscle, even in the near dark.

"I would much rather read about this kind of adventure," she whispered. The wind shifted and her stomach rumbled. "Is that beef I smell?"

"They're cooking supper over a spit. I can see the light,"

he whispered in return. "I'm guessing one of Lorenzo Davis's cattle."

Her eyes had begun to adjust to the heavy darkness. She saw an old well house not far away, a stable made of rough logs where one of Olly's lackeys was hitching Burke's horse with others, and Pa's unhitched delivery wagon. Faint shadows shifted behind a wooden corral. Probably what remained of Lorenzo's stolen livestock.

In the other direction, the ghostly dance of firelight waxed and waned. The cookout must be on the other side of the shanty. Men's voices murmured, pots clanged, steel forks scraped on enamel plates. An argument broke out over the best piece of steak.

"I can't get us out of this." Burke's whisper came chocked with emotion. "They took my guns, my knives, even the one I keep in my boot."

"I left my guns and knives at home," she quipped. What was wrong with her? She was on the edge of hysteria. She closed her eyes and tried to stay calm. She had to think. There had to be a way out of this. The books she read always offered a solution.

"When they untie us, I want you to run," Burke's tone dropped below a whisper, barely audible as a cooling wind gusted. "Run and don't look back. No matter what, I will hold them off."

"With what? You are unarmed."

"I intend to improvise. Don't worry. I'm good at it."

"But what about you?"

"Me? I don't matter. Your freedom does." His voice broke, betraying a hint at the depth of his affection for her. An answering tenderness welled within her, sparkling pure.

"Can you reach one of my hairpins?" She arched her neck toward his bound hands. "How about now?"

"What do you want with a hairpin?" His fingertips brushed the silken crown of her braided topknot.

"Just pull out one and try to drop it into my hands."

"I don't see the reason for it." He twisted as far as the bindings would allow. His spine popped. His ribs protested. His knuckles brushed against her textured braid. "It's not going to cut the rope or break the chain."

"Yes, but I read this in a book once." She tipped her head slightly.

"There." He had to concentrate to work the thin metal clip out of the thick braid. When it came loose, he managed to twist his neck just enough to see the curve of her shoulder and the back of her head. Her hands would be behind her, directly in line with her spine. He released the pin. "Here it goes."

"I didn't get it." She didn't sound perturbed. "So close. It just barely glanced off my fingertips."

"Try it again." While he worked, he kept his senses alert. The clatter at the fire pit grew louder. Everyone must be gathering around to eat, so the guards on them would be at a minimum. He couldn't see anyone watching in the dark, his eyes were still adjusting, but guards had to be somewhere. Neither Olly nor Dobbs would trust him alone, even unarmed and chained to a pole.

"Got it." Lila's whispered triumph was replaced by silence. He felt her inching closer to the post, closer to him. The chain binding the both of them drew tighter as she fought for more give. She went after the padlock.

C'mon, Lila. You can do it. He gritted his teeth as the chain threaded through his bindings shortened and the ropes cut flesh and clamped on bone. The pain was nothing, not when he thought about what would happen if she didn't get away. He'd seen it before. He lived with the

Cheever gang for a year. He knew what ruthless men did to a female captive.

Regardless of any he deal struck, any he bargain made, Burke knew Lila would be beaten, raped and shot. He wouldn't be there to save her because they would have already put a bullet through his brain.

"Ooh, almost!" she muttered. The faint click of chain links might have been loud enough to carry, but the wind gusted again, hard enough to rattle the trees and send the boughs of the surrounding forest swishing and creaking. Cold air sang through the limbs, needles rustled and the faint starlight overhead eked out. Huge, scattered drops of rain plopped to the earth like popcorn popping.

Just a little more help, Father. Please. The sky was dark, as if Heaven no longer watched but he did not feel forsaken. A dark silhouette separated from the inky shadows. A guard patrolling the distance from the cluster of horses to the captives was getting closer.

The metallic snick told him she'd done it. She'd picked the lock. Adrenaline spilled into his bloodstream. The gunman was pacing closer, not hurried. He hadn't spotted Lila yet, but he soon would. The chain whispered as she snaked it out of the bindings holding one of his ankles to the post and a foot was free.

The shadow drew closer. He was a tall and skinny scarecrow and it could only be Slim, the head of the gang. Burke's pulse cannoned. Danger closed in only ten yards away. Nine. Eight.

Hurry, Lila. He willed her hands to go faster. He pulled at his wrists, but they were bound. He was helpless to move, helpless to protect her. Six yards. Five.

He felt the slither of the chain against his palm and his wrists came free from the post, but his hands were still bound. Slim carried his rifle, relaxed in the crook of his arm, rain dripping off the wide brim of his hat. Burke tensed, ready to move as the rope tugged and abraded his wrists as Lila worked at the knot. Three yards. Two.

"What the—" The outlaw's gaze dropped to where the woman ought to be. The rope slid free, Burke stepped forward on his free leg, grabbed the nose of the gun while Slim was too startled to move and rammed the flat of his palm directly on Slim's sternum. Without a word, the mighty outlaw crumpled and slid to the puddled ground. The tiniest splash was the only sign he'd been taken down.

"Is he...?" Lila gasped. "Did you—"

"I don't know." He only knew the man was unconscious. Maybe he'd stopped Slim's heart, maybe not, but he'd stopped him. He ripped the chain from his ankle, scanned the perimeter and grasped Lila by the forearm. He pulled her hard against the side of the shanty where the shadows were the deepest.

He had a gun, so he had a fighting chance. He hauled her to the corner of the building, searching the foliage, ears peeled for the slightest footfall or the tiniest splash of a puddle. Nothing. The merriment around the campfire continued, talk turning to how they were going to spend the mill's payroll once they'd stolen it. Whiskey and women seemed the most popular choice.

"Run." He covered her while she dashed across open ground to the shelter of the well house. He followed her, walking backward, gun raised, finger on the trigger. The horses were feet away, tied loosely to a long rope anchored between trees. He chirruped and Lucky answered with a low nicker.

"So far so good." He swiped the rain sluicing down her forehead and into her eyes, just to have one last reason to touch her. He wished for moonlight to see her by. He wished for an eternity to love her through but it was not to be. At least he had the chance to know her and to love her. He was grateful for that. "Untie Lucky as quick and as quiet as you can. Can you ride bareback?"

"I've never ridden," she replied in her low, dulcet alto. "But I've read about characters who did. I can do it."

"Good." He covered her lips with his. One last kiss. Pure love blinded him. Pure devotion filled his soul. He released her, sure it was the last he would see of her. "The second you get on his back, you tell him to fly. You hold on, and you don't look back. No matter what. Do you promise?"

"Will you be right behind me?" Her voice trembled.

"Promise, Lila." He shook her gently. They had no time to waste. He didn't hear danger approaching but that could change in the blink of an eye. "You ride to town and find Jed. Tell him to wait for my boss. Now, go."

"But—"

"Go," he growled. "If you love me, do this."

"I love you. I do." She stumbled back, torn by what he asked, lost in the shadows. "I didn't believe what those men said about you. I know they lied. You are the best man, Burke."

"Go!" He sounded strangled, almost angry. Of course he was. Every moment she delayed put them both in more jeopardy, so she did as she promised.

She raced past the stable, slipped between the horses, untied Lucky and climbed awkwardly, slipping and sliding onto his back. With both hands full of black mane, she leaned against the horse's neck and whispered, "Fly."

The mustang snorted, gathered his muscles and leaped away from the others. She had no bridle to guide him, no saddle horn to grab. She squeezed with her knees just like she'd read about in so many Westerns and clung with all her might. His power glided beneath her and moved through her as he sailed across the yard. Surely Burke would grab one of the horses and follow.

But the rhythmic pounding of Lucky's hooves brought men running. The forest came alive. Gunfire echoed like cannons. Shouts rang and bodies thudded to the ground. The gunfire did not end. That's when she knew Burke wasn't coming. He'd never intended to do anything but defend her so she could escape.

How could he have done such a thing? She broke her promise and glanced over her shoulder. Burke pushed himself out of the mud and onto his knees with rifle raised. He must have been shot. He fired again and again before he tumbled backward, hit a second time.

"Stop!" she screamed but Lucky did not obey. He knew his duty and carried her far away into the night, where black clouds roiled across the endless sky and no outlaw rode out of the dark to chase her.

Chapter Seventeen

He had hit the ground hard and feared he couldn't get back up. The first bullet had sliced through his side, grazing neat as a pin between two of his ribs. The second burrowed into his left shoulder. He'd heard bone crack and pain radiated everywhere. Up his neck, across his back and chest, down his arm which hung limp. He couldn't feel it. If he hadn't been able see his arm, he wouldn't know it was still there.

You have to get up, Hannigan. He was still breathing. As long as he lived, no one would charge down this road after Lila. His senses told him someone was untying some horses, a few men remained probably hunkered down behind a rock or a log making sure they were safe before venturing out. He'd lived and worked with criminals enough to know they put themselves first and wouldn't risk an unnecessary bullet wound unless they had to.

That gave him a few seconds to gather his strength and figure out a way to get off the ground. He clenched his jaw and heaved upward.

His body stayed flat in the mud. Wet and cold seeped through his shirt and trousers. Rain pelted his wounds and sluiced down his face. His gun became slick with rain, mud and blood beneath his grip.

He had two more bullets left. He'd taken down four men. That meant five were still alive and gunning for him. He didn't like those odds. It sounded like two were ready to mount up, which meant one thing. He was out of time. He had to stop them right now. *Lord, Lucky has a head start. Now give him wings.*

He exhaled so his shot would be steady, straightened his right arm, drew the rifle an inch to line up a shot with the road and squeezed. The first rider tumbled off his mount and hit the ground. Another shot stopped the second.

"I told you he was still alive, boys," Cheever bellowed. "Now stick your chicken necks out and cover me."

Rain blurred his vision. Weakness made his teeth chatter. He turned his gun toward the squish of boots in the muck, splashing closer in a slow measured step that told him his nemesis knew he was out of bullets.

Defenseless, he stared up at the Heavens, infinitely black and cold. At least Lila had a fighting chance of making it back to town. Even if Cheever's men mounted up, Lucky had too big of a head start. It was a good chance they couldn't catch up with him. That meant Lila was probably safe.

She's worth it, Lord. He gladly gave his life for hers. He coughed and felt a stream of blood rush warmly down his shirt. For the first time since he was fifteen, he was proud of his life and of what he stood for. He would die with love in his heart, not guilt and not emptiness. Love.

"Looks like we have a score to settle, Burke." Olly towered over him, gun in hand.

"Guess we do." He stared at the barrel of the .45 aimed at his heart. "I wouldn't have shot your pa if he hadn't shot me first."

"You got what you deserved then and you'll get it now. Only this time I'll make sure the job is done right. This time you will be good and dead." Olly spat a spray of tobacco juice, thumbed back the hammer and exhaled, ready to take his shot.

That summer so long ago rolled back to him, the scent of growing grass and sun-scented wind and daisies nodding lazily. Before Olly's betrayal, before a life of crime, before his soul had shattered. He could almost feel the boy he'd been, lost and lonely but innocent.

One last try, he pushed with all his strength. Surprised his body responded, he didn't move fast enough. The gun went off, but he grabbed it out of Olly's hands. Before his old friend could draw his holstered second shooter, he fired. He knew it wasn't a fatal wound, he wasn't trying for it. Light bled from his vision, sound from his ears and he hit the ground he could not feel. Darkness claimed him, cold and final. His last thought was of Lila and the first time he'd stumbled into her store and asked to buy a bandage. It was her beautiful face he saw and then there was no more.

He knew nothing for a long while. Pain invaded out of the darkness even when he could not reach consciousness and finally the pain vanished, too. In dream, he heard the rustle of wheat in a mild breeze. Ripening fields rolled around the shanty in every direction. The Dakota sky stretched blue overhead and puffy white clouds sailed through it. The warmth of summer wrapped around him as he pulled a blade of grass from its leafy sheath and popped the raw stem between his teeth. The green taste filled his mouth.

"What are you doing, son?" Pa looked up from hoeing Ma's garden, strong and healthy and whole, his easygoing grin wide.

"I'm lookin' at the cloud pictures." When he tipped his head again and held his hat to keep it from falling, he saw shapes just like his pa had taught him to look for. "It's a wagon!"

"Let me see." Pa came around to look and sidled up close. His big comforting hand settled on Burke's shoulder, engulfing it. "Yep, you're right, son. It's a covered wagon. Looks to me like it is heading west."

"And there's the horse that goes with it." Excited now, he poked his finger toward the sky. "But it's grazing. They must be done travelin' for the day."

"I wonder who they are and where they are goin'?" Pa swept off his hat to rake his hand through his hair.

"Rob, what about my garden?" Ma asked in her gentle, amused way. "Thistles are trying to take over my green beans."

"I see a thistle up in the clouds, too. Want me to weed it?" Pa quipped and everyone laughed.

Ginna came running from helping in the garden. She dusted the dry prairie dirt off her hands and brushed it from the corner of her apron.

"I see a little girl." Her braids bobbed as she tipped her head to study the entire sky. "I see a family stopping to camp for the night. A happy family."

Something warm brushed his jaw and settled on his forehead, a soothing comfort that drew him up out of his dream to surface. Before his eyes opened, pain invaded. He couldn't feel his arm or his shoulder, but everything else hurt. That had to be a good sign. It meant he was alive.

He clenched his jaw, grinding his teeth, to endure it. He did not want to sleep, not even to escape the agony. Gradually he became aware of a rocking movement, the incandescent glow of starlight and the faint flutter and snap of a skirt hem as the winds snatched at it. His eyelids fluttered knowing she was near. His Lila.

"You came." The words croaked out of his dry throat. "You disobeyed me."

"I'm difficult that way, ask Eunice." Humor polished her. She'd never been more beautiful. Gratitude stung his eyes. He'd never thought he would see her again. God had been kind to allow him to gaze upon her one last time.

"The doc says you are hurt pretty bad. You had to go and play the hero, didn't you?" She brushed at his hair, smoothing it out of his eyes, her touch infinitely caring. He heard what she did not say.

"Only a fool lets himself get shot at." Words that were too vulnerable caught in his throat, and he could not say them.

"Exactly. The day I met you, you had two bullet wounds. The day I say goodbye to you, you have three bullet wounds. I'm starting to think you are a dangerous man to be around."

"Finally." The smile cost him, and he couldn't hold it for long. He held up his hand for her to take. Her soft fingers fit between his, a perfect fit. Love brimmed over, leaving him defenseless. "I tried to tell you."

"Everybody did." Her fingers tightened around his in a single affectionate squeeze. "I didn't believe it for a moment."

"You should have." He wished he could sit up. All he could see was the patch of starry sky overhead beginning to gray. Dawn was not far away. "You should have believed it, because it is true."

"Hardly." She looked at him as if he'd hit his head, as if he were talking nonsense. "Just close your eyes. We should be in town before long."

Then he didn't have much time. The wagon bounced

and jostled on country roads, making the wagon bed bite into his spine. He lifted his head a scant inch off the blanket he was lying on. It looked like Jed was driving. She must have rounded up half the town when she'd arrived back in Angel Falls. Ardent concern and unspoken affection polished her, made her more lovely than ever. He cleared his throat.

"I was an outlaw. When I was fifteen I rode with Cheever in his father's gang for a year. We robbed stages and banks, innocent folks and not-so-innocent folks. What Olly said was true." He nearly choked on the words. He wished he could erase that time from his memory. He wished he'd never picked up a gun. "I'm wanted for the murder of a deputy in Wyoming. I've committed crimes in the Dakotas, which I've never paid for."

He watched while she shook her head adamantly, fighting disbelief and denial. Her denial wouldn't last. His words would sink in and she would believe him. Her love would die, her regard for him vanish. What would his life be without her love? He was about to find out.

"But you are a Range Rider." Even in the thick dusk, he could see her feelings change. Distance settled between them like the leading edge of a storm. She sat up straighter, away from him, still in denial. "I saw your badge."

"Yes. We had a job go wrong. Olly's pa was furious at me because I refused to gun down anyone else. I'd been pushed too far. I was a kid, but I grew up. I finally learned how to have the courage to stand up to someone that terrifying and tell him I was out. He shot me. So I shot him. The gang left me to die." He could remember the chill of that cold December day when he'd been left for dead in the snow. "A unit of Riders from town got there just before I lost consciousness. I knew they recognized me. I knew I was looking at a hard prison sentence or worse."

"You murdered people?" She shook her head, as if dazed, as if she couldn't make the pieces fit.

"I tried to hurt them instead of kill them, but the one deputy died of his injury anyway." Remorse and guilt of the strongest kind battered him, greater than any physical pain. He would never forget opening his eyes that day and seeing the Rider towering over him, hands on his hips, starkly familiar. "One of the Riders was the first man I'd shot. I thought he'd died, but it turned out the bullet missed his heart and he lived. He remembered me. He saw what Old Man Cheever did to me. He offered a deal and got the governor to agree. If I worked for them and made up for what I did, I would have the chance to earn clemency for my crimes in Montana."

Here is where she would say she despised him. She would turn away. Perhaps regret ever knowing him. He steeled his heart. He gathered his courage. He was man enough to face her rejection, although it would hurt.

"That explains why you are so good with a gun." The sorrow haunting her belied the attempt at humor. "Jed said it was incredible shooting you did."

"I tried my best." For her. All that mattered was her. That she would have a happy future. She deserved a good man to love her, children and a fairy-tale ending to her life. He would give anything to be that man.

Not in Your plan for me, I know, Lord. He swallowed hard, his confession done and his strength, too. *But I wish.*

"I never wanted you to know." His eyelids drifted shut, he couldn't keep them open. "But you needed the truth. The man you think I am doesn't exist."

"You are wrong, Marshal. In novels, the hero always has a past." Her fingers in his did not move away but remained strongly entwined. "I saw the man you are on the day you stumbled into the mercantile shot and bleeding, on the day you drove the delivery wagon to keep me safe and last night when you took bullets for me."

"All flukes."

"Hardly." She straightened her spine, let the cool early-morning breeze buffet her face and the first rays of dawn brought illumination. "A character's true nature is revealed in the choices he makes through the book. I have seen yours."

"You saw me kill men right in front of your eyes." A muscle ticked along his clenched jaw, as if that tortured him. "You saw me being violent."

"I saw you being protective. We both know what those men would have done to me. You were the only thing stopping them." Her love for him renewed. It felt as fresh as the new day, as hopeful as the pearled light shining over the world.

"You were the one who picked the padlock holding us," he argued as if determined to be humble. "You could have escaped all on your own. I was unnecessary."

"Yes, well, you are a man," she quipped, too choked up to say what she really meant. Although his eyes were closed, he pressed his jaw against the curve of her palm and she knew he heard the symphony of love in her heart.

He did not speak again as unconsciousness claimed him. She sat at his side until the wagon rolled up to the depot. Jed, Dr. Frost, Mr. Winters and Pa carried him to the platform. The whistle could already be heard. She leaned against the edge of the depot building and watched as the train rumbled to a stop, a unit of Riders disembarked and that was the last she saw of the love of her life.

Chapter Eighteen

"Whatcha doin', Earlee?"

"Nothing that would interest you." She tapped the excess ink off the pen on the side of the bottle. She'd left the bread dough to rise in two big bowls on the table beside her, covered with light cloths. The yeasty scent already made the kitchen end of the living room smell homey.

"I was hopin' you could come play fort with me." Edward folded his forearms against the table and leaned in. "Everyone's workin'. I'm bored."

"Enjoy it while you can. Next year you will be old enough to help with some of the farmwork." She set the pen on the paper and marked the date, August 30, 1884. "Tell you what. After I walk back from seeing my friends in town, I'll take you down to the creek."

"Honest?" That lit him up. "I sure do like the creek. I wanna watch the crawdads again. Can we have a picnic supper there? Oh, boy. I'm gonna go tell Ma!"

Edward's bare feet slapped across the floorboards. Already he was calling out to their mother, who was resting comfortably in the shady backyard.

She smiled as her brother leaped out the door, all little boy energy. The day ahead held so much promise. An afternoon spent with her best friends, supper by the cool shady creek and while the children played she would start penning her new story. She itched to get her idea down on paper and there was nothing more pleasant than sitting in the whispering grasses with the sounds of her family all around her while she imagined up a fictional adventure.

But first, her letter. With her pen loaded, she set it on the page to write.

Finn,
I know you are concerned for me and feel associating with you might not be in my best interests. I appreciate your concern. It tells me you are still the McKaslin boy I remember, kind to all, liked by everyone before you started spending time with people who weren't good for you. I am certain that part of you is still there, for good is never truly lost. So you will simply have to endure my friendship, as I like to write letters and you are too far away to stop me.

She drew a smiling face so he knew she was smiling as she wrote. She chronicled the changes on the farm since she'd last written.

The fluffy yellow chicks have tripled in size and are gangling instead of cute, the way they used to be, but always funny. Pa built a summer enclosure for them to scratch in and chase after bugs. They dash around after a prize bug, so focused they run into the screen fencing and each other, bounce off and keep going. The baby calves have grown, too, adorable with their big brown eyes and curiosity. The kittens have taken over the barn, sliding down the remains of last harvest's haystacks like otters at play.

She added a few anecdotes from Edward's latest exploits and the news of the Range Riders in town and the sheriff's arrest. Lila's pa's horses and delivery wagon were returned. Some of Lorenzo's cattle were recovered. Several towns-people who'd been threatened and intimidated by Dobbs had come forward. Good news, all in all.

She signed the letter with a flourish, addressed the envelope and went to dig for her stash of pennies hidden in the room she shared with her sisters. She would stop by the post office on her way to Lila's. That way the letter could go out on the afternoon train.

"The bread is ready." Her sister Beatrice sailed into the shanty. "Don't worry, I'll get the dough kneaded and in the oven. You go have a great time with your friends."

"Thanks." She went in search of her Sunday calico and her shoes. Hopefulness filled her heart. Her and Finn's story wasn't over yet.

Lila waited for the dust from the teamster's wagon to clear before she stepped off the boardwalk and crossed the busy Friday afternoon street. It had been three weeks, almost four, since the sheriff's arrest. Dobbs had been replaced by Clint Kramer, who had been sheriff before he'd lost the rigged election. The Range Riders had hunted down the remnants of Slim and Olly's gang, two of which had fled when Cheevers had been shot and the others had been out setting up to rob the nearby logging company's considerable payroll. Peace and order had returned to Angel Falls. The only thing missing was the gigantic piece of her heart Burke had taken with him.

"Lila, how's the new job?"

She stepped up onto the boardwalk and glanced around. Recognizing the older man seated on a cart pulled by a donkey, she broke into a grin. "Perfectly, Mr. Grummel. How's Mrs. Grummel?"

"Wishing she didn't live next door to that stepmother of yours." He hollered over the clatter of another teamster's loaded wagon rumbling by. "Do you know what business is going in across the street? I heard the storefront was rented but not by who."

"I have no idea." Lila shifted the bakery box she carried to her other hand. "I didn't even know it was rented."

"These days everything changes." Mr. Grummel shook his head. "Nothing stays the same. People come, people go. Oy."

"Have a good afternoon!" She called before the donkey took him out of talking range. Mr. Grummel's hat tipped in answer and his cart rolled away.

She spun on her heels to face the mercantile. The harvest window display Eunice had set up was quite effective. Canning jars and lids, big kettles and drying screens, knives and peelers and a pretty assortment of kitchenware.

Her hand hesitated on the door handle. On the other side of the glass midway through the store she caught sight of her father. Eunice fussed with his hat, tugging as if at a stray thread, perhaps talking about the steps necessary to mend it, a look of adoration plain on her face. A look of contentment on his.

Lila turned the knob, the bell chimed and she crossed the threshold into the store.

"Lila!" Lark bolted out from behind the counter, arms wide and leaped into a quick hug. She rocked back on her heels, bursting with pleasure and flicked a braid behind her shoulders. "Lila, I'm doing real well taking your place. Eunice is letting me post all the sales to the accounts."

"Good job." The store looked the same, but different. Better, brighter and she could still picture her mother at the fabric counter, chatting with customers as she cheerfully measured out bolts of colorful fabrics.

"There's my girl." Pa came over, pride showing. "Cora Sims was just in telling us what fine work you are doing for her."

"Yes," Eunice agreed. "I told her it was the way you were raised. Hard work, lots of discipline. You've made yourself a fine reputation, Lila, but remember, you can come back anytime."

"Thank you." She was content with her decisions. She was her own woman. With a start, she remembered the time. "I'm in a rush. I need to pick up some berries for my sewing circle this afternoon."

"I'll get them." Eunice paraded over to the buckets of fresh blueberries and chose the nicest one.

"I'll put it on your account!" Lark rushed to pick up a pen and ink it.

"I've got deliveries to make," Pa said, giving her nose a tweak. "Don't forget to visit your old man more often."

"How about I come over for Sunday supper?"

"That would be just fine." Pa nodded, cleared his throat and ambled away.

"I'll make pot roast," Eunice decided, "and my sourdough biscuits you like so well."

"I'll forward to it." Lila took the pail of berries, waved goodbye and pushed out onto the street. She was late, late, late. Her friends would be arriving any minute.

As she hurried down the blocks and neared Cora's dress shop, a pretty little buggy pulled to a stop. She recognized the mare, Miss Bradshaw, being tied to the hitching post.

"It's Meredith!" Lila squealed as she spotted her dear friend, lifted her skirts with her free hand and raced in a very unladylike manner, weaving around perfectly innocent pedestrians on the boardwalk. Oh, how she'd missed her friend!

"Surprise!" The willowy blonde in a fashionable cotton print dress pushed away from the post and came running. The jaunty tilt of her hat brim flapped slightly with her gait as she flung her arms wide. "It's so *good* to see you!"

Lila set the box and pail on the bench outside the dress shop so her arms were free. They met in the middle of the boardwalk, hugged and hopped up and down in their excitement. They caught hold of hands, the way they used to do when they were little schoolgirls. "You look wonderful, Meredith. You're positively glowing."

"I'm happy." Joy lit her up, making her lovelier than ever. An engagement ring sparkled on her finger, a beautiful diamond and emerald setting which suited her perfectly. "I blame Shane for it. My happiness is entirely his fault."

"Is he still training your father's horses?"

"Yes. Pa is pleased with his work, and you know my mother. She can't stop fawning over poor Shane. I think he drives out to visit me on the weekends just to escape her flattery." Meredith laughed, her bliss contagious. "I don't see an engagement ring, so Burke hasn't returned to town to propose?"

"Pro-pose?" she sputtered at the notion. Her happiness at seeing her friend evaporated. The misery of losing Burke and the anguish of missing him through the past three, almost four weeks seized her again. In truth, she did not even know if he lived. She tried to smile, tried to keep her heartbreak hidden. "No, Burke was never serious about me. I told you that in my letters."

"Yes, but the heart follows its own path." Meredith gently squeezed Lila's hand, her understanding and support unshakable.

"Meredith! It's Meredith!" Fiona leaped from the wagon seat while it was still creeping up to the boardwalk, leaving her grandmother and her husband behind with a wave. The horses sped along again as she squealed up the step. "You came! You're really here!"

"I couldn't stay away. I missed you all so much!" Meredith laughed, and Lila did, too, as Fiona set down her sewing basket and caught them both. They circled into a three-person hug, skirts swishing together, arms tangling right along with their peals of laughter.

"Let me in!" Kate bounded up, dropped her sewing basket and joined in the squealing and the hugging. "Meredith, this is the best surprise ever. Are you staying in town over the weekend?"

"Yes. I have to squeeze in all the time I can with my friends while I'm here. Letters are great, but they aren't the same as being here with you. Kate, what is going on with you? You haven't written me hardly at all."

"I have a letter right here. I finally got to town to mail it, but now you're here so you may as well take it with you." Kate pulled an envelope from her skirt pocket and her gaze landed on someone else hurrying up the boardwalk toward them.

Lila glanced over her shoulder. "Scarlet!"

"Ooh! I had hoped you would be here, Meredith!" Her red curls bounced as she set her sewing basket alongside the others. "I loved your last letter about all your little students. They are so funny."

"And fun. I love being a teacher, but I've missed my friends." Meredith reached out to bring Scarlet into the hugging circle. "My next job must not be so far away."

"It's fine to be your own woman," Lila spoke up, "but life is better when you are close to your friends."

"Exactly." They all harmonized, glad to be all together again.

"Hey, is there room for me?" A shy, soft-noted voice asked.

"Ruby." Lila let go of Meredith, breaking apart the circle to make a space. "There's always plenty of room for you."

"Always," everyone chimed.

Ruby flushed prettily, not used to so much attention, and joined them. She was such a pretty person no one noticed the careful patches on the elbows and skirt of her red calico dress. "And to think I almost didn't come. Meredith, I would have been terribly upset to have missed seeing you."

"Is there a problem at home?" Scarlet asked.

"Only of the wild animal kind. I've been run ragged trying to keep the jackrabbits out of the garden," Ruby explained with good humor. "If I don't keep an eye out, they are nibbling on my carrots. Pa took pity on me and agreed to pay the neighbor girl to chase away the bunnies while I'm gone."

Across the street, Lorenzo Davis caught the gentle sound, stopped in his tracks and turned toward them. His gaze landed on Ruby and only on Ruby. His wide shoulders straightened and his chiseled face became dreamy. No one else noticed, just Lila. She wondered if a romance between the two of them was in the future.

"We have rabbit problems, too!" Earlee squeezed into the circle, shaking Lila from her thoughts.

"Hey, you aren't even late," Fiona said in her gentle manner. "For once. I'm shocked."

"No one is more shocked than me." Earlee's gold curls glinted in the sunshine. "Lately I have been so busy with the house and the farm, I don't know if I'm coming or going."

"You should have been named 'Late' instead of 'Earlee,'" Kate quipped and they all laughed together, just like old times, like the schoolgirls they used to be.

So much in life changed. Little girls grew up, they became young ladies who found jobs, married or helped support their families. They were all finding their way in the world, but she knew the best things in life stayed the same. Their friendship was stitched together with the thread of love, a bond too strong to break.

"Come inside," she said. "I don't want to waste a single moment of our time together."

The sun brightened, as if even God agreed. They broke apart and gathered up their sewing baskets. Their merry chatter rose like lark song as Lila retrieved the cookies and blueberries and led the way.

"I don't think the doc was right." Jeremiah Kane pushed his chair away from his desk. The scrape of wooden chair legs against the oak floor echoed in the Helena office that headquartered the territorial Range Riders. Jeremiah rose to his impressive six foot plus height. "You aren't ready to come back, Hannigan. You can't use your arm."

"If I can stand, I can work." Burke leaned back in the corner chair, stretched out his legs and crossed them at the ankles. He wasn't intimidated one bit. "Sure, my arm is in a sling. It's not my shooting arm."

"That's not the point." Jeremiah cornered his desk, came to the front of it and leaned against it. He folded his arms over his chest, a casual stance, but there was nothing casual about his glare. "You push yourself too hard, Burke."

"I have a lot to make up for. What I did was wrong. I was coerced, I was forced, but I still did it." He was a man, unbowed, not that kid who had been frightened into submission. That didn't erase the past. The thing is, the past felt more distant, as if it truly were in the past. "You know it, Jeremiah. You were the first man I shot."

"You shot many, but you did your best to wound, not kill. Not many outlaws take up that philosophy. That says something, too." He paused a moment. The front door swung open, voices rose and fell near the entrance, and the door closed again. They were alone. "I understand why you are driven, but maybe it's time to ask yourself one question. When is it enough? How do you know when you have paid your debt?"

"Never." The answer nearly choked him. He wanted it to be different, but wanting didn't make it so. Reality was reality and no amount of wishing could change it. How could he let go of what he'd done? "What I took can't be replaced. I caused harm. I took a life."

"That's true. But you've spent almost a decade stopping harm, stopping criminals." Jeremiah, tough as nails, boomed out the words as if with anger, but there was no true anger in them. "Think of all the harm you stopped from happening. The justice you helped to find for honest folks who were victimized. You saved countless lives by getting violent outlaws behind bars before they could hurt anyone else."

"It doesn't feel like enough." But he wanted it to be. He ached with the wish down to the marrow of his bones.

"It is. I've spoken with the governor and you are officially pardoned. Your debt to this territory is paid in full." Jeremiah softened, a rare show of emotion. "Maybe it's time to forgive yourself. I have, the government has and I'm reckoning even God has."

He thought of Lila kneeling in the wagon at his side, coming back from Slim and Cheever's hideout. She'd hardly blinked an eye when he'd told her his story. He'd been so sure she would hate him, that she would never understand, that she would see what he saw in himself.

"You are no longer that scared kid. You were never like Cheever. You were a good kid in a bad situation, but you grew up and you rectified what you could of your mistakes. You've made a difference. No one could have done more." Jeremiah shoved off the desk. "It's time to let you go. It's been an honor serving with you."

"Go?" They were letting him off the hook, just like that?

"You are free to be whatever you want. A farmer, a shopkeeper, a railroad worker." Jeremiah held out his hand, palm up. "Son, I'm going to need your badge."

His badge. He pulled it off his shirt and ran his thumb over the raised shield. He traced the rifle and horse imbedded in the silver. Those symbols had come to mean protection and commitment and duty. The raised words above proudly proclaimed, Montana Territorial Range Rider.

It was his identity, all he had wanted to be as a boy. He could still remember the feel of the splintered fence against his palms as he stared between the boards in the orphanage yard, watching strong, impressive men ride by on their fine horses. The Range Riders had been briefly in that town, but the impression they'd made remained.

"I want to keep it." He couldn't give up this life he'd earned, the job God had led him to. Besides, he had nowhere to go, nothing else he wanted to be.

"I'm glad you feel that way." Jeremiah almost smiled, a rare show of mirth. "I hear from the boys you found yourself a pretty little calico in Angel Falls."

"I did." Lila's beautiful image washed into his mind like a cool splash of water on a hot July day. Her soft oval face, her cinnamon-brown hair, her green-and-blue eyes shimmering with love for him.

Have You forgiven me, Lord? The prayer rose up straight from his soul. *Are You really giving me a chance?*

"As it turns out, we are making a few changes around here." Jeremiah opened his top desk drawer and pulled out a shining new key. "The governor has decided he wants a branch in Angel Falls. The railroad has brought more population into that area and a lot of crime has followed. We need someone to run that office. Are you interested?"

Chapter Nineteen

A new day's sunshine cheerfully sparkled on the windows of Cora's dress shop. Lila considered the display she'd just arranged, adjusted the angle of the darling straw bonnet and plumped the silk ribbon bow. There. The pretty, summery dress Cora had designed as a sample draped perfectly, surrounded by lovely coordinating accessories. That ought to have passersby stopping in their tracks to take a look.

Monday mornings were slow and Cora had said to take advantage of it. So Lila threaded her way around a table of reticules to the front counter, where a fresh sheet of parchment was waiting. She uncapped the bottle, inked her pen and bent to start her latest letter to Meredith.

I hope you are settled back in your schoolroom teaching your adorable students, all seven of them. We loved hearing about them when you were here. I know we miss you already. Things are good here. It's not exactly an adventure novel these days, but I'm enthusiastic about my life. God may be the One to set my path, but it is up to me to make it all it can be.

The musical chime above the door sang out a melody and let in the sounds of the street and the whistling arrival of the morning train several blocks over. Lila put down her pen and greeted her first customers of the day with a smile. "Good morning, Noelle. Matilda."

"Good morning," the cousins called in unison. Matilda with her dark curls and quiet manner led blind Noelle through the doorway.

"Are you looking for anything in particular?" Lila asked, capping her ink bottle.

"Matilda saw the bonnet in the window display and we were suddenly overcome with the need for new hats," Noelle explained happily. "How is your father, Lila? I meant to catch up with your family at church yesterday and ask about him, but my aunt got a hold of me."

"Pa is fine." Noelle's husband, Thad, had been the rancher who had found Pa after he'd been beaten and rushed him to town and rode for the doctor. "His black eye is gone, his nose is nearly healed. The blow to his head turned out not to be as serious as Dr. Frost first feared."

"Now that the outlaws are rounded up and arrested, he can make his deliveries without fear," Matilda added. "It was frightening for a while. Thank goodness the new deputy turned out to be a great help and we are all safe again."

"Yes," Lila agreed, ignoring the hammering blow of grief that struck hard at the mention of Burke. She didn't know if he'd survived his injuries, or if he was well or if he thought of her at all. He had made a great difference to this town and a lasting difference to her. Pride filled her, chasing away some of the sadness. "We have a new shipment of bonnets from back East. Come with me and I'll show you. I just set them out this morning."

"Perfect," Noelle said happily and with her hand on

her cousin's arm wove through the store almost as if she could see.

The front door chimed again and Cora breezed in, looking joyful, as she always did these days. Her wedding was less than two weeks away. She was marrying a very handsome bounty hunter. "Noelle! Matilda! How wonderful to see you. Aren't those bonnets adorable?"

"I have to have one," Noelle answered her dear friend. Cora gave Lila a nod, as if to say she would handle the sale, and hurried over to chat with her friends about hats, the upcoming nuptials and Noelle's baby boy, Graham, who was home with his proud papa.

The door swooshed open with a jingle and a gust of dusty air. Tingles skidded down her nape and trickled along her spine. She turned toward the doorway and stared at the man with shoulders braced, boots planted, one arm in a sling. Dark brown unruly hair framed a face so rugged it could have been carved out of stone. The silver shield pinned to his white muslin shirt glinted in the morning sun.

No, it couldn't be. It was her imagination playing tricks on her. Wishful thinking conjuring up the image she cherished most. Her knees buckled and she grabbed the counter for support. She blinked, but he didn't disappear. The ring of his gait, the power of his stride, the love in his gaze made her see. He was no dream or image but a real, live, flesh-and-blood man striding through the shop toward her.

"Burke." She choked out his name. Tears bunched in her throat. Joy dawned within her. The deep grief and the pain of missing him vanished. She gathered her skirts, dashing toward him, drinking in the sight of what she'd missed most. His handsome face, his physical strength and his mighty honor. Integrity radiated from him like the goodness of his heart. "You came back."

"To you." His chiseled mouth tugged up in the corners,

softening the hard planes of his face. His midnight-blue eyes radiated a depth of caring that betrayed him. He held out his good arm in an invitation. "I came for you. Only for you."

"I lost hope." She stepped into his embrace and laid her cheek against his chest. "I thought I would never see you again."

"For a while there, I did, too. It took a while for me to heal." His jaw settled against the side of her head, a pleasant pressure that made her feel sheltered and safe. He was steely muscle and solid bone against her cheek, and she could feel his heart beating oddly fast and heavily, belying the calm he projected. "I couldn't stay away."

"I thought you were a lone wolf. A man who had no ties and liked it that way." She smiled into his shirt, holding him tight, so very tight.

"I don't want to go through life with nothing to show for it. Loving someone and being loved in return is the only real living there is." His voice smiled, layered with warmth and affection and conviction. His heartbeat slowed, one reliable thump at a time. "I was merely existing until I met you, Lila. Loving you changed me. A lot of things have changed."

"Like what?"

"I'm a free man. I've been granted clemency from the government. So I looked at God and where he seemed to be leading me and then I looked in my heart. Do you know what I found?"

"I'm breathless to know."

"My love for you. There is nothing but my love for you without condition and without end in my heart and in my soul." He breathed in her lilac scent and savored the silk of her hair against his jaw. She felt *right* in his arms, as if this moment was meant to be. Gratitude filled him and he held her tight. So very tight. "There is going to be a new office here in Angel Falls and I'm in charge of it. Since I'll be staying in town, I was wondering if you could do me a favor."

"Oh, I don't know about that. I've done quite a few favors for you. I've read to you, made soup for you and saved your life, twice. You are out of favors with me." Her rosebud mouth curved upward. Her green-blue eyes shone luminous with her love for him.

Her beautiful, precious love. His throat tightened with emotions too great to measure. For so long, he'd believed love happened to other men. That he wasn't good enough to deserve it, that it was something he could lose and vulnerability he couldn't allow. But he'd been wrong. God was giving this one chance, the one he'd prayed for. He would not waste this chance for Lila. He could make his life new and have the happiness he'd once known and lost as a little boy.

"Maybe you can see your way to granting me one more favor anyway. It's a wish, really. The one thing I want or ever will want." He gazed down at her, not used to being vulnerable, but he was tough. He was strong. He could open his heart without condition or end. "You as my wife. Will you marry me?"

"Marry you?" Humor flashed in her smile. Happy tears filled her eyes. Unspoken love glowed there, the greatest gift he could ever receive. A single tear slid down her cheek and she swiped at it. "It would be my honor to take you as my husband. Yes, I will marry you. Absolutely, with all of my heart."

"I love you, Lila." He brushed away another warm, salty tear with the pad of his thumb. "I love you with all I am and all I will be. I will do my best to protect you and cherish you, my best never to let you down."

"I know, because that's you. The best man. My best man." Infinite bliss seemed to lift her from the ground. His lips met hers with the softest kiss that was sweet, pure and true, just like their love. Theirs was a romance story, after all.

Epilogue

It was a perfect day for a wedding. Green leaves rustled musically in the warm breeze that blew through the Lawson family's buggy. Cheerful sunshine made the clear blue sky bluer and highlighted the white church where her beloved waited inside. Lila could barely wait for her pa to draw the horses to a halt. Excitement flitted through her like hummingbird's wings. She was getting married! Today she would become Burke's bride.

"Everything is perfect," Eunice declared from the front seat. "I made three trips to the church this morning to make sure everything has been done to my specifications."

Leave it to Eunice to take charge. Lila knew her stepmother meant well. "Thank you for everything you've done, Ma. You, too, Pa."

"Are you nervous?" Lark leaned close to whisper. She looked adorable in her lavender lawn dress, the one they had sewn together just for the wedding.

"No, I'm not nervous at all." It was a big step to marry anyone, but she was certain of her choice. Burke had told her the entire story of his orphanage years, how he had fallen in with the Cheever gang and the near decade of hard service he'd given as a Range Rider. The test of time had proven his character. He was honorable, righteous and brave. "I keep pinching myself, sure that I am dreaming."

"I can't believe it, either," Pa spoke up. While she and Lark had been talking, he had helped Eunice down and now offered his hand to her. "My little Lila is all grown up. It's hard for a father to face."

"I'm grown up but I'm not growing away, Papa." She swooped down from the wagon, landing lightly on the grass. "Burke and I will be just down the street above Cora's shop. It's not far at all."

"I know, but this is a hard day for me. I have to give you away." He cleared his throat, hiding emotion, and helped Lark down next. "At least it's to a good man. I see that now. I wouldn't have gotten back my horses and wagon if it weren't for him."

"Oh, Pa." Lark rolled her eyes. "You might as well say it. You take him fishing. You said last night at supper Burke was like a son to you. Go ahead and admit it."

"I'll keep my feelings to myself, missy." Pa gently tweaked her nose. "Lila, the door is open. They are waiting for us. Are you ready?"

"Almost." She looked up expectantly. Shadows moved inside the doorway, rushing toward her and took shape. Scarlet with her red curls in a summery dress dashed down the steps. Everyone followed her—Kate, Fiona, Earlee, Meredith and Ruby. Laughter filled the air like a lark song, voices rose and fell with merriment, arms wrapped around her and before she knew it, they were in a circle, arms locked together, her dear friends.

"You look as excited as I felt on my wedding day." Fiona with her dark curls and ready smile looked especially happy this morning. She practically danced in place. "I know you and Burke will be exceptionally happy together."

"If only I had known who he really was, I never would have warned you against him," Scarlet said.

"Or me," Kate agreed. "He's good to you, Lila. He'll make you very happy."

"Yes, he will." She was already transported. Just through that door, her bridegroom was waiting for her. Her engagement ring, a sapphire set between two sparkling diamonds, caught the light at that moment, like a sign from above.

"Is it me, or do you look a little pale, Fiona?" Ruby asked in her gentle, concerned way. "Do you feel all right?"

"Oh, I am probably pale," Fiona said casually. "But I'm not sick."

"Oh!" Meredith was the first to start leaping. "You're expecting!"

"The baby is due around May." Fiona blossomed with happiness. "I have a lot of sewing to do."

"We'll help," Earlee volunteered. Congratulations rose on the wind. So much was changing for them all, such good things. Life, love, families.

"Come, Lila," Pa said. "It's time."

There was a flurry of excitement, her friends gave her more hugs, funny advice and good wishes before they dashed back inside the church. Later there would be a supper party at home for her friends and family with Burke at her side.

Every step she took along the path and up the stairs felt monumental. Sunlight sparkled through stained-glass windows, adding jeweled beauty to the sanctuary. She hardly registered the full pews of well-wishers, or Reverend Hadly at the pulpit or how shy she usually felt in front of so many people.

Her gaze arrowed to Burke waiting for her. How dashing he was in a black suit and white shirt, his thick dark hair tamed for there was no wind inside the church to blow it. He looked vibrant and masculine and invincible, and he was hers. Hers to marry, hers to love, hers to cherish for all eternity. Bliss filled her and her shoes didn't touch the floor as Pa accompanied her down the aisle.

The minister began to speak, but did she notice? Not a chance. All she could see was Burke and the unshakable affection warming his midnight eyes to a gentle blue as he turned toward her.

"Her mother and I do," Pa answered the minister.

In a daze, Lila realized her father released her. Burke gathered her hand in his.

"I'm not nervous one bit," he leaned in to whisper. "Are you?"

"No, only ecstatic. I get to marry you."

"That's my line," he chuckled. "God has blessed me richly today."

"And tomorrow and the rest of our lives." Her confidence touched him down deep. Once Arthur was settled, the minister continued the ceremony. He could only half listen, he had a hard time focusing on anything other than Lila. She looked beyond beautiful in a white print dress sprigged with tiny yellow flowers—sunflowers, he realized.

Thank You, Lord. He sent a prayer Heavenward. It wasn't easy to forgive himself for that dark time in his life, but he felt that God had. The Lord had looked inside his heart and brought him to Lila. Gratitude left him speechless as he realized the minister was waiting on him.

"I do," he vowed. Never had a man meant those words more. He intended to love, honor and cherish his wife through any hardship and every happiness until he no longer drew breath. She gazed up at him with unfailing love and he had everything he'd ever wanted.

"I do take this man as my husband," Lila breathed, tears glittering in her eyes. "I so do."

Love lit her softly, the same way happy endings came in a fairy tale. With happily-ever-afters and promises that were always kept, never broken.

It was easy to see the future when he looked into her eyes, their loving future. A pretty house for her to make into a home, a close marriage laughing and reading and watching thunderstorms. A baby in a bassinet, maybe another on the way. He saw the years pass, a little boy looking up at the sky to see the pictures in the clouds, a little girl hurrying to join in as Lila tended her flower beds and he hoed up the weeds for her.

A happy family.

Although it was not that time in the ceremony, Burke cupped her chin in his free hand and kissed her sweetly, his wife, his love and the best part of his soul. Understanding laughter rippled through the crowd, the minister cleared his throat and Lila beamed up at him, her infinite love gentle and honest and true.

The sun chose that moment to brighten. Rich light tumbled through the windows and fell like grace on the noble lawman and his calico bride, Heaven's assurance of great happiness to come.

* * * * *

WE HOPE YOU ENJOYED THIS BOOK!

Love Inspired SUSPENSE

Uncover the truth in these thrilling stories of faith in the face of crime from Love Inspired Suspense. Discover six new books available every month, wherever books are sold!

LoveInspired.com

SPECIAL EXCERPT FROM

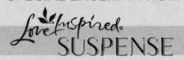

Love Inspired.
SUSPENSE

*When a rookie K-9 cop becomes the target of a
dangerous stalker, can she stay one step ahead of this
killer with the help of her boss and his K-9 partner?*

Read on for a sneak preview of
Courage Under Fire *by Sharon Dunn,*
the next exciting installment to the
True Blue K-9 Unit *miniseries, available in
October 2019 from Love Inspired Suspense.*

Rookie K-9 officer Lani Branson took in a deep breath as
she pedaled her bike along the trail in the Jamaica Bay
Wildlife Refuge. Water rushed and receded from the shore
just over the dunes. The high-rises of New York City,
made hazy from the dusky twilight, were visible across
the expanse of water.

She sped up even more.

Tonight was important. This training exercise was an
opportunity to prove herself to the other K-9 officers who
waited back at the visitors' center with the tracking dogs
for her to give the go-ahead. Playing the part of a child lost
in the refuge so the dogs could practice tracking her was
probably a less-than-desirable duty for the senior officers.

Reaching up to her shoulder, Lani got off her bike and
pressed the button on the radio. "I'm in place."

The smooth tenor voice of her supervisor, Chief Noah Jameson, came over the line. "Good—you made it out there in record time."

Up ahead she spotted an object shining in the setting sun. She jogged toward it. A bicycle, not hers, was propped against a tree.

A knot of tension formed at the back of her neck as she turned in a half circle, taking in the area around her. It was possible someone had left the bike behind. Vagrants could have wandered into the area.

She studied the bike a little closer. State-of-the-art and in good condition. Not the kind of bike someone just dumped.

A branch cracked. Her breath caught in her throat. Fear caused her heartbeat to drum in her ears.

"NYPD." She hadn't worn her gun for this exercise. Her eyes scanned all around her, searching for movement and color. "You need to show yourself."

Seconds ticked by. Her heart pounded.

Someone else was out here.

Don't miss
Courage Under Fire *by Sharon Dunn,*
available October 2019 wherever
Love Inspired® Suspense *books and ebooks are sold.*

www.LoveInspired.com

Looking for inspiration in tales
of hope, faith and heartfelt romance?

Check out **Love Inspired®** and
Love Inspired® Suspense books!

New books available every month!

Nick took his seat next to her and picked up the reins, but before moving onward, he said, "I don't understand it, Lucy. Why is my caring about you such an awful thing?" His voice was quivering and Lucy felt a pang of guilt. She knew she was overreacting. Rather, she was reacting to a heartache that had plagued her for years, not one Nick had caused that evening.

"I don't expect you to understand," she said, wiping her rough woolen mitten across her cheeks.

"But I want to. Can't you explain it to me?"

Nick's voice was so forlorn Lucy let her defenses drop. "I've always been treated like this, my entire life. *Lucy's too weak, too fragile, too small, she can't go outside or run around or have any fun because she'll get sick. She'll stop breathing. She'll wind up in the hospital.* My whole life, Nick. And then the one little taste of utter abandon I ever experienced—charging through the dark with a frosty wind whisking against my face, feeling totally invigorated and alive… You want to take that away from me, too."

She was crying so hard her words were barely intelligible, but Nick didn't interrupt or attempt to quiet her. When she finally settled down and could speak

LIEXP0919

normally again, she sniffed and asked, "May I use your handkerchief, please?"

"Sorry, I don't have one," Nick said. "But here, you can use my scarf. I don't mind."

The offer to use Nick's scarf to dry her eyes and blow her nose was so ridiculous and sweet all at once it caused Lucy to chuckle. "*Neh*, that's okay," she said, removing her mittens to dab her eyes with her bare fingers.

"I really am sorry," he repeated.

Lucy was embarrassed. "That's all right. I've stopped blubbering. I don't need a handkerchief after all."

"*Neh*, I mean I'm sorry I treated you in a way that made you feel…the way you feel. I didn't mean to. I was concerned. I care about you and I wouldn't want anything to happen to you. I especially wouldn't want to play a role in hurting you."

Lucy was overwhelmed by his words. No man had ever said anything like that to her before, even in friendship. "It's not your fault," she said. "And I do appreciate that you care. But I'm not as fragile as you think I am."

"Fragile? You? I don't think you're fragile at all, even if you are prone to pneumonia." Nick scoffed. "I think you're one of the most resilient women I've ever known."

Lucy was overwhelmed again. If this kept up, she was going to fall hard for Nick Burkholder. Maybe she already had.

Don't miss
Her Amish Holiday Suitor by Carrie Lighte,
available October 2019 wherever
Love Inspired® books and ebooks are sold.

www.LoveInspired.com

LIEXP0919